THE SAFFRON FIELDS

Also by F. K. Salwood

The Oystercatcher's Cry

THE SAFFRON FIELDS

F. K. Salwood

HEADLINE

First published in 1994
by HEADLINE BOOK PUBLISHING

10 9 8 7 6 5 4 3 2 1

British Library Cataloguing in Publication Data

Salwood, F. K.
Saffron Fields
I. Title
823 [F]

ISBN 0-7472-0996-0

Typeset by Keyboard Services, Luton

Printed and bound in Great Britain by
Mackays of Chatham PLC, Chatham, Kent

HEADLINE BOOK PUBLISHING
A division of Hodder Headline PLC
338 Euston Road
London NW1 3BH

This novel is for Jacqueline and Charles Hall

Acknowledgements: Thanks to Chris and Jim Lillie, and the *Venice Simplon Orient-Express* by Shirley Sherwood (Weidenfeld & Nicolson) for information regarding the VS-O-E journey from London to Venice.

Chapter One

Jane Transon was twenty years of age when the war in Europe came to an end at last. She watched the faces of the men as they drifted back from the trenches in France to their farm cottages in the Essex countryside. These men carried the spirit of the land within them and that spirit was brutally scarred. Their trust in their leaders had gone. She knew they felt betrayed by those who had stayed at home, even the waiting womenfolk; she knew too that it would be a long while before their confidence in themselves would return and they would be able to conduct normal lives again.

Courtney himself did not return home until the spring of 1919. Still serving as a commissioned officer in the regular army, he was among the last to home back. But one of the first things he did was to visit Jane and her father at their cottage in the hamlet of Howlett End. She was glad to see his sense of humour had not been completely snuffed by further experiences in the trenches, though she perceived a certain iron in his soul. There was also a second physical wound which had left him with a slight limp. He dismissed this with a short laugh and wave of his hand.

'Nothing much,' he said. 'Didn't touch the bone this time, thank God, so nothing was broken. Not like the arm. Just a few muscles torn, around the thigh. I'll survive.'

They were sitting in the conservatory overlooking the single-acre garden. Henley Transon, Jane's father, was standing before his easel on the sunlit lawn, painting a picture of a swathe of daffodils that separated three crooked apple trees. His main forte was the natural world. Not landscapes as such, but a landscape in microcosm: a blaze of poppies, a woodland path lined with bluebells, a cherry blossom branch, a bank of herbs. He was at his best painting plants in bud or in bloom. Henley's face was creased with concentration. He was not one of those artists to whom the work came easily. While he held a brush in his hand, he did not seem to be able to relax for one second, but constantly shifted his balance from one foot to other.

The two onlookers watched this display with different feelings. Jane was thinking how tired her father was looking around the eyes lately: it seemed to her he needed a good night's rest. Courtney was admiring the deftness of the hand with the brush and thinking how fit the older man appeared.

In answer to Courtney's last remark, Jane said, 'You'll survive, but still it must have been quite awful for you. I'm glad I'm a woman.'

'Women have to face other horrors,' said Courtney. 'I'm glad I'm a man.'

She turned her eyes from the figure of her father to glance at her new friend. Courtney was in his uniform, bearing the insignia of a captain in the Essex Regiment. His lean, smooth face was still a slightly jaundiced yellow, and he had a short, barking cough, picked up in the trenches, he told her, for which he had apologised once or twice. His dark curly hair had no parting and was unfashionably long. It occurred to Jane that he was in fact quite attractive, though she had no illusions about anything more than a friendship developing between them. For one thing, Courtney was from an upper-class family. While Jane's father was respectable, he was nothing more than the son of a wealthy farmer, though Henley Transon certainly had no pretensions to rank or privilege. Indeed, he looked upon the aristocracy with undisguised distaste, regarding them as arrogant leeches who used the working class to keep themselves in the style to which they were accustomed.

Jane and Courtney had met by chance. She had helped with convalescing soldiers in a Kent nursing home during the last year of the war. Though not a trained nurse, she had been given menial tasks at the home and had carried them out as cheerfully as she was able. Courtney had passed through the home after his shoulder had been hit by shrapnel, leaving his left arm impaired. They had discovered, during a short conversation, that they came from the same area of Essex, between the towns of Thaxted and Saffron Walden.

A friendship had formed between them during Courtney's brief stay, and he had promised to visit her once he had arrived back at his home, Stanton Manor, the estates of which rivalled those of the more famous Audley End. Stanton Manor lay some seven miles east of Wildrose Cottage, where the Transons lived.

'Well,' said Jane, smiling, 'it's probably a good thing we're happy being what we are then. Would you like some more tea? Or some more cake?'

'No thanks, very kind of you, but I've got to be going soon. I've really enjoyed our chat, but I'd better be getting back to the old homestead. You must visit us there sometime.'

'I'd like that.'

Jane had sensed the unspoken: *Once I have had time to prepare my mother and father.*

Outside the skies had begun to darken, and Jane's father suddenly threw down his brush and strode across the lawn towards them. He entered the conservatory from the garden side, stopping for a moment to glare at Courtney before walking past him to a chair in the corner.

'You still here?' he asked, glowering from beneath dark, bushy brows.

'Don't feel privileged,' said Jane, before Courtney could answer. 'My father is rude to everyone, gentry and peasant alike.'

Courtney did not look in the least offended. He simply murmured, 'I'm about to leave, sir.'

Henley threw himself into a wicker chair in the shady area of the conservatory. He completely ignored his daughter's remark, and also that of his visitor and began grumbling about the light outside. 'Keeps damned well changing,' he said. 'My yellow looks like runny mustard when the cloud comes over. I need to wait for the sun to come out again. Is there any tea left?'

'Yes, Father, but I want you to be nice to Courtney while he's here. He's had a bad time in France and deserves a little civility, even from grouches like you. Say something sweet to him, or you'll have to pour your own tea.'

'Strawberry jam to you, young man. Now can I have my tea?'

'Father, you're incorrigible.'

Jane poured Henley some tea, while the older man studied his daughter's visitor. 'So you're Courtney Stanton?' he said finally. 'Met your father once, at some pig and horse show. I have to tell you, young man, that I don't approve of you people. Ordinary flesh and blood is what you are, nothing more. Nothing special. The *real* people are all around you, working their knuckles to the bone. Farmers, coopers, farriers, publicans, yes, even *artists*. Those are the real people. Your lot feed on efforts of the rest of us . . .'

'My people are farmers too, Mr Transon,' said Courtney in a calm, quiet tone. 'We farm some eight-hundred acres.'

'Not *you*. Your tenants do the work.'

'Some of it, but we get our hands dirty too, these days. All right, my grandfather never touched the soil while he was alive, but that's not true of my father and my brother.'

Jane handed her father his cup and saucer, and gave him a warning look, but Henley took a sip of his tea and said, 'Only because your labourers were dragged off to the war.'

'That was the start of it, I admit, but these are hard times for all of us. My father has found he enjoys the physical work; I doubt he'll give it up, even now some of the men have returned. Many, of course, will never come home.'

Henley growled over the top of his cup. 'Don't try to make me feel guilty, young man. I didn't start the damn war and I didn't send the young men over there to be slaughtered like birds at a shoot. What about you? What are you going to do now it's all over? Play a bit of tennis? Wait around for a bit before taking up a seat in the House of Lords?'

'Father!' snapped Jane, but Courtney laughed and said, 'It's all right, Jane.'

Then he turned to Henley again. 'I have an older brother who will inherit the baronetcy: the seat will be his, not mine. I dislike tennis, probably because I'm no good at it. At the moment I'm still in the army, but what I should like to do above all things is take up painting.'

Though this announcement was as much a surprise to her as it was to Henley, Jane was amused to see that her father almost dropped his cup and saucer. Some of the tea spilled into Henley's lap, but since he was still wearing his smock, already smeared with ochres and siennas from his pallet, she did not feel it necessary to run for a dishcloth. She simply watched as he composed himself again.

'Painting?' growled Henley. 'You think painting is something you can pick up, just like that?'

'No,' replied Courtney, 'I expect to serve some sort of apprenticeship. I'm no fool, Mr Transon. Most of my work so far is quite unworthy of any attention but my own, but I intend to improve, given time and practice. The only pieces I would even contemplate showing to anyone are a number of sketches which I did in the trenches.'

'I thought all you fellows were damn poets,' snapped Henley.

'There were many poets, I admit,' replied Courtney, 'but I preferred the medium of the sketchbook and pencil.'

'Hummph,' muttered Henley, but Jane could see that her father was impressed by Courtney's forthright attitude, and by his determination not to be ruffled by Henley's boorish manners.

There was silence for a few moments, then Henley said to Courtney, 'What are you going to do about this great love of art you've discovered, young man?'

Courtney smiled at Jane, rather than at the person who asked the question. 'I have to persuade two stubborn people that I was not born to follow a life in the military.'

Jane knew that Courtney was referring to his parents. Courtney had told Jane that his father had been a brigadier and expected Courtney, the younger of his two sons, to reach at least as far up the military hierarchy. Stephen, Courtney's older brother, was expected to inherit the Stanton estates and was therefore being groomed towards that end. Julia, their young sister, was at eighteen already married and expecting her first child. The baronet was apparently determined to relive his life through his children: the eldest taking on the duties of his civil rank; the second following his career in the army; the third providing him with descendants.

'Your father is a strong character,' said Henley, 'I know that much of him. You have my sympathy.'

Jane saw Courtney's jaw stiffen a little. 'I don't need your sympathy, thank you, sir. I am my own man and can handle my affairs tolerably well.'

Henley's eyes sparkled, knowing he had scored a hit. He took a sip of his tea and then said, 'I'm sure you can.'

Jane quickly changed the subject, not wanting the two men to form an antipathy towards one another so soon in the course of their acquaintance.

Turning to Courtney she said, 'One of father's projects is to paint a field of saffron crocuses, but to do that he would have to travel to the Mediterranean countries. Now that the war's over, perhaps it would be possible. What do you think?'

'Why the Med? Why not here?' asked Courtney, straightening his injured leg and causing the rattan seat to squeak. He looked stiff and awkward in the basket chair, but Jane knew that he would refuse it if she offered to bring an easy chair in from the main part of the house.

'*Sativus*,' snapped Henley. 'The saffron crocus. Hasn't been grown seriously in Essex for over a century. Once upon a time we had fields of them around here – hence the town of Saffron Walden, of course – but not any more. One needs to go to Spain or Italy for the sight of saffron in bloom.'

'I realise that,' said Courtney, 'but what's to stop you planting your own?'

Henley stared at Courtney for a long time, seemingly studying his features, perhaps to try to gauge whether the young man was making fun of him. Jane looked apprehensively from one to the other, wondering whether there was going to be an explosion from her father, as often happened when he felt he was being mocked or spoken down to. To her relief Henley finally smiled broadly. Courtney too was grinning.

Henley said, 'I think you've got something there, Stanton. I've sold off the main part of the farm I inherited – what does an artist want a farm for, after all? – but I still own twenty acres of land. It's mostly pasture, rented out to graze cattle, but it's good land, rich loam, and no doubt has grown the *sativus* at some time in its long history. It could be planted with bulbs this coming July . . .'

Jane caught some of the enthusiasm that was passing between the two men. She became excited at the vision Courtney had created for them. Fields of flowering saffron, here in Essex, for the express purpose of providing her father with a subject! She remembered that before the war, while on holiday from school, her father and she had travelled down through France, painting the fields of sunflowers.

6

Jane recalled a childish delight in discovering that sunflowers turned their heads all one way, in the direction of the light, as if they worshipped its source. Another time they had visited the tulip fields at Haarlem in Holland, and here in Essex he had painted the brilliant acres of flowering mustard. But she knew that Courtney's idea had really fired her father's imagination.

'Well,' said Courtney, rising stiffly from his chair, 'I'll leave you to think about it. Now I must be going . . .'

'I'll see you to the door,' said Jane. 'Father, the sun has come out again. You can go back to your painting.'

Henley looked out through the glass and frowned. 'Yes, but for how long? Look at those dark clouds coming up from the south. Bloody English weather, no staying power. Constantly changing. I'd better just bring my stuff indoors for today.'

Henley flicked a wave at Courtney and went out into the garden.

At the door to the cottage, Jane shook hands with Courtney and apologised for her father's manners.

'Don't worry, I like eccentrics,' smiled Courtney, collecting his cap from a peg behind the door. He put it on his head. 'Anyway, he seems to like me now, doesn't he?'

'Because of your marvellous idea. It'll keep him excited for ages. Thank you, it will give us both a lot of pleasure to grow those crocuses. I'm sure father will produce something worthwhile on canvas too.'

Jane did not add that she had other more serious reasons for wanting to keep her father's mind occupied.

Courtney waved away the thanks and promised to call again in the near future. Jane watched him stride away in his knee-high brown leather boots. He went down the lane, towards the field where he had tethered his horse. She saw him mount, give a last wave, and then canter off over the meadow rise. She remained in the doorway of the cottage, breathing in the fresh spring air. Overhead the clouds were lowering again, drifting down to meet the landscape.

A motor car was weaving along a distant ridge, its roof just visible above a dry-stone wall, following an ancient, meandering road. Jane watched it disappear into the folds of the hills. The contours of the countryside around the cottage were like deep ocean swells, rising and falling gently into each other, breaking occasionally into a dark patch of woodland. These spinneys stood mostly on the crowns of knolls, where flints had come to the surface, making the soil difficult to cultivate. Nodes of chalk rose like albino whales, just sliding their backs above the arable loam.

Even as she watched, the clouds suddenly broke, the rain spilling forth from their undersides. Within minutes, the storm that had been skirting the area finally carried out its threat. It attacked the countryside below with a fury. Now the landscape heaved and tossed in the violent mood of the weather, the light running away, the darkness rushing in. The copses on the knolls turned from benign dark patches to sinister black entities, seemingly intent on over-powering all around them by sheer force of will.

Poor Courtney, thought Jane, he'll be soaked through. His general state of health seemed already at a low, and a chill would do him no good at all. She hoped he had a cape or something with him.

Jane closed the door and went to help her father carry his easel and paints to his studio on the ground floor at the end of the cottage, where the large french doors let in plenty of light. Extra horizontal windows had also been fitted high up in that room, for the same purpose. In summer the studio could become insufferably warm, as the sunlight streamed through the glass. Then the french doors would be flung wide and a gauze hung over the opening to stop insects from flying in and sticking to the paintings. But during the cool and cold seasons it was the favourite haunt of both humans and cats. Jane would go there to read while her father worked.

When they had finished, he thanked her and told her he was going out for the evening.

Jane's heart sank at these seemingly innocent words. 'Why don't you stay in, Father? I'll cook us some nice supper of green fish. We have that trout you caught early this morning.'

'No, no. I'd prefer to go out. You cook something for yourself, Jane. Don't worry about me.'

But she *was* worried about him, because she knew exactly where he was going.

Just before her father left the house, Jane heard a knock on the front door of the cottage, then male voices. She was in her bedroom, so she hurried downstairs to find Mr Driscoll – a tall, willowy gentleman – talking to her father. Mr Driscoll had been to the cottage three days earlier. He was visiting Saffron Walden from Yorkshire and said he wanted to buy one of Henley's paintings, but could not make up his mind which one. Mr Driscoll owned a factory and seemed reasonably wealthy.

Jane believed her father should nurture prospective buyers, but instead he tended to become irritated with them. He called them 'plebs', and had been known to tell customers to their faces that they did not know a good painting from a horse's backside. Jane knew that her father wanted only to paint, and could not be bothered with the business side of things. She would gladly have handled that part, but often the purchasers wanted to meet the artist in person before they actually let go of their money.

Henley sounded grumpy. He was leading the way to his studio.

'As you know, Transon,' Driscoll was saying in ponderous tones, 'I first saw one of your paintings in the Guildhall, at Thaxted. Most impressive. Very impressive indeed. Lovely colours, if I may say so. You seem to have a way with colours. Of course, ha-ha, you being an artist and all, I expect you've studied colours quite closely, one way or another. I know about dyes, you see, because that's my business, but you painter chaps work in different mediums. If asked – which I likely will be by the wife – I'd say the difference between your colours and the dyes I use is in the *tone*. You understand what I'm saying here, Transon? Mellow, I'd call your tones. That's why I want one of your works. I'd like to take one home to the wife, back in Sheffield, but I can't quite make up my mind, you understand? I like the tulips, but I also like the roses . . .'

'Hello, Mr Driscoll,' said Jane a little breathlessly, falling in at the end of the line.

Driscoll looked down over his shoulder and smiled. 'Oh, hello, Miss Transon. I was just saying to your father here . . .'

'Yes, yes,' said Henley with an impatient edge to his voice. 'You don't have to go through it all again.'

'Quite,' said Driscoll, turning to stare at Henley's back.

Inwardly, Jane groaned, wondering if she could keep her father under control until the purchase was made. The money from the sale of the farm was almost gone. They needed some income if they were to maintain their comfortable lifestyle.

'Father,' said Jane, when they were all standing in the studio, 'why don't you go to your appointment? I'll help Mr Driscoll choose his painting.'

Driscoll shook his head. 'No, I need your father's expert advice. I can't quite choose between the tulips and the roses, you see . . .'

Henley took the two paintings out from a stack in the corner. He placed them one beside the other, propped against the old couch he used when resting during work periods. Then he stepped back and folded his arms. Driscoll put on a pair of spectacles, crouched a little, and began peering, first at one painting, then the other. Jane felt sure it was all going to end in disaster. She could sense her father's hackles standing on end.

Finally, Driscoll straightened. 'You couldn't . . .' he said with a slight smile, 'you couldn't see your way to doing a new painting with both tulips *and* roses, all in the one picture?'

'What?' exploded Henley.

Jane stepped in front of Mr Driscoll. 'What my father is about to say is that he can only work with a live subject, and the roses are not quite . . .'

'Surely,' interrupted Driscoll, becoming a little heated himself now, 'you can just prop these two up somewhere and copy them both on to one canvas? I'll pay you good money for the result. I'm not short of a bit of brass, you know.'

Jane knew that all was now lost. As predicted, her father lost his temper.

'Get the hell out of my studio, you oaf!' he shouted. 'What do you think I am, some kind of interior decorator? Out! Out! I'll paint bloody roses and tulips for you. I'll paint them on your arse. Get out of here.'

Driscoll went red in the face, swore at Henley in broad dialect, called him several names – some that Jane understood and some that she didn't – then stormed past her, through the living room and out of the cottage.

Jane shook her head at her father. 'You'd better go out,' she said, tight-lipped. 'You've done the damage.'

'I will not be spoken down to,' said Henley. His voice was now quiet, though still taut.

'I rather think it was the other way around,' Jane said. 'He wasn't going to get you to come down from your high horse whatever he said, now was he?'

'Don't talk to me like that, Jane.'

'Oh, Father, just go.'

Jane went back up to her room, her mind seething with annoyance at her father's intransigence. It was some while before she managed to cool down. When she did, she made certain plans. She would follow up on the idea Courtney had given her father. It would be up to her, she knew, to make the idea blossom into something more than an enthusiasm. If they *could* manage to grow several acres of saffron crocuses, it might absorb her father's attention and help to draw him away from his vice.

Chapter Two

It was nearly four miles to the Old Pig and Whistle, but luckily the rain stopped shortly after Henley began the walk, so by the time he arrived he was almost dry again. He went straight through the main part of the pub, nodding to one or two acquaintances at the bar on his way, and through to the rear. Henley was not a serious drinker. He seldom paused to get anything on his way past the bar.

Once at the back of the inn, he made his way to a private room. On entering, he saw that there were already three other people sitting at the table: Deaf Johnston, Al Wallingford and Petre Peake.

Henley nodded coolly in their general direction. 'Evening,' he said, and received the same in kind.

Al Wallingford was a local cutler, whose firm made knives, forks and spoons. He was a little round man with a red button nose. His wife did not know he gambled. She believed he was propping up the bar with his cronies. If she ever came to the Pig and Whistle, one of the men in the bar was instructed to nip upstairs and get him. Wallingford could then enter the bar doing up his flies, as if he had been to the toilet at the back. A half-full glass of ale stood on the bar, ready for him to pick up as if he had just left it. So far he had not needed to put this simple plan to the test, since no emergency had arisen in the Wallingford household which required his immediate attention.

Deaf Johnston and Petre Peake had been back from the front for close to six months. Deaf had been an artillery gunner, and had spent the war behind the lines, shelling the enemy from a distance and being shelled in return. During his time in the army he had collected two unwanted items. The first was a set of corporal's stripes, which he had thrown away with his tunic in disgust once his discharge papers had come through. He had no use for the army, and he was glad it no longer had any use for him. The second was a brace of damaged eardrums from the almost constant thunder of the field guns: hence his nickname.

Petre Peake, lean, tanned and hard-faced, had been an army aviator in the Royal Flying Corps. He had shot down seven enemy aircraft with his Sopwith Camel Browning machine-guns. He had refused all promotions beyond lieutenant because he said he hated responsibility for others and preferred to worry only about himself. Of the three men at the table, Henley actually *feared* Peake. There was a story that Peake had strafed a German pilot who had managed to land his damaged Fokker on an open field. The German had actually stood by his aircraft and waved, so the tale went, as Lieutenant Peake stooped to kill, probably thinking that the Englishman was diving in order to check that his adversary had landed safely, as any gentleman would do. Instead, the Browning machine-gun bullets had ripped into the turf, into the Fokker bi-plane, and finally into the incredulous German pilot, caught in mid-wave.

'War is about killing the enemy,' Peake would say, 'not about playing games.'

As Henley sat down at the table, Peake said, 'About time. We'd given you up. Jason Banbridge can't make it, so there's just the four of us.'

Henley settled down comfortably. When, a few moments later, the barman poked his head around the door, Henley ordered a double cognac. This was Henley's weekly game. Once a month he took the train into London for a more serious evening at his favourite club. Here at the Pig and Whistle they played a form of baccarat (which Johnston insisted on calling *chemin de fer*, since he had been to France and discovered they were the same game). It was a hardened gambler's game.

Henley played baccarat because the others wanted to. He actually preferred card games in which the players held lots of cards in every hand, but Wallingford, Banbridge and Johnston – the regular players – were not interested in the aesthetic pleasures that cards could

14

provide. They were there to win money, and disdained fancy games. Peake would play anything so long as high stakes were involved, and he usually won. If the stakes were too low, he became bored: in this way he was prone to losing trifling amounts of money.

Occasionally Henley found some people who would play bridge for a penny a point, but then the main excitement was missing: the high stakes. (No one he knew with any skill at bridge would play for a shilling a point.) Henley liked the feel of the cards, the texture, the look of them. He enjoyed the skill of riffling and shuffling the pack, dealing smoothly and cleanly, fanning his own hand. Since only two people held cards during a hand of baccarat – the banker and one of the punters – and then only two cards each, all of these (albeit *minor*) enjoyments were denied him. However, his main enjoyment, surpassing all others, was the betting: he was prepared to forgo small pleasures for the greater thrill.

Wallingford was the talker at the table, always keeping up a flow of low, mainly one-way conversation. Occasionally one of the others would answer a question, though not Johnston, who refused to ask for a repeat and rarely heard anything the first time. Wallingford, like Henley, had been too old to fight in the war, but unlike the artist, the cutler was fascinated by the savage death-toll that the battles had produced.

'. . . terrible,' he was saying as Henley took his turn as banker and dealt two cards to himself and two to Peake, 'what that Haig and the Kaiser's done between 'em. The cream of British youth, all gone in just a few short years. Cut down like wheat stalks, eh? My own two sons among 'em.'

'Just pay attention,' snapped Peake to the speaker, 'we're waiting for your bet.'

Wallingford made his bet then said to Peake, 'You come through it all. You were lucky . . .'

Peake's head shot up. He stared at Wallingford with a venomous expression on his face. 'Lucky? Luck had nothing to do with it, man. I survived because I have no fear.'

Henley was shocked at these words. It sounded almost as if Peake were accusing other men, Wallingford's sons perhaps, of being cowards. They had died because they were afraid, not because they were hit by a stray round, or because they were unfortunate enough to be in the way of some shrapnel, or because they were brave enough, although shaking with terror, to charge an enemy machine-gun.

Peake, as if sensing the disapproval around the table and probably not wanting to spoil the evening from the outset, smiled thinly and added, 'No fear – and no conscience.'

'Ahhh,' breathed Wallingford. 'There, you've said it.'

'But,' Peake said, 'I say it again. It was my lack of fear that got me through.'

Deaf Johnston, who had managed to catch the last sentence, said loudly, '"*Fear knocked on the door, Faith answered, and there was no one there.*"'

Peake sneered and said sourly, 'It's got nothing to do with religion, you idiot.'

Deaf Johnston chose not to hear this remark, and concentrated instead on the cards.

Henley, as ever fascinated with the deadly, cobra-like soul of Petre Peake, inquired further. 'If you do not attribute your lack of fear to an embracing of the Christian faith, then what?'

Peake said, 'It's said that men are born with only two fears – fear of falling, fear of loud noises – all others are *learned* fears. I have never managed to learn any new fears, and I conquered my fear of heights and falling, and my fear of loud noises, by flying a Sopwith Camel in a war. Now I am without fear.'

Without emotion of any kind, thought Henley, but he pursued the conversation. 'Where did you learn this theory – about the two inherent fears of men?'

Peake shrugged impatiently. 'Oh, I don't know. Freud, Jung, one of those people. I read so much I can't always remember where my knowledge originates. I read because I do not sleep. When one does not sleep, one lives two lifetimes; the second has to be filled with something. So I read.'

'You've got to sleep *sometime*,' said Wallingford.

'Why do I have to?' snapped Peake. 'Oh, I *rest*, but I rarely close my eyes. Sometimes –' there was suddenly a faraway look in his eyes,

16

– 'I dream on my feet. The strangest dreams, yet I'm still awake. It all gets mixed in together, the real and surreal.'

He shook himself. 'Enough of this. Are we playing a game of cards, or chattering like old women? Come on. Let's see the colour of your money, artist, and you, cutler, and the reluctant corporal. Let's get to it, damn you.'

So the chatter ceased, although Wallingford could never completely dry up, and occasionally opened a quiet monologue when he felt the others, or more specifically Peake, would not be distracted by it. Once or twice during the evening, Peake grunted sharply and, taking this as an objection, Wallingford fell silent in the middle of a sentence.

When the evening was over, Henley had lost over thirty pounds. He almost always did lose. It was a constant source of mystery and grief to him. Johnston had come out more or less even. Wallingford had lost heavily. Peake, of course, had won, though his method of betting had seemed ludicrous at the time. Somehow Peake's mistakes turned miraculously into winning plays, and his shrewd guesses were almost always correct. It seemed he could not lose, no matter what he did. If baccarat had not been so difficult to cheat at, Henley might have entertained some nasty thoughts about his main opponent at the table.

As Henley walked home along the dark lane towards his cottage, he reflected on his habit. Gambling was certainly an obsession with him; he admitted that much to himself. He loved it. It was the breath of life. All his other actions and thoughts during each passing day were somehow directed towards the moment when he would be sitting at the card table again. On those rare occasions when he walked away from the table with a substantial win, he felt like a king. The world shone in every corner and there were no shadows.

Painting *never* did that for him. Painting was hard work: ditch-digging in comparison to gambling. To win! It was the headiest, most wonderful feeling in the world, and it acted on him like a drug. For days, even weeks afterwards, he contemplated giving up painting altogether and becoming a professional gambler, for each time one of those rare winning streaks hit him, he believed it would never end; that he had finally found the secret.

That was the answer of course, he told himself as he walked beneath the dark boughs of the solitary oaks that studded his walk: there was a *secret*. Peake knew the secret. Peake had found that cryptic entrance to the golden world of the winner. How had Peake discovered it? Henley puzzled over this unanswerable question. Character came into it, Henley was wise enough to see that much, but there was an additional element. It had something to do with the ice in Peake's blood. Did one have to experience war to find it? Surely not. Johnston had been away to war too, and he did not have it. It was almost as if Peake had gone through a secret initiation and was now the possessor of hidden knowledge. He seemed to be able to read men's thoughts, see into their very souls.

Perhaps, thought Henley, if I saw more of Peake, invited him to the house, maybe I could study the man, discover the source of his understanding?

He decided that the next time he met Peake he would ask the man to dinner. Henley would become friendly with him. It would be like befriending a shark, but what of that? Perhaps one had to *become* shark-like in order to see into that otherworld of the winner?

More cheerful now, Henley began to whistle as he made his way through the night. Jane would be in bed, he guessed, though probably waiting for the sound of his key in the lock before she fell asleep. Jane. She was a good daughter to him, though a little too demanding sometimes. It was in her nature. Her mother, his darling wife Rosemary, had been the same. Too domineering by half, or had tried to be. He would not put up with that nonsense. There could only be one master in the house, and that was of course the husband and father. It was the way things were meant to be. It was *his* house, after all, and his money that ran it. He was entitled to do as he pleased with his own money, whatever the damn females might think. They were always trying to tell a man what to do.

Rosemary. She was at rest now, bless her, in the churchyard at Thaxted. Her headstone dropped in naturally on the first piece of graveyard turf at the end of the narrow alley of Stony Lane, which itself led down to Town Street, past the Tudor cottages which grew out of the north-east wing of the Guildhall. Thaxted's architecture was like that: it was all one, each Tudor house or pink-wash cottage growing out of or into its neighbour, snake-eat-tail, like a wall with no beginning and no end. A town with a single, octopus-like building, which was in reality dozens of dwellings. Rosemary had loved Thaxted. She had been a Thaxted girl. It was right that she should be buried there, in the shadow of its magnificent church.

Henley suddenly found himself outside his front door. As he fumbled in his coat pocket for his key, a light appeared behind the bull's-eye pane in the door; then the latch was lifted and the door opened. A female in a long white nightdress was standing there holding a lamp, the soft light illuminating her beautiful features, her black, waterfall hair. Henley started: absorbed as he had been with thoughts of his dead wife, for a moment it seemed she was here, now, young again, waiting at the door as she had so often done in the early part of their marriage.

'What . . . ?' he said, stepping backwards.

'Father, are you drunk?' said the figure, and he saw it was only his daughter, not a ghost, and he recovered his wits.

He stepped inside and said gruffly, 'You startled me. I wasn't expecting you to wait up.'

'Sorry, Father,' she said. 'I was doing some accounts and I heard you walking down the path.'

He grunted, not wishing to inquire further about the 'accounts'.

She made him a drink of hot milk, and then prepared to go to bed. Henley sat in the dark by the dying fire, staring into the embers and the last of the flames. Just before Jane left the room to go upstairs, she said to him, 'You thought I was Mother, didn't you?'

He looked at her and nodded slowly. 'Yes, I did. It . . . worried me for a moment, that's all.'

'*Worried* you?'

'Yes.'

'I'm sorry. Goodnight, Father.'

'Goodnight.'

She left him alone.

He tried to penetrate the fire with his thoughts, tried to understand his own feelings. It *had* worried him, but when the apparition had turned out to be his daughter, not the spirit of his wife, he had felt something else too. It was an emotion he experienced quite often these days; one with baser origins than the emptiness he had lived with since Rosemary had gone.

He had felt disappointment.

Chapter Three

Jane had put on a coat and boots over a summery frock, and had taken a footpath from Howlett End towards Thaxted, over the rising and dipping shallow-bowls of the landscape. In her part of Essex there were no flatlands like those out towards the east and south, but none of the ascents were very high either. To her it was an in-between land, not flat nor really hilly, though when you were in one of its dips you could see nothing beyond the gently breathing slopes of the gradients around you. She believed it truly a motherland, a country of feminine curves.

Jane had been reading: studying various books concerning the *crocus sativus*.

She had discovered that the saffron itself had a long history of association with mankind's vanities: it had been used variously as a dye, a perfume strewn in Greek and Roman cities, and of course as a spice, mostly in rice and fish dishes. Once upon a time, in the thirteenth century, it had been worth more than its weight in gold. Even now, in 1919, it was still the world's most expensive spice.

However, since she had no intention of harvesting the stigmas from the flowers, she had concentrated her studies on the growing of the bulbs. She had found it was an autumnal flowering crocus, as her father must have known, for he had mentioned July as a time for planting. Since it was now only the end of April, there was still time to send for the bulbs and get them in the ground.

On reaching Thaxted, Jane made straight for Coleman's Seed Company. The building stood at the point at which Town Street split and flowed into Mill End and Orange Street, positioned to attract the attention of the many farmers who would have to pass the company on their way to and from the market on Saturdays. Jane climbed the steps and entered the clapboard-cladded office of Mr Saltash, the manager of the firm.

She was confronted by a female secretary. 'Yes, can I help you?' asked the woman, looking Jane up and down, and no doubt finding her particularly lacking in terms of farmer's dirt or calloused skin.

'My name is Jane Transon. I'd like to see Mr Saltash, please.'

'Mr Saltash is very busy at the moment. I take it you do not have an appointment?'

Jane faced this imperiousness with dignity. 'No, no appointment, but I'm sure if you asked Mr Saltash, he might find me five minutes. I wish to speak to him about some bulbs . . .'

Mentioning wares was a great mistake, as Jane realised almost immediately. It helped the secretary to categorise her: the secretary clearly decided she was not worth a great deal of money to the company, that she was only a lady gardener needing advice on the planting of bulbs in her cottage garden. It was certainly not worth disturbing the great Mr Saltash for her needs: he would probably be extremely irritated.

'Our hardware shop is just along the street,' smiled the secretary, rising and opening the door. 'Why not inquire of the counter assistant there? Mr Saltash only sees farmers who wish to order in bulk.'

Jane ignored the open door.

'I may not look like a farmer, Miss . . . ?'

'*Mrs* Bignall.'

'. . . Mrs Bignall, but my order would be a bulk one. I need to plant some eight acres of land with about one thousand bushels of *crocus sativus*. Do you think Mr Saltash would be interested in such a piffling amount?'

For a moment Mrs Bignall shrivelled a little before Jane's eyes. 'I can't say for certain,' she said, rapidly regaining some of her former composure, 'but I shall certainly inquire.'

A minute or two later, Jane was being ushered into the office behind the frosted-glass door.

A large, knobbly man, around fifty years old, rose and offered a hand. Jane shook it, finding it surprisingly soft. Why not, she thought? Mr Saltash was not a field-worker, he was a businessman.

22

He just happened – probably luckily for his kind of import-export company – to look like a man who had laboured outdoors in all weathers.

'Sit down, Miss . . . yes, Miss Transon.'

Mrs Bignall was certainly efficient; she must have remembered Jane's name and passed it on.

Jane took the polished wheelback chair in front of the desk: worn smooth, she imagined, by the tweed-covered bottoms of a thousand farmers. She rested her elbows lightly on the arms of the chair.

'I understand you wish to purchase a thousand bushels of crocuses . . . some say croci but I find that a bit pretentious in my line of work,' said Mr Saltash.

Very efficient, Mrs Bignall.

'That's correct,' said Jane. 'Autumnal crocuses. The *crocus sativus*, to be precise. However, I exaggerated a little in order to get past Mrs Bignall. Actually, I only want to plant a single acre – even that might be too much.'

'Did you now, did you now? That's not important. Trade is trade.' Mr Saltash frowned a little. 'We don't get much call for crocuses, and certainly not that one in particular. Refresh my memory with the more familiar name, if you will?'

'It's the saffron crocus,' explained Jane.

Mr Saltash's expression brightened. 'Ah, so it is. I remember that now. Well, that hasn't been grown around here since God . . . for heaven knows how long. We certainly wouldn't have any in stock. We'd have to send for them.'

Jane's heart sank. It might take an age. It might cost a fortune. Either could ruin her plans, for her father was a man of the moment, whose enthusiasms died with the seasons.

'Where? Who would have them? Would they have to come from a long way away?'

'Excuse me a moment, Miss Transon.'

Mr Saltash took out a stack of papers and magazines and began sorting through them, stopping occasionally to leaf through a magazine, or turn the page of a document. He took quite a long time, glancing up with an apologetic expression every so often before immersing himself in print again. Finally, he looked up and smiled.

'Not so far,' he said. 'Holland. We could probably have them over here in six weeks.'

Jane heaved a sigh of relief. One hurdle over. 'And the cost?'

'That would take a little more time to work out, but I can give you a rough figure if you like.'

He consulted his papers again, and scribbled in the margin of a magazine with a pencil. When he had finished, he looked up. He gave Jane a figure which elated her.

'I work it out to six shillings and ninepence per bushel. So a thousand bushels, plus shipment costs, would cost about three hundred and fifty pounds.'

Jane blinked. 'No, I'm sorry, you misunderstood what I said. I corrected my earlier figure. I was thinking perhaps a hundred bushels. That would be around thirty-five pounds, wouldn't it?'

Mr Saltash tapped his pencil on his desk top while he stared at Jane with a serious look on his face. She expected to be upbraided for wasting his time. Instead he said, 'Look, Miss Transon, can you *afford* three hundred and fifty pounds? I know you said you really only wanted enough corms for one acre, but if you've got eight acres, you should plant them. It's much more cost-effective. It doesn't really matter to me. I can order a hundred bushels, if that's what you really want, but I'm not sure it's the best thing for you.'

'Well, to be quite honest with you, Mr Saltash, I'm not growing these plants for the saffron – not to make a profit from them. I have another reason. One acre is as good as eight acres for my purposes.'

He sighed and threw down his pencil. 'That's a shame . . . that's a great shame. You'd not lose anything by it, you know, except a little more energy. The corms can be planted in order to reproduce themselves, so even if you didn't use them to make saffron, you could still make a profit.'

Suddenly Jane saw a way of banking her money so that it was out of her father's reach. Even if he begged her for a loan, she wouldn't be able to give it to him if her money was all in saffron bulbs and buried beneath the earth. He was hard to resist. She knew Henley's financial situation was coming close to the point where he would be looking for money from anywhere, even from his daughter, such was his gambling sickness.

Three hundred and fifty pounds was a large sum, but it *was* within her means to meet such an amount – and a little more, if necessary. However, she wanted to be sure she was getting the best deal.

'All right, Mr Saltash, you've got me interested, but is there no discount for ordering in bulk?' she asked.

'We're already talking about half the retail value of the bulbs,' Mr Saltash replied.

'Even so, you must be making a handsome profit or you wouldn't be so eager to do business with me.'

Mr Saltash stared at her for a moment without blinking. Then he nodded slowly. 'I'll tell you what I'll do. I'll stand the shipping costs, which will bring the price down to three hundred and thirty-seven pounds and five shillings. How about that?'

Jane took a deep breath. 'Let's not talk any more about rough figures – you've obviously worked it out precisely. I'll pay you three hundred and twenty-five pounds in total on delivery of the bulbs.'

Mr Saltash leaned back, picked up his pencil again, and tapped the desk top for a moment. '*Corms*,' he said. 'We prefer to call them corms rather than bulbs. I like you, young lady,' he said. 'Normally I'm not fond of women who put themselves forward, play men's games. They're often too concerned about getting the upper hand rather than striking a bargain which leaves both parties happy. But you've got a good head on your shoulders, if I may say so. Three hundred and twenty-five pounds it is then. Shake on it.'

Once again she shook the large, soft hand. 'That's wonderful, Mr Saltash,' she said, hardly able to contain her excitement. 'Could you please order one thousand bushels of *crocus sativus* corms – I'm afraid "crocuses" doesn't work when you use the full Latin name – and have them delivered to Wildrose Cottage at Howlett End?'

Mr Saltash seemed to hesitate before scratching his head and raising his eyebrows a little.

'What's the matter?' asked Jane.

'Well, we don't usually have young women coming in here ordering such large amounts of seed,' he said weakly.

Jane sensed there was something more. 'That's not it, Mr Saltash. We've just been through all that. You said you thought I had a good head on my shoulders. Come on, be straight with me. You were quite happy until I said "Howlett End".'

The bulky man looked decidedly unhappy as he answered. 'Well, if you want the truth of the matter, Miss Transon, it's your credit I'm concerned about. I know your father, if he's Henley Transon. Leastways, I know *of* him. A good painter – I've seen his pictures in and about the town – but not a good *payer*, if you get my meaning. He's known to be a bad debtor . . .'

'My father always pays his debts,' said Jane hotly.

'Oh,' said Mr Saltash, looking very uncomfortable, 'I expect he does, but *when* is the question. I don't doubt he's an honourable man and intends fulfilling all his obligations, but he's a card player, Miss Transon, and a poor one at that, so I understand. My own friend Allan Wallingford plays with him. They're two of a kind – they'll both lose their souls one of these days.'

Jane swallowed her anger and indignation with difficulty, but she managed to control her emotions. 'This is *my* money we're talking about, Mr Saltash, bequested to me by my mother. I shall make a down-payment on the shipment now. You can wait for the cheque to be honoured before you order the bulbs – corms – from Holland. I just want them here before July so that we can get a crop this year.'

'I shall need twenty per cent of the total cost.'

'Good,' said Jane, taking a chequebook from her bag.

As she was leaving, Mr Saltash held open the door for her. 'If you decide to harvest your crop,' he said, 'I shall be interested.'

Jane had not thought too much about that side of things. The primary reason for planting was of course to obtain a vast show of saffron crocuses for her father to paint. Still, if there was money to be made, she might as well do her best to make it.

'Could you resell the corms for me when we dig them up again?'

'So far as I recall, the corms themselves only last three years, but if you want me to get rid of their offspring, I can certainly do my best.

'However, Miss Transon, I wasn't thinking of the plant itself, I was thinking of the harvest. You'll surely be gathering in your crop of saffron chives?'

She chided herself for her ignorance in these matters, not having researched that side of things.

'Yes . . . yes, of course,' she said vaguely. 'But would it be worth it? Eight acres? You see, it's the flowers themselves that I'm interested in. I need a good showing for my father to paint.'

Mr Saltash had obviously been reading about more than the price of the saffron crocuses in his magazines and papers while Jane had been sitting waiting for him to name a sum. He nodded sagely. 'Ah, I see, then it might be politic to order corms that have already given off a crop.' He looked down at one of the magazines. 'According to this, more flowers appear in the second and third year.'

'Oh, really? I didn't know. In fact I'm woefully ignorant on the subject. Can we do that?'

'I don't see why not. We're the customers. If they want our business, they should give us what we want.'

Jane smiled at him. She felt a warmth for this basically old-fashioned man of commercial affairs, who was prepared to keep an open enough mind on matters of business to make a transaction with a member of the opposite sex.

'And I'll bear that in mind, Mr Saltash, what you said about harvesting, though I'm inclined to think it would be better just to raise the new corms and sell them. I don't know anything about gathering the saffron itself. Thank you again for all your help.'

'You're welcome, Miss Transon. The pleasure was mine.'

Jane was fairly light-hearted as she walked along Town Street, then up the cobbled, sloping Stony Lane, to the churchyard where her mother was buried. She said a short prayer over the grave of the woman who had been taken by influenza in her thirty-fifth year. Since her mother's death, Jane had lived a fairly liberated existence for a girl. Her father, while loving and generous, was a very careless parent. He had allowed his daughter many freedoms which, had her mother been alive, she would most certainly have curbed.

In her adolescent years, Jane had been very much a tomboy, romping around the Blatchers' farm, roaming over the fields, paddling in streams. She had copied the boys in their tree-climbing, wild games, and antics with wooden weapons. It was she, along with two young village lads, who had helped set light to the heathland west of the hamlet, by allowing a small fire on which they were roasting stolen potatoes to get out of hand. Later she had been trapped in a barn by a youth, and had realised she wasn't like the boys at all, though she had escaped virtually untouched by brandishing a sickle and screaming loudly enough to startle the chickens in their coops two hundred yards away.

After this frightening incident, which she had not revealed to her father, she had begun to shed her hoydenish ways. She stayed in the cottage more, began to read novels and poetry, and adopted dress more suited to her sex. Her father, being less distracted by his art and pastime than normal, somehow noticed the change in her. It had made him take his responsibilities a little more seriously, and he had removed her from the village school and sent her to a private college for young ladies, which Jane secretly hated. The girls there talked about nothing but boys, and even went silly over casual visitors like the builders brought in to do repairs to the college buildings.

When Jane had returned home at the age of sixteen, Henley had become more engrossed than ever in his own private world. She was still allowed as much freedom of movement as she wished, but now she wanted to use this independence wisely. She had asked Henley if she could study to become a doctor. He had agreed in principle, but had told her to wait until she was older. By the time she *was* older, she had changed her mind, probably realising she did not have the dedication necessary for such work.

She promised herself that one day soon she would train for some sort of profession, but for the meantime she slipped into a routine of caring for her father, keeping house, managing the household finances, and seeing to all the practical tasks necessary to running a home. Apart from normal housework and shopping, there were gutters to fix and clear of dead leaves, gardens to garden, doors to paint, wasp nests to get rid of, drains to unblock – none of which they could afford to employ workmen for. She had even repaired the roof tiles and flashing on the chimney after a terrible storm. What she did not know she found out from books. She became a passable plumber, a good painter and decorator, and a reasonable restorer of broken furniture.

She was still allowed to do many things which shocked her father's brother, Uncle Matthew, who ran a more orthodox household, but she defended herself by saying that women were more sensible and responsible than men like Uncle Matthew gave them credit for.

'You think we're just empty-headed creatures that will do the silliest things without men to guide us, but you're very wrong, Uncle.'

'There you are,' he had said, obviously stung by this remark, 'no young woman would have *dared* to call an older man *wrong* when I was your age. They might have suggested, somewhat timidly, that perhaps we could be a little mistaken, a little less harsh in our judgement, but they would never have been so blunt as to call a man "wrong".'

'Well, that just goes to show how silly *men* were in those days, doesn't it?' she had said, taking him fondly by the arm. 'I hope you've progressed a little since then, my dear old fuddy-duddy uncle. Otherwise there's no hope for you. You'll go to that terrible place to which all unrepentant misogynists go.'

He had snorted in exasperation, but had diluted his apparent disapproval by patting the hand tucked under his arm.

Now, today, she had become a grower of saffron flowers. Her mother would probably have liked that. Rosemary had been very fond of flowers.

Jane left the graveside and walked around the great church to the porch which opened on to the north aisle.

Many East Anglian churches were on an extraordinarily grandiose scale when viewed alongside any possible size of congregation. Some were almost of cathedral proportions, boasting tall spires supported by flying buttresses, magnificent examples of high stained-glass art, timbered ceilings that an archbishop might have envied and vast vaults of stone supported by multiple pillars that one had to crane one's neck to follow from foot to head. Many of these lavish giants stood outside small villages, as if lifted from a great and wealthy city during the night and dropped into the middle of nowhere. It was said that their construction had been funded by the wool trade of earlier centuries, when Suffolk, Norfolk and Essex were rich fit to bursting, and East Anglian people, having satisfied all their worldly needs, turned their excess money into spiritual symbols.

The small town of Thaxted had one of these great monuments to a time of local prosperity, built (Henley was fond of telling Jane) from wealth provided by sheep, for the use of sheep. Henley was an atheist; Jane was merely a sceptic. She doubted, but she was not sure enough to actually reject religion. In fact she had recently become quite a regular visitor at the church. She found it peaceful inside: a place where she could think through her troubles slowly and clearly. She was beginning to tell herself that, if she turned to God when she had problems, she would have to start acknowledging Him once things were all right.

The vicar, who went under the unlikely name of Reverend Conrad Le Dispenser Noel, had listened to her once or twice when she had asked for advice on how to deal with Henley's obsession with gambling, but he could offer nothing more than words. He told her that she should help her father to turn to Christ, but when Henley steadfastly continued to prefer to turn to the green baize table and the deck of cards, this did not offer a very hopeful solution.

Perhaps the saffron fields might wean him away, she thought as she knelt in prayer, just long enough to break the habit? If he could become engrossed by another obsession for a while, the cycle might possibly be broken. That Henley was a man with an obsessive nature was not in question. To give him something else to lock on to: that was her goal.

Chapter Four

A week after his visit to Wildrose Cottage, Courtney Stanton was already planning a second visit. He had decided to make exercise his excuse for making the journey so soon after his first visit to Howlett End, though this was only half the truth. It took him a while to admit it to himself, but he *did* find Jane Transon very attractive. His parents, he knew, would not approve of the friendship, but their opinions no longer influenced him. He had long since passed the point of challenging their values; he now felt them to be unacceptable. The war, or rather being away at the war and amongst men of other classes, had altered his opinion of both his parents and himself. He was not ashamed of his parents, but their views were not his any longer, and he felt he had to assert himself if he were going to be true to his own feelings.

There was another reason for wanting to revisit Wildrose Cottage. He desperately wanted some guidance with his sketching and painting. So he needed to see the father and the daughter, for different reasons.

On the day of his proposed visit, while his father was absorbed in his newspaper and his brother Stephen absent, Courtney told his mother that he was going to ride over to Wildrose Cottage. His mother asked him who lived there, and suddenly and rashly Courtney told her about Jane and his interest in Henley Transon's daughter.

'The daughter of that dreadful artist fellow?' she said plaintively and, he thought, rather predictably.

'You know them then? The Transons?'

'I know *of* them,' said his mother, a painfully thin woman who wore drab colours as if to do so was her patriotic duty. 'That's an entirely different thing.'

31

'What do you know of them?' demanded Courtney.

Lady Constance gave the coffee pot a withering look. 'I understand the man is a card fanatic.'

Courtney laughed at this piece of information. 'Why, so are *you*, Mother. And Father. Eh, Charles?'

Sir Charles Stanton flicked the newspaper, seemingly unwilling to join in the conversation.

Instead, Lady Constance explained, very carefully, the difference between fanaticism and enjoyment, concluding with, 'Your father and I play bridge, sometimes a little whist, purely for pleasure.'

'You never play for money, I suppose?' said Courtney, knowing very well that they did.

'Of course we do,' snapped his mother, losing her poise, 'but we do not mortgage the estates in order to do so. Honestly, Courtney, since you've come back from that war, you've been enough to try the patience of a saint.'

That war. As if there were a dozen wars to choose from and he had picked the wrong one. Perhaps, thought Courtney bitterly, I should have been in Africa, or India, or somewhere exotic, and then I wouldn't be such a trial to her?

'Mother,' he said, 'you are no saint.'

'Don't be impertinent. Charles?'

Sir Charles reluctantly lowered his newspaper revealing the wary eyes of man being dragged reluctantly into combat like a minor buffer state caught between two great warring nations.

'What?' he said.

'Your son Courtney has returned from Europe with strange ideas concerning civility towards his parents.'

'Good Lord, Mother,' snapped Courtney, 'I'm twenty-eight years of age. I simply want to know what you've got against the Transons. You infer, but you never state. If there's something unsavoury about them, for goodness' sake say so.'

Sir Charles narrowed his eyes and spoke. 'If you are referring to Henley Transon, the artist, your mother is correct. The man is a waster. He sold his father's farm for two-thirds of what it was worth, simply to pay off his gambling debts.'

'If he had a right to sell it, then it must have been *his* farm, not his father's.'

'What I'm saying, Courtney, is that the man never used the farm for what it was. He never set foot in the farmhouse, nor did he do anything with the land. He simply sold it off as soon as he could.'

'That's not surprising, is it, since he's an artist and not a farmer?'

Sir Charles tightened his lips. 'When something is passed from father to son, it should be held sacred. At times like this I think I'm rather glad you're not the eldest, Courtney, or we might find that Stanton Manor and its estates would be sold off to the first buyer the moment I'm in my coffin.'

Lady Constance shushed her husband. 'Don't say such things, Charles. But your father is right, Courtney. This man Transon might very well be a nice person, but he has a reputation. I expect his daughter's charming in her way and you're very taken with her, but I'm sure there are other lovely young creatures around, just as pretty.'

She spoke as if her own sex were roe deer rather than human beings. Courtney was exasperated with her, with both of them. He didn't mind them being choosy about their *friends*, but he resented being told with whom he could associate, especially at twenty-eight years of age. He winced as he thought what he must have been like at the age of twenty-four, when he had gone away to the war: a gauche, immature naïf, an extension of his parents.

How his father had managed to rub shoulders with men of the lower classes and still retain that undented belief in his own divinity was beyond Courtney's understanding. Charles Stanton had risen from lieutenant to brigadier during his army career; at least in the early years he must have had contact with every kind of man, from farm labourer to blacksmith. Had he not seen that these men were as noble and honourable as himself, that there was nothing special about being the son of a baronet, or even a baronet himself? Or was the old man so thick-skinned that no reality ever penetrated his hide: an aristocratic pachyderm whose armour could resist all the arrows of truth?

'Trashy stuff, anyway,' said the baronet, resuming his interest in his paper.

'What's "trashy", Father?'

'Fellow's pictures. Garden scenes, or something. All a load of rubbish.'

This was the last straw. 'Father, you know a lot about many things, but you have never taken any interest in art. I'm sure you know very little about it.'

Lady Constance gasped, and the paper came down from the baronet's face with a sweeping gesture. 'I beg your pardon, Courtney?' spluttered the old man.

Courtney climbed awkwardly to his feet, for his wound always hurt him a little after sitting for a long period on a hard chair. 'I should jolly well think you ought to, Father. You've not studied art in any depth. Do you know the difference between Daumier and Millet? Pissarro and Pirandello? I think not.'

'I know they're all dead,' roared the baronet, going red.

'Really,' said Courtney, calmly. 'Pirandello is dead, is he?'

His father glared at him for moment, realising he was trapped.

Lady Constance sniffed and then fell all the way into the pit. 'What your father means is that Pirandello might as well be dead, for all his paintings are worth.'

'I shouldn't think his paintings are worth anything at all,' smiled Courtney, 'since Pirandello is a writer, not an artist.

The baronet looked away, but Courtney could not tell whether in embarrassment or anger. He suddenly felt very cheap, having played his trump card and won. His mother was looking a little horrified, as if she had just discovered she had reared a viper in place of a son.

Courtney tried to smooth things over. 'I'm not trying to put you both down, I'm trying to point something out to you. There are men you regard as clods in the village who know more about art than all three of us put together. Joseph Smith the farrier, for instance. Those gates he made for you, Father, for the driveway, are originals. He *invented* that form of centripetal you so much admire and point out to your guests. Do you understand what I'm trying to tell you?'

Sir Charles stared at his son again. 'I understand *what* you are saying, Courtney. I'm trying to comprehend *why* you're saying it to me. No one thinks more highly of Joseph Smith than I do, and when

I'm boasting to my guests, I never fail to mention that Joseph was the farrier who wrought the gates. In fact he tells me he is quite grateful for the business which I put his way. I do not seek to gain praise at his expense, and I am fully aware of his talents.'

'If that's so, I'm glad, Father. Look, I'm sorry we're all out of sorts with one another, but I'm just trying to say that artists deserve as much respect as anyone. I regard Henley Transon as a good artist, certainly the best we have around here. What he does in his private time has nothing to do with his art.'

'Surely,' said Lady Constance, 'the reputation and the art are one and the same thing?'

Courtney smiled. 'Mother, some of the wickedest people in history have been the best artists.'

She took a sip of her coffee and replied, 'That may be so, but it doesn't mean we have to associate with them.'

Despite his mother's remark, Courtney left the table shortly afterwards in better spirits. It was true he had found his parents difficult since he had returned from the war, but he was beginning to believe that it wasn't so much that *they* had altered from the people he knew as a younger man, but rather that it was he himself who had changed so much.

He decided after all to take the family car, and drove along the lane towards Howlett End. Courtney drove very slowly: he had only just learned to drive, and the last time he had taken the vehicle out he had put it in the ditch. He was not very good with mechanical things. They were cold and artificial, and he much preferred riding to driving. But the discussion with his parents had delayed him, and he had to admit that using a car was quicker. His horse could travel almost as fast, but took longer to saddle up.

As it happened Courtney did not have to go all the way to Wildrose Cottage to meet Henley. About four miles from Stanton Manor, he noticed the figure of Henley painting wildflowers in the corner of a pasture.

Courtney parked the car by a field gate and walked across the meadow to greet Henley. 'Morning! On your own?' he called.

Henley looked up. He did not seem at all pleased to be interrupted. Courtney kicked himself mentally, knowing he should have just strolled up without saying anything and left the other man painting.

'Don't let me disturb you,' he said to Henley. 'I'll just prop myself up against that fence post and watch.'

Henley let the pallet drop from his hand on to the grass, then he wiped his fingers on his smock. He was wearing a straw hat which had once belonged to his wife – so Jane had told Courtney – and he removed this and skimmed it away from him. Then he picked up a basket which contained, among other things, a bottle of milk and a loaf of bread.

'Don't worry,' said Henley. 'I was thinking of stopping soon anyway. Come and join me in a glass of milk.'

Henley sat down on the damp grass, and Courtney had little choice but to follow suit. The sun was shining, but it was not warm enough for the dew to have dried. Shadows from the trees and hedges were still quite long, and tended to shade the corners of fields. He knew his bones, not long rid of the fever, would ache on rising. However, he told himself in amusement, one had to suffer for one's art.

Courtney took the glass of milk offered him. Henley drank out of the bottle. The artist then broke the small loaf in two and left half for Courtney, who was still not yet recovered from his breakfast.

'Jane's gone into Thaxted,' said Henley.

'Well, actually, I came looking for you as well,' Courtney said. 'I want to see Jane too, of course, but I wanted to talk to you – about your painting.'

'What about it?'

'Well, for instance, what school do you consider influences you?'

Henley smiled and stuffed a piece of bread in his mouth, then washed it down with milk.

'Who do *you* think influences me?' he asked.

'The impressionists? Renoir mainly, I should say.'

'Why Renoir especially? Why not Cézanne, or Van Gogh, or Seurat?'

'Well, you seem to give your work a deep underlying structure of horizontal and vertical lines, in the way that Renoir often does. I admit you use similar colour tones to Cézanne – those ochres – but your subject matter is less abstracted than Van Gogh's work, and you are certainly no pointillist.'

Henley took another bite of his bread and stared hard before saying, 'Did you write that down?'

'I beg your pardon?'

'Before you came here today. Did you write that speech down, practise it before a mirror?'

Courtney felt himself colouring up, but he managed to say in a level voice, '*You* gave me the list of artists. I didn't prepare them beforehand.'

'That's true,' said Henley, suddenly smiling. 'And you're quite right, the impressionist form of painting is the most exciting thing to happen to art. What else could I be? A Japanese woodblock cutter, I suppose, except that I'm not Japanese, and I'm no good with sharp tools.'

He smiled again and took a withered apple from the basket and began to peel it very efficiently with a penknife.

"I'm no Utamaro, me,' Henley laughed.

Courtney felt rather put out by this show. 'I'm glad you find me so amusing.'

Henley shook his head. 'No, you misunderstand me. I thought we were actually getting closer to each other. I was only half joking with you. I'm flattered that you've taken such an interest in my technique and I agree with you over some of the points you make; but you have to understand, I am my *own* man. I don't mind people pointing to my influences, but at the same time, of course, I seek to be original.'

'You are, very much so,' said Courtney. 'That's why I want your advice. So far I've mostly sketched, but I want to paint too. I've been thinking of taking up watercolours.'

Henley made a face. 'Watercolours are all right for Sunday painters, but if you're serious, oils is the only medium.'

Courtney was surprised. 'There are some very famous people who've used watercolours.'

'Only as an exercise, I'm sure. How many of the world's great paintings are in watercolours?'

Courtney shrugged.

'There you are then,' said Henley.

Courtney took a piece of the bread and chewed it, even though he did not feel hungry. It was necessary to do something with his hands and he wished he had a cigarette. He did not smoke often, but there were occasions when he wanted a cigarette above all things.

'So,' he said, 'you think I should plunge straight into oils?'

'Waste a few canvases. Paint a few dozen pictures that you intend showing to no one. Go into the hundreds, if you can afford it. *Gradually* find your way into a style you like the best – find your own method of perception. Chuck them all away once you start to hate them, which you *will* believe me. At first you'll think, 'That's not bad', then as time goes on you'll begin to be irritated by the flaws, and finally you'll be sick to death of them. Then's the time to paint over them. I take it you've got a bit of money?'

'A bit.'

'Good. Then there won't be any problem setting yourself up with equipment and paints, will there? Now, what do you want to show me?'

Courtney was genuinely perplexed. 'Show you?'

'The sketches you did in the trenches. You surely want my opinion of them?'

'They're in the car.'

'Then run and fetch them, there's a good chap. I want to get back to my work.'

Courtney rose and limped quickly over the field, retrieved his sketchbook from the car, and carried it back to Henley.

Henley took it and began turning the pages, frowning as he did so.

Henley had always avoided violence, to the point of not reading newspapers and magazines. He had not been in the army and had never experienced war. Whatever else Courtney's sketches might be, they were certainly vivid, and as Henley studied the horrible conditions under which soldiers had lived in the trenches, and the suffering they had undergone, he felt sickened. Headless corpses, detached limbs lying casually in muddy pools, torsos without appendages, these were depicted on page after page, the realism stark and shocking.

'Good Lord,' he said in a hollow voice, 'was it as bad as that?'

Courtney had been viewing the sketches over Henley's shoulder, not really seeing the carnage, the gore, the devastation, until Henley had spoken. All Courtney had been aware of until then was an uneconomical line, a stroke too many on a crumpled figure, or too much shading around a severed leg. Now he looked at the sketches through Henley's eyes, seeing the utter waste of human life, the misery, the terrible mutilations of the young men.

'Yes, I suppose it was.'

'Disgusting,' said Henley, showing anger. 'Absolutely bloody appalling.'

'But surely you heard? You read the newspapers?'

'Nothing quite comes home to me unless it's a piece of visual art. The newspapers printed photographs, of course, but they were not as candid as these. I expect the editors considered it unpatriotic or obscene to publish pictures of this nature. I read Sassoon's *Counterattack*, but it didn't hit me with the same force as these sketches.'

'Does that mean they're all right?' said Courtney, hopefully.

Henley expression changed.

'I haven't had a chance to look at them that way yet. The subject matter is too overwhelming initially, but . . . yes, they're not awful. Mind you, you'll never get one artist to appreciate fully the work of another, especially if he's a young upstart.'

Courtney grinned. 'Is that what I am, a young upstart?'

'You will be, if people start saying you're better than I am. No, seriously, these are fair, nothing more. You haven't really practised enough, have you? Forget all that rubbish about talent. You need to sketch a thousand sketches before you do one worth keeping. You need to exercise your *creative* muscles, the way a tennis player exercises his arm muscles. You wouldn't expect to play half a dozen games of tennis then go out and win a championship, would you? In the same way, you need to be able to draw instinctively, not self-consciously, so that the correct line is second nature. Does this depress you?'

'No, it excites me. I've never been very happy with the idea of inspiration, or talent, because I don't believe I've got that much. Hard work sounds more to my liking. I remember reading that Jack London said you have to go after inspiration with a club.'

Henley nodded. 'So long as you stick to that idea, you won't go far wrong. Even if you have bags of talent, it won't do you any harm to ignore it. Talented people who rely on their genius usually end up being lazy and doing very little. Now buzz off. I've got work to do.'

Courtney did as he was told, staying just a short while to watch Henley applying the strokes, but realising he was disturbing the older man simply by being there, he soon crossed the field again to his car.

Henley had mentioned that Jane was in Thaxted for the day, so Courtney made up his mind to drive in and see if he could give her a lift back to her cottage. After cruising through the streets two or three times, he failed to chance across her, and he was just about to give up when he saw her coming out of the church. She was dressed in a blue coat with a high collar, her black hair up on her head somehow, under the fur hat. Courtney regarded the exposed, elegant neck, and wondered how she could look so entirely different each time her saw her. One day she might look simply pretty; another, like today, she appeared absolutely beautiful – so fresh and lovely it hurt him to look at her. He drew up alongside her, just outside the churchyard.

'Jane? Can I offer you a lift?'

Jane turned and regarded the shiny vehicle with a slight smile on her lips. 'Oh, Courtney. This is very posh, isn't it? Is it yours?'

'Family's, but you never know, once I get the hang of the thing I might buy one of my own.'

'You mean you can't drive properly yet? Should I come with you, or will I be in danger?'

He laughed. 'I'll try not to hit anything. I don't go fast enough for that, anyway. Old Jake Crampthorne overtook me in his pony and trap on the way here.'

Jake was well known locally for allowing his pony to move at snail's pace along the by-ways.

'I don't believe you.'

'It's true, he flashed past. Or so it seemed.'

'In that case, I'd better walk. I want to be home by nightfall.'

Having spoken these words however, she allowed Courtney to open the passenger's door from the inside, and she climbed aboard. Courtney set off, a little faster than usual, heading for Howlett End. He was wondering how his mother could possibly disapprove of such a wonderful girl as Jane Transon.

Chapter Five

Henley only remembered to tell Jane that someone was coming to dinner as she was cutting vegetables for the two of them.

'Oh, Father, not tonight?'

'Yes, tonight. I forgot to tell you.'

'But I've only bought enough stewing steak for the two of us. What am I going to do?'

Henley shrugged. These situations always left him at a loss.

Jane wiped her hands on her apron and said she would run up to the farmhouse and see if she could get some kidneys. They could have steak and kidney pie. The Blatchers, their nearest farm neighbours, were often willing to help out in an emergency. Jane knew that they had slaughtered a pig just a few days before: she had heard the terrible squealing, terminated suddenly and followed by deep silence. Having lived near the farm all her life, she knew the meaning of that sound and the subsequent silence well.

She put on her coat over her apron and took the path alongside the corner field. Blatcher's wife Sally was feeding the chickens when Jane arrived. A short, stout woman of great strength, she listened to Jane's request, nodded pleasantly and said, 'You carry on with this, lovey, while I go and get you the kidneys. I don't like to break up their feeding because it upsets 'em so.'

Jane took the bucket of feed. It was so heavy it almost wrenched her arm out of its socket. Sally Blatcher had handed it over as if it were a basket of flowers. When Sally had gone into her back kitchen, Jane put the bucket on the dirt floor of the yard, only to find that the chickens swarmed all over it. She had to lift it up out of their reach again with one hand, while scattering the feed with the other. She was very relieved to see Sally again.

41

'You can pay me some other time,' said Sally. 'Just pop it up when you can, lovey.'

'Thanks awfully, Sally, you always come to our rescue.'

Sally waved away the thanks with a shy smile.

Jane dashed back to the cottage, carrying the bloody kidneys at arm's length. Sally had wrapped them in newspaper and the package had soon become a sodden, leaking mess. Once back in the kitchen, Jane put them on a plate and then got to work on the pastry. When she was rolling out the crust, there was a knock on the door.

'Can you get that, Father?' she yelled.

There was no answer, so with her arms covered in flour she went to the door and opened it.

A tall, fair-haired man stood there. 'Henley Transon's house?' he inquired.

'Yes, I'm his daughter.'

'He didn't say anything about a daughter. I'm Petre Peake. I believe I'm invited for dinner.'

The alarm she felt must have shown on her face, for he added after a moment, 'You weren't expecting me?'

'Well, yes I was, but not so early. Father said you wouldn't be here until about seven-thirty. It's only just six. Do come in, anyway . . .'

Peake remained where he was standing. 'He told me six, but I can go down to the pub and be back for seven-thirty.'

'The pub's miles away. How did you get here?'

'By horse-carriage.'

'Actually, dinner won't be ready until about eight, probably later. My father – well, he forgot to tell me we were having guests. So the pie is only just about to go into the oven. Do please come in. I'm sorry if I seem so unwelcoming. I'm not really, I'm just a bit flustered.'

'Of course.'

He stepped inside and removed his trilby. Jane took it gingerly between white thumb and forefinger and put it on a peg behind the door. As it was, she saw that she had left a thumbprint on the brim.

'Sorry,' she said. 'I won't shake hands. You'll get flour all over you.'

He nodded, and she saw that his eyes were such a light shade of blue that she found difficulty in looking at them.

'At least you didn't immediately apologise for your appearance,' he said to her. 'I like that. It would have been the first thing most women would have done.'

Jane had been about to do that very thing, and clamped her jaws together tightly, suppressing a desire to laugh. She glanced again at the guest, who seemed quite at ease, totally comfortable in what was for him a strange house. He looked as though nothing would ruffle him. She noticed that he was smartly but plainly dressed in a dark suit with a coloured tie. There were no frills about him, Jane noticed.

Something else she had already observed about him. He had not smiled once.

She showed him into the living room and then went to fetch her father from wherever he was hiding. She knew what the problem was: Henley hated the smell of kidneys cooking – he said the odour of urine made him feel ill – so he was probably out in the garden somewhere.

While she was gone, Peake glanced around the living room, at the sparse furnishings and little feminine touches that his own lodgings in Saffron Walden lacked. The lace curtains, for instance, and the little doily things on the sideboard. He reached over and picked one up. 'Thaxted 1918' had been worked into a corner of the pattern. Such items were not part of Petre Peake's life, and he found it strange that someone had been crocheting these flimsy bits of nonsense while men were being shot to pieces in a filthy trench half filled with stinking water. It didn't upset him. He simply found it ironic that such a useless activity, the production of a frippery, had employed someone's time while the fate of the world had been held in balance.

Peake replaced the item and then stared at some photographs on the mantelpiece. There was a woman he did not recognise, which he took to be Transon's dead wife. There was also a fairly recent picture of Jane Transon. He liked the look of her; and she seemed a sensible woman to him. He tried to imagine what it would be like to be married to such a woman. There were aspects of such a situation which appealed in some ways, but of course for him it was an impossible scenario.

At that moment, Henley entered the room.

Jane, after finding her father in the potting shed and informing him of the early arrival of their guest, had gone back to the steak and kidney pie, potatoes and cabbage.

Later, the three of them were seated around the dining-room table, about to start their meal. Jane was becoming rather fascinated by Petre Peake. There was something very deep and sorrowful about him, beneath the diamond-hard exterior, and she wondered if he had had some unhappy affaire. He appeared like the stone statue of some forgotten god, waiting and hoping for worshippers to return to his shrine. She tried not to let her interest become too evident, but Henley must have noticed the way she was studying the young man, because he gave her a little frown.

Jane ignored this and directed a question at their guest. 'You live in Saffron Walden then?' she said.

Peake nodded curtly. 'Lodgings. Not as comfortable as this.'

'And what do you do now that you're out of the army? I take it you *have* left the army.'

'Royal Flying Corps. Yes, I left when it became the Royal Air Force, last year. I now have a private income, so I have no need to work.'

Henley said, 'You resigned your commission?'

'It wasn't a difficult thing to do. I was never an army officer at heart. If I'd have had my way I would have stayed a ranker, just like Johnston.'

Henley shook his head vigorously. 'Not like Johnston, surely? You're an educated man.'

No one felt inclined to argue with that statement, least of all Jane, so they began to eat their meal. There was no wine on the table – it was too expensive for Jane's purse – but there was a jug of beer which had been cooling on a slate shelf in the larder. She poured a glass for each one of them, then lifted her own glass and said, 'To peace, may it continue for ever.'

They all lifted their glasses and drank, but afterwards Peake said to her, 'An optimistic toast – impossible, of course.'

'You don't think that was the *last* war we'll experience?' Jane said.

'In addition to taxes and death, war is inevitable.'

'But after what people have seen? The terrible losses amongst the young men. The *slaughter*. The disabled. And for what? Don't you think the futility of war has at last been plainly revealed for everyone to see?'

'For those of us who took part in it, perhaps. *We* mightn't want another war. But there'll be generations who will have no experience of war and they will begin it again.'

Jane could not accept this. 'But we have a written history of the horrors . . .'

Peake stared at her with his intense blue eyes. 'If history prevented wars, we'd have stopped fighting each other thousands of years ago. We have a written account of the Battle of Marathon, which was a bloody slaughter – thousands dead, thousands maimed. *That* didn't stop the next battle, which I believe was Thermopylae, only ten years later.

'I personally *enjoyed* the war. It allowed me to exercise a skill at which I am particularly efficient. Ordinarily, one is not permitted to kill people – not without punishment. In a war, however, this is precisely what is required of one. I am very competent with weapons.'

Jane felt a chill go through her at these words. 'You're joking with me,' she said, attempting a smile.

Henley said, 'No, he isn't, my dear. Mr Peake is a ruthless man.'

Peake allowed his mouth to curve slightly upwards at the corners. Jane would not have called it a smile, but it was close to it.

'Your father's right,' he said, 'I am completely without ruth, which makes me valuable during times of aggression, when one's country is threatened by an enemy. Now that it's over, am I supposed to deplore my hour of glory? Am I supposed to say that it was a necessary but horrible task? I'm sorry, I can't do that. I actually felt like a king. People looked at me with admiration in their eyes. Young men envied me. Why should I now deny all that and condemn the circumstances which brought about my golden time? Without the war, I would be nothing.'

'But you came through it whole,' Jane said, feeling a little angry with him. 'Some did not.'

'Did I?' he said, rather sharply.

Jane was taken aback by the hardness in his tone. 'I'm sorry,' she faltered. 'I assumed you had.'

45

'No one comes through a war whole. There is always a loss, either mental or physical, or even spiritual. I lost something, I'm not sure what to call it. Perhaps one might call it "humanity", for want of a better word, though that doesn't really describe it.'

Henley said, 'You lost your *humanity*?'

'I said it was not accurate, but yes, for want of a better term.'

They ate in silence for a while after that. Jane was now even more fascinated by this young man, who seemed to be have the same kind of amorality as an avenging angel. He killed because it was required of him and he was good at it. He killed not out of enjoyment, but without conscience. It was a particular vocation, a skill to be exercised in the same manner as the skill of a carpenter or blacksmith.

Her eyes must have said something, for he spoke again after a while. 'I've disturbed you,' he said to her.

'No – yes, yes you have, but I don't wish to discuss the subject any further.'

'As you wish.'

When Jane cleared the table and took the dishes into the kitchen, Henley felt able to broach the subject which had precipitated the invitation in the first instance. He had to be careful, though, for he still had to play cards with Peake, and did not want the other man to regard him as a complete innocent.

'You said something which interested me the other evening,' Henley began.

'What was that?' asked Peake, lounging back in his chair.

'About luck. You said you didn't rely on luck at cards. That must mean you have some system or other.'

Peake took out a packet of cigarettes and offered one to Henley. They both lit up. Peake took a long pull on his cigarette before answering.

'No, no system.'

Henley felt a twinge of frustration. 'A secret then. Some cryptic insight, perhaps? A way of looking at the cards, gauging the strength of others? Perhaps you have a photographic memory?'

Peake suddenly leaned forward and stared into Henley's eyes, making Henley feel that same chill which had travelled through Jane just an hour or so previously.

46

'Transon,' said Peake, 'the secret is not caring.'

The hairs rose on the back of Henley's neck. 'Not caring?' he repeated.

'That's it. Not caring. Not caring when you kill your fellow man. Not caring whether you live or die yourself. Not caring if you win or lose. War, cards, love. There are certain things which men desperately care about. The more they care, the less successful they are. If you went into a card game not caring what the outcome might be, I don't doubt you would win – but the trouble is you're not equipped, mentally or physically, for not caring. You'll be thinking to yourself, what if I *lose*, and consequently you *will* lose.'

'Is it that easy?' Henley said.

Peake laughed out loud, humourlessly. '*Easy?*'

Henley thought about it. Could he really go into a game not caring – *really* not caring – about whether he won or not? Wouldn't there always be some little spark, deep inside, which would nag him during the play? Wouldn't that *hope*, that sometimes *desperate* hope, which accompanied the turn of the card, be there whatever mindset Henley tried to adopt? Of course it would. That was why he played. For that thrill, that electric feeling he experienced on every turn of the card. If he didn't care, why would he want to play at all?

Something else was bothering him now. 'What do you mean, not equipped mentally and *physically*? I can see how a mental attitude . . .'

Peake's eyes had gone cold and hard. 'You need to be born without a heart, Transon.'

Just then, Jane walked back into the room, and something in the way Jane looked at Peake caused another icy thought to cut through Henley's mind. In Peake's list of things other men cared so much about, and Peake not at all, had been the word 'love'. Had he employed this term spontaneously, or was there some deeper motive in using it as an example?

When his daughter had left the room again, Henley cleared his throat and said, 'Jane is very fond of a young man recently returned from France.'

'Really?' said Peake. 'Why are you telling me this?'

'No real reason. It just occurred to me, while she was clearing the table.'

'Who is this man?' asked Peake.

'Stanton. Courtney Stanton.'

'I don't believe I've ever met him.'

'His father is a baronet. You know Stanton Manor?'

'Oh, that place. Yes, I've passed it once or twice. In that case it's very doubtful I would have met this Stanton. We hardly move in the same circles, do we?'

Henley shrugged. 'Courtney Stanton is a captain with the Essex Regiment. I thought you might have come across him that way.'

'No.'

When Jane came back into the room she found conversation had ceased between the two men. It was a strange kind of quiet which had settled between them, not so much peace as silence, for the atmosphere was still charged with a kind of unspoken anger. Shortly afterwards Peake's transport was heard clattering its hooves on the flint road-surface outside the cottage.

'Time to go,' Peake said, stirring himself.

Jane said, 'Back to your lodgings in Saffron Walden?'

'That's right.'

'Do you have family in Essex, Mr Peake?'

He stared at her in a strange way for a few moments before answering. 'My parents are now both dead. I was an only child. I'm on my own.'

Jane said, 'Oh, I'm sorry. Don't you have any relations who might be close to you?'

Peake gave her a tight smile. 'You're very inquisitive, Miss Transon. Yes, but those people are nothing to me. Now, may I leave to catch my lift?'

Once Peake had gone, his lean dark figure disappearing along the path to the lane, Jane said to her father, 'What a strange young man. He looks so tortured . . .'

Henley said quickly, 'He's not a lame rabbit, Jane.'

'I know that, Father.'

'So long as you do. I know you. You'll take in any creature if you think it needs care. That young man is dangerous.'

'In what way?' asked Jane with interest.

'He's like dynamite on a slow fuse, waiting to explode. There's too much contained anger in him. I don't want you getting mixed up with such a man.'

'You brought him home,' said Jane, suddenly feeling angry.

Henley looked a bit shame-faced. 'Well, that was for reasons of my own.'

Jane left it at that, realising that Henley was becoming defensive. When he did that they almost always ended up arguing with one another. She finished the rest of the tidying up and then bade her father goodnight and went to bed. As she undressed her thoughts were on Petre Peake. As she pictured his hard, lean form striding away from the cottage, she shivered involuntarily. Yes, he was a strange man, an enigma. In one way he was vulnerable, a wounded animal, and in another he seemed invincible, unforgiving, a man of stone. He was obviously a harsh, exacting man with other men, men like her father, yet she sensed something – not really compassion, but something still human – at the core of his heart, something locked inside the granite, sealed away from the world and himself.

But whatever he was, she thought to herself as she climbed into bed, he was definitely an exciting man.

Chapter Six

The bulbs arrived at the beginning of July, thousands of them, just in time for the planting. Henley was astounded by the number of sacks which had to be stacked in the back garden. He kept asking Jane how much they had cost.

'None of your business, Father. These were bought from my own savings,' she said over breakfast, the day after they had arrived.

Outside, it was a beautiful summer's day with only a few pieces of white, buoyant cloud in the sky. The sunlight streamed through the leaded windows that overlooked the rolling farmlands and sparkled on the breakfast dishes. Jane felt immensely happy. There was nothing her father could say or do today which would upset her. She was set on enjoying this time.

'If you are determined to waste it, I could use that money to pay a few bills,' Henley grumbled.

Jane poured herself another cup of tea. 'It hasn't been wasted, it's an investment. An investment in your art, Father.' She did not add that if she had given it to him, it would not have been spent paying bills, but more likely thrown away on the turn of a card. Henley was grieving the loss to his gambling, not to the household expenses.

'There are plenty of wildflowers for me to paint, without you spending a fortune on these corms. I'm astonished. I really think it was an appalling thing to do.'

'Father,' said Jane, still smiling, but through gritted teeth, 'you are the most ungrateful man alive. When Courtney Stanton was here you became *very* excited over the prospect of painting fields of saffron crocuses. This is my gift to you, and I don't expect to have it flung back in my face.'

'Excited, yes...' He looked up into her eyes and seemed to falter. 'Well, you're right,' he said. 'I do appreciate it, but Jane, we've got an awful lot of work to do. Do you realise? These have to be planted if they're to grow. Just the two of us?'

'I've already thought of that,' replied Jane smugly. 'I've hired some field-hands through the Blatchers. They use gypsies at picking time, for the peas and potatoes, and Sally has sent word to them. They work for next to nothing, Father, the gypsy women. They're due to arrive in three days' time.'

'And what about the preparation of the fields?' said Henley drily. 'It's mostly pasture. It has to be ploughed.'

'Oh,' cried Jane, pretending she hadn't thought of this and putting on a crestfallen look, 'what a fool I am.'

Henley wagged a righteous finger.

Just at that moment there came a knock on the door and Henley rose from the table and went to answer it. Jane heard the door being opened, then her father's voice saying, 'Young Stanton? Were we supposed to meet today? I don't remember...'

Then Courtney's voice saying, 'Jane asked me to come. I'm supposed to be helping her with some ploughing or something. I must confess I'm no expert, but she says Blatcher will loan us his team of Suffolks and a man to show us how to use them.'

She then heard her father's short laugh as he and Courtney entered the room.

'Good morning, Courtney,' she said. 'Thanks for coming.'

Courtney was dressed appropriately in slacks and collarless shirt rolled up at the sleeves. 'I may regret this,' he smiled.

'Would you like some breakfast before we go?' she asked him.

'No, I've already had some. It's a glorious day. Let's get out there and churn up the county.'

The three of them left the cottage and walked up the hard earth track to Blatcher's Farm. There they duly collected two Suffolk Punch horses, complete with harnesses, and a farm-hand, John, to manage them. The plough had already been delivered by cart that morning and was standing in the corner of one of the meadows when they arrived.

They were shown how to hitch the horses to the plough, a method which only Courtney grasped the first time. Henley himself was looking bewildered and out of his depth. He simply stood and watched as the technical details were passed on to his daughter and Courtney. Jane herself was determined to master at least the knowledge, if not the skill, of ploughing.

When John had shown Courtney the art of ploughing a straight furrow the length of the field, and Courtney had tackled three or four himself, though with less accuracy, Jane wanted to try.

'I don't think you'm strong enough, miss,' said John doubtfully. 'These brutes are gentle enough, but they'm hard on the handling.'

'I think he's right,' said Courtney. 'My muscles are aching already, Jane.'

Jane gave both men a cold stare. 'I want to try,' she said, simply.

Henley called out, 'Better let her have a go, or you'll never hear the last of it.'

John shrugged and Courtney said, 'All right then, but I'll walk beside you, just in case you need someone to take over.'

She didn't object to this. Jane felt a rush of adrenalin as the excitement built inside her. She was going to plough a field! She felt suitably dressed, having put on a heavy skirt and boots, both of which were already splattered with the rich loam. She rolled up the sleeves to her dark blouse, copying Courtney's style.

'Right,' she said. 'I'm ready.'

When she was directly behind the plough she was suddenly aware of how large the two horses were in their great leather collars. It was true they seemed very gentle animals, but they towered above John, who held one of the traces to keep them still while Courtney showed her where to put her hands on the plough.

'All right,' said Courtney, 'now give them the signal.'

Jane's heart was beating fast as she yelled at the horses, 'Giddy-up, giddy-up.'

They remained motionless until John flicked the trace and growled, 'Giddap, you'm lazy beggers.'

The beasts suddenly lumbered forward, as if coming out of a trance. Jane almost had the plough jerked out of her hands, but she gamely held on, her heart still racing a little. What had looked relatively easy when John had been doing it, suddenly became impossible: to keep the ploughshare slicing through the turf in a straight line. Jane felt sure there must be something loose between the horses and the plough. The plough seemed to want to go in different directions to the Suffolks. It skidded along the surface of the field, hardly cutting a slit in the turf, until Courtney said, 'Bear down on it, bear down. It needs your weight to get it into the earth. Bear down.'

Bear down? What was she supposed to be doing, giving birth or ploughing a field? She put all her weight on the handles of the plough and was rewarded with a mild success. All her heart-racing and trembling had gone now as she utilised every ounce of strength she possessed in getting the ploughshare to bite into the turf. She was elated, but at the same time angry that her physical strength was not the equal of Courtney's. John was different. He had been doing this all his life, and had formed the muscles for it. But Courtney himself actually didn't look a strong man. It all seemed most unfair.

The ploughshare suddenly struck something hard, jolting the plough out of the furrow. She fought to keep the heavy wooden implement upright. The horses, suddenly finding their burden lighter, jerked forward involuntarily.

'Keep it straight, keep it straight,' yelled Courtney, as the plough began to bounce and veer to the left.

'Don't shout at me,' she shouted, trying to keep the plough on course. 'I hit a flint.'

Courtney used his shoulder to help the plough back on to its former course. 'There are flints all over the place,' he said. 'You just have to plough through them, knock them out of the way.'

'Listen to the expert,' Jane panted breathlessly as she fought against the forces of the earth. 'How long have you been at it?'

'I'm only repeating what John told *me*.'

John was now stationed at the top of the field with his arms folded, watching their progress through narrowed eyes. Henley was standing next to him, his mouth agape as he watched his daughter struggling with two beasts of burden, a flint-covered field, and her own frustration.

'It looks so easy when he does it,' Jane groaned. 'Why does it keep bouncing out of the rut like that? I'm not that light, am I?'

Courtney laughed. 'You could do with a few more pounds for this job, Jane.'

The end of the field trundled slowly towards them, and suddenly Jane thought of something. 'Oh my God, how do you *turn* them?'

She need not have worried. When the Suffolks reached the ditch at the end, having received no order to the contrary, they simply came to a halt. Their great hooves thumped into the earth as they waited restlessly for some sort of command. They were sensible beasts, not given to the kind of flighty behaviour indulged in by Courtney's mare, Sheba.

Courtney grasped a trace and led the horses round until they faced the other way. 'Do you want me to take them back up the field?' he asked.

'No,' said Jane, though her muscles were aching like fury, 'I'll take them up.'

She began the journey again, trying to stay as close to her first furrow as possible. Flocks of seagulls and rooks had descended from out of nowhere, having somehow received the message that there was fresh food to be had. They followed her snaking progress up the field, making a racket as they did so. To Jane it sounded as if they were being critical of her efforts. *Even the birds are against me*, she thought.

When she reached the top she almost fell away from the plough, but she was happy. She had done some of the work and she would do some more once she recovered. Looking back down her two furrows, they didn't seem all *that* crooked beside Courtney's. You could have fired an arrow down John's furrow, of course, and not hit the sides, but Courtney's were only just a little bit straighter than her own.

'Well done, miss,' said John. 'Now you and the gentleman have got the hang, I'll be gettin' back to the farm.'

'You're going to leave us?' she said, her eyes opening wide.

'You'll be all right. Mr Stanton here knows how to handle horses, and these 'uns are only just a bit bigger than the one he uses hisself.'

'That's all right, John,' said Courtney. 'We don't want to hold you back from your work.'

When the farm-hand had left, Courtney said, 'I suggest we have some lunch then really get stuck in.' First he led the horses to a patch of grass in the unploughed part of the field and left them munching. Then he returned to where Jane was recovering and lay down level with the ground to look along one of his own furrows.

'Looks like the damned River Chelmer,' he said, 'meandering over the countryside like that.' He looked up. 'Yours isn't bad though, Jane. What do you say, Henley? She did well, didn't she?'

'If I utter anything even faintly like praise she'll tell me I'm patronising her,' said Henley. 'You can get away with it, being a friend, but I can't.'

Jane was unpacking the picnic basket. 'It's going to be hard work,' she said, 'but we'll get it done. I'm sorry I lost my temper out there, Courtney. You're getting some glimpses of the real Jane Transon – a bad-tempered she-devil.'

Courtney sat down, picked up a sandwich, and grinned at her. 'I deem it a privilege.'

Henley said, 'Say that at the end of the day. There are several more acres to plough yet. As for me, I'm going home after lunch. I'll leave the turning of the earth to you youngsters.'

'That's very kind of you, Father,' said Jane.

'Not at all,' he replied, her sarcasm bouncing off him without having any effect.

When they had eaten, Henley made good his word and left them to it. They took turns, doing about ten furrows each. It was backbreaking work for those not used to it, but Jane found she was thoroughly enjoying herself. Until now she had done little physical work, apart from housework, and she was surprised at how rewarding it was. At Horsham St Faith's School for Young Ladies, they had not encouraged physical activity. Until she reached the age of eighteen she had played some games like lacrosse and tennis, but other than that had indulged only in gentle rambles over the Norfolk countryside with the rest of her nature class.

Some of the enjoyment was of course derived from the fact that she had company. It would have been a lot less fun alone. Courtney kept making jokes, keeping her laughing, mostly about their amateurish efforts at farming. She noticed that his limp became more pronounced as the afternoon wore on, and his arm was obviously giving him pain, but he said nothing about either. He quoted Gray's

Elegy written in a Country Church-yard right through, stumbling only once or twice, which impressed her, even when he told her that it didn't matter if you got the order of the lines mixed up, it still sounded right because they stood on their own.

They started a hare from its form once, and watched it zig-zag across the field towards the ditch.

'Oh, we've destroyed its home,' said Jane. 'I feel like Robert Burns must have felt when he crushed the nest of the little harvest mouse.'

'No, it's not that serious,' Courtney said. 'He'll scrape himself another one in a few moments. They're very adaptable.'

Towards evening they saw a fox sneaking along the ditch, and Jane again became worried about the hare, until Courtney assured her that any self-respecting hare would not be caught napping and could outrun a fox any day.

'Foxes don't catch many large mammals, unless they're young or sick,' he said. 'Hares are especially difficult to catch because they have all-round vision. If a hare sees a fox skulking round he'll simply stand up tall on his hind legs, and stare at the fox. He's saying, "I see you, Foxy, and you know I can outrun you, so don't even bother trying." No, unless a fox is right on top of a hare before he's seen, he doesn't stand a chance of catching it.'

'Well, how do foxes eat, then?'

'Foxes catch a lot of mice, grubs, worms, things like that. They'll eat vegetables and fruit too, if they can't get anything else.'

'You seem to know a lot about the countryside.'

'I grew up here,' he said.

'So did I, mostly, but I'm very ignorant about the wildlife.'

He grinned at her. 'The trouble is, you're a girl. As a boy I was allowed to roam at will over these fields, which I expect you were not. I was a lonely child too. I wasn't allowed to mix with the village children, so I used to go out on my own. You see a lot, hear much more, when you're on your own.'

'A lot you know, Courtney Stanton. No one realised I was girl until I was fourteen. I was into everything, from ponds to ditches to hayricks.'

He smiled and shook his head. 'I can't believe that, looking at you now.'

'I wasn't always this shape – or this feminine.'

As they talked they unhitched the team and started back over the undulating fields towards home. The sky was red, which promised a good following day. Clumps of elms patterned the skyline as the weary pair trudged along the Chelmer valley, the hills around them like fragments of brown and green eggshells. There were no ridges, no crags or cliffs to throw long, sharp shadows. Only the smooth swell of a gentle landscape fading gradually into darkness. Here and there, in the late evening, they saw lamps lit in solitary cottages.

They delivered the horses to Blatcher's farm and asked if they might use them again in the morning. Blatcher said that would be all right. Courtney then rode home on Sheba and Jane had a little supper and fell into bed. Henley was out for the evening and she did not hear him come home.

When Jane woke the next morning, she could not move without extreme pain. Every muscle in her body hurt her. Simply lifting one arm caused her excruciating agony. She called for Henley.

'What's the matter?' he said brusquely, coming into her bedroom.

She managed to turn her head on the pillow, but it hurt her neck to do so. 'I'm . . . I can't do anything,' she said. 'I hurt all over, Daddy.'

She hadn't called him 'Daddy' for many years, except when deeply troubled by something.

Henley looked at his daughter. A pang of conscience went through him. He had come into her bedroom expecting an argument over him not wanting to join them in ploughing the fields today. Instead he found his daughter looking as if she had been trampled by an elephant.

'Would you like me to make you some breakfast?' he asked. He always felt awkward around any kind of illness. Women seemed to know what to do instinctively, and did it without fuss, but Henley felt at a loss. He wanted to help, but he also wanted to get away from the sickroom as quickly as possible.

'No, no breakfast. Is Courtney here yet?'

'I think he's just arrived. I heard his horse just as I came up the stairs.'

'Could you . . . could you thank him for coming and say we'll have

58

to leave it today? I really don't think I can get out of bed.'

'I'll pass the message on and then make you some tea. You look as if you need *something*.'

Henley left the room quickly and descended the stairs. There was a knock on the door and he went to answer it. As expected, Courtney Stanton was on the step.

'Is Jane ready?' he asked.

'Come in, Stanton,' said Henley, much more confident now he was dealing with a healthy male. 'Jane's not too good. I think she overdid it yesterday. She's asked me to pass on the message that she wishes to postpone the work today.'

Courtney limped through the doorway. 'Feeling bloody stiff myself, to tell you the truth. However, we've booked the team of Suffolks and I suppose we ought to use them. They might not be available next time. I would have stayed in bed a bit longer myself if I hadn't promised to come over. Now that I'm here, I think I'll do a bit of ploughing.'

'Would you like to tell Jane that, while I'm making her some tea?'

'Thank you, I will.'

Henley called up the stairs. 'Rogue male ascending! Make yourself decent.'

He grinned at Courtney and left him to go up.

Courtney climbed the stairs, feeling every movement in his muscles. The pair of them really had overdone it the day before, and he was not surprised they were out of sorts this morning. In a rather perverse way he felt immensely satisfied with that fact. It was something to do with feeling alive.

When he entered her bedroom, which he did not without experiencing some shyness, he found Jane half sitting up in bed with the bedclothes up around her armpits. She looked white and drawn and there was pain in her eyes.

'Good Lord,' he said, 'you're not going to die on us, are you?'

'Not funny,' she said. 'I think I'm coming apart at the seams. I can feel myself tearing every time I move.'

'I know. I'm the same.'

'At least you can get up and walk around.'

'With immense difficulty. I suppose my muscles are just a bit more used to harsh physical exercise than yours are. Give it a day or so and you'll be right as rain.'

She suddenly looked miserable. 'We'll never finish the ploughing at this rate. It's Tuesday today and the gypsy women are coming on Thursday to do the planting . . .'

'Don't worry,' he interrupted, 'I'm still going to the fields. I'll take John the labourer with me if I can get him. I bet he could plough up what's left in no time at all.'

She looked at him with dark eyes. 'Oh, Courtney, are you sure? Even if you're suffering only half as much as me, you must be in pain.'

'Bit of pain won't kill me.'

She suddenly seemed to realise something and buried herself more deeply under the bedclothes.

'What's the matter?' he asked.

'I must look a sight. I haven't even brushed my hair.'

'Who cares,' he smiled. 'You look fine to me. I could ravish you at this moment.'

She turned her head slowly in his direction. 'What?' she said, looking at him strangely.

Realising he had overstepped the bounds of propriety, he immediately apologised. 'I'm sorry, wasn't the thing to say when you're feeling vulnerable, was it?' He tried to play it down, gesturing around 'Not used to being in a young woman's bedroom. Makes me feel awkward, say awkward things. Looks like a different world to my place. Even smells different.'

'What's your bedroom like?'

'It's *cold*,' he replied in a definite tone. 'Even in the summer. It's in the north wing of the house and it's made of stone throughout. It keeps the winter locked inside it.'

'It's a big house. I've seen it from the outside. Why don't you change your room?'

He laughed. 'Sounds simple, doesn't it? But if I were to suggest it, my parents would think I was queer in the head. In my family you put up with things like cold rooms without a murmur of complaint; it wouldn't enter their heads to consider changes. Besides, nearly all the rooms in the rest of the house are just as cold. It's the way the manor's built. One is meant to suffer – in silence. It builds character.'

'I thought it was nice being rich.'

'Well, in the first place we're not rich – not in the way you imagine; and secondly, it's only nice if you can do what you like with it. I certainly can't, and neither can my family really. We're constrained by our own code of frugality. Those who come after us must be left enough to keep the family estates intact. We must ensure the family line. We're an ancient family.'

'Aren't we all? I mean, isn't everyone from an ancient family? We all go back to the first man and woman, after all.'

Courtney laughed. 'I suppose when you put it like that, yes, we must be. We aristocrats like to believe we're special, however, and talk about things like pure bloodlines.'

'Pure poppycock.'

'Again, I agree with you.'

She smiled at him, then winced as a muscle reminded her of its presence. At that moment Henley entered with some tea and Courtney took his leave.

'Rub some liniment on those arms and legs,' he said before he left. 'It'll help.'

Jane remained in the house until the time came for planting the saffron corms. When she got to the fields with the first waggonload of corms, she found them all ploughed ready to be sown. She silently thanked Courtney for his hard work.

Also at the fields, waiting patiently, were the gypsy women who were to do the planting. Jane noticed how vibrant they were, their hair tied up in bright scarves, wearing their multi-hued dresses. It gave Jane's heart a lift just to see them get to their feet and make their way towards her. There were children too, dozens of them, and one or two lurchers dashing in and out of their legs. A circus could not have been more colourful.

She stood on the back of the cart and gave them their instructions. 'The corms must be planted three to four inches deep. I've cut some sticks the right length and I'll pass them around. There's enough for at least one each. They should also be planted about four inches from the next corm. We've got about eight acres to cover, so we'd better start straight away.'

The women needed no more telling. They each grabbed a sack of bulbs, heaved it high on to their backs, and set off for the end of the first field, chattering like starlings.

Jane watched happily as the first *crocus sativus* for a hundred years were planted in her father's fields.

Towards evening, when the grey-blues of the day began to drift into mauves and purples, the gypsies made preparations to leave. Jane was well satisfied with what they had done, with very little supervision from her. She gathered up her own things – a headscarf and the remains of her lunch – and set off over the undulating fields towards her home. Half-way there, in a shallow valley between hills, she looked up to see a figure standing on a ridge by an oak, stark against the skyline. She recognised the figure as Petre Peake.

Since she would have to pass within a few yards of him, Jane realised it would be impolite not to stop and talk. She felt embarrassed at having to do so, however. There seemed something a little contrived about this meeting. Besides that, the evening had turned now to scarlet and black. The spot was a lonely one, amongst the combed and rolling land, creating a confidential atmosphere. It made a meeting between a young man and a young woman too intimate.

Nevertheless, uncomfortable as she felt, Jane was too concerned about courteous behaviour to ignore him.

As she approached, he had his back to her, one hand on the trunk of the oak. He seemed to be staring out over the landscape, lost in contemplation. There was a moment when she felt she could sneak past without even being seen, but that quickly passed. He must have noticed her coming from a long way off.

'Mr Peake?' she said.

He turned and stared at her. 'I watched you come up over that rise. It was a magnificent sight – like some warrior queen returning from a victory – Boudicca in modern dress. I half expected an army to be following you, banners flowing in the wind, drums beating, faces full of triumph. Do you always stride so purposefully? I wish I had your confidence in myself.'

'I think,' she said, trying not to smile, 'you are far too romantic for your own good, Mr Peake.'

'Petre. Yes, I think you're right.' He turned to stare out again over the fading landscape. 'I was just imagining a world without pain. Wouldn't that be something worth fighting for? One would think that after over four years of war, things would be better – but they aren't, are they? In fact, it seems worse. There's pain everywhere you look.'

'Is there?' she replied. 'I thought people were beginning to heal and rebuild things.'

'Superficially we seem to be rebuilding, but underneath there are terrible festering wounds, Jane. It'll take generations to heal them. Even our sons and daughters will bear the scars . . .'

There was something very tragic about this magnetic man, who stood so straight and tall, yet had such contempt for mankind, had such a cynical stamp upon his features. Jane felt a longing to repair the damage the war seemed to have wrought within him, but then she felt that way about all those who had come home from the war with disfigured souls. Their bodies were lean and youthful and full of vigour, but their hearts were a thousand years old.

'Perhaps you're right,' she said, 'but there's a point where feelings need to become tasks, and we begin to tackle the problems instead of brooding over them.'

He turned and smiled. 'The practical woman. I like that. It fits with my image of the warrior queen. "The Romans have raped my daughters, stolen my lands, demeaned my tribespeople? Why, let's not stand around and bemoan our lot, let's get out there and give them a thrashing."'

She smiled too at this description of herself. 'Do I seem like that to you? I'm not, you know. I'm just as terrified of life as everyone else.'

'Well, you certainly don't show it.'

'None of us likes to reveal the person inside,' she said meaningfully.

He nodded. 'You're right.' He half turned. 'Goodnight, Miss Transon.'

She felt as if she were being dismissed, but was unable to think of a suitable way to counteract this. 'Goodnight,' she murmured weakly.

She set off again, over the darkening downs, towards the lighted cottage in the distant. When she had gone a few yards she turned to see him staring again, at the distant horizon.

'You won't change the world just by thinking about it,' she called.

'I lied,' he called back. 'I don't want to change the world – I want to change *me*.'

Again, she had no suitable reply.

Chapter Seven

Once the corms were planted, Jane took to visiting the fields almost every day at first. She could not help but be excited by the prospect of the autumn crocuses. However, since there was very little to see except brown earth, the thrill of the trips to the fields soon palled, and she resolved to go only once a week.

At the beginning of August, her two cousins, Jonathan and Nancy, came to stay at Wildrose Cottage. Jane had one surviving uncle, her only living relative apart from her father, and these were his children. Jonathan was fourteen and Nancy just over eighteen. Jane liked them both, though she found Jonathan could be a nuisance. He was at the age when he was very impressed by guns and hunting and kept asking Jane to take him shooting over the fields.

'In the first place, I don't own a shotgun, Jonathan, and secondly, I dislike shooting things,' Jane told him after the third or fourth request.

'Oh, but shooting things is natural!'

'It might be natural to you, young man,' said Jane grimly, 'but not to me.'

'But just think, someone has to kill the meat you eat, Jane, so, why shouldn't I do it for you? I could bring home a rabbit easily, I should think. Or even a hare.'

'And who's going to skin and gut it? You?'

Jonathan looked a bit doubtful about this. 'I've never done it, but I could try. Maybe we could get some local person to show us how? There must be hundreds of people around here who know how to skin a rabbit.'

Jane shook her head emphatically. 'Whether there are or whether there aren't, I'm not going to take you hunting. And it's no good asking your uncle Henley, because he doesn't like guns either.'

Jonathan had no intention of asking Henley, of whom he was a little bit afraid. Henley was inclined to be brusque with his niece and nephew, and both Jane's cousins took this as a sign that their uncle did not like them. In fact Henley had no feelings for them either way. They were simply there for a short time and once they were gone he would forget them.

Nancy Transon was a slim girl with wispy fair hair and almost transparent skin. Jane could see the fine blue veins beneath her cousin's arms. Nancy had the kind of looks which lead to being chosen to play a fairy extra in *Midsummer Night's Dream*. Her eyebrows and eyelashes were so fair that in some lights they were invisible. She had virtually no hips, narrow shoulders and slim, tapering fingers that appeared to be made from tallow.

Nancy allowed her fine hair to hang over her face, like a curtain. She was intensely shy, and confessed to Jane that she always felt as if people were staring at her.

'Why would they do that?' asked Jane.

'I don't know,' said Nancy, her voice rarely rising above a whisper. 'I just feel their eyes on me.'

Jane, who occasionally enjoyed being the centre of attention, had difficulty in understanding this fear of Nancy's. Still, the girls got on quite well together, and certainly Nancy was not shy with Jane herself, once she had been in her company for a day or so. Jane enjoyed having a companion whom she could take for walks over the fields, or into one of the two towns.

On Wednesday, the two of them decided to go into Thaxted. Jane wanted to show Nancy the Guildhall and the John Webb's windmill, as well as the church. They hitched a ride on a farmer's wagon into Thaxted. Jonathan had asked Henley if he could accompany him to the Chelmer River, where Henley intended to paint.

'I could bring my fishing rod,' he told his uncle. 'I made it yesterday out of a tuppenny bamboo pole. Do you think there're roach in the Chelmer?'

Henley saw no real reason not to take Jonathan, since the boy could hardly get up to much mischief down by the river. If a bit of fishing was all it took to keep him quiet, then it would do no harm to relieve Jane of the youth. After several days of Jonathan's pestering, she needed a break from him.

So, the two males went one way, out into the countryside, and the two females the other, down to the town.

Nancy professed a desire to look in the shops first, so they went to Jelham's Fashions, a small store in the centre of town. Nancy was amazed that so tiny a place sold silk stockings, though she told Jane that they were more expensive here than in Green Lanes on the outskirts of London, where she and Jonathan lived. The girls also looked at several dresses, and Nancy eventually bought a pleated skirt.

Next they went to the Guildhall, built by the Guild of Cutlers in around 1390. Nancy was not impressed by the building, with its many woodwormed beams and upper storeys jettied out over the streets. She told Jane she did not like stuffy old places that were falling to bits.

Once this piece of information had been imparted, Jane decided not to take Nancy to the mill, which had been derelict for over ten years. The local children had begun using it as a playground recently, and it was falling more and more into disrepair as they knocked bits off it. Instead, Jane took her to the church, which Nancy said she liked because it was big and airy and had a lot of light inside.

'So many country churches are gloomy, aren't they?' she said.

'I don't know,' Jane replied. 'I haven't seen that many.'

When they became hungry, a little later on, they visited the tea-shop opposite the church. Jane ordered Earl Grey tea and scones for both of them.

Nancy asked Jane in a confidential tone, 'Have a lot of the young men been killed in the war? From around here, I mean?'

The question surprised Jane. 'Quite a lot, I suppose. Why do you ask?'

'Well,' said Nancy, peering out from behind her curtain of hair, 'I haven't seen any, that's all.'

Jane was inclined to think that, if they had seen a young man, and had he so much as looked at them, Nancy might have fallen down and had a fit.

'I expect they're all at work on a weekday,' said Jane. 'Most people around here work on the farms. Some are employed in the cutlery industry. I expect if you went into one of the pubs you'd find a few there, too.'

'I don't want to go into a pub,' said Nancy.

'I wasn't going to take you into one. It would start a few tongues wagging if we did. But surely, Nancy, you're not that desperate to meet boys?'

'Not boys,' she said fiercely. 'Men. I've had enough of boys. They're worse than me for being shy. I want to meet someone who . . . who isn't.'

Again, Jane was surprised by her cousin, but she also sympathised with what Nancy was going through. Although she herself felt quite natural with most people, whether they were men or women, she had known one or two shy girls at her school who had seemed to go through agony when they met someone new. Jane realised that if Nancy met only boys who were like herself, then the pair might sit for days without speaking or looking at one another. It conjured up an amusing picture, but only for the onlookers.

They got a ride back on a gig in the late afternoon, walked to the cottage, and were met at the open door by a triumphant-looking Jonathan, who had obviously been waiting impatiently for them to return from town.

'Captain Stanton is going to take me shooting!' he cried. 'Isn't that marvellous?'

'Can we get through the door, please?' asked Nancy, ignoring the announcement completely.

Jonathan's face remained flushed with pleasure, despite his sister's lack of response, and he sidestepped out of the way to let the two girls over the doorstep. Suddenly, Nancy stopped dead in her tracks, and Jane, not expecting such an abrupt halt and coming in behind her, walked directly into her.

'Nancy, for heaven's sakes . . .' said Jane, rubbing her nose where it had collided with Nancy's bony shoulder.

Nancy turned, apparently in confusion, and managed somehow to squeeze behind Jane and push her cousin forward into the hallway. Jane then saw Nancy's problem. Courtney was standing at the end of the hallway, seemingly about to leave. He crossed the short distance to shake her hand.

'Hello, Jane,' he said breezily. 'Ran into your father out in the meadow. He's promised to have a look at some paintings I've done. How are you, anyway?'

'I'm fine,' said Jane, smiling. 'So, Father's promised to look at some paintings and you've promised to take Jonathan out killing things.'

'That seems to be the deal,' he laughed.

Jonathan was standing beside Courtney now. He puffed out his chest. 'Captain Stanton says we might even get a crack at some rooks that his gamekeeper wants out of the way. You can't really eat rooks, though, can you – not like pigeons? Leastways, I've not heard of them being eaten. So I hope we can shoot some rabbits too.'

'So long as you do as I say,' cautioned Courtney, 'and we don't disturb the game birds, we should be all right. Shooting is a serious business.' Courtney turned to Jane. 'I've got an old .410 this young man can use. A twelve bore would be a bit heavy for him.'

'Oh, I don't know . . .' began Jonathan, but Courtney interrupted him with, 'A four-ten is a good beginner's weapon.'

Jane noticed that Courtney was in his riding clothes. He was looking rather handsome, with new colour in his cheeks and a clear look to his eyes. He peered over Jane's shoulder.

'Who's this then? Ah, the other cousin. Are you going to introduce me, Jane?'

Jane's arm was clutched from behind. It felt like a raptor's talons digging into her flesh. She peeled away the fingers and half turned. Nancy had hunched into herself, her head was down and she was staring at the floor with wild eyes. However, there was nothing else for it but to carry out the introductions. Nancy was trapped in the narrow hallway, and to take any other course of action would have been excessively rude.

'Courtney,' Jane said, 'this is my dear cousin Nancy. Nancy, this is Courtney Stanton, a friend of the family.'

Remarkably, a hand crept out from within the recesses of Nancy's clothes and Courtney shook the thin fingers.

'Very pleased to meet you,' said Courtney.

Nancy made some inaudible comment in kind.

Courtney led the way back to the living room. 'I hope my presence here didn't startle you, Nancy?' he said over his shoulder. 'I know how alarming it can be when you're not prepared for someone. It used to upset me, meeting people unexpectedly.'

Nancy's head came up at once. 'Did it?' she whispered, with gratitude in her tone. She following the group into the room but remained close to the door and her escape route.

'Oh, terribly,' Courtney confirmed. 'Used to make me panic and want to run away. Then the war came and of course I had to meet all kinds of people. I suppose it's just a matter of practice really. Getting used to it.'

Once he had said this, Courtney turned his attention to Jane. She knew he had done this deliberately to allow Nancy some time to recover her poise, and Jane was touched by his kindness. They chatted briefly, catching up on each other's news, and then he said he ought to be going.

'You won't forget, though?' Jonathan said.

Jane cried, 'Jonathan, stop it!'

Courtney smiled. 'No, I won't forget. I'll call by here Friday morning and pick you up at about eight o'clock. How's that?'

'Wizard!' cried Jonathan.

'Oh, forgot to tell you, Jane. Your father's staying to catch the last of the light. That's why I brought the young rascal home.'

'I came home on the back of Captain Stanton's horse,' said Jonathan, proudly.

'Thank you, Courtney,' Jane said as she saw him to the door.

'You don't want to come with us? On Friday, I mean?' he asked.

She shook her head, smiling. 'You won't want me squealing in your ear every time a gun goes off.'

'You don't like guns?'

'No.'

'Neither do I, really,' he said, seriously. 'Had enough of the blasted things in France. Still, the boy seemed to want to so desperately.'

'It's extremely kind of you ... that, and the way you treated Nancy.'

He shrugged. 'She's a pretty girl, or would be if she came out from behind that screen.'

When he was gone, Jane went back to her cousins in the living room. Jonathan was aiming an imaginary gun out of the window and making popping noises with his mouth. Nancy was sitting on the sofa, looking at her laced hands on her lap.

'He's a nice man, isn't he?' said Jane, conversationally.

Nancy looked up at her with wide, brimming eyes. 'He's *wonderful*,' she breathed.

Jonathan, too, spared no compliments. 'I think he's terrific. I bet he's the best shot in the whole of Essex. I just bet he is.'

Well, thought Jane, Courtney has certainly made his mark here today. She wondered, though, whether her family were not taking up too much of his time. Surely, she thought, he has better things to do than take young Jonathan shooting? He must really want to learn to paint very badly to devote so much of his leave to us: first in ploughing and planting the crocuses, then in amusing her cousin. Or perhaps there was another attraction? Jane wondered a little about that, then dismissed it from her mind.

On Friday, Courtney duly arrived with two shotguns: a double-barrelled twelve-bore and a single 'threepenny bit-barrelled' four-ten. He had also two game bags, picnic lunches, and various other necessities. Jonathan was ecstatic. Jane had warned him not to be too effusive, but it seemed he could not help gushing when the shotgun and game bag were presented to him.

'I'll hand you the cartridges when we get out in the fields,' said Courtney. 'I want to give you a few lessons on how to carry and handle the weapon first. Leave the gun broken while we're in the house, then you'll know it's absolutely safe.'

'Oh, yes, of course, Captain Stanton,' said Jonathan. 'I understand, sir.'

While this was going on, Nancy sat on the sofa and watched the proceedings. Finally, when the pair were about to leave and Jane was showing them to the door, Nancy said, 'I don't suppose I could come?'

The group had been moving out of the room, and they froze where they stood, forming a tableau for a moment.

Then Jonathan cried, 'Oh, sis, why do you have to spoil everything?'

71

Nancy, wearing a print frock, stared at her brother. 'I don't want to spoil anything. I just want to come with you.'

Jane said, 'Nancy, you'd *hate* it. The guns banging away and some poor creature being shot. What on earth do you want to see that for?'

Nancy jumped up from the sofa and went to the corner of the room, where she stared at a bookcase. 'Oh, well,' she said after a few moments, 'I expect I would spoil it.'

Courtney spoke now. 'I don't think it's that at all. We'd like you to come, but Jane's right, I don't believe you would enjoy it very much, tramping through the brambles and hawthorns. You'd need some other clothes, or your cotton dress would be torn.'

'You'd get scratched to ribbons, Nancy,' said Jonathan.

She turned and gave them a faint smile. 'Yes, I would, wouldn't I? Never mind, you go. It was . . . just a thought.'

'Perhaps another time?' said Courtney, and he ushered Jonathan out of the room. When they had gone, Jane returned to the living room. Nancy was back on the sofa again. 'I'm sorry, I shouldn't have done that, should I?' She seemed very pleased with herself about something, and Jane was surprised that her cousin had got over her disappointment so quickly.

Jane said, 'No, it was a bit silly. This was really Jonathan's treat. And in any case, if you had desperately wanted to go with them, you should have put on a heavy skirt and your boots.'

'Yes, but I wouldn't have looked nice then, would I?' said Nancy in an aggrieved tone.

Jane did not reply to this, but a little later it sunk in that Nancy was actually interested in attracting Courtney. She had not really wanted to go out shooting, or even for a walk with her brother. She had simply wanted to be with Courtney. Thus, the girl had put on her prettiest frock in order to catch the eye of Captain Courtney Stanton.

Oh God, Jane thought, the girl's got a crush on him.

That Nancy was playing games was confirmed later in the day, when the hunters returned in triumph, saying they had shot two rabbits. Nancy had again changed her dress. This time she had on a skirt and an embroidered blouse. She was sitting in the same place on the sofa, reading a book, or pretending to, when Jane showed Courtney into the living room.

Jonathan was close behind, glowing with pride. 'Sis, you should have seen me . . . us. I bagged a rabbit, I really did. It popped out of a hedge and ran along the top of a ditch and I got it first shot, didn't I, Captain Stanton? They're in the kitchen, on the draining board. You can come and see them if you don't believe me. Captain Stanton killed the other one, but mine's the biggest. It tried to run but I just aimed and fired and the blast knocked it head over heels, didn't it, Captain Stanton?'

'A magnificent shot,' confirmed Courtney. 'My gamekeeper would have been impressed.'

Jane laughed. 'That's a bit thick, isn't it, Captain?' she said.

'No, not really. The lad is only using a four-ten, which has a limited range, and he's not an expert in the use of firearms. I'd say it was a pretty remarkable shot for a beginner.'

'See!' cried Jonathan.

'Yes, well, we have to learn to be modest about our achievements,' Jane said sternly.

Jonathan looked suitably abashed, and seemed at last a little subdued. 'I know, I know,' said the boy. 'I'll be modest in a minute.'

They all laughed.

'Well,' Courtney said, turning slightly to include Nancy in his audience, 'have you managed to amuse yourselves without us?'

'Yes, thank you,' said Nancy.

'Good. Then all's well that end's well. By the way Jane, we met a fellow called Johnston on the way home. Said he knew your father. Seemed a bit hard of hearing. He admired our rabbits and offered to skin and gut them for us on the spot, so we let him. I think he'd been out himself, because he had a sack with him . . .'

'Deff Johnston is the local poacher, Courtney. Didn't you know that? He uses snares.'

'I sort of guessed it, though he didn't seem at all worried at meeting us. Anyway, I thought you'd be pleased that you didn't have to go through all that messy business. All you have to do now is wash them and stick them in a pot.'

'That's all there is to cooking rabbits, is it?' said Jane, amused.

'A few herbs and spices, I suppose,' smiled Courtney. 'I'm not much of a cook.'

'Yes, well. Oh, but didn't you cook for yourself in the trenches?'

'Not much. Someone used to make me tea once in a while, but I have to confess I did little for myself.'

Nancy broke in hotly with, 'Captain Stanton is an officer. Officers don't have to cook for themselves.'

'I don't suppose it would damage them if they did so, would it?' Jane said.

'Of course not,' laughed Courtney, 'but you're right, Nancy, we don't. Perhaps someone will teach me one day.'

'I could teach you,' said Nancy, quickly.

Courtney nodded. 'Thank you, Nancy. I may take you up on that. In the meantime, I've got one week's leave left before I rejoin my regiment. I'm meeting with Henley tomorrow, Jane, to show him my latest paintings.'

'Are we allowed to see them too?' she asked.

'I'd rather not. They're apprentice works, you see. Once I feel confident, I'd like to show you something.'

She nodded. 'All right. Would you like to stay to supper? I believe we're having rabbit stew.'

He laughed. 'No, better be going. I'm expected at dinner tonight. We've got some stuffy people coming and they want me there to make up the numbers.'

He said goodbye to everyone, pausing to give Nancy a broad smile, which made Nancy flush with pleasure. Jane thought, perhaps he really does like her? Nancy had that kind of pallid fragility which attracted men; there were those who preferred vulnerable women precisely because such females needed looking after. Perhaps Courtney was such a man, Jane thought.

It brought directly to mind Jane's own feelings about Courtney, which normally she studiously ignored. She found him very attractive, liked his sense of humour, enjoyed being with him, but quickly retethered any romantic feelings which unleashed themselves in her breast. Jane could have fallen in love with Courtney very easily, was perhaps a bit in love with him already, but she was terribly conscious of their different stations in life. He was the son of a peer of the realm, and she was the daughter of an artist and profligate gambler. They might be friends – especially since Courtney was

74

interested in her father's work – but she could not hope for anything stronger or deeper. Even Nancy's family was marginally more acceptable than her own, Jane's uncle being a respectable business-man without a reputation for wild excesses on the gaming tables. She *loved* being his friend, and told herself she was content with that situation.

Courtney waved away Jonathan's profuse thanks and said he'd be happy to do the same at any time. Jane made a mental note to tell Jonathan that this was a remark made out of politeness and not to be taken literally. She had visions of Jonathan sending messages to Stanton Manor every five minutes, asking if Courtney could come out hunting again.

Finally he went, and Jane set about cooking the rabbits for their evening meal.

Over the next few days, Courtney was a frequent visitor at the house. Ostensibly he was there to talk with Henley, but it seemed to Jane that he spent a lot of time talking to Nancy. Jonathan was there too, and Courtney did not leave him out, but Nancy was the one who commanded most of his attention.

Once, on the third and last day he was there, Courtney came out into the garden where Jane was doing some work.

'Can I help?' he said.

She shook her head. 'No, I'm quite happy on my own. It's only light work, nothing that needs muscles.'

He smiled. 'You're still annoyed about the ploughing.'

'Why should I be?'

'No reason, except that I know you found it hard. I can't help being a man, you know. It was my parents' fault.'

'Not even theirs. They didn't get a choice.'

He laughed. 'That's true. Look, you seem to be avoiding me. Have I done something to offend you, apart from being fit and well the day after the ploughing?'

She suppressed a laugh herself. 'You keep on about the ploughing. I don't think you did any more than me. John probably finished it off.'

'I must admit, he did do a lot of it.'

She stuck her trowel in the ground and stared at him for a moment.

She was just about to suggest a walk when the french doors flew open and Jonathan came running out on to the lawn.

'Captain Stanton,' he called. 'Nancy says are you going to come and finish our game of cards?'

Courtney half turned towards the house, then said apologetically, 'I'd better give them full measure. I promised your cousins a chance to get their own back. I won the first game, you see.'

'Even though you were trying to lose?'

'Something like that. You know me too well.'

'I'll come inside in a moment,' she said. 'I just want to finish the weeding.'

'All right, but don't leave it too long. We need a fourth for partner whist.'

He left her to her gardening; though there was very little weeding to do, Jane did not go back into the house. She found herself irritated for some reason, mostly with herself. It was not a feeling she could precisely analyse; she finally put it down to a general irritation about having her cousins to stay for so long. She had been glad to see them, but their prolonged visit was putting further strain on her and her father's already parlous financial situation. She also needed to make long-term plans, and needed quiet and space to do so.

Henley's bank-manager had sent a note the previous day, which Henley had left exposed in the writing bureau, and Jane had seen. It stated that, unless funds were forthcoming to reduce Henley's current overdraft, legal proceedings would be initiated in order to recover the debt. Jane was aware that this was probably normal banking procedure, and that they were trying to frighten any hidden assets out of her father, but nevertheless she was concerned. There were no hidden assets and, while the bank could not take what they had not got, they could still make life uncomfortable for her father.

Jane knew that, once the saffron flowers had bloomed and Henley had painted them, she could retrieve the corms and resell them. She did not wish to settle her father's debt, because she knew that would only encourage him to gamble away large sums again, but just having the money available would give her a sense of security. It meant they would not starve. In the meantime she hoped her father could sell some more of his paintings. She knew that he was going to take some pictures to London soon, and she told herself that perhaps some would sell there. After all, they were good paintings and people seemed to like them.

The following day, Jonathan and Nancy were collected by Jane's uncle, to be taken back to Green Lanes. They were full of protestations about how much they had enjoyed their stay and how good Jane had been to them, and she felt a little guilty that she had wanted them to go home. After a few hours, she had even begun to miss them a little. The cottage seemed so quiet without Jonathan roaring through it, and Nancy was not there to appreciate Jane's efforts with her appearance. Henley never noticed what Jane wore, or what kind of state her hair was in. She could not share anything like that with her father.

She went out for a walk to escape the lonely atmosphere of the house. The summer ditch was crackling with dried weeds in the heat. Dust hung in the air over the hedgerow. She took a winding lane through open landscape, intent on studying the life in the by-ways of her county. Jane was not a woman who was instinctively in communication with the natural world: she was normally too busy doing things. But when there was time on her hands, she found she could appreciate beauty. She could enjoy the thrush-egg blue of the sky, the stylish flight patterns of the martins, the differing shades of green in the landscape.

A butterfly which she recognised because of a painting her father had done – a purple emperor – fluttered around the wildflowers in the hedgerow. Jane liked the rapid movement of colour amongst the weeds as it busied itself in its task of redistributing pollen.

As she rounded a corner, Jane came upon the Bull Inn and decided to rest on one of the seats in the back garden. She could not go in – not as a woman alone – but there would be shade in the rear which she could enjoy. She walked through the small gateway, the open gate hanging from one leather hinge, and followed the winding path around to the back of the pub.

Half-way round she stopped. At the far corner of the house, a man was washing himself with the water from the rain-barrel. He had his shirt-sleeves rolled up. His shirt collar and tie had been removed and placed on a windowsill nearby. The front of his shirt was open, so that much of his chest was bare. He was splashing his face, neck and upper chest with the cool water from the barrel. There was something familiar about him.

Jane felt intensely embarrassed by the scene, but there were also other feelings there too. She did not turn and walk away, because any movement from her – now that the man had finished his ablutions – would have brought attention to herself. Besides, there was something mesmerising about the sight of a young man's torso bared to the day: a hard lean chest to match the sinewy arms. It stirred something deep within her, an excitement which shocked and frightened her a little.

Then, as she gazed, he looked up. The moment he saw her, she recognised him and felt herself flush from head to foot. It was Petre Peake. He stared at her, astonished.

She wanted to run, but realised that would look foolish. Instead she half turned away, saying, 'I – I'm sorry, I didn't realise anyone was here. I was just going to sit in the shade.'

'You don't need to apologise to me,' he said. 'I feel just as embarrassed as you do. I had a drink too many in there – needed to cool off before walking home.'

He rolled down his sleeves and buttoned his shirt.

She made as if to go and he called, 'Do stay for a moment. Perhaps I can walk with you for a while?'

'I don't think that would be a good idea,' she said.

'Why not?'

'It – just wouldn't, that's all.'

He stuffed his shirt collar and tie into his trouser pocket and hung his jacket over his arm. 'Improper, you think? You know, I find you very attractive. How do you find me?'

She flushed with shock, then turned on him, saying, 'You're very blunt. I don't think I encouraged such advances, did I?'

He walked over to her and gripped her arm lightly. 'No – but how *do* you find me?'

She shook her head and took her arm from his grasp, not knowing the answer to that herself. 'I don't know, and I certainly shouldn't say so if I did. It's very unfair of you to ask such questions on so short an

78

acquaintance. As a man you can say such things, but you mustn't expect an answer. That certainly *would* be improper.'

'But there was something in your expression – when I looked up from washing – otherwise I wouldn't have asked.'

She began to get angry now. He was trying to trap her into saying something which might commit her. If she had felt anything, it was not something she wished to admit, and certainly not to him. He *was* being unfair. She didn't like it one bit. Control wasn't something she relinquished happily.

'I'm going now,' she said, walking determinedly to the gate.

'Can't I walk you?' he called, almost plaintively.

'No, you may not. I came out for a walk by myself, to gather some thoughts together. Goodbye.'

There was no answer, and she kept walking, wondering if he would follow her along the lane. Her heart was beating rapidly. All she could hear was the click of her own heels on the surface of the road. When she dared to look back, he was nowhere in sight, and she slowed her walk to a stroll again. It was an unfortunate meeting in more ways than one. It had given rise to some peculiar feelings in Jane which she knew were not at all within the bounds of propriety. Initially it had surprised her and now it worried her. It was something she was going to have to guard against carefully in the future.

She passed an old man in the lane and nodded absently in his direction, her mind a tangle of disturbed thoughts.

After Jane Transon had gone, Petre realised how clumsy his addresses had been. He knew he was far too blunt and forward for most people. It was not something he could do very much about, since he reacted instinctively to any form of aloofness. He had in fact intended to be as accommodating as possible when he met Jane Transon again, but once more he had been too direct.

Wanting to repair the damage, he quickly finished dressing and hurried after her. By the time he was clear of the pub, he could just see her at the end of the lane. He stepped out, hoping to catch her before she reached the main highway. There was another figure between them. An old man was wending his slow, weary way towards the pub.

Half-way along the lane, Petre met the old man, who had stopped and seemed to be in some sort of distress. He had dropped his walking stick and was rubbing his right eye. Indeed, he seemed to have made it quite sore.

Petre hesitated. The fleeing Jane was many yards ahead of him, unaware that she was being pursued.

He stopped and turned to the old man. 'What's the problem?' he said.

The old man looked up, one eye half closed and a little swollen.

'Got a fly in me eye,' he said, plaintively. 'Can't get 'er, I can't. She's paining somethin' awful.'

Petre took a last look at the end of the lane and saw that Jane had now disappeared from view. Damn, that woman can walk fast, he thought. If he ran he could probably catch her, but he would have to leave the old man to his fate.

Petre sighed and took out a handkerchief. 'Here, let me have a look,' he said, peering into the old man's rheumy eye. 'Wait a bit – I see it. Little midge swimming in the corner there.' He made a twist in the corner of his handkerchief. 'Head up, hold still, I'll soon have it out.'

The old man submitted trustingly to Petre's ministrations, and then blinked rapidly once Petre had said, 'Got it. All right. You should be fine now. Don't rub it.'

'Ar, that's what my old gel would say,' said the old man. 'Don't rub 'er. Thank 'ee, sir.'

'Just close your eyes next time you go through a swarm of midges,' said Petre, picking up the old man's stick and handing it to him.

With that he strode off, in the direction that Jane had taken, but with little hope of catching her up now.

Two days after Jane's encounter with Petre Peake, Courtney called on Jane to say, '*au revoir*'. He was rejoining his regiment in Yorkshire and would not be home again for some time. He looked rather stiff and formal in his uniform.

'Would you write to me occasionally?' he asked. 'I should like to hear all your news.'

'I'll try, if you want me to,' she said, doubtfully, 'but I'm not good at writing letters.' She was wondering if he had asked Nancy to write to him too.

Courtney looked puzzled. 'Of course I want you to, that's why I'm asking.' He paused, then said hesitantly, 'Are you still angry with me?'

'I'm not angry with you.'

'You seem to be. I must confess, I've searched my mind for a reason, and I can't think of anything I could have done to upset you; but if there is something, I do wish you'd tell me what.'

Jane shook her head and smiled. 'Oh, Courtney, you are silly sometimes. I'm ... I'm really quite fond of you, if you want to know the truth. I'm sorry if I've seemed a little stand-offish lately, but I've had one or two things to worry about – domestic problems. Nothing terrible, but enough to distract me, I'm afraid.'

He put his hands on her shoulders, lightly. 'I'm sorry about your worries. I take it you don't want to share them, or you would have done so. Are you really fond of me? The feeling's mutual you know. So you will *try* to write?'

'All right, I will,' she laughed, enjoying his touch, 'but they'll be pretty boring letters. Nothing much happens round here, you know that.'

'Nothing could be more boring than the army,' Courtney said with feeling, 'believe me. And in any case, I shall want progress reports on the crocuses. I put a lot of effort into those little devils. I'm entitled to a day-by-day account of the growth of their green shoots.'

'I'm not writing to you *every* day,' she protested.

'Of course not,' he grinned, dropping his hands. 'Once every other day will be fine.' With that he kissed her lightly on the cheek, strode off towards his mare, his limp hardly in evidence.

Jane suddenly felt rather sad. She went indoors to look at the newspaper. She had decided it was time to get some sort of a job, even if it was part-time, to help them with their financial problems. She supposed the melancholy stemmed from a lack of sense of purpose now that her childhood was over. Still, once she found something, she would have little enough time to sit around and mope for her lost youth, she told herself. There was nothing like hard work for chasing away self-pity.

Chapter Eight

In the last week of August 1919, Henley crated up seventeen of his pictures. These were taken by carriage to the station on the Monday, and thence transported by train to the picture gallery in London's Charing Cross Road. Henley followed them two days later, promising Jane he would return before Saturday, hopefully with some sales under his belt. The exhibited paintings were to be on view for the first time on Thursday evening, at a cocktail party thrown for potential buyers, the press, and the new people from the wireless.

Henley had failed to receive good notices from the art critics, ever since an important one had labelled his painting 'pure candy-floss', early in Henley's career. Henley's work had never recovered from this attack and, while he remained bitter about it, he could no longer get passionate about a bad notice. Mostly the critics ignored him these days, which suited him fine. If they could not say something positive, then Henley was not interested.

Henley's paintings still sold in reasonable numbers, though of course the amount he charged for them might have been considerably higher if they had attracted rave notices. His fresh, vibrant paintings – fields of wildflowers, poppies, sunflowers and tulips – had an appeal, despite the critics.

Henley was not the only artist whose paintings would be displayed in the gallery's current exhibition. There were five artists in all, one of them another Essex painter who specialised in beach scenes with boats. None of them was famous, but all were able to sell, which was what the gallery owner, Nicholas Marchant, cared about.

Henley always stayed at the Princess Louise Inn, a pub in Holborn: it was reasonably near the gallery, and close to the Colonial Club, which was where he gambled while in the city. Once he had dropped his overnight bag at the Princess Louise, Henley visited Nicholas Marchant to make sure his pictures had arrived, then went immediately to his club. He had dinner there on Wednesday evening and played cards until the early hours of the morning, winning a substantial amount.

On Thursday evening, Henley was required by Nicholas to be at the gallery for the opening of the exhibition, but he was anxious to be back at the green baize tables, and managed to get away about ten-thirty after seeing eight of his paintings sold.

He found the same group of men playing at the club. Henley joined them, intending to remain at the table until six the following morning. He played recklessly with the four hundred pounds he had won the previous evening, since it was money he had never expected to have and would not need to account for to Jane.

Amazingly he won again, a great deal, and by the time he went up to his bed he was feverishly elated, imagining that he had at last found the secret formula he had desired all his life. The other men around the table – London bankers, stockbrokers and lawyers – were asking him how he did it, wanting to know the key to his success. He felt like a king – greater than a king: he would not have changed places with anyone that morning.

It was not just a matter of staying calm and cool and betting substantial amounts. He believed that previously he had been too cautious, too obviously anxious not to lose. This was the secret, he told himself. One had to desire to win, not just hope one would not lose. There was a great deal of difference in the two attitudes.

When he woke at four o'clock in the afternoon, he bathed and dressed with care. There was no hurry now that he was a winner. He could afford to be leisurely in his activities. He chose his shirt and tie with care; both were more colourful than those he normally wore to the tables. Then he counted his winnings, an exercise he had been savouring until he could perfectly enjoy it, having rested and completed his ablutions.

The amount came to two thousand three hundred and forty pounds. He had started the first game with only thirty pounds in his pocket: an advance from Nicholas on the sale of his paintings.

'My God,' whispered Henley to himself. Such an amount would enable him to clear all his debts and have at least fourteen hundred pounds left over. Jane would be ecstatic when he told her.

Henley was due to catch the train at eight o'clock the following morning. He still had a whole night's play ahead of him, which he began to look forward to with relish.

I shan't take the whole amount to the table, he told himself, because that would be foolish. My luck might run out tonight, although such runs often come in threes, and this is my third evening.

He believed he was certainly owed more than three sessions worth of *good* fortune, considering the innumerable times he had played and been cursed with *bad* fortune.

When he went to the Colonial Club for his dinner, Henley asked the club steward to put two thousand pounds in the safe. The remainder, some three hundred pounds, was to be his playing money. This was thirty times more than the amount he had started with, and would be ample for his needs, even if he should lose that evening. Once it was gone, if it were to go, then he would simply return to the Princess Louise and go to bed. Now that he knew how to win, it was not essential to do so *every* time he sat at the tables. He could afford to allow himself a loss occasionally, so long as he was sensible and knew when to stop.

Once he had dined, he found his regular group, who greeted him with groans and rolling eyes.

'Not Lady Fortune's bedmate again?' said one. 'Are you sure you wouldn't prefer to sit at another table?'

Henley smiled at this, recognising it as a compliment. 'Give you a chance to win back your losses,' he said. 'Least I can do.'

'Please, no favours,' said another. 'There are richer men than us in the room. I think you've earned your place at a more lucrative table.'

'No, no,' smiled Henley. 'This one will do fine. I like you gentlemen, all of you.'

'Please,' said the first, '*hate* us, if you have to.'

The banter went on for a few minutes before the play began in earnest once again. The game was draw poker, and for the first hour or so Henley's luck continued to be good. He began to feel invincible and bet on everything, even the most ludicrous hands.

A string of poor hands followed, but Henley continued to bet when clearly others held better hands. He bluffed them into throwing in their cards by raising the stakes higher than usual: this worked once or twice, since he had been unassailable until now. Then the player to his left paid to see his cards twice in row, and the others began to discover that he was indeed bluffing much of the time.

From that point on he began to lose heavily. His irritation grew with every loss. The other players seemed to become more cheerful, which only increased Henley's annoyance. He wanted to get back to his former relaxed state of kingship, the state in which they deferred to him, but he felt the five other men around the table were beginning to conspire against him, gibing at him with every increasing loss.

'Ah, the Lady has deserted you, artist. I can feel her on my arm now,' said the player to Henley's left.

'She's not that fickle,' growled Henley, in an attempt to rejoin the banter he had enjoyed so much while he was winning.

'I'm afraid you're wrong,' sniffed the banker on the far side of the table, 'she's extremely fickle. In fact, I'm amazed she stayed so true to you for such a long time. Two days is almost a marriage where she's concerned.'

Henley snapped, 'I don't think we're done with each other yet.'

A stockbroker muttered, 'Oh yes, I think so.'

It was this kind of conversation which put Henley's teeth on edge and made him want to hit someone. He was determined that they should all change their tune. To make that happen he had to win.

By ten o'clock, Henley had been up to the club steward twice and lost both amounts. The third time he went he took all his money out of the safe. He was amazed to see he only had just over half of the amount with which he had begun the evening. He split this into two again, putting one half in his jacket pocket. Six hundred pounds was still a lot of money to take home to Howlett End. There would still be some glory attached to such a homegoing. And of course he would have a story to tell the country gamblers at the pub.

As he was walking back to his table, Henley happened to glance into a side room, where another game was in progress. Sitting on the far side of this table, half hidden by a red velvet curtain, was Petre

Peake. Henley hadn't known he was also a member of the club, though in fact there were only five gambling clubs in the whole of London, so it really wasn't all that surprising.

Realising he had not been noticed, Henley stopped to watch the game through the partly open door for a few moments. Peake seemed to be winning, just as he always did back in Saffron Walden. As usual, the young man had that bored expression on his face which Henley knew so well: a look which did not change even as Peake raked in his winnings with a casual arm.

Well, I'm doing it too, tonight, thought Henley. *You're not the only brilliant player, Mr Peake.*

The sight of Peake winning so easily heartened him. They were from the same school, Peake and himself, and here they both were in London, showing the other club members how it was done. There was something in that, some common bond between the two of them. Henley went back to his own table, buoyed by his new-found enthusiasm. All he had to do, he told himself, was to bet low stakes on his bad hands until his luck changed. Then he could begin to retrieve his losses.

That way, he thought, I won't lose.

Unfortunately, every time his luck seemed to change, it did so only for a hand or two. It then slipped back rapidly into its early-evening pattern of poor hands. Henley began drinking brandy at about one o'clock: he needed to relax, as he seemed to be wound up too tightly to alter the course of his luck.

At two-thirty he reached into his pocket to pay his debts and realised with a shock that, once he had settled this particular account, his pocket would be empty. Having settled up, he tried the other pocket, the one in which he had put six hundred pounds, but found that empty too. In a panic now, he was about to call the steward and complain of loss or theft, when he remembered that he had been dipping into that particular pocket for over an hour.

The cards began to blur before his eyes. He felt numb, stunned. He threw in his next hand, even though it was a good one – three queens – knowing that he would not be able to make good any further bets. He was absolutely broke.

Mumbling, ' 'Scuse me,' he rose from the table and made his way to the bar. His mind was spinning now. The cards. The cards had been getting better, steadily, for the last few hands. He felt cheated. They *had* been getting better. Three queens! If only he had just a hundred pounds more. Fifty even.

He searched his pockets again, hoping to find a sizeable amount tucked away somewhere. There was nothing but a little loose change. Enough for a brandy. He bought the brandy and stared about him, moodily, at the other people in the bar.

The place was full of fools, jabbering away at each other, oblivious of his plight. Men with red bloated faces, talking nonsense about politics, religion or women. Men who filled trousers and suit jackets with nothing but hot air.

The cards. The cards were on the change. They're like the ocean tide, he told himself, once they begin to move the other way there is no force on earth that can halt their progress. If he had still been at the table he would be winning by now, back on the way to retrieving his lost two thousand pounds.

The brandy went straight to his head. He felt heavy, drunk. His brain was like a lump of lead in his skull. He tried his pockets again, less hopefully this time.

Nothing.

Then he remembered the art gallery. Nicholas Marchant would have sold some more of his paintings by now. There would be more money to come. If he only had that money now! Well, it was his, wasn't it? Why shouldn't he have it? All he had to do was go and ask Marchant for it. If it was his money, it should be in his pocket, not in Marchant's. The art dealer was probably obtaining overnight bank interest on Henley's money. Henley decided this was not right. Not right at all.

He left the club. The cool air hit him in the chest and head with such force that he staggered down the steps. It was not a particularly warm night for August. He had forgotten to put his coat on, but the brandy would keep him warm for long enough to collect his money.

Henley made his way unsteadily along the dark streets. When he reached the gallery, it was all in blackness, and at first Henley was at a loss as to his next move. Then he remembered that Nicholas Marchant lived in a flat above the gallery. Locating the flat's bell,

Henley pressed it until someone opened a window above.

'Who's that?' cried Marchant's shrill voice. He sounded frightened or annoyed, Henley wasn't sure which.

Henley gulped in air. 'It's me, Henley Transon.'

There was silence for a moment, then, 'Transon? What on earth do you want? It's three o'clock.'

'I want my money.'

Marchant's voice grew shriller still. 'Money? What money? Are you mad? It's the middle of the night, man.'

Henley began to get angry. 'I want my money, damn you. Do I have to kick the door in? I bloody well will if I have to.'

'I'll be down in a minute,' hissed Marchant, 'but you'll regret this, Transon.'

For a second Henley's conscience pricked him. He realised he was committing an unpardonable breach of good manners. Marchant's threat could easily be carried out, by refusing to allow Henley to sell paintings at the gallery again. Still, it was his money, and he *needed* it.

The door opened and Marchant motioned for Henley to step inside. The gallery owner was in his dressing-gown. He looked infuriated.

'Now, what is it?' asked Marchant.

'Have you . . . have you sold any more of my paintings?'

'Is that it? You want the money for your paintings? At *this* time of the night?'

'I . . . I need it. I haven't got any money to pay for my lodgings.'

'Surely they're not asking for it in the middle of the night? You could have come to me tomorrow. I'm not going to run away, you know.'

'No, no,' said Henley, thinking quickly, 'but I have to catch a train very early tomorrow. Five-thirty. I would have had to wake you anyway. I . . . I lost all my money at the tables.'

'I guessed that much, Transon. Wait here.'

Marchant disappeared into the back of the gallery and left Henley standing in the darkness by the door. Although Henley could not see more than two feet in front of his face, he strained his eyes in an attempt to see if there were any more red spots on his pictures which would denote that they were sold.

Suddenly the light went on, blindingly, and Marchant strode across the room. 'Here,' said the gallery owner. 'Forty-seven pounds.'

'Is that all?' Henley muttered, disappointed, counting the money as it was handed to him.

'It was only one day, Transon. There're still two weeks of the exhibition left. You'll probably sell some more, I don't doubt. However, this is the last time you'll exhibit at *this* gallery, you can be sure of that.'

The money safely in Henley's pocket, arrogance took over from anxiousness. 'I wouldn't exhibit here again in any case. There are other galleries in London. In fact, I'm not so sure you've been entirely honest in your dealings with me.'

'What?' exploded Marchant, taking a step back. 'What are you accusing me of . . . ? How *dare* you, you . . . you Sunday painter. To think! My God, I ought to throw your trashy paintings out on the street now. Get out! Get out of here. I don't want to see your face in my gallery again.'

Marchant was shaking with anger. His slim hands were balled into fists and Henley, who was by far the stronger of the two, wished the gallery owner would try to strike him. Henley badly needed someone to hit, but he wasn't drunk enough to do it without direct provocation. However, Marchant must have realised what he was thinking, because a moment later the fists uncurled.

Henley growled, 'Call my paintings trash? Do it again! Call me a Sunday painter again. I'll knock your head off!'

'I'll call the police, that's what I'll do,' cried Marchant, his voice growing very shrill. 'You're nothing but a stupid little gambling addict.'

This incensed Henley beyond endurance. Reaching out, he slapped Marchant across the face. The blow was so hard that the gallery owner spun away and crashed into the wall. Some paintings were dislodged and fell to the floor. There was a splintering sound as a frame cracked.

Marchant cried out in pain. 'You swine. You hit me! I'll have you thrown in jail. I'll sue you, you thug.' He filled his lungs with air and then shrieked, 'Help! I'm being attacked!'

Seeing that one of the paintings which had fallen was a Henley

Transon, Marchant kicked out savagely and sent the framed canvas sliding across the floor to smash against the wall on the other side of the room.

Henley stepped forward again, a red haze before his eyes, but before he could reach him, Marchant ran away into the back of the gallery. Henley realised Marchant would have a telephone in his office, and he decided it was time to go.

Henley walked quickly out of the gallery and along the street. His mind was in a turmoil, but he was sensible enough not to go back to his lodgings, which was presumably where Marchant would send the police. Fortunately he hadn't told Marchant the name of his club, so Henley felt he would be safe there for the next few hours, until he could catch his train in the morning. The few clothes he had left in his room at the Princess Louise would just have to remain there. They could keep them in lieu of payment of the bill.

On reaching the Colonial Club again, Henley entered and went straight to the bar. He ordered a double brandy. His hand shook as he lifted it to his lips. As he sat there drinking it, the enormity of what he had done finally sank in. He had attacked another man, his erstwhile benefactor, and moreover a man who would not hesitate to take him to court. Henley could foresee a messy time ahead. It was not the scandal he was concerned about so much – a bit of scandal did not usually hurt a painter; indeed it sometimes helped with publicity – but the costs might be crippling. Then there was Jane. She would be dreadfully upset. He had let her down, and the memory of her mother.

Henley finished the brandy and returned to the table he had left. It had already broken up; the other members had either gone home, or to bed in lodgings. His two thousand pounds had gone with them.

Henley could not give up. His blood was tingling again. He needed just an hour's play to settle him, then he would leave for the train. He decided that when he got home he would call Marchant and apologise profusely, saying he had had a temporary brainstorm and that it would never happen again. But for the present he needed a game to settle his nerves.

The only game in progress was the one in which Peake was

participating. Henley presented himself before the table, nodding at Peake, who seemed only mildly surprised to see the artist.

'Do you have room for another?' asked Henley. 'I need just a few hands before I return to my lodgings.'

A fat man sitting next to Peake grunted. 'If you sit in here, you play seriously. We're not here for a few bedtime hands.'

'Of course,' snapped Henley. 'I always play seriously. It was simply a request.'

'Sit down, Transon,' said Peake. 'Play as many hands as you like.'

There was an uncomfortable shifting of buttocks from the man next to Peake, but no one argued with the young man. It was obvious to Henley that the king of this table was his acquaintance from Saffron Walden. The others would follow his lead. Henley nodded gratefully to Peake and then took a chair from an adjacent table. The others made room for him and he found himself sitting opposite Peake, which suited him fine.

The way in which they handled the money at the Colonial Club tables was set down in the club rules. No money was allowed on the table during play. The players kept a sheet on the debts, which were settled every half-past the hour, or when a member decided to leave the table for good. The sheet was kept by the player directly on the left of the dealer.

At first Henley played in a kind of fog, simply following his instincts and not really concentrating on the play. He could not shake off his memory of the scene in the gallery when he had struck Marchant. It all seemed so stupid now. What an idiot he had been! Yet it was difficult to contain one's temper, he acknowledged to himself, when someone was being deliberately abusive. He had struck out blindly, without considering the consequences, and now he was in trouble.

When the sheet reached him, Henley glanced down and noticed with surprise that he was winning. His forty-seven pounds had turned into two hundred. Once again the elation surged through his veins. He was on another winning streak.

His luck continued to hold out for another hour, during which he was paid two lump sums, and a surge of happiness coursed through him.

His winnings mounted.

Just before half-past five, he found himself in a contest between himself and Peake alone. All the other players had thrown in their hands. The stakes were climbing rapidly as Henley refused to yield to his old adversary. Henley had been dealt three sevens, a two and a king. He had exchanged the two and had drawn a second king. He thus held a full house. Recent hands had been such as to suggest that a full house could not be touched. Henley guessed Peake held a flush, as the young man continued to raise the stakes and Henley followed, sometimes raising them himself.

The pot began to reach dizzying heights, and everyone else around the table was as still as death. Only their eyes moved as either Henley or Peake spoke, adding to the enormous amount with each new bet. Henley's hands began shaking a little when the pot reached several thousand pounds. He realised then that Peake was not going to budge. The young man would continue to raise the stakes until one of them keeled over from exhaustion. Henley, although sure of winning, decided something had to be done or they would be there all night. It was up to him to end the contest and collect the pot.

'Your two-fifty and see you,' said Henley when it was next up to him.

The man with the sheet scribbled frantically, and then everyone waited for Peake to lay down his cards.

His eyes emotionless, Peake placed his hand carefully on the table and spread the cards.

Relief flooded through Henley's body. It was as he had thought. Peake had been holding a flush, in diamonds.

'Full house,' he said, trying not to smile as he placed his own hand on the table and spread the cards.

Peake nodded grimly, and then said, 'Hard luck, Transon. It was a good battle. Best of the evening.'

Henley felt a chill go through him. What was Peake talking about. Hard luck? It was as if he were commiserating with Henley, yet Henley had won, hadn't he?

Henley stared at his own hand, then looked at Peake's again. He suddenly saw what was actually there, instead of what he had wanted to be there. The cards began to swim before his eyes. Yes, there was a run. Oh Christ! Not a flush. Not just a flush. *A running flush*. Seven,

93

eight, nine, ten, jack in diamonds. Peake had won. Peake had beaten him. He felt he was going to be sick. He had to get out of the room quickly.

'Well done, Peake,' he said in a tight voice, taking out his handkerchief and covering his mouth. 'Won't be a minute. Just got to go to the toilet. Be back in a jiffy.'

Somehow he managed to push back his chair, rise and cross the room without throwing up. Once in the toilets, however, the bile came rushing to his mouth. He vomited into the washbasin several times.

Once he had splashed water on his face, washing away the sweat that had gathered there, Henley thought coldly about his position. In his pocket he had seven hundred pounds. He owed Peake something in the region of three thousand eight hundred. It was an impossible situation. Impossible. He could *never* hope to pay the man, let alone immediately, as the club rules demanded. They were strict on that score. If you did not have the money, you could not bet. Then there were his debts at the bank to consider, and possibly the costs of a court case brought against him by Marchant. It was all a ghastly nightmare.

What was he to do? What was there to do?

He stared at himself in the mirror above the washbasin for a few moments. His pale, haggard features stared back at him, the eyes like dark, deep pits. Suddenly he made a decision. He hurried quickly from the toilets, slipping across the hallway before one of the players from the table came to look for him. He left the club, walking south towards the river. It was not far to Waterloo Bridge, where a second decision had to be made.

When he reached the Thames, however, and looked down into its murky waters flowing coldly by, he knew he could not contemplate anything like suicide. It was not in him, to throw away his own life. A rat-infested prison was more acceptable than death.

Still, he found he could not go back and face the music. He did not know what to do. So he simply walked eastward along the river, occasionally staring moodily down into the water at the barges and traffic moving up and down. Finally he found himself at the docklands.

It was past six o'clock, and a grey dawn was creeping over the sky. There was another way out, he realised. Making his way to the merchant marine office, he inquired about which ships were due to leave.

'There're three leaving on the tide, at approximately eight-fifteen,' said the clerk. 'Two cargo vessels, and a liner bound for Hong Kong.'

'Can I purchase a ticket for the liner here?' he asked.

'No, sir, you'll have to go to line's offices in the Strand for that.'

'But I haven't time. It's nearly seven now.'

'In any case,' said the clerk, 'the offices probably won't be open until nine. You could go directly to the ship itself and have a word with the purser. Sometimes, if they're not fully booked, they'll take passengers at the last minute.'

Henley thanked him, inquired as to the position of the berth, and then made his way towards the ship, the SS *Dunera*. He found the place bustling. He explained his circumstances to the man on the gangplank, who duly sent for the purser. The purser arrived and listened to Henley, then asked him if he had any luggage.

'Er, no, I was hoping it would be here, but it must have gone astray. I sent it on by carriage.'

He pressed a ten-pound note into the purser's hand. The purser palmed the note with a practised movement.

'I see,' said the purser, staring at him for a moment. 'There's no problem with the police is there?'

'I beg your pardon? No, nothing like that. If you like to call them, you can check.'

The purser shook his head. 'No, that won't be necessary. You can purchase some more clothes on board. I take it you have enough money with you to pay for your passage and any extras you may require?'

Henley fingered the seven hundred pounds in his pocket.

'Yes, adequate. I have cash. I shall need to put some in your safe, if I may?'

'In that case,' smiled the purser, 'welcome aboard, sir. We sail in just over an hour. Come with me now and I'll allocate you a cabin. It'll be on the lowest deck, but you'll find the ship doesn't rock so much down there. We're told there's a storm out in the Bay of Biscay at the moment, so you might find that a blessing.'

'Thank you,' said Henley.

At eight-twenty, Henley was leaning over the rail, watching Tilbury slide by on the port side. It looked a grey, forbidding place, with derricks and other contraptions dominating its skyline. Henley thought about Jane, and a great wave of guilt washed through him. He would write to her once he was established somewhere. There was no need to go all the way to Hong Kong. He could stop off in Malta, Aden, India, or any British Colony on route. However, his instinct was to get as far away from England as possible, so he might very well go all the way, perhaps even further, to Australia or New Zealand. Who knew?

'Excuse me?'

He turned from the rail to face a middle-aged woman wearing too much make-up.

'Yes?'

'Do please forgive me for intruding on your thoughts, I wonder – are you travelling alone?'

'Yes, I am,' he said without hesitation.

'There are three of us, two ladies and a gentleman, and we need a fourth for canasta. Do you play card games at all?'

Henley felt something lift inside him. 'I most certainly do, madam.'

'Then perhaps you'll oblige us?' she said with a smile.

'I most certainly will,' he replied, leading the way back to the main lounge. 'With the greatest of pleasure.'

When Henley Transon didn't return to the table, Petre Peake made his excuses to the other players and went to look for him. He saw Henley leave the toilets and make straight for the doorway to the street. Petre was just about to shout, to ask where the hell Henley thought he was going, when he decided to remain silent. He followed Henley outside, into the cold air.

Henley Transon hurried off through the streets. Petre stood for a moment, lighting a slim cheroot, then followed the man who owed him money. By this time Petre had a good idea what had happened. Henley was in way over his head and couldn't settle his debts. It was in Petre's nature to feel cold about that, to demand the money owed him or threaten exposure, but Henley was something more to him than just another gambler.

For one thing Henley had shown Petre a certain kindness by inviting him to his house, even if he had had other motives for doing so. For another, Henley never spoke of or alluded to Petre's reputation as a callous flyer in the war. There were plenty of stories, but Henley had never asked him if they were true, nor had he censured him without inquiry. According to Henley a man's past was his to reveal or conceal, which ever he chose. That meant a lot to Petre: the fact that he had not been judged.

Thirdly, there was Jane to consider. Petre found her lively and intelligent. He was very attracted to her. She made him feel whole again. He had already offended her with his abrupt manner. Petre did not want to do anything further to jeopardise his relationship with Jane.

Petre threw away the smoking cheroot as he realised Henley had got quite a way ahead of him. The older man was hurrying now, and Petre saw where he was heading. The river.

'Good God, he's not going to . . . ?' Petre muttered to himself.

Petre waited in the shadows as Henley leaned over the parapet, looking down into the Thames. Then the artist suddenly straightened and began walking east along the river bank. Petre relaxed now, knowing he was not going to have to rush forward and prevent a man from committing suicide.

By the time Petre reached the gates to the docks, Henley had disappeared. Where had the man got to? What did he want at the docks? A ferry to France or Spain perhaps, to allow time for things to cool down? That would be it. Was there any point in following him further? Petre didn't think so; he didn't want to confront the older man when he was clearly broke. It would be to no avail. He would wait a while.

Petre walked slowly back to the club, noticing how cold and grey London looked in the dawn light. He thought he might take in a concert before returning to Saffron Walden. He wondered if the Philharmonic were doing something by Albinoni, or perhaps Bruch, or even Sibelius? – all three favourites of his. Of all the arts he preferred music. It didn't make him angry like paintings or poetry.

The poetry being published now was mostly about the war. There were some very good war poets – Sassoon for one – and that posthumous protégé of his, Wilfred Owen. But some very bad poets were cashing in on the war theme, as were some very bad painters. They were making money out of the dead and the maimed. It left a bad taste.

Music, on the other hand, soothed him, spoke the truth to him, was sublime and eternal. You couldn't write a crash-bang piece and call it 'The Somme' or 'Attack at Ypres' and hope to make money out of it, unless it was really good and therefore deserved to be successful. Petre found solace in music; he tried to fill his tortured brain with it as often as possible, to drive out the demons that inhabited that region of himself.

As he walked along the strains of Bruch's 'Scottish Fantasy' filled his head, and he allowed them to wash through him.

Chapter Nine

When Henley did not return home on Saturday, Jane was not overworried. Her father was not the most reliable of men and, as they had no telephone at the cottage, he had no way of getting a message to her. Several times within Jane's memory he had been up to three days late returning home from somewhere.

By Wednesday she was beginning to fret a little, and walked three miles to a house with a telephone. The people who lived at the house, the Batemans, had bought a couple of Henley's pictures and were a very obliging couple. Jane called the art gallery first. She had met Nicholas Marchant only once, when she had accompanied Henley to one of his exhibitions, and had found him a rather distant man.

'Mr Marchant? This is Jane Transon, Henley Transon's daughter. My father hasn't returned from London yet. Do you know where he is?'

'No, I have no idea.'

There was more frost in the reply than Jane's simple question warranted, so Jane guessed there was something wrong. 'Did he say where he was going?'

'Miss Transon, I have absolutely no interest in your father's whereabouts. Now I'm a very busy man. Do you mind?'

Oh God, thought Jane, they've had a fight. 'Mr Marchant, I take it by your tone that you and my father have had an argument of some kind. I'm sorry for that, but my father hasn't come home. He was due back on Saturday and I'm trying to find him. Can you help me at all, please?'

There was silence on the other end of the line for a moment, then Marchant's voice came back, considerably softened. 'Look, your father acted very strangely, very strangely indeed. In fact, I'm thinking of suing him for damages, both to my property and my person. He attacked me, Miss Transon. He attacked me in the middle of the night, after getting me out of bed and demanding money. Now I don't know . . .'

'He did what?' said Jane, faintly.

'I beg your pardon? Oh, well, as I say, he attacked me physically. Then he ran off. This was at about three o'clock in the morning. He woke me up to ask for money. I'm sorry to have to tell you all this, Miss Transon. Henley and I have dealt with each other reasonably well in the past. I know artists are unstable people sometimes, but this is a bit too much. I'm afraid I'll have to take it further. Another artist's painting was ruined when your father struck me and knocked me against the wall.' There was a pause, then, 'I wish I could help you further, but I don't know where he went to. He said something about his club, I think.'

'I'm sorry, Mr Marchant. Sorry to have bothered you. I'll try elsewhere.'

'When you find him, tell him to call me. I'm not a vindictive man, Miss Marchant, but we've got to sort something out about this.'

'I'll tell him.'

Jane put down the telephone and sighed heavily, her feelings confused. Mrs Bateman put her head through the doorway into the hall and asked, 'Is everything all right, dear? Have you had your call?'

'Yes, thank you, Mrs Bateman. I wonder could I make one or two more calls? I'll pay for them, of course.'

'Certainly, dear. You can ask the operator for how long, you know. They do that for you.'

'I will, thank you.'

Jane telephoned the Colonial Club next and got the steward on the line. 'Miss Transon?'

'Yes,' said Jane, 'I'm trying to find my father . . .'

'He's no longer a member of this club, I'm afraid.'

Jane felt bewildered. 'Of course he is. I wish he weren't, but he is.'

'No, not since Friday last. Goodbye.'

There was a click as the receiver went down at the other end.

Good God, thought Jane, what on earth has he been doing? The art gallery and his club, both upset with him?

Finally she telephoned the Princess Louise. She was told that her father had not returned on Friday night, had not paid his bill, and had left his luggage. The owner of the Princess Louise had of course informed the police. Mr Transon was an old patron of theirs, said the owner's wife, and she did not believe he had simply skipped without paying the bill, especially since he had left all his clothes behind. The owner's wife said she would have informed Jane if she had known whom to call. Jane thanked the woman and said she appreciated her concern.

Jane settled with the Batemans without telling them about the disappearance of her father. Her mind was in a whirl and she did not know what to do. She intended contacting the police, of course, but since they already knew he had vanished, she doubted they would have any new information to offer, or they would have got back to the owner of the Princess Louise. It was perplexing and horrible.

Half-way back to the cottage, she realised she should have called the police while the telephone was handy, but she had been so upset by her talk with the owner of the Princess Louise that she had not been thinking straight. She decided to go back to the cottage, then go into London herself. Telephoning people was not enough. She had to be there and talk to people properly. She felt miserable and confused, and she turned things over and over in her mind as she walked, not really seeing where she was going, but finding her way back by instinct.

When she arrived back at the cottage, there was someone waiting for her. Petre Peake was standing on the doorstep, looking thoughtful. He seemed about to walk away, when he noticed Jane coming towards him.

'Hello,' said Jane, taking her key out of her handbag, 'I'm afraid my father isn't here at the moment. In fact,' she could not stop the tears from coming now, 'I think he's lost somewhere. I don't know. I can't find out where he's gone.'

Peake stared at her, stone-faced, letting her cry for a moment. She found a handkerchief in her handbag and blew into it, trying to pull herself together.

Peake said, 'Perhaps we'd better go inside.'

She nodded and handed him the key. He opened the door and Jane stumbled inside. She went to the kitchen and put a kettle on the range automatically. Peake stood in the doorway of the kitchen, watching her.

'I just can't think where's he's gone,' said Jane, the tears having stopped now. 'It's all so stupid.'

Peake said, 'I think I know *why* he's gone.'

She turned and faced him.

'You do? Was it because of his fight with Mr Marchant? How do you know? Were you in London?'

'I don't know any Marchant, but yes, I was in London at the same time as your father. We belong to the same gambling club, though I didn't know it before Friday. We got into a game together at about three-thirty or thereabouts, I never keep proper track of time . . .'

'In the afternoon?'

'In the early morning. Anyway, he won a certain amount, probably about eight hundred or so.'

'Pounds?' cried Jane.

Peake gave her a strange smile. 'Why yes, of course, pounds. What other currency would we be using?'

'No, I'm sorry. It's the amount that shocked me,' said Jane. 'We don't have that kind of money, you see.'

'Then you've got a bigger shock coming. Would you like to sit down?'

Jane gripped the edge of the sink. 'Tell me.'

'I think the reason Transon – your father – has disappeared is because he owes me a lot of money. After losing a hand on which he had betted extremely heavily, he made the excuse to go to the toilet and never returned to the table. The club steward saw him leave the club and hurry down the street.'

'Oh no,' said Jane, feeling weak. 'I think I will sit down. Do you mind?'

She went into the living room and sat on the edge of the sofa. Peake followed her and stood by the door.

Jane said, 'Won't you sit?'

'No thanks. I'm fine.'

'How much was it? How much did my father lose?'

'Nearly four thousand pounds.'

Jane felt numb all over. 'Oh my God,' she said in a whisper. 'Oh Lord. What are we going to do?'

'As I said before, he did have some money on him. I know he won at least seven hundred pounds, probably more. I came here today to tell him I would accept some on account and work out some kind of arrangement for payment of the rest.'

Something stirred deep within Jane. 'You're going to hold him to this debt?' she asked.

Peake looked a little surprised. 'Of course. However, as I say, we can work something out for the actual payment . . .'

'A stupid gambling debt,' Jane said, working herself up into a fury. 'Not a debt for services rendered, or payment for goods, or return of a loan. Simply something said over a game of silly cards.'

'That's the way it is,' said Peake slowly, his eyes going very hard.

Jane's anger boiled over. 'It might be the way it is in *your* world, Mr Peake, but not in mine. It's an empty debt, and the people who promise such payments, and demand such payments, are empty people. It comes out of *nothing*, can't you see that? It's immoral. To expect someone to pay you four thousand pounds simply because a card was red or black, hearts or clubs. People say the silliest things in the heat of the moment. How can you hold someone to such a debt? Especially a weak man like my father.'

Peake said, 'Your father wasn't weak when he collected nearly three thousand the night before.'

This took the wind out of her sails for a moment, but she soon rallied. 'Of course he was. I'm not talking about whether he wins or loses, I'm talking about the whole principle behind the thing. You're an intelligent man, you ought to know better.'

'I'll thank you to remain civil, Miss Transon,' snapped Peake. 'I'm not going to be lectured to, by you or anyone else. Men and women have always gambled. There are those who've been ruined – aristocrats who've lost their entire estates, businessmen who've thrown away all their wealth on the turn of a card. It's a fact of life. I'm not going to argue the niceties of such behaviour with you, and I don't apologise for taking part in it. I simply will not be spoken to like a schoolboy.'

She did not feel like apologising to him. 'Perhaps you'd better leave,' she said, standing up. 'It's obvious why he's gone, though where he's run away to is another matter. I don't suppose he'll come home until his money has run out.'

'You underestimate his problem, Miss Transon.'

'Whatever do you mean?'

'I mean, if he has seven to eight hundred pounds in his pocket, he'll attempt to turn it into eight thousand. I wouldn't be surprised if he's not at some race meeting in France right now, trying to back the winner that will get him out of the pit he's in.'

She stared at him for a moment, then said, 'Why in *France*?'

Petre Peake stared back at her and finally said, 'Because he went to the London docks after he left the club. I didn't want to tell you this because it reflects badly on me, but I followed him. I wanted to make sure he didn't do anything foolish – like jumping into the river.'

'Why should it reflect badly on you?' she said, softening a little towards him. 'I think you did the right thing.'

Peake shrugged. 'Well, I don't like spying on another man, but that kind of money's not worth *dying* for, that's for certain. Anyway, I lost him once he reached the docks. I just guessed he was taking a boat somewhere, to allow things to cool off a little. I thought he might even be back by now. It's been over three days.'

'He hasn't been home.'

'I'm sorry. If he does, please tell him to contact me and we'll make some arrangement which will not be too burdensome to you both.'

When Peake had gone, Jane sat and considered what he had told her. She had suffered a series of shocks in the last hour or so, and their impact on her spirit was enormous. More than likely her father had gone to France or Spain and, as Peake had said, would now be trying to gamble himself back into society. What he would do once he had lost all his money, she had no idea. There was nothing she could do but wait for him to return home.

104

Chapter Ten

By mid-September, Jane knew that Henley was not going to come home. After spending agonising weeks waiting for news, Jane finally received a letter from him. It was posted in Gibraltar and it said that he was not going to return for reasons which would have become obvious to her now. The letter said that he was seeking a home elsewhere in the world and would write to her once he had settled, but when he did she was not to reveal his whereabouts to anyone.

'. . . I'm sorry to cause you all this distress, Jane, but I know you'll be all right. You're a competent girl and will manage. In fact, you'll probably be better off without me around. Say a prayer over your mother's grave for me. I enclose a banker's order for fifty pounds. I wish it could be more, but alas I'm almost stony broke. The captain has asked me if I will give talks to other passengers, perhaps demonstrations, on painting. I might have to do that. In the meantime, my dear, look after yourself, and try to forgive your foolish father.'

The letter ended 'with love', below which was a flourish Jane recognised as her father's signature.

Jane was less upset than she expected to be by this letter, because in a way it had cleared her mind of all sorts of horrors. She was angry with her father, certainly, but at least he was alive. Henley was a survivor, she realised that now, and he would not permit himself to be driven to suicide. He was right about one thing: he *was* a foolish man. She gathered he was on some kind of voyage, but after paying the fare to anywhere in the world there would still be a great deal left out of seven hundred pounds.

He's been gambling while he's been on board, she told herself. It was hopeless. Henley would never change. He would always be obsessed by the cards or, if not by them, then by something else on which he could throw away his money.

The day following the arrival of the letter, Jane fell into a deep depression. Recent days had been grey and damp, and did nothing to bolster her spirit. Having little to keep her at home, she packed her bag and travelled by horse-carriage, steam train and finally motorised bus to number 110 Green Lanes, Hornsey, where her aunt Sybil and uncle Matthew lived. Normally this would have been an experience in itself, since there were no such machines out in the country, but Jane was feeling too low to appreciate it.

It was six o'clock in the evening when she arrived. Her cousin Nancy opened the door, and her eyes widened when she saw that it was Jane.

'Jane, what are you doing here? You look *awful.*'

'Thank you, Nancy,' said Jane wryly, stepping into the hallway, 'I can always rely on you for a few uplifting words when I'm feeling down. Is Uncle Matthew at home?' Jane's uncle was an insurance salesman and was away from home a great deal.

'Yes, he's just come in. He's in the living room.'

Jane put her suitcase down in the corner of the hallway and Nancy took her coat and scarf. Jane then made her way to the living room of the Victorian terraced house. As she entered the room, her aunt looked up from her knitting and evinced the same expression of surprise that had been shown by Nancy at the door. Like her daughter, Jane's aunt Sybil had an almost translucent complexion and fine, fair hair. Now in her late forties, Sybil Transon had begun to fade into a ghost-like apparition. This physical obscurity was matched by a mental vagueness and lack of verbal expressiveness.

Instead of greeting Jane, Sybil said, 'Matthew?' in a very soft voice.

Matthew Transon was a small man with a tight little moustache above a little rosebud mouth. He wore his wire-rimmed spectacles as if he had been born with them attached to his face and would need to have them cut away from his nose once the prescription had to be changed. He was scribbling furiously on some papers, presumably to do with his work, and he looked up with an irritated expression.

'Yes, what is . . . Jane?'

His face immediately broke into a smile. Jane was a favourite of his. Then his expression changed again.

'What is it?' he said, standing up. 'What on earth has happened? Is it Henley . . . ?'

Jane suddenly found herself sobbing as the pressure of the previous few weeks finally found a vent. Her aunt stood up and took Jane in her arms, hugging her and crooning, 'There, there, Jane. Don't fret love. We're here.'

Jane allowed herself to be cuddled and fussed over for a few minutes while she choked back her tears. Matthew stood by and looked on, a little helplessly. Nancy went to make a cup of tea in the kitchen. Jonathan came downstairs from his room and was immediately waved back upstairs again by his father.

'So,' said Matthew, obviously fearing the worst, 'Henley . . . what's happened to him? Is it his heart?'

Jane shook her head and wiped away the last of her tears with the handkerchief given to her by her aunt.

'No, Uncle. I'm sorry if I've worried you. He's well enough, but he's gone.'

'Gone?' echoed Matthew, looking bewildered. 'Gone where?'

'That's just it. I don't know. He went into London about three weeks ago, to sell some paintings, and got into a card game. Apparently he lost an awful lot of money – thousands of pounds – and of course we can't pay it. So he just walked off somewhere and caught a boat. I don't know where he is now. I've had one letter from him, postmarked Gibraltar.'

'Good heavens. What a bloody fool. Excuse me, my dear,' he said, apologising to Sybil for his swearing.

'That's all right, Matthew,' Sybil said. 'The news provoked you.'

'It did indeed, it did indeed,' snorted Matthew, thumbs in waistcoat pockets and beginning to pace the room. 'Gone away and left you, just like that, has he? Irresponsible man. We made allowances for him, because he's a genius, but he's always been an irresponsible man. Thousands of pounds! Good Lord. It's monstrous. Leaving his daughter to fend for herself.'

Jane shook her head at this typical reaction. 'Uncle Matthew, I don't want you to say things about my father that you might regret later, because I know you're fond of him. He's irresponsible, yes, but I'm well able to take care of myself, really. And if I can't, I should be able to. I'm nearly twenty-one, after all. And you're far too generous with your praise. He's a reasonably good painter, but he's not a genius.'

Jane took her aunt's hand in hers. 'Aunt Sybil, I haven't come to foist myself upon you for ever. I've just come for a few days' visit . . .'

'You can stay as long as you want,' said Matthew firmly. 'I'm sure we can find room.'

'No, you'd soon become fed up with me – and anyway, I don't wish to be a nuisance. I just got upset and needed a bit of company for a few days. Is that all right?'

Nancy came into the room with a tray of tea and set it down before the fireplace, which at the moment held a vase of flowers. Jane's aunt and uncle did not light fires until 1 November, no matter what the weather, and they ceased having them precisely on 31 March. Sybil busied herself pouring the teas while Matthew paced up and down.

They discussed Henley and the circumstances in which he had left Jane until late in the evening. Jonathan was allowed into the room once Matthew was certain Jane had stopped crying: he did not feel it was seemly to expose his son to a weeping woman; it was uncomfortable enough for him, a grown man.

There was very little Matthew could do for Jane financially. He was not a wealthy man. He was able to keep his own family in a certain amount of comfort by working very hard, but though he might be able to let Jane have a few pounds here and there, he was not able to be thoroughly generous. Although he was now a sales manager, he still had to keep his 'team' on their toes and to do that he needed to be everywhere at once. His family did not see a great deal of him.

'How could Henley *do* this?' he kept saying. It was not something Matthew could understand at all. As a man who was thoroughly conscientious, completely law-abiding, and with a horror of besmirching the family name, he could not comprehend the actions of his brother.

Jane told him, 'You're different kind of men, Uncle. I know my father doesn't understand you, and you don't understand him, but that shouldn't stop you from loving one another.'

'Love' was not a word Matthew would use in referring to his feelings for his brother. He was not comfortable with that kind of language. He would often say he was fond of Henley, and that Henley had been 'a good brother to him', but that was as deep as he would allow the words to go.

Henley had in fact not been 'a good brother' but a very thoughtless and unreliable one, causing Matthew a great deal of pain at times. Moreover, Henley had been their father's favourite. Henley was the exciting one, the artist, while Matthew was a plodder. As favourite and senior, Henley had inherited seven-eighths of the farm. Matthew's older brother had squandered most of that, while Matthew himself had used his one-eighth of the inheritance to buy a London home for his family.

Despite all this, Matthew would not allow himself to think less of Henley than he felt he should. Henley was his brother, and it was Matthew's duty to maintain certain emotions regarding their relationship, no matter what Henley did. Those feelings involved fondness and regard, for Henley was the elder and entitled to respect, but the word 'love' smacked too much of false and sloppy sentimentality for Matthew's liking.

Having unburdened herself of her own feelings, Jane was able to go to bed that night feeling a great deal better. A firmness of mind began to set in which would help her over the next few months.

When she stayed with her aunt and uncle, Jane shared a room with Nancy. As they got ready for bed that evening, Nancy questioned Jane about recent events at Howlett End.

'Have you seen Courtney lately?' she asked, slipping into an ankle-length nightdress.

Jane did not like the way Nancy was using Courtney's first name, as if Nancy were thoroughly familiar with him, but then decided she was just being churlish and Nancy was innocent of nothing more than trying to share Jane's friends.

'Courtney has rejoined his regiment, in Yorkshire,' said Jane.

'Oh, I know that,' said Nancy, airily. 'I had a letter from him just the other day.'

'Did you?' said Jane, wondering why she felt so irritated by this piece of information, since she had received three letters herself.

'Then you probably know more than I do.'

'He said he was trying to get back for a weekend. I was hoping Dad might let me go and stay with you, so Courtney and I could see each other. Has he been home recently?'

'Not to my knowledge,' Jane replied stiffly.

'Well, I'm sure he'll call on you when he does, because you are quite good friends, aren't you? He said he's dying to see me again.'

'Dying?'

'Well, he didn't use that word of course, but the meaning's very plain . . .'

After this exchange, Nancy altered the subject and the girls were able to talk more easily.

Later, before she fell asleep, Jane thought over what Nancy had told her. Why had Courtney written to Nancy? It was perfectly possible that Nancy had written first and Courtney felt obliged to answer. Or probably he had promised Jane's cousin that he would let her know how things went in response to a request from her.

However, the mystery to Jane was not really why Courtney had written to Nancy, which might be explained by a number of reasons, but why she, Jane, was slightly angry that he had done so. After all, she herself had received letters from Courtney, though she had only sent one short note in reply. She was not, she admitted, a good correspondent, but it was *she* who was Courtney's friend, not Nancy, and that was the main reason for her feeling of chagrin. He was not yet a long-standing enough friend for her to want to share him with her cousin Jane. *That* was the crux. She was afraid that Courtney might like Nancy better than her, and become better friends with Nancy.

That's silly, she told herself, *Nancy's still a schoolgirl.*

Yet Nancy was very pretty, in that pale, vulnerable sort of way which certain men found attractive. They wanted to protect such girls: it probably made them feel big and brave and needed. Was Courtney that kind of man? Wasn't there something of the protector in *all* men?

And why didn't Courtney tell her that he had written to Nancy? Was there any reason why he should tell her, though? What exactly, thought Jane, is our relationship? We have seen each other not more than half-a-dozen times, yet I think we can call ourselves *good* friends. I suppose what I would like to be, Jane told herself honestly, is a *special* friend. But Courtney's writing to Nancy had put her cousin almost on the same level as herself, hadn't it?

Finally Jane was completely exhausted and fell into a fatigued sleep. She spent a restless night full of disturbed dreams and awoke the next morning feeling only partially refreshed.

The following day she went with her uncle to Marchant's gallery and retrieved three of Henley's unsold paintings. There was also some money, since two more paintings had sold. It was not much, but Jane took it gratefully.

'I'm sorry you and my father have fallen out,' she said to Marchant.

'Miss Transon, I have no quarrel with you,' he said, 'but right at this very moment I don't care whether I ever see your father again.'

'I don't think any of us will see him again,' she replied as she walked away, 'whether we want to or not.'

Over the next few days, Jane gradually relaxed. By the time she felt it was necessary for her to return to Wildrose Cottage, she had shed her terrible depression. She was not happy, but at least she did not feel so utterly dejected. She was able to say goodbye to her cousins and thank her aunt (her uncle had been working away over the previous two days) for putting up with her, and travelled back to Audley End by steam train. From there she took a horse-carriage back to the cottage.

Once again Petre Peake was waiting for her.

'If you've come for your money,' she said coldly, 'I haven't got it, but you can be sure I'll get it for you as soon as I'm able.'

'I'm not interested in the damn money,' he said. 'In fact, you can tell Transon the debt no longer exists.'

'Why?' she said, suspiciously.

'Because I say so,' he snapped. 'The money is owed to me. I'm entitled to say whether I want it back or not.'

She shrugged, unable to fathom this strange man whose eyes haunted her, even when he was not there.

'I don't understand why you're doing this, but I'm very grateful.'

He said, 'I doubt whether it will bring him home again, you know. Even though I've wiped out the debt, he probably won't accept that fact. It's all right to run away from a gambling debt, but it's not all right for me to say it no longer exists. That smacks suspiciously of charity. Henley won't like that. Men very seldom do. In his mind Henley's probably telling himself that he'll settle the debt one day. It's a matter of honour.'

Jane shook her head slowly. 'You mean, it's all right to evade a gambling debt – that's honourable – but not to accept that it's been dropped?'

''Fraid so. Right at this moment he will hate me for holding the winning hand. It would be impossible for him to be beholden to the man who's responsible for his present circumstances. I'm the one to blame, you see, not him. If I had held a simple flush in my hand, instead of a running flush, he would be crowing like a rooster now, instead of running like a dog.'

Jane shook her head again. 'As long as I live, I'll never understand gamblers,' she said. 'Now, would you like a drink while you're here?' she asked, opening the front door with her key. 'A cup of tea?'

'That would be welcome,' he said.

The tea took some time to make, since there was no fire in the kitchen range. Peake insisted on making the fire, though he had to be shown where to find the kindling and coal. Jane unpacked while this was being done. When she returned to the kitchen he had a kettle on the hob. Later, they sat drinking their tea before a glowing fire.

'You called here for something?' she prompted him.

'Yes. I came to tell you and your father that the crocuses are in bloom, up on your land.'

She had forgotten about the crocuses. A sudden melancholy hit her, which must have been visible in her features, because Peake said, 'What's the matter? Have I said something wrong?'

'No, no. It's just that I planted those saffron crocuses for my father – to give him something to paint, something different and exciting – and now he won't see them.'

'He's not coming back?'

'I don't think so.'

'Where is he?'

'Who knows?' Jane sighed.

Peake stared at her intently. 'I'm sorry,' he said.

112

Jane said, 'Because of your money?'

'Because of you.'

This took her by surprise and she didn't know what to say. Instead she looked into the fire and tried to quell her feelings. There could be no mistaking the way in which he'd said it, but she was confused. Why should Petre Peake be concerned about her? Why should he worry if she missed her father or not? Why wouldn't he take his eyes off her? She could sense them boring into her.

'Don't stare at me like that,' she said, without looking at him.

'Why not?'

'Because it makes me feel uncomfortable.'

He shrugged. 'I meant no harm.'

They lapsed into silence after that, until finally he stood up and made a suggestion. 'It's a bright day. Why don't we take a walk up to the saffron fields and have a look at them? I'm no judge of beauty, but they look quite startling. It's the numbers, I think. Like the poppies on the fields of Flanders. Flowers don't normally interest me, but when you see them in their hundreds of thousands, they can have quite an effect.'

'What a good idea,' said Jane, getting to her feet. 'Yes, let's do that.'

To have something to do was better than a medicine for her sadness. She suddenly felt brisk and energetic. A long walk would do her good, she thought.

They set off from the cottage at a reasonably fast pace, with Jane doing most of the talking as they walked. She was suddenly conscious of the closeness of their bodies, for he was one of those people who constantly brushed her with his shoulder as he strode beside her. Once or twice she surreptitiously glanced up at him.

She couldn't help comparing Petre with Courtney, with whom, for some reason, she was a little angry. Whenever she recalled how she and Courtney had ploughed the saffron fields together, a wave of tenderness went through her, but this was quickly washed away by the thought that Courtney seemed to be playing a double game with her and her cousin Nancy. She had little real evidence of this, apart from Nancy's implications that feelings were beginning to run deep between them.

Intellectually, Petre and Courtney seemed on a par with one another. Both appeared to have a fairly keen insight on life, and seemed equally quick-witted. There were barriers in both of them, guarding certain areas, but Jane guessed this was the result of the war. A lot of men had returned with hidden wounds which they did not wish to open or reveal to anyone at home. In fact many seemed incapable of communicating on certain subjects and she wondered if this were the fault of those who had remained behind, rather than those who had experienced the war, since many people at home were totally unable to imagine the horrors of the front.

Petre was a tall man, a little taller than Courtney, and there was a litheness about him which seemed to contain a terrible strength. Their colouring was totally different, of course, since Petre was blond and blue-eyed, and the dark-haired Courtney's eyes were a liquid brown and softer-looking – or so she remembered them. Their complexions, too, were different. Petre had an olive, Mediterranean-type skin despite his fair hair, while Courtney's was much lighter.

None of these outward comparisons really emphasised the principal difference between the two men, though, she decided. The real dissimilarity was in their nature. Petre's darkness was internal, within his character and personality, while Courtney was open and easy. There was something about Petre which both frightened and fascinated her. He seemed capable of anything; perversely she found that exciting.

'Now it's you who's staring,' he said, without looking down at her.

'Yes,' she agreed. 'I was wondering. We know so little about you. Where do you come from? Have you lived in Essex all your life?'

'Ah, questions. The army asked me a lot of questions.'

'And did you have answers for them?'

'Not all of them. I don't think people should ask questions unless they're invited. Not questions like that. It sometimes stirs unwanted thoughts.'

This reply and its lack of information intrigued her.

'How old are you?' she asked.

'How old do you think I am?'

She stopped and he halted with her. She stared at him openly now.

114

What struck her was how ill-suited he seemed to the outdoors. He seemed not to fit in with the rolling countryside, the sweeping brown-velvet fields, the tree-studded crests of the soft, low hills. He looked completely out of place, which was strange, for he had a gypsy appearance about him, as if he *should* be a traveller on the road, part of the landscape.

'Well?' he reminded her. 'My age?'

'I'm sorry. Oh, I would guess at about thirty, perhaps a little older.'

'Close. I'm thirty-five, I think.'

'You *think*?' she said, surprised.

His eyes, which had begun to soften a little, suddenly turned to flint again. 'That's not something I'm prepared to discuss.'

He walked on then, a long stride, and she had to hurry to keep up with him. Jane was even more intrigued now. *He didn't know his own age.* It obviously upset him, too, that he was not certain about it. What was he, a changeling, a child left by the fairies? She thought briefly of saying this to him, jokingly of course, but she was certain he would be extremely angered by it. Now there was the difference: Courtney would probably have laughed and agreed with her. *Yes, the fairies had taken away the real heir to the Stanton estates, and left him in its place.* But not Petre. Petre, she believed, would fly into a rage and accuse her of ridiculing him. So she wisely remained silent.

They crossed deep ditches, like wounds between the flesh of the hills. Rooks had gathered in their hundreds on various fields and scattered noisily on the approach of the two humans. There were other smaller birds amongst them, which Jane could not recognise from a distance; but they voiced a softer sound, in contrast to the harsh 'caws' of the rooks.

They passed spinneys, mostly beech and hornbeam with an undergrowth of blackthorn, hawthorn and elder. Solitary oaks guarded some of the hedgerows, and elms appeared to walk the ridges like roaming giants. Above and around them was the wide curve of the sky that touched earth in some fantasy world far away on distant horizons.

When they reached the saffron fields, the sight of the flowers took Jane by surprise. 'They're beautiful,' she breathed.

'Yes, I thought they had something,' said Petre, breaking a stick

115

from an ash tree and using it to point. 'Look over there. They look like lakes of perfume, don't they?'

His attempt at poetry was reasonably accurate: Jane immediately saw what he meant. The lilac saffron fields, which lay in a huge, shallow bowl of land at the bottom of the slope on which they were standing, appeared to be liquid, and Jane had to suppress a desire to immerse herself in their beauty, to run and throw herself into the vast pool.

The colour was not strong, being of a pastel hue, but it covered such a large area that it dominated the whole landscape. Low clouds above the bowl of fields reflected a delicate mauve shade on their undersides. The sweet perfume of the blooms drifted over the chalk-soiled fields in gentle waves.

'What a pity father can't see this,' said Jane. 'He would have captured this scene so well on canvas.'

'Is he a good painter?' asked Petre.

'Yes, a good one. Not brilliant, but good. Haven't you seen any of his paintings?'

'Yes, but I wanted your opinion of him as an artist.'

Jane didn't want to continue this discussion of her father. Instead, she said, 'I think I'm going to swim in those flowers. Come on!'

She ran across the meadow in which they were standing until she reached the ditch on the far side. Then she scrambled through a hole in the low hedge and found herself amongst the mass of six-petalled blooms on the far side. Shedding her inhibitions completely, she rolled down the gentle slope, crushing the blooms beneath her as she went. She heard herself laughing as she inhaled the sweet smell, until she came to a halt at the bottom of a dip. There she finally lay still amongst the crocuses and stared up at the sky.

The clouds moved overhead, stained with lilac light.

Suddenly, Petre appeared above her, looking down on her. There was something in his expression which made her heart begin to race. She felt strange: light-headed and light-bodied. It was almost as if she were looking down on herself, seeing herself through his eyes. Her blood began to quicken in her veins, as she watched him standing there, motionless, a tall, blond warrior home from the war. There was a raw need evident in his eyes, which, although she was a virgin, she recognised instantly. This obvious craving in him fuelled something deep within herself too: a fire that had never sprung into flame before. Her breasts began to feel hot, her thighs began to burn.

She felt the need to say something, to break the terrible silence.

'The flowers are so beautiful, aren't they?'

For a few moments he simply looked at her, his eyes unfathomably deep. Then, incredibly, she saw that he was crying. He turned away, as if to walk off, then back again, to stare down at her. She sat up and opened her arms, wanting to comfort him in his distress. He fell to his knees and then they were holding each other, his tears wetting her cheeks.

When he spoke his voice was dangerously low and hoarse, as if the saffron pollen was dust in his mouth.

'I'm sorry,' he said.

She could have said something, in a normal tone, to change the mood. The spell would have been broken immediately and they could both have walked away without losing face. But she could not. Instead, she remained silent in his arms: felt the blood banging in her temple. Her own breath tasted musty in her mouth and there was a curious ache in her stomach, as if she had tensed the muscles and couldn't relax them, even though she tried.

When he lay down beside her, her legs began trembling violently, and he must have felt this against his own thigh, because he whispered to her not to be afraid, that he would not hurt her, that he would be very gentle. After a few minutes he sat up and took off his clothes until he was completely naked, his long, lean body dark against the white flesh of her arm. Curiously, she reached out and touched the hard ridges of muscle on his abdomen with her fingertips, and then quickly withdrew her hand as she inadvertently brushed the darker, aggressive stem below, surprised by its presence there.

When his warm hands began undressing her, she bit the inside of her cheek in panic, and tasted blood. Curiously, this had the effect of calming her fears, and once he had begun stroking her breasts and stomach, felt the soft skin of his palms on her nipples, the terror subsided completely. In its place was a mixture of loving feelings and the enlightenment of a new kind of passion for this blue-eyed man whose fingers now explored her most cryptic places. Gently his explorations covered her whole body, stroking her abdomen with the side of his face now, breathing her, tasting the salt from her skin, as if lost in some wondrous search for a pleasure which both of them would enjoy.

Her skin began to tingle violently as he kissed her neck and face, her nerve-ends alive. Then she felt him gently part her legs with his hands. As he entered her, slowly, there was some pain, which made her tense herself, but she heard him whisper, 'Relax, don't worry, I'll try not to hurt you . . .'

Her next thought was that he had lied. She wanted to shout at him in anger. In the beginning, before they had started, he had promised no pain at all, that he would not hurt her in the least. Now he was saying the pain was inevitable, that it was supposed to hurt. These were passing thoughts, however, swifter than the birds flying across the clouds above. They were gone in a moment, and after a while she actually began to enjoy the easy rhythm of those movements, his olive-skinned movements, inside her. She felt as if she enveloped him, possessed him, held him prisoner with her body. He was wholly hers.

'Help me,' he whispered urgently, and this simple request fuelled her desire.

She began working with him, their legs entwined, their arms around each other's nakedness. She stroked the hair on the back of his head and neck, encouraging him. She smelled the odour of his skin, on his narrow shoulders, which mingled with the scent of the saffron blooms. She felt the power of his muscled form, sinewy and serpentine, locked around hers.

There was a kind of hunger being satisfied within her, but not with the fullness she had expected. It seemed as if something was missing, something vital, and even amongst the enjoyment of their love-making, it worried her. She wondered whether she was failing, in some way, to *give* enough to him. Perhaps, she thought, I shall learn the art of total abandonment to the pleasures of this act, and then I won't feel this lack of fulfilment?

Then, finally, he made a sound in the back of his throat and his body turned to iron. She felt him clasp to her completely, as if it would take a great force to part them afterwards. Then, after a moment or two, he simply relaxed and slid from her. He lay on his back, looking upwards, breathing deeply and noisily.

Jane felt an intense need to communicate with Petre on an important level. So far they had said nothing to one another of any consequence, and she needed to understand him, to make him her own. To do that, he had to let her inside him, as she had let him inside her. Hers had been a corporeal lowering of the gates; his needed to be metaphysical.

She went up on to her elbows to look at him. His body, wet with perspiration like hers, was covered with lilac-coloured petals where they had rolled amongst the flowers. When she looked down at her own breasts, red styles and yellow stamens decorated them, as well as the petals. She felt like the princess of some pagan tribe, adorned with nature's ornaments. And Petre was a great warrior, out of the rainforest, his skin printed with floral tattoos. She used this to break the ice in order that they could open a discussion on a higher level.

'Look at us,' she laughed. 'We're children of the earth.'

He glanced at her, and suddenly she was shocked by the lack of lustre in his eyes. There was a dullness there, as if the passion had been so fleeting it had simply been a surface sheen. It was then she realised that it would be useless to try to find each other in a spiritual sense. There would be no practical end to it. It had been a transient ardour.

She turned from him and dressed quickly. Now that the physical part was over, she saw through it. She understood her feelings of dissatisfaction, those faint concerns while they had been making love. He had been gentle, she thought, but spiritually passionless. She could not love a man who was so empty of passion.

The disappointment that this revelation brought her was enormous. Jane realised she had been looking for love, hoping it was there between them, allowing all her defences to fall in the belief that love would come storming through and take her completely. It was a strange, unsettling experience, giving herself physically, yet withholding the essential ingredient. It left her with a huge, hollow feeling inside, and she felt like bursting into tears.

'You're upset,' he said. 'What is it?'

She opened her mouth, and then decided she could not tell him;

not bluntly, because it would hurt them both.

'Nothing, I'm all right.'

'You didn't enjoy it? I'm told women rarely do the first time, but it's supposed to get better. Don't be disappointed.'

'It's not that. I know – at least, I can imagine that it will – get better.'

'What then? Was it more painful than you imagined? You seemed all right after a while.'

She looked him directly in the eyes, knowing she had to say something now. He had to know what she was thinking, whether it was hurtful to them or not. Otherwise she knew she would allow the affair to grow into a shapeless thing that neither of them enjoyed but were unable to control.

'Petre, I'm sorry, but this can't happen again.'

He suddenly looked mystified and very vulnerable, and she knew she was wounding him.

'Whyever not?' he said.

'Because – because we don't love each other.'

A look of comprehension came into his eyes. 'You want to get married – is that it?'

'I have no intention of getting married, to anyone. What I'm trying to tell you is that this occurred during a moment of thoughtlessness. I . . . we were both caught unawares. It didn't come out of anything deeper than . . . than a desire to bury our disappointments in each other. I'm feeling at odds with the world at the moment, and you – well, I think you've always felt bitter, at least since I've known you. It seems deeply rooted. Anyway, we have to forget this. I'm sorry.'

He snorted, 'Don't feel sorry for me. I don't need that kind of thing. Pity? You can shove it.'

'Please don't be angry,' said Jane, not really knowing how to defuse the situation, and saying anything. 'I *did* enjoy it with you. I did. But I can't do it again, that's all. Can we be friends?'

'If you think we can be simply *friends*, after just making love in a field of crocus flowers, you must be out of your mind,' he said. 'We just crossed the Rubicon and there's no going back.'

As he pulled on the last of his clothes, something dull and heavy dropped from his jacket pocket and stuck in the soil. Jane was horrified to see that it was a gun. Petre quickly picked up the weapon, wiped the mud from it, and stuffed it back into his pocket. The movement was almost unconscious.

'What's that?' she asked him.

He looked at her. 'You saw what it was – a revolver. It's my old .38 service revolver, from the war. I kept it when I left the RFC.'

'What do you need it for, Petre?'

He shrugged, not looking at her now. 'I don't know. I feel a need for it, for some reason. Not for protection or anything like that. I'm not intending to shoot anybody, if that's what you think. It's for . . . an emergency.'

Jane said, 'I don't know what to think. If you don't carry it for protection, who *is* it for? What kind of emergency?'

He turned those terrible eyes on her. 'I told you, I don't know. Just an emergency. If I knew the nature of it, I probably wouldn't need the gun. You ask too many questions for someone who just wants to be a friend.'

With that, he strode off, heading for the road over a mile away.

Jane straightened her own clothes and followed some way behind. She could not keep up with him, however, and soon he was lost amongst the folded hills. Slowing her pace, she idled as she finished the journey back to the cottage, thinking about what had happened to her, and about her fields of saffron. There was nothing she could do about the former, but the latter required her attention, and could be dealt with. In one way, making love had liberated her from something. She was not quite sure what, but she felt vaguely energised. The task she had to tackle was clear, and she felt eager to confront it.

Tomorrow, she promised herself, I'll go into Thaxted and see Mr Saltash. Her capital was buried under four inches of soil at the moment, and she had to dig it out. She needed Mr Saltash's advice about raising the saffron bulbs and reselling them.

Once practical decisions had been dealt with in her mind, she dwelt upon the fact that Petre carried a gun. She really did not know what to make of this. Was he more dangerous than anyone thought? Or perhaps lots of young men stole their service revolvers to keep by them for some sort of imagined security need? Jane supposed that going through a war where thousands of your comrades had been slaughtered around you like cattle would make for terrible traumas, many hidden anxieties, vulnerabilities of which she could not conceive. To survive such an ordeal would be to carry enormous guilt. Perhaps for some reason, unknown even to Petre, the gun made him feel safe, kept the nightmares at bay? A talisman of sorts?

Jane decided it was really none of her business anyway, since Petre had effectively rejected the lesser relationship she had offered in place of love. She doubted whether she would actually hear from him again. It would probably be best if they avoided one another in the future.

She began to feel the pressure of guilt, at the back of her mind, for allowing what happened to happen. Of course he expected more. But then again, he was so unwilling to give anything of himself, his *real* self, to *her*. He was not allowing her inside. How could she even begin to love a man who built walls around himself and refused to let her look behind them? He wanted to *take*, but not *give* anything.

Petre seemed to believe that a physical show was all that was needed, to prove that deep feelings existed. He hadn't even *mentioned* the word love. When she had talked about friendship, he hadn't said, 'But I love you, Jane.' She was glad he had not, because she could not have replied in kind, but it surely gave some indication as to the nature of his feelings for her? Let *him* feel guilty, she thought, for taking advantage, not of her, but of the moment. Why should she be the one to bear all the blame for what had happened?

Having settled this in her mind, she began to cheer up and look forward to some manual work. That would take her mind off all these emotional problems, she decided. She remembered how her muscles had been after the ploughing of the fields. When you ache from head to toe, you have no time to consider whether you feel depressed or happy. You just live.

Chapter Eleven

When Jane woke the following morning, she felt a little sore and recalled the events of the previous day. In the cold light of the morning, she wondered how it had happened. When she had walked with Petre to the saffron fields, there had been no intention on the part of either of them to make love. Or had there? Had Petre planned it? No, she couldn't believe that. It had to be chance. Petre was a strange, cold man, but he could not be so conniving as all that. It was an accident, pure and simple, and she was inclined to think that it had happened so fast that neither of them actually knew what was happening until it was all over.

Jane stared out of the window at a grey, blustery day.

It *had* been fast. One minute they had been discussing the saffron flowers, and the next they had been rolling amongst them. She regretted it now: not so much the act itself, but the raw emotions that had been exposed. She regretted it more for Petre's sake. He had taken the act as a pledge, a sign that her feelings for him ran deep. They did not. She found him physically attractive – startlingly so – but when she thought of spending the rest of her life with him her feelings wilted. She had been selfish and indulgent, seeking comfort from him without taking into account *his* feelings. She had used him, and in doing so she had awakened something in him which she could not now respond to. She realised the wrongness of her actions now, and wished she had not sought refuge in his arms.

Jane knew, too, that she would regret it even more if she became pregnant. This cold thought sobered her a little. That was another risk she had not taken into account in the heat of the moment. *I've been poking around in the dragon's nest*, she thought, *and I'll count myself lucky if he hasn't been woken.*

123

Then there was the business with the gun. Jane shivered when she thought about it. The fact that Petre carried a weapon might make him more exciting to some women, but not to Jane. She had felt very vulnerable, her confidence had gone, and she had needed comfort. There had been an unwarranted feeling of guilt within her, caused by her father running away from his responsibilities. Jane had no idea *why* she should feel bad about that, because he hadn't run away from *her*, but deep down she did. She had needed to feel wanted, blameless, so she had followed her instincts rather than her good sense.

She rose, dressed and breakfasted. Then she went out on the road and hitched a lift on a farm wagon into Thaxted. There she went directly to the office of Mr Saltash. This time she was admitted immediately by the formidable Mrs Bignall.

Mr Saltash stood and reached across the desk to shake her hand. 'Miss Transon,' he said warmly.

A flush of pleasure went through her. 'Oh, you remembered me?'

'Of course. I have to say it's because I don't get many young ladies in here. Especially young ladies as pretty as you, if I may say so.'

This reply disappointed her a little. 'I had hoped you'd remembered me because I was good at doing business,' she said ruefully.

He laughed. 'Ha! Men will get up to all sorts of tricks to be remembered in the business world. Being memorable because you're a woman doesn't make you any less of a hard bargainer, now does it? I remember that part, too – how you beat my price down.'

She laughed at this as she took the seat he was offering.

'Now,' he said, regaining his own seat, 'what can I do for you? Have the crocuses flowered?'

'Yes, but I have to dig them up again. I've ... I've fallen into financial difficulties. I'd like to resell the corms now. Can you help me?'

Mr Saltash pursed his lips and leaned back in his chair. Jane wondered what was going through his mind. She thought perhaps he was going to offer her a low price for the bulbs, now that she had revealed she had problems.

Finally he spoke. 'Is there any reason why we can't harvest the saffron itself?' he said.

Jane said, 'I remember you mentioning that before. But I only have eight acres of crocuses. Surely it wouldn't be worth harvesting that amount? I imagine they have thousands of acres in the Mediterranean and in India.'

'Hold on a minute.'

He got up and went to a shelf with some files bulging with papers. Eventually he found what he was looking for and took one down, rifled through it, and came out with a single sheet of paper. Looking satisfied with himself, he returned to the desk and put the piece of paper in front of him.

'After you left, last time, I went and looked up some facts and figures,' he said. 'It seems you get about one pound of dried saffron from five pounds of wet. Now, you might be surprised to know that dried saffron retails at about twenty pounds a pound these days.'

Jane nodded. 'That sounds a lot of money, but how much could I expect to harvest from eight acres?'

'Well, normally in the first year the yield is only two pounds of dried saffron per acre, but if my memory serves me, we used corms that had already given off a crop, so if you're lucky, something in the region of twelve pounds an acre.'

Jane's eyes widened a little.

'Well, if my sums are right, that would mean nearly two thousand pounds?'

'One thousand nine hundred and twenty pounds, to be precise,' said Mr Saltash.

'That's six times my original investment.'

'Just a bit less.'

Jane began to feel excited by these figures, then something struck her. 'Saffron hasn't been grown here since the late 1700s, has it? If it's so valuable, why did the industry die?'

'Well, at one time it was used for all sorts of things, from getting rid of pimples to curing sleeplessness. Finally, when all the old wives' tales were put to rest, it was only used in cooking and dyeing. That's the case today. As a consequence, there was a glut on the market.'

'So the market was over-supplied?'

'Not just that, though. The main reason it died out here was because of the gathering and drying. It became too expensive. Labour costs went up through the roof during the industrial revolution, when all the farm-workers went to the factories in the towns. But I think we can get round that. I know someone with a couple of oast-houses – you know, for drying hops? Since there's no hops grown in Essex now, the oast-houses are idle. We could probably hire them for a few pounds.'

Jane's excitement grew. 'That sounds good, but what about the picking?'

'Who did you use for the planting?'

'Gypsies.'

'Well, there you are then. Gypsies are not farm-hands. Once the fruit picking's over, the gypsies usually move on. Heaven knows where they go to – Scotland? Cornwall? Anyways, gypsies will be the cheapest pickers. You'd better bone up on harvesting the flowers. I've got a book somewhere..'

He got up and began rooting amongst his dusty shelves once more, until he finally came up with a roughly-printed pamphlet. 'It's old, but I shouldn't think much changes in the way of harvesting saffron. You sit here and study this while I get us a cup of tea each. Sugar and milk?'

'Just milk, thanks.'

Jane took the pamphlet and began to read, as Mr Saltash went to the door and called to his secretary for two teas. It seemed that the whole six-petalled crocus flower was picked initially. These were dried before the three orangy-red styles, or 'chives' as they were popularly called, were extracted from the blooms and again dried, this time between sheets of paper, for each chive was precious. If any of the yellow stamens got mixed in with the red chives there would be a dilution of the product, so it was necessary to weed these out before the process went any further, and the saffron was pressed into cakes.

As she drank her tea she talked again. 'Well, from what I've read here, we'll probably have to dry the flowers in the oast-houses, then remove the chives.'

'How's that done?' asked Mr Saltash.

'Two methods, apparently. One is labour intensive and involves picking out the chives by hand. The other is by beating the flowers lightly with sticks then immersing them in tubs of water. The chives float to the bottom. This second method produces a saffron which is less pure, called "mongra".'

She looked up. 'If the gypsies are willing, we'd better plump for the first method. We don't want to find we have to sell our saffron cheaply because it's of a low quality.'

'My feelings exactly.'

'And how much do you require for your services, Mr Saltash?' asked Jane, finishing her tea.

He smiled. 'How much do you think I'm worth?'

Jane pursed her lips in the way he did himself when she asked him questions. 'For helping me so far, and for a promise to help me with the oast-houses and possibly a kiln to dry the chives – five per cent?'

He leaned back in his chair. 'You think that's enough, considering my contribution?'

'Yes, I think it's very fair. You'll make a hundred pounds, or close to it.'

'Quite right,' he smiled. 'I accept.'

They shook hands on it, and Jane asked him to go ahead and arrange the oast-houses.

'There's a brickfield nearby, with a kiln,' he said. 'I'll see about that, too.'

'Good,' Jane replied. 'I'm off to see about hiring the labour.'

Jane had to walk most of the way back to Howlett End, but she finally got a lift from a baker's van pulled by a very sprightly little roan. She went directly to the farm and spoke with Alex Blatcher, who promised to have a word with the gypsies who were doing his apple picking for him.

'I'm not sayin' they'll want to do it, mind. I don't know as if any of 'em will of heard of saffron pickin', but we can but try, dear.'

It turned out that the gypsies had in the past picked saffron in Italy, after they had left the English orchards, so they were more than willing to remain and pick in England, especially since the war had prevented them from going to Spain or Italy for the past few years. Jane did not even have to organise them very much, because they had their own hierarchy and worked things out amongst themselves. They were a different group from the ones who had planted the corms, and were a great deal noisier and more demonstrative, but they seemed to know what they were doing.

Blatcher supplied a couple of carts at very low cost, so all Jane had to do was transport the flower heads to the oast-houses. A telephone call to Mr Saltash supplied her with the whereabouts of the oast-houses, some six miles away on the bank of the Chelmer River. Arrangements had been made, said Mr Saltash, and she could go ahead with her plans.

The next two weeks were heady with excitement. Jane spent her time running from one part of the operation to another, supervising something about which she knew very little. The gypsies helped a great deal, especially one elderly woman called Rona, who *seemed* to be in charge. Jane wondered about who was actually giving the orders, because the women pickers always appeared to be arguing with each other over who should do what, who had picked the most, who was the boss, and a variety of other disputed things. They shouted, threw their hands in the air, waved Rona away as if she smelled of rotten fish, stood their ground stubbornly when ordered to work, flounced off occasionally, spat on the ground at Rona's feet, and demonstrated their distaste for either Rona and the work in a dozen other ways.

When she asked Rona about it, the gypsy woman said, 'You don't want to worry. I'm the one in charge. They do as I say.'

'But they're always quarrelling with you over the work.'

'Oh, yes, they *talk* too much, but then I threaten them with things.'

'What things?'

'I say you won't pay them nothing,' said the burly gypsy woman, folding her arms, 'even if they've already done work, I say, they will get nothing, not one penny.'

Jane was a little concerned by this. 'What do they say when you tell them that?'

Rona snorted in contempt. 'They say they will cut off your head and feed you to chickens, if you no pay them. It's just the way they talk.'

'I certainly hope it is,' answered Jane, alarmed. 'I like my head where it is.'

'Sure. Don't you worry, dearie. Rona knows these old crows. She gets them working.'

So Jane left it to them to sort out themselves. She had to admit, the work got done somehow, despite one or two interruptions. One woman even went behind the hedge and delivered a baby without interfering with the main flow of work, though two others went with her to assist in the birth. Jane wondered about hygiene and insisted on the mother and child being taken to the cottage and washed down with warm water, but though they humoured her, they seemed to regard this as a bit of a lark, and it was accompanied by a lot of laughter. The mother and her baby were eventually installed in her caravan and the picking continued throughout the whole episode.

There was something very picturesque about a long line of colourful gypsies working their way up through a field of mauve flowers. They chattered like starlings as they stooped near to each other, their broad aprons bunched at the free end to form a kind of hammock in front of them, into which they could flick the flower heads with minimum effort. Their bright clothes contrasted sharply with the brown and green landscape surrounding the saffron fields, yet they seemed more a part of the natural world than the brown-and-green gamekeepers who wandered past, or the farmers and their labourers.

It seemed strange to Jane that these people who owned no land themselves should be closer to it than those who did. But with their swarthy faces and hands they could have sprung from the very soil in which they toiled. In the saffron fields, Jane was the odd one out, with her comparatively dull clothes and clear, pale complexion.

The whole scene was tremendously vibrant, and Jane felt charged with energy by it. It was a living kaleidoscope, the patterns for ever changing before her eyes, as the women in their handwoven fabrics with dynamic designs constantly moved from one place to another, a shifting mosaic of colour. She was able to enjoy it more once her period had arrived and relieved her of the worry of being pregnant. For the first time in her life she was glad of it coming, even if the timing was awkward – it always weakened her a little on the first two days.

The wagons were loaded with the purple flowers and transported to the oast-houses, where they were scattered on wire trays in racks, so that the air could circulate around them freely, and dried. Mr Saltash came to the fields and accompanied one wagon to the oast-house, even helping to unload it.

'I've taken this project to my heart,' he said to Jane as he assisted her with the trays of blooms. 'It's more than a hundred years since saffron was grown here commercially. It feels like history repeating itself. Kind of appropriate with Saffron Walden just along the road.'

'That's what I thought,' said Jane.

Mr Saltash put his hands on his hips and surveyed the vast numbers of flower heads. 'Extraordinary,' he said, 'quite extraordinary. How many blooms are drying in the houses right at this minute?'

'Approximately sixty-four thousand.'

'Incredible. Enough to make just one pound of saffron. All in all, you'll have over six million flower heads pass through here. You're going to have to work terribly hard, lass, for your money.'

'We'll make it,' smiled Jane. 'The women are wonderful. They talk a lot, but they work like Trojans.'

'How many are there?'

'Oh forty or more on a good day. Sometimes they don't all turn out, especially if the weather's bad, but I've never had less than thirty-five. They bring their children, too, although the younger ones don't work, they play on the edge of the field. I think they're a smashing lot.'

Mr Saltash frowned and murmured, 'An average of forty pickers a day. That means each picker will have to gather one hundred and fifty thousand crocus heads.'

Jane laughed. 'You and your numbers.'

'I've got some more for you. Let's say they pick one bloom a second. That's sixty minute, which is three thousand six hundred an hour. At this time of the year you're not going to get more than about ten hours' work out them, including breaks, which means thirty-six thousand flower heads per day. You should have them picked in just over four days,' he said, with a smug look on his face.

'Four days? That's if everything goes like clockwork, but we'll be lucky to get them all gathered in under a fortnight. We have to stop for rain, and various other acts of God and nature. No, I shall be happy with two weeks.'

Mr Saltash looked a little concerned by this.

'I hope you're paying them piece-work,' he said, 'and not by the hour. Otherwise they'll string it out until for ever.'

'Of course I'm paying them piece-work. They wouldn't have it any other way. I pay them by weight. They're all right, don't you worry about that. Rona keeps their noses to the grindstone . . .'

Mr Saltash seemed satisfied with this arrangement, not that it was really anything to do with him, thought Jane. He was due his percentage, whatever came out of the fields.

Mr Saltash stayed the whole day, sometimes standing back and watching, but at other times, when it seemed necessary, he threw himself into the work with a great deal of energy. At the end of the day he told Jane he hadn't enjoyed himself so much for a long time.

Jane went home tired that night, as she did every night after the picking and drying, but this kept her mind off other things. She had a routine for these days which she stuck to rigidly, because she needed her sleep, and in order to get her full eight hours, everything had to run smoothly.

Someone had put a note through the letter-box. After lighting the lamp she picked it up and glanced at it. It was from Petre, saying he would like to see her again, to apologise and to work something out.

Apologise? For what, thought Jane? Surely not for making love to her? That needed no apology, because she was mostly to blame – she had wanted it to happen at the time. And what was there to 'work out'? As far as she was concerned, nothing. She went to bed feeling very weary, and hoping that Petre would not come around again. She did not really want to see him.

As she fell asleep she concentrated on other matters: on the enjoyment she was getting from her 'business'. Jane had never been so industrially involved before, and she found it suited her temperament. Previously she had been to school, did a little nursing in the war, kept house for her father, but had never been fully immersed in something that interested her. Now she felt this work had an importance to her beyond just making her busy and helping her forget her problems.

It was a learning process in which she not only discovered things about the saffron trade, but about herself too. She found she had depths of enthusiasm for something. It gave her determination and a confidence in herself which had lain dormant.

And the more she learned, the more she wanted to learn. She felt she was grasping an expertise she did not want to waste. At the moment she was just flirting with the idea of becoming a saffron farmer, but at the back of her mind was an idea that one day she might take it up fully, seriously, if she could convince herself it was worthwhile, and if she could increase her knowledge of the trade. A farmer's granddaughter, she had it in her blood, she thought as she drifted into sleep.

Chapter Twelve

Once the gathering and drying of the flowers was completed, the really hard work began. The women had to pick out the red chives from the centre of the flower and press them between large sheets of absorbent paper, which Mr Saltash had supplied at cost price, before Jane transported them to the oast-house kilns for the final drying process.

The women sat in groups, chattering away as usual, taking the blooms from the baskets in front of them, picking out the chives, then tossing the useless flower head over their shoulders. The piles of spent crocuses were eventually taken away and heaped in the corner of a field ready to be burned.

Jane wasn't sure about the burning of the spent saffron crocuses. It seemed a terrible waste of beauty, just to set light to them. In the beginning she had grown them for their beauty alone, and now that resplendence was a waste product of a commercial enterprise. Sometimes natural beauty and business did not mix; money always seemed to win in the end.

However, the flowers were all but dead by the time they were thrown on the pile, and Jane could not think of a use for the lilac petals. If there had been a wedding, they might have been needed as confetti, but no one was getting married, so up in smoke they went, like autumn leaves.

Before that happened, though, the gypsy children used the giant mound of petals as a soft landing after jumping out of the old oak in the corner of Blatcher's field. Jane watched them squealing and laughing as they threw themselves from a bough, to land in the crocus heads, sending petals up in showers, some to float away on the wind. She sighed, thinking that the joy of childhood was all too soon over, and glad that they were able to make the best of their careless years.

Once the threads of saffron were dry, Jane knew she was supposed to make them into cakes or bricks, but since she had no idea how to go about this, she simply packed some old chocolate boxes full of the now precious chives. The boxes had been begged from a neighbour, who had collected them because of their pretty tops. She was half-way through this final stage when she saw Courtney riding towards the kilns. Immediately she felt guilty because she had not written to him as she had promised, and wondered if he was going to be annoyed with her for not doing so. At least she *thought* her guilt mainly stemmed from the fact that she hadn't written, though there were other sources.

Courtney tied his mount to a post and came up to her, smiled, and then looked serious. 'Jane, how are you? The gypsies told me where you were. You look absolutely wonderful. I heard about your father...'

'What did you hear?' she said, rather too quickly, thinking Courtney was referring to Henley's debts.

Put on the defensive, he shrugged. 'Only that he had gone away and left you to fend for yourself. However, I see you're doing very well without him.'

This was a compliment and she smiled at him now. 'I'm sorry, I didn't mean to snap. It's just that Father left me in a bit of a spot, and I imagine everyone's been talking about us.' She reached out with her hand. 'How are you?'

He shook the proffered hand. 'I'm very well, very well. The army is as tiresome as ever, but I'm working up to telling my father I want out. Bit of a coward when it comes to things that I know will cause a great row in the family. Anyway, I'll survive a little longer, I think. But look at you! The flourishing businesswoman! All our efforts were not in vain, eh? The planting of the corms. I remember it well. Dirt under my fingernails for the first time in my life.'

'Oh, don't be silly,' she laughed. 'You were in the trenches. You were wallowing in mud over there, weren't you? I saw pictures of that terrible landscape.'

'Well, perhaps there was a little grime, but this was muck from honest toil, wasn't it? Do you remember? The ploughing of the land? Quoting Robert Burns to each other until we were sick of hearing about field-mice and other vermin?'

'I remember my aching muscles. Oh, Courtney,' she said, 'it *is* good to see you. So much has happened since you left I believe a hundred years have gone by.'

She suddenly wanted to be taken and hugged by him, but the pair of them just stood there and smiled at one another. Then the moment was over, and she walked past him and stroked the nose of his horse, receiving a wet nuzzle in return.

Courtney came and stood by her side. 'Well, I *am* sorry about Henley. Has he really left you with problems? You don't have to tell me, but as a friend I would like to offer some help if I can.'

She did not answer this straight away; instead she said, 'I'm sorry I didn't write to you. I've been very busy.'

'Oh, don't worry about that, I understand. Your cousin Nancy made up for it. She's showered me with letters. It was from her that I heard the news about Henley.'

Blabbermouth, thought Jane. Trust Nancy!

'I'm glad *someone* wrote. You realise Nancy has a crush on you, of course?'

He appeared to be slightly embarrassed, but also seemed to digest this information thoughtfully.

'Has she? No, I didn't realise. She's very young isn't she?'

'Eighteen, going on nineteen.'

'Oh, I thought she was younger than that. A very pretty girl. She shouldn't go getting crushes on old men like me.'

'You're not so very old,' Jane laughed.

He grinned at her. 'No, I suppose I'm not. I'm glad you think so. What do you think I ought to do about this crush of Nancy's? Perhaps...'

But Jane never did find out what was to come next, because they were interrupted.

At that moment Rona and one of her companions arrived with a tray of wet saffron chives. They plonked it down on the path to the kiln, cocked their heads, and stared at the couple. Jane called, 'Be with you in a minute, Rona.'

'You take your time, love,' called back Rona, while her friend giggled. 'If you want to do hanky-panky with the gentleman, it's no skin off my nose.'

Jane coloured up and took a step towards them. Courtney said, 'I'll come to the cottage this evening, if that's all right. I have a proposal to make to you.'

'All right. Before eight o'clock though. I get pretty tired these days.'

'I imagine you do. I'll be there.'

Courtney arrived at the cottage at six. She made them both some toast and tea and they sat in the living room.

'Are you missing your father?' asked Courtney.

'Yes, I miss him,' Jane answered truthfully. 'And I'm a little worried about him. Not *too* much, because I know he can take care of himself. Henley is a survivor. Still, we've been living together for all my life. The house seems empty without him. I'm sure he's all right, though.'

'I'm sure, too,' said Courtney, reassuring her. 'He's probably giving someone a terrible ear-bashing right now about their lack of artistic taste, don't you think?'

Jane laughed. 'I'm sure you're right. Anyway, at least I've got the cottage. It has memories of him tucked in every corner. Some of them very amusing.'

Courtney stared at her seriously for a moment, then said, 'You pay rent on the cottage?'

'Yes, it's not ours. Father kept some of the farmland but sold the old farmhouse. Still, as you saw, we're harvesting the saffron, so I'm hoping to have a good deal of money soon. It was Mr Saltash's idea. He's the man who runs the seed . . .'

'Oh, I know old Saltash. Nice old codger. He supplies my father. He suggested you harvest it, eh?'

'He's been marvellous. I think he likes me.'

Courtney smiled at this ingenuous remark. 'Of course he does. I'd like to meet the man who could resist your charms.'

Jane was a bit startled by this remark. 'Oh, I don't charm him, not in the way you mean. Anyone would think I was a monstrous flirt.'

'No, no. I didn't mean that. I meant just by being *you*. You're a nice person, Jane. People like you.'

'Good old Jane,' she grunted.

'You can't have it both ways,' he said. 'Either you're good old Jane or Jane the monstrous flirt. In fact, you're neither. You're an attractive woman with an easy open manner and few prejudices. Saltash probably enjoys conversing on his own terms with someone young and pretty, rather than have some simpering female chatter on about pansy seeds, or a gruff farmer about crops. You probably make a refreshing change.'

'I think it's the project he likes. It's captured his imagination. Saffron-growing in Essex.'

'Perhaps it's a bit of both,' conceded Courtney. 'So, anyway, what are you going to do now? You'll earn some money from this venture, but from what I've heard – and it's general gossip so don't jump down my throat – your father left a few debts behind with the bank. If I know you, you'll settle them first, which will leave you short again, won't it?'

'I'll grow some more saffron.'

Courtney nodded. 'But that can't happen until next autumn. What will you do in the meantime?'

She felt she had to be honest with him for some reason, though it was really none of his business. 'I'll have tough time of it, I admit,' she said, 'but that's nothing for you to be concerned about.'

'Isn't it? I see I'm being put in my place. However, I refuse to stay there. You know I said this morning I had a proposal to make? Well it's this. My sister's husband Mark is leaving for India soon, and Julia has just given birth to their first child. Mark doesn't want Julia to join him until he's become established out there. He's going to run a tea plantation, but there are no facilities yet for a wife and child. The last man in charge was a bachelor, and apparently he wasn't too worried about the state of his living quarters . . .'

'What's all this got to do with me?' asked Jane. 'You want me to got out to India and build them a house, is that it? I may be able to work the fields like a man, but you need certain skills to be a house-builder.'

He laughed. 'Must you joke about everything? No, no. What it is, is this. Julia's coming back to live with us for a year. She'll need a companion and someone to help with the baby. I wondered if you would consider taking the post?'

Jane was a little taken aback. 'Post? You mean, just chatter with your sister all day long?'

'And help with Stephanie, the child.'

'But I don't know anything about children – babies especially.'

'Oh, well, there'll be a nurse too, of course – you know, a nanny. But Julia will want someone to share her excitement over the baby with. I mean, she's very young – still eighteen – and she gets lonely. I often wonder if that's the reason she married so young in the first place. She has very few friends at Stanton. It's so isolated, you see.'

'What about your mother? Surely Julia can talk with her?'

'Well, she can and she can't, if you see what I mean. Mother is not a very maternal sort of woman. She has very limited interest in these things, and she's not very flexible either. We were handed over to nannies and governesses when we were young. Mother had very little to do with us. She tells us now that she couldn't abide us until we could hold a sensible conversation with her. That's just the way she is. Julia just gets on her nerves, talking about the baby, and mother has no interest in her grandchild whatever, except to look horrified every time Stephanie so much as mewls. When that happens she leaves the room quickly, in case there's more noise to follow.'

Jane was astounded. When she thought of the loving home in which she had been raised, where her parents fought each other for the privilege of cuddling her, reading stories to her, and taking her out for walks in the country, she had difficulty imagining what the Stanton home must have been like for the three young children. Cold, she told herself. It must have been cold. She said as much to Courtney.

'Cold? No, not really. We have different ways of showing our affection, that's all. We're not demonstrative people.'

That sounded even worse, but she didn't tell him so. If they couldn't hug and kiss their own children in the privacy of their own home, they were certainly the most undemonstrative people Jane had ever heard of. No wonder Courtney hadn't held her this morning: he probably didn't know how to. Jane believed these things had to be learned, in the way that most other things were. However, Courtney seemed reluctant to discuss it further, and repeated his request that Jane should come and stay with them at Stanton Manor to keep his sister Julia company.

'It will be a paid position, of course, that's why I'm suggesting it. If you don't come they'll advertise in some awful magazine anyway, so it's not as if I'm offering you something out of charity.'

'Can I think about it?'

'Well, can I tell Mark and Julia that you are considering it, so they don't go and get someone else?'

She smiled at him. 'Yes, you can do that. What's your sister like, is she fun? I'm sure she is.'

'Julia, oh, she's all right. Not much wrong with Julia.'

'Good, solid, brotherly judgement.'

'Well, what would you expect me to say? That she's a bundle of laughs? Not in our house she isn't, though she may be in her own. It seems like only yesterday that she was running around the nursery, she's grown up so fast. But then, I've been away for some time now, and you notice these things more when you come and go infrequently. She was only fourteen when I left home to go to the war.'

'Well, I'm sure I'm going to like her, if she's anything like you.'

'Thank you. I'll accept that compliment.'

At that moment there was a knock on the front door, and Jane excused herself to answer it. She wondered whether it was Rona or one of the gypsy women, come to cry off tomorrow's work. They did that occasionally. When she opened the door however, she almost jumped backwards. It was Petre.

He looked down at her reservedly. 'I thought I'd come and see you,' he said.

Jane felt a surge of panic go through her. 'It's not convenient at the moment, I'm afraid.'

He frowned a little. 'Not convenient? I'm here, aren't I? I walked all the way from Saffron Walden.'

'Well, I'm sorry about that, Petre, but I don't want to let you in. I'm sure you know why. It wouldn't be good for either of us.'

His penetrating blue eyes flashed dangerously. 'Don't tell me what's damned well good for me. It meant nothing, did it? The other day? Nothing at all.'

'Petre,' she said, desperately trying to keep her voice down, 'this is just not convenient. I've got a visitor in the house and I don't want this broadcast. What are you trying to do to me?'

'What are *you* trying to do to *me*, more like? Goddamnit, can't you see I want you? I want you, for Christ's sake. You let me make love to you, then you treat me like a leper. Was that all you wanted? Was it? I can give you more of *that* . . .' he spat, contemptuously.

She was absolutely devastated to hear that he wanted her, because she had no such feelings to return to him. A few minutes' thoughtless passion had turned into something enormously complicated. She felt sick at heart and now wished it had never happened.

Petre stepped towards the doorway and she barred his way, saying, 'Petre, I'm sorry. I was caught up in something, a confused state of mind. It just happened. I don't regret it, not in the way you think, but I realised afterwards it was a mistake. I'm truly sorry. I like you, but we can't see each other again. I can't change my feelings. They are what they are . . .'

A voice came from behind Jane. 'What's the problem, Jane?'

Petre's face turned to stone as Courtney appeared. She could see the cold anger in Petre's eyes. She could see the way he tensed into something quite frightening – a wild animal – beneath his clothing. Jane prayed that he would not make a big scene in front of Courtney. She realised now that she had acted very stupidly in allowing this strange man to make love to her, but she could not turn back the clock.

'Ah,' Petre said, 'so that's how it is?'

Then he turned and strode away, along the path towards the road. Jane wanted to run after him, try to talk things out with him, explain how she felt now. It was all so cruel, this business of loving. When someone loved you, all they wanted, the *only* thing they wanted, was for you to love them back. Anything else – any explanation or apology – was utterly useless to them.

Courtney said; 'Who was it?'

'Oh, someone my father brought home from one of his gambling nights. He's – he was very kind to me after father went away.'

'He sounded rather upset.'

'Yes, he was,' she replied, turning to look at Courtney in the gloom of the hallway. 'It's rather personal.'

'Right. Keep my nose out.'

He was obviously still intrigued, but too polite to inquire further into what he realised was a very private matter.

They went back into the living room, but Jane was too fraught to talk any more. She promised Courtney that she would think about taking up the post of companion to his sister. Then she showed him to the door.

Courtney made his way to where he had tethered Sheba to the old oak beyond the cottage. He took the reins and said, 'All right, old girl, we'll take it easy along the road. We don't want you stepping into any potholes in the dark.'

Just as he swung himself into the saddle, a figure stepped out of the bushes behind the oak. In the deep, heavy gloom, Courtney recognised him as the same man who had just called at the cottage. Courtney watched, curiously, as the man advanced, wondering what he wanted.

'Who the hell are you?' said the man.

Despite himself, Courtney was rather taken aback by the abrupt and ill-mannered approach. He rallied quickly, falling back on the upper-class defence of treating his attacker with cold contempt. He spoke severely and curtly.

'Unless you identify yourself, sir, you will receive nothing but the sight of my backside. I'm not in the custom of replying to such a lack of civility.'

The man stood with his hands on his hips, looking up at Courtney with a similar contempt in his eyes. Courtney was immediately wary of the stranger, seeing in his stance and demeanour a dangerous type of personality. Courtney sensed he was being confronted by a man with few scruples, if any, and wondered if he were going to have to defend himself physically before the encounter was over.

The man spoke again. 'Ah, class, are we? That public school accent doesn't work on me, chum. I've heard too many of them to be intimidated by them. You've got a point, though. My name is Peake. Now what's yours?'

A cold chill went through Courtney as he recognised the name of a notorious lieutenant in the Royal Flying Corps.

'Not Lieutenant Peake of the RFC?'

'That's me,' said Peake. 'I see my fame has reached the gentry. You're obviously back from the Front, or you wouldn't know who I am. I'm still waiting for your name.'

Courtney again gathered his mental reserves together and put on a steely front. 'Why do you wish to know?'

'Because I want to know what you were doing at that cottage,' said Peake. 'I have an interest in the family. Henley Transon is a particularly good friend of mine. He's away at the moment and I promised I would keep an eye on his daughter for him. Does that answer your question?'

'I'm sure Jane is well able to look after herself, but even if she weren't, I too have an interest in the family. Henley is also a friend of mine. To set your inquiring mind at rest, Peake, my name is Courtney Stanton.'

'Ah, one of the Stantons. I didn't know any of you had been at the Front until Jane told me.'

'There's no reason why you should have done. My name wasn't bandied about: I didn't shoot down any unarmed prisoners in cold blood.'

Peake's hand went into his right pocket. He took a sudden step towards the other man at these words, and Courtney's mount shied a little.

Peake said, 'You watch your mouth, Stanton. You listen to too many tales and take them as you hear them. That's how people get persecuted. We were at war, the enemy was the enemy, and I killed as I was supposed to. That's what it was all about.'

'You murdered a man on the ground, so I hear.'

'If I hadn't shot that pilot when he climbed out of his cockpit, he might have killed me the next time we met in the air.'

'I'm told you could have taken him prisoner.'

'I forced him down behind his own lines, not ours. I couldn't land

and take him prisoner – I would have been captured by all the German troops that were milling around like ants. It wasn't a game to me, like it was to you lot: the playing fields of Eton and all that rubbish. He was the enemy and he had to die.'

Courtney's view of this cold-hearted aviator began to falter. 'He waved to you as you stooped to kill.'

'He shook his fist at me. That's a very different gesture. We were often sent out to strafe troops on the ground. What's the difference between splattering humble soldiers in the trenches and shooting some arrogant bastard sauntering away from an aircraft? I don't see it was any different. I didn't believe in that "knights of the air" rubbish, any more than I did in "knights of the trenches". Aristocratic nonsense, invented by Richthofen and bluebloods like him. That pilot was the enemy. Do you think a German machine-gunner would stop mowing down soldiers because they lost their rifles? That's all an aircraft is – a weapon. He lost his weapon. He died for it.'

There was, Courtney admitted, a certain amount of logic in what Peake was saying. Still, he could not help himself arguing for what he felt should be preserved: that there was something noble about the art of flying an aircraft. That the war in the air was not as barbaric as the war on the ground. He said as much to Peake, who looked back in disdain.

'So you think it's all right that Private Entwhistle should be executed for leaving the battle scene – on going mad when the air is humming with bits of hot metal – but when Von Schinken or the Honourable Charles Trelawny does it, it's considered the act of a civilised man? That pilot I shot was the enemy. I had been sent out with the specific task of killing him. If a soldier got out of a broken-down tank and began to walk back to his lines, and I failed to shoot him, I would have been put on a court martial for neglecting my duty. Can't you *see* it, Stanton? Of course you can.'

Courtney felt at a loss, but he put his side of it. 'I was in the trenches, Peake. I fought *that* war. All the while I was wallowing in filth, and wondering whether the next time I went over the top I would be turned into meat fit only for flies. I thought of you chaps in the air. It kept me going, knowing that at least in some part of that war there was *honour* and *decency*.'

'Honour and decency,' sneered Peake. 'The generals wouldn't give us parachutes because they didn't trust us not to jump out at the first opportunity. Men were getting mangled with their machines – men who could have been saved to fly again – simply because they were not trusted, *on their honour*, to do their duty.'

There was silence between the two men then, as they regarded one another in the near darkness. Courtney felt as if he had been bested in an argument by a man he wanted to despise. He had no doubt that Peake was a man with little conscience, but this was not something he could hold up for examination. Peake had answer for everything and there was no way of Courtney knowing whether it was the truth or not.

Peake stunned him with his next remark. 'Raped any peasant women lately?'

Courtney felt the anger well up inside him. 'What the hell are you talking about? I've never hurt a woman in my life. I ought to knock you down for that.'

Peake smiled. 'Oh, I see. You don't have to prove your innocence because you're Courtney Stanton.'

'What do you mean by that?'

'You were judging *me*,' said Peake. 'Who the hell do you think you are, sitting up there in judgement on me? I don't have to defend a single thing I've done, not to you, not to anyone. There are skeletons in everyone's past – mine, yours, everyone's. Why is it *my* character that's being assessed here and not *yours*?'

'I haven't done anything I'm ashamed of.'

'Neither have I. Now, next time you want to brand a man, make sure you have proof, instead of just listening to gossip and taking it as fact. No one knows what really happened on the day I killed that German, except me and the Germans, whose propaganda machine was pretty effective, considering the number of times I've had to defend myself against the same accusation. You and your kind can go to hell, Mr Stanton . . .'

'Captain Stanton.'

'Still a military man, eh?' said Peake in a pleasant tone. 'Well, whatever, I'll say this – if Jane complains about you bothering her, I'll come and find you, and when I do I'll snap your neck with no more

144

thought than if you were a rabbit. Understand?'

With those words firmly in place, Peake walked away into the darkness, leaving Courtney fuming.

Courtney took the road home carefully, not wanting to injure himself or his horse. He considered Peake's arguments calmly and thoughtfully and decided that, unpleasant as his manner was, the man had a good point. Everything about Peake was hearsay. It was true, there were more stories about him than just the shooting of the pilot on the ground, but then once a reputation has been earned, others tend to embellish upon it, especially during wartime, when legends are formed out of the most smoky details. Courtney was a fair-minded man and he judged himself to be in the wrong with his unfounded accusations.

However, that having been admitted, he still did not like Peake, and still considered him a menacing man. There was that final threat about snapping his neck to consider too. Most rational men would not make threats like that during a confrontation over who was a lady's appointed guardian and protector, unless the relationship between Peake and Jane went a lot deeper. Courtney found that surprisingly wounding. He could not believe that Jane was fond of a man like Peake, whose whole being shrieked of torment and violence.

Still, he thought, now I'm judging Jane without proof. That was not right either. Courtney hoped Jane would accept his offer to come to the house: he hated the thought of her living alone in a remote country cottage. At Stanton she would be looked after: Courtney would make sure of that.

The electric generator was pounding noisily at the back of the stables when Courtney stabled his horse. This powered the bulbs which adorned almost every corner of the large house, though the light they provided was quite dim and had to be supplemented by coal-gas burners, candles and lamps throughout the manor.

Courtney went indoors and changed his clothes, then proceeded down to dinner. His mother and father were there and his brother Stephen and sister Julia. The baby was with its nurse in some other part of the house.

During the soup, Courtney spoke to Julia. 'I've had a word with Miss Transon, Julia. She's considering the matter.'

'What's this?' asked their mother, breaking bread and spreading crumbs all over the cloth.

Courtney knew he was in for a battle, but he was well prepared. 'Julia and Mark asked me if I knew anyone who might consider the position of companion to Julia. You remember they have been attempting to advertise the post?'

Lady Constance stared at her son. 'Don't your father and I have a say about who comes into this house?'

'Of course, Mother,' said Courtney, 'but it's Julia who's employing the woman, and you haven't taken any interest in the applicants so far. I can't see what objection you can have to Jane Transon, in any case. She's not going to walk off with the family silver.'

'Don't be flippant,' snapped Lady Constance. 'You know very well what my objections are – we've had conversations about these people before.'

'This *person*, Mother. Her father is no longer living with her. He abandoned her when his debts became too burdensome, and I think she and Julia would find each other good companions. Jane is at this moment trying to work off her father's debts, even though they're nothing to do with her personally; I think that shows a degree of character which even you can't fail to acknowledge.'

Stephen said, 'Pass the salt please, Julia. If you want my opinion, I think Courtney's right. One shouldn't advertise a post like this. Best to get someone we know.'

Courtney glanced over at his brother gratefully. Stephen was always taking his side in arguments against his parents. Since Stephen was a great favourite with both parents, while Courtney and Julia took second place, his interventions did Stephen no harm at all, and helped Courtney considerably.

'Do we actually *know* this woman?' asked Sir Charles.

'*I* know her,' said Courtney, 'and I think she'll do admirably. She hasn't said yet that she'll come. She told me she would think it over very carefully, and of course Julia will have to approve once she meets her. What do you say, Julia?'

Julia was never happy about taking sides against her mother and father because her mother had ways of making her suffer for it later. Very simple, subtle ways that were only detectable by the two people

146

involved: a remark about a hairstyle, or the colour of a dress, or the quality of one's motherhood, or the potential of one's husband. Nothing that could be flung back afterwards without being countered by a surprised, hurt expression and a, 'But Julia dear, whatever can you mean?' However, in this instance Courtney knew his sister had interviewed a dozen candidates for the post and found none of them suitable. She was weary of looking and trusted her brother's judgement implicitly.

'From what you've told me about her, Courtney, I think I shall like her a lot.'

Lady Constance glared at her daughter before saying, 'Well, it seems I'm to be outvoted again by my children. There was a time when my word meant something around here, but it seems all that is history now you've reached adulthood. I suppose I'll have to bow to your wishes.'

It was left to Stephen to smooth things over. 'Mother, you know how much we all admire you, so why do you put yourself down like that? Courtney's just trying to help Julia, that's all. If you don't like this Jane Transon, you can soon ask Julia to dismiss her, can't you?'

The ruffled feathers were allowed to settle again. 'I don't know why your father doesn't say more during these family discussions,' said Lady Constance. 'He just sips his soup and lets it all go over his head.'

Sir Charles said, 'Can't abide all this bickering. Don't see why I have to. What follows the soup?'

'Asparagus tips. I hope they're to your liking?'

'They'll do,' said Sir Charles, non-committally.

Courtney went to bed in a satisfied frame of mind. If he could get Jane into the house he need not worry about Peake any longer, for Jane would be under the protection of the Stantons. The manor was like a fortress with its army of gardeners, stable boys, gamekeepers and household servants, and Courtney very much doubted if Peake would try to contact her while she lived there.

Courtney decided he did not want Peake anywhere near Jane. It wasn't just that he found Peake strange and threatening – a dark character with a dark mind – but his presence at the cottage had aroused something in Courtney tonight. If asked, Courtney would have called it 'the protective instinct in me' but anyone else would have recognised it for what it was: jealousy. Courtney did not like the fact that another man was paying attention to Jane. He did not like it that Jane seemed to be more deeply involved with Peake than she was prepared to admit. Courtney had decided his own interest in Jane went deeper than friendship and his battle nerves were tingling.

'I'll be damned if I'll lose her to a man like that,' said Courtney to himself. Then he added thoughtfully, 'To *anyone*, for that matter.'

Petre made his way back quickly to Saffron Walden after his encounter with Courtney Stanton. Alone, in the dark, he allowed his unhappiness to come forth. It would have shown on his face, had he met someone with a lamp along the road, but the night kept his feelings hidden safely from others.

Petre was now desperately in love with Jane. It seemed to him that she was the answer to all his feelings of wretchedness and hopelessness. The war had torn him apart, certainly, like most wars do to most young men, but he remembered a time before that when he was just as unhappy. Not *remembered* exactly, but certainly *felt*. With Jane he had discovered a different person within himself: a nobler Petre Peake, a man he quite liked.

She *must* love me, he thought. How could he feel so much for her and she feel nothing for him? It wasn't possible. There must be something there which could be nurtured, and if given space and time, which could grow. She had let him make love to her! They had shared their bodies with each other! Surely they had shared their inner selves too?

Perhaps she was waiting for him to prove himself to her? he thought. He was quite willing to do that. He was willing to do anything to win her. He would look for his opportunities and use them. He would prove his love for her if it was the last thing in the world he ever did.

A small flame of hope was rekindled in his breast. There was something to live for, after all. There was love of Jane to live for. There could be a future to look forward to.

Chapter Thirteen

When Jane went to see Mr Saltash in his office, three weeks after the saffron had been gathered, dried and delivered to him for sale to a contact he knew, he presented her with one thousand seven hundred pounds.

'It's a bit less than we anticipated, but not much, and I've already taken my percentage.'

'I think it's a wonderful start,' said Jane, excitedly. 'We've still got next year's crop to go before the corms have to be taken up. Do you think we can do as well next year?'

'Better, I hope,' smiled Mr Saltash.

As she left his office, he held the door open for her. 'You know, young lady, I have a great deal of admiration for you. I was saying to Mrs Saltash the other night: that young woman's going somewhere in this world.'

Jane felt extremely pleased by this. 'Thank you, Mr Saltash,' she said. 'You've made me feel as if I'm worth something.'

'You?' he laughed. 'I wish I had a dozen like you, working for me.'

Jane walked up Town Street towards the church with a warm feeling inside her. She did indeed feel valuable to herself. She, Jane Transon, had made almost two thousand pounds. But not just that. She had used the earth to produce something. She had taken the seed, planted it, watched it grow and harvested the crop. It was a miracle: the miracle of the recycling of life.

Jane was experiencing the same feeling farmers felt about the land, about growing crops. One could get rich by farming, but more often than not one simply just got by. To farm the land and just get by – a hard, sometimes gruelling life – one needed a motive other than financial reward. One needed the fierce pride which comes from owning a piece of soil and bringing forth its produce.

Her grandfather had been a farmer; her father had always maintained that grubbing around in the dirt was for peasants, not painters.

Looking up at the guildhall brought her father forcefully, and not unwelcomingly, to mind. She nursed certain memories of him, since she liked to think of him sometimes without feeling annoyed with him. It was easy to be angry with her father; but she loved him despite his faults, and she enjoyed entertaining herself with recalling some of his more harmless excesses.

Henley had once painted the famous guildhall for a local man, though he had hated doing so because it was not his usual kind of subject. In fact she recalled that he had thrown a cup of tea dregs at the painting in temper – a final tantrum born out of frustration – before it was dry. The mark on the paint remained at the sale. Henley refused Jane's pleas to put it right out of sheer cussedness.

Henley had explained it away to the buyer by saying the brown stain was the reflection of the guildhall roof on the cloudbase. It had been a ludicrous statement, but Henley had got away with it as usual, with a bluff and bluster that many men felt they could not challenge without causing a great fuss.

Jane smiled at the memory: she could not help but admire her father's perverse nature – he was an individual if nothing else – even when she didn't approve of it.

A motor car passed her as she crossed the road and the driver honked his horn, a brass affair with a big black rubber bulb. Jane wasn't in his way, but she understood that motor-car drivers honked their horns on every occasion that presented itself. They seemed to like the noise, and of course it drew attention to their vehicles, which were becoming much more common in Thaxted and Saffron Walden. Someone had even started up a bus service between the two towns using a motorised vehicle.

She went straight to the bank and asked to see the manager. In a few minutes she was standing before him in his office.

'What can I do for you Miss Transon?' he said in a brisk, but not unfriendly tone.

'You will remember I wrote and told you that my father had gone away.'

The manager leaned back in his chair, and a non-committal expression appeared on his face. 'The bank has done its own investigations, Miss Transon. Your father owes us just over a thousand pounds, so you understand we had to look into the matter, though of course I myself was prepared to take your word. I'm afraid we can't lend you any more money though.'

'I'm not here to borrow, I'm here to pay back the amount my father owes you,' Jane replied with some satisfaction.

The manager, who was quite a young man for the position, shot forward abruptly in his chair. 'I beg your pardon? You're not destitute?'

'Far from it. I've started a business in saffron growing, you see, and so far it's been extremely successful. Mr Saltash . . .'

'So *you're* the mysterious business woman he's been bragging about?' cried the manager.

'Has he?' said Jane, the warm feeling growing.

'All over town. Says you're going to be the mayor before you're finished. Personally I think that the day we get a woman mayor – excuse me, but I have my opinions – the guildhall will come tumbling down.'

Jane handed over the money she owed the bank, and the manager called in a teller to receive it. A receipt was made out and handed over to Jane. The young bank manager then shook her hand.

'I must admit, Miss Transon, I never expected to see that money again. You've restored my faith in human nature. If ever you want a loan, for business purposes, don't hesitate to call on me.'

'I'll bear it in mind,' she replied.

She left the bank feeling enormously satisfied. From there she went to the old mill, where Rona and the gypsies were waiting to be paid. They lined up for their money and gave Jane a little cheek when she paid them. Then it was all over and they were on their way.

'Next year, missus,' called Rona. 'We come again next year.'

'I'll be looking for you,' said Jane.

The men were all waiting on the colourful waggons, with the pots and pans hanging from the sides, and the children hanging out of the back doors and windows. The women joined them and the group set off towards the south. Rona had told Jane they were heading for Spain, for the winter. Jane envied them the warmth they would be getting over the winter months. She wondered how they crossed the channel, but she supposed they knew the boats with the cheapest fares. Spain was the country most of the gypsy horse-dealers went to, for the summer festival in Andalusia, so the route would be a well-used one.

Jane still had a few hundred pounds left, though she had one or two bills outstanding. There was the use of the oast houses and kilns to pay for, and a little for the Blatchers, but when these had been settled she expected to have one hundred and seventy pounds. With careful management, it could see her through the winter. However, she still had the job Courtney had offered to consider. There was a reason other than financial for contemplating the post of companion to Julia: it would put Jane out of Petre's reach. He would not try to see her if she lived at the manor, she was sure. It might be she would be better off at Courtney's house, for a few months at least.

She took the winding path back from the windmill to the church and went into the peace and quiet of the interior. She kneeled in the south chapel, the church's Lady Chapel, and said a prayer for her father. Then she sat in one of its pews and thought seriously about Courtney's offer.

There had been little time to think about that evening when she had last seen Courtney. Petre Peake had almost turned it into a bad one for her. It had been pure coincidence that he had turned up during Courtney's visit, but his appearance had been distressing for all three of them. She felt guilty in some way, for being unable to return Petre's regard for her. She did not believe it was love, but *he* seemed to think it was. And what was worse, it was making him bitter. Why couldn't he just forget what had happened in the saffron field and leave it at that? But of course, she told herself, human nature wasn't that simple. Starting a relationship was like tying a thread to a tree in a forest, then running around haphazardly, letting the ball unravel. Pretty soon there's an unholy tangle.

That's what it is, she told herself, *an unholy tangle*.

Then there was Courtney, who seemed just a true friend. I don't want any lovers now, she thought, I just want friends at the moment. Courtney was fine because he kept his distance and didn't crowd her. She hoped their relationship would stay that way always. It was much simpler having him for a friend. There was no awkwardness between them, no uncomfortable moments, and they could just relax in each other's company. What was it Emily Bronte had once written? 'Love is like the wild rose-briar, friendship like the holly-tree – the holly is dark when the rose-briar blooms but which will bloom most constantly?' That's what it was all about. Love was something deep and intense, but it did not last, whereas friendship was always there, reliable and undemanding.

Jane thought about the money her father still owed Petre Peake. She felt frustrated about the fact that she could not repay such an enormous sum. She had changed her mind about the debt having no connection with her. It was now something that bothered her considerably. It did not help that Petre no longer wanted it settled. She felt it tied them closer together. It was another knot in the tangle; if it were settled then she would have one less thread to connect her to Petre Peak. There was nothing she could do about it for the foreseeable future, but one day, she told herself, perhaps I'll have enough to settle it?

She stared at the brilliant colours of the stained-glass window, and all of a sudden she decided to take the post which was being offered her at Stanton Manor. Courtney had written to her from Yorkshire. He was coming home again this weekend, and he had said he would call at the cottage for her reply. Well, she was ready to leave Wildrose Cottage at last! She wondered whether she should keep it on, just in case the arrangement with Julia did not work out. She decided that would be a wise thing to do.

Jane left the church and did some shopping. Then she returned to the churchyard and, after placing some flowers on her mother's grave, took the new motor bus back to Howlett End. It was a rattling, bumpy experience, since the road was not in the best of repair.

That evening, Courtney came round to the house in his father's new motor car, a bright, shiny Daimler. Jane heard the car coming up the lane and went outside to see a shaky Courtney step from the vehicle and wipe his face with a handkerchief.

He said, 'Well, I'm getting more used to it, but I have to say I still prefer horses. You can talk to animals, calm them down when they get too skittish, but if that thing decides it's going to stick a wheel in a rut and head towards the ditch, it doesn't listen to a word you say.'

Jane laughed. 'I would have thought the opposite. I mean, I haven't done much riding, but I've found that sometimes you can pull the reins to turn the horse left and it turns right. Now, as I understand it, if you turn the wheel of a motor car left, the whole machine follows suit, automatically.'

'Unless, as I say, it's in a rut.'

Jane said, 'Like a lot of us, I expect. How are you Courtney? You don't seem to be limping as much as you used to – perhaps your leg is improving?'

'I'm very well, thank you, old friend, very well.'

She was glad he had called her that. It made her feel very safe with him. It was just an expression, of course, and one used more by Courtney than most, but it was a good expression, one that put her at her ease.

Courtney slapped his leg. 'Yes, the beast is getting a little better. Mind you, I think the winter will set me back a bit – cold weather usually does – but, hey ho, there'll be a summer to follow.'

'There usually is,' Jane smiled at him.

Being October, the weather was very changeable, and though the day had been warm, the late afternoon began to chill. Still, they stayed by the gate for a while, Jane in the thick Irish shawl she had thrown on to greet him, and he in his driving coat. They watched the low scarlet sun with its weak light moving down to the horizon, behind a nearby orchard. The sky was a watery blue-grey, and it seemed the sun's delicate rays were trying to reach out and give the heavens some colour before it left. It was more successful amongst the trees, and the two watchers stood and marvelled at the tints of the leaves.

'How different they all are,' said Jane. 'Look at those cherry-plum leaves – distinctly yellow, aren't they? But some of the pear-tree leaves are a brilliant red. I wonder what scientific reason lies behind that phenomenon?'

'Scientific reason!' exclaimed Courtney. 'There's no such thing. It's all *art*. The art of nature. Nothing to do with acids or alkalis, or anything like that. Beauty, pure and simple, with no science in it.'

'You're just an old-fashioned romantic.'

Courtney smiled. 'I should hope so too. I saw enough of science at work, at Ypres and the Somme. Artillery, field guns, nerve gas, bombs. Science changed a beautiful landscape into a quagmire, a wasteland, within weeks. Science covered the landscape with dead souls and left others crippled. Give me art any time.'

'*Now* I know why you don't like your motor car,' she said, quietly.

He turned to her and smiled. 'I shouldn't make too much of it. We'll all get over the war one day. It's a bit too close at the moment. Just at this time I'd rather see the world through the eyes of art, not science, that's all. It'll probably wear off when next year's shoot comes round.'

As they turned to go inside, a pair of pigeons flew up from an elm overshadowing the cottage, startling them both. They watched the birds turn and wheel over the orchard.

'Such noisy things, pigeons,' said Courtney. 'They're either bleating just outside your window early in the morning, disturbing your sleep, or they're frightening the life out of you with that thrashing sound amongst the trees.'

'Listen to the romantic,' she said.

'Nothing romantic about pigeons. They're pests.'

When they were inside the cottage, Courtney suddenly took Jane by the shoulders and looked very seriously into her eyes. 'There's something I wish to say—' he blurted, but Jane had also started to speak and stopped him in mid-sentence. She was saying, 'I wanted to thank you, Courtney, for being a good friend to me during a bad time. It means a great deal, your friendship. It feels so comfortable and warm, without all those messy feelings that go with . . . with another kind of relationship. I was at the church today, and thinking about you, and those were the thoughts I had. Sorry, didn't mean to interrupt you, what were you saying?'

Courtney continued to stare into her eyes for a moment, then let his hands drop. 'Oh, nothing really.' He turned away from her and laughed abruptly, then said, 'Yes, yes I was. I wanted to ask you if you'd made a decision yet? About Julia?'

'Of course, and the answer is yes please.'

He turned to look at her again, his face shining. 'Really? You really want to?'

'Well, I think it's up to your sister, don't you? She might not like me in the least. Have you any idea when she'd like to see me?'

'I've arranged it for tomorrow. Oh, of course, I would have cancelled the appointment if you'd said no, but I think it should be done as soon as possible. Julia will *love* you, I've no fears about that. Why shouldn't she?'

'Courtney, you really are a romantic, you know. Just because you and I like each other, doesn't mean your sister will view me with the same eyes. Women don't always hit it off, you know.'

Courtney nodded and said very seriously, 'I noticed something like that in the officer's mess the other day. There's one of the wives, a young, bright-eyed woman who is adored by the officers themselves, but the other wives don't seem to like her at all. A most extraordinary thing, I thought.'

Jane laughed. 'You mean she's an outrageous flirt! Of course the women don't like her. She probably doesn't give a damn about whose man is dangling after her.'

'Really?' said Courtney, even more ponderously. 'I wouldn't have guessed it. She seems to me to be a sweet lady, and I told her so. She said we had a lot in common and asked me if I would show her the garden, which I was happy to do.'

Jane, who had surprised herself by feeling a faint pang of jealousy as he spoke, suddenly saw his face break into a wicked grin and realised that he had been leading her on. She punched him on the shoulder. 'You're teasing me, Courtney Stanton. I won't have it, do you hear?'

They went into the living room, where Courtney asked about the saffron harvest.

She turned to him, beaming. 'A brilliant success,' she said, 'with knobs on. Really. I've paid my father's debt to the bank and still have some left over. Next year...'

'Next year?'

She nodded emphatically. 'Next year we shall make even more, because the crocus yield gets progressively higher each year.'

'So in ten years' time you'll have them coming out of your ears?'

She laughed. 'No, silly. The corms have to be lifted after three years and you start again.'

Courtney seemed to think about this for a moment, then he said, 'But if you plant more land now, you'll be in your second year with one crop when the present one has to be lifted. What about that then? Who said I wasn't a farmer?'

'Certainly not me, but there's a problem. I'm using almost all the land my father owns already. I might ask Blatcher if he might release some land, but I'd better have a word with Mr Saltash first. I don't want to drag other people into this and then find there's no market for the saffron. We might have been lucky this time.'

'I would ask my father,' said Courtney, 'but I know what his answer would be. He's such a traditionalist. He'd think we were trying to be fancy – copying the Far East. Father loves Asia, especially Ceylon, but he doesn't think their farming practices are worth tuppence.'

Jane said, 'Anyway, this calls for a celebration. I bought a bottle of whisky in Thaxted today, and some soda water, so let's get a little merry, shall we?'

She went to the sideboard and took out two whisky glasses and the bottle she had purchased at the grocery store. Mr Wilkins the proprietor had been quite happy to sell it to her, of course, although young women did not usually buy hard liquor.

Jane poured them each a generous measure topped up with soda water and then Courtney lifted his glass in a toast. 'To the saffron lady,' he said, 'may she be happy during her stay at Stanton Manor.'

Jane followed suit, muttering, 'If she gets the job.'

The following morning, Jane dressed in a smart dark suit, the only one she owned, and a small pillbox hat with a little black veil covering half-an-inch of her brow. She had applied her make-up with great care, in the way that she had often seen her mother do when she was alive. ('Why don't you make your lips bigger and redder, like Mrs Durber does, Mummy?' 'It's not *how much* you use, sweetheart, but how *little*. The skill is in making it appear that you're not wearing any at all.')

157

Finally, when she was ready, she waited in trepidation for the sound of the Stanton family's motor car. She wished at such times that she smoked, but having tried it once, and had a terrible coughing fit, she had never touched a cigarette again.

It seemed she had been sitting on the edge of the sofa for an eternity, afraid to move in case she creased her skirt, but finally she heard the sound of the engine coming down the lane. She picked up her handbag, rose, and went to the door.

Courtney was just opening the gate as Jane left the house. He gave a long, low whistle. 'So that's what the well-dressed saffron farmer is wearing these days?' he said, holding open the gate for her.

'No silly remarks, if you please,' she said.

He smiled at her. 'You look incredibly beautiful.'

'You don't think I look too tarty?' she said, coquettishly.

'You know you don't. You're fishing for more compliments. Well, I've got a whole bunch of them if you like, but the fact is, you don't need 'em. You must have spent hours . . .'

'Oh, I just threw it on in seconds.'

He laughed and held the door of the car open for her. She climbed in. Then, just as he was about to start the Daimler, she thought of something and turned to him. 'You don't think I *need* hours?'

He laughed again, fiddling with various chokes and switches on the dashboard.

'You don't need a thing to enhance what you have. No cosmetics, no smart suit, no funny little hat. You'd be just as beautiful whatever you decided to wear . . .'

The subject was dropped as the car exploded into life and, as Courtney eased the handbrake down, it began trundling along the uneven, muddy lane. The brief exchange had disturbed Jane a little, not because of the nature of its content, but because Courtney had revealed something which she was not sure she could deal with at the moment. He was fond of her, in more than an old-friend way. She realised that now.

The drive was pleasant from the aspect of seeing the countryside slip past. The trees were rapidly baring themselves, and red and yellow ochre leaves decorated their roots, like discarded clothes. Most of the fields were bare too, of course, since the crops had been gathered in long before. There were some winter cabbages in neat rows of thousands, dipping and rising with the contours of the landscape, but most of the land was brown combed earth. Pastures made a change, sliding greenly past the windows of the motor car, sometimes containing horses that danced to a music in their heads.

However, the ride was not the most comfortable Jane had ever experienced. The bad roads were in some part compensated for by the smooth action of the car and its good springs, but she was not used to going so fast. It was on the one hand exhilarating, yet on the other terrifying. She felt sure they would terminate the journey by mating savagely with some tree.

Courtney's grim visage, as he clutched the wheel determinedly, and negotiated corners as if they had in some way affronted his honour, did nothing to inspire her confidence. She was glad when they reached the gatehouse to the manor and drove up the long driveway to the house itself, a beautiful building, the architectural style of which reminded her of a French chateau.

'You were brought up here?' she breathed.

Courtney raised his eyes from the driveway for a moment to regard the house.

He knew its history, which had been drummed into him by his mother from when he was an infant. Stanton had been built in 1865 for Courtney's great-grandfather. It was actually Jacobean in style, with jagged bow windows, dormers and with chimneys placed with careful asymmetry. A many-spired gabled tower marked the position of the grand staircase, and there was a huge sundial over the front doors made in the Arabic style. It was said to have been built by Anthony Salvin, but since Manley Stanton, Courtney's great-grandfather, wished to keep the architect's name a secret for some reason, this could not be sworn to by anyone living. Courtney believed it, because he had read somewhere that there was said to be a coldness about Salvin's later houses and Stanton Manor was certainly cold enough.

'Eh? Oh yes, looks very romantic, doesn't it? Wait until you're getting up on a cold winter's morning and the bedroom is about three degrees below the temperature at the South Pole on a bad day. Then see how romantic you feel about it.'

'You just take it for granted, because you've always known it.'

'Yes and no. At least, I did before I went away to war, but since I've
been back, I can see it with fresh eyes. It is a very imposing residence,
and has a lot to commend its architecture, but there's a lot of cold
memories caught in its nooks and crannies, as well as draughts. You
can't separate the bricks and mortar from childhood . . . Ah, there's
Mother, waiting for us just inside the doors.'

Jane looked up as they were drawing adjacent to the steps up to the
house and saw a thin, grey-haired woman in a tweed skirt, twin-set
and black beads, standing like a statue between two open double
doors. Her expression was rather severe and Jane steeled herself for
the encounter.

Courtney led the way up the steps. 'Mother, this is Jane Transon,
the young woman who's going to keep Julia company. Jane, this is my
mother, Constance.'

Jane saw Lady Constance's eyes widen slightly at the mention of
her Christian name unheralded by her title.

Jane smiled and shook the thin fingers, surprisingly warm, of the
proffered hand. 'How do you do? I'm sure that, as an employee, I
should call you Lady Constance, not simply Constance.'

'I think that would be preferable,' said Lady Constance with a tight
smile directed towards her son. 'How nice to meet you, Miss
Transon.'

Jane said, 'Those beads look fascinating. May I ask where you got
them?'

Lady Constance looked down at herself and fingered the single
strand of black, multi-faceted beads. There was a look of pleasure on
her face, and Jane knew that she had asked the right thing.

'These? They're from the slopes of Mount Vesuvius. They're made
of black lava, would you believe, and were given me by a dear friend,
Count Buccino. He's a visitor here at the moment. If you decide to
stay, you'll no doubt meet him.'

'Well, they're lovely.'

'Thank you. Now if you'll follow me, I'll show you to the nursery.
Julia is there with Stephanie, my granddaughter. She's just three
months, you know, but such a bright, intelligent child, as you'll very
quickly deduce. I don't know where she gets it from, because my own

children were all rather slow. I often think that intelligence must skip a generation . . .'

'Mother!' said Courtney in a warning tone. 'If you're going to run us down, I'm off. I'll be in the stables with Sheba if you want me.'

'Sheba's his horse, you know,' whispered Lady Constance, as if this confidence was akin to revealing that Courtney still went to bed with his teddy bear.

Jane was led through the maze of passageways to a room with a huge fire, before which sat a young girl on a rug, playing with a baby.

'Julia,' said Lady Constance, not entering the room, 'this is Jane Transon. I'll leave you to talk.'

With that she left the two young women alone.

Julia rose, picking up the baby as she did so. Jane saw that she was a slightly plump girl, with the same pale complexion as Courtney, but with a beautiful head of auburn hair which fell around her shoulders like a waterfall of bronze. Julia put the baby in a cot, where it lay and gurgled, windmilling its legs and arms, and stared at the ceiling. Then the young woman motioned for Jane to take a chair by the fire.

'This is my favourite room these days,' said Julia. 'Mother insists on having a fire going most of the time, for Stephanie of course. She says babies are delicate.'

'Don't you agree?' asked Jane, as Julia took the chair opposite.

'Yes, it's just that Mother – well, we were not given the same treatment, my brothers and I. It seems that grandchildren are much more delicate than children.' Then she smiled. 'But I'm not going to bore you with family sagas. Heavens, that's a nice suit. Did you get it around here?'

Jane laughed. 'No, my father bought it for me when he went to London on one of his gambling sprees – on one of the rare occasions when he won, that is.'

'Your father is a *gambler*? What, professionally?' said a wide-eyed Julia.

'He would like to think so, but no, he's very much an amateur. So much so that he's had to flee the country because of his debts. I'm not very proud of him at the moment.'

This frank revelation concerning a parent obviously impressed Julia. Jane struck her as refreshingly open and honest about something her own family would have hidden with great determination. And Jane did so without any apparent embarrassment too. In some people such revelations might have been vulgar, but not in Jane. Julia knew that Jane was ashamed of her father's actions, but was not going to hide behind white lies in order to protect herself. Julia could not help but admire that in her.

There was something else she admired so much she was in awe of it. 'I don't think I've ever criticised my father out loud,' said Julia, wonderingly. 'Even when he's deserved it.'

'You don't approve?' asked Jane.

'It's not that – if it ever got back to him he would never forgive me. Neither would Mother. That sort of thing isn't done – especially a female member of the family criticising a male member.'

Jane laughed. 'Oh, Henley would *encourage* it in me. He's a terrible man in many ways, but he isn't a hypocrite. He knows he's incorrigible. In fact, he indulges himself with his obdurate nature, and thinks he's entitled to do so because he's an artist. I tell him that's a selfish trait. No, Henley doesn't back away from his shortcomings. If it's the truth, then whether it is his daughter or Ghengis Khan who says it, it is no matter to him. It's a quality I love him for, though he has several serious faults.'

'You can say your father has faults *and* that you love him? I couldn't say either, though both are true in a kind of way. The second would be regarded as a silly statement in this household – not worth mentioning.'

'Love?' cried Jane. 'Silly? Family love?'

'I'm afraid so.'

Jane thought of the strong loving relationship she had with her father, which both would have admitted at the drop of a hat, and of their own particular flaws, again which he would have no hesitation in pointing out to anyone who would listen. She decided she was lucky in many ways. She would have hated a cold relationship with secret, unmentioned defects.

'Your mother's dead, isn't she?' said Julia, breaking the silence. 'I'm sorry. But I want to ask another thing about your father. You say he bought you a suit in London. Weren't you with him? How did he know your size? My father wouldn't *dream* of buying me anything –

162

nor would my husband. They wouldn't have a clue.'

'My father, when he's not gambling, is quite a good artist. He likes to think he knows his textiles too, and often buys me clothes. He's a very generous man. He has an artist's eye, and though he doesn't know my size, the things he brings me always fit. I suppose it's a gift.'

'That's amazing,' cried Julia. 'Gosh, I wish I had a father like that.'

'Well, as I've said half a dozen times, he's got his faults too.'

'Haven't they all, but at least yours has got something to offer too. My father – well, he'll tell you the gauge of shotgun at a glance, or where the fastest foxes are to be had during hunt time, or the best type of land for beet, but he can hardly dress himself with any taste, let alone his females. There, I've criticised him for the very first time – and to a stranger. I feel awful, and you've got me at your mercy.'

Jane was amused at this, and found herself liking Julia more and more by the minute. They chatted until tea was brought by one of the servants, then played with Stephanie for a while, until Julia's mother appeared in the doorway. They had been laughing uproariously over an expression Stephanie had made because of wind, with Julia comparing it to her father's face on tasting coffee without his beloved sugar.

Lady Constance stared at them for a moment as they tried to control their giggling, then said, 'You two seem to be enjoying one another's company. I take it Miss Transon has got the job?'

'Oh, *yes*,' cried Julia. 'She *must* stay. That is,' she looked appealingly towards Jane, 'if you want to, Jane.'

'I would very much like to, but I must be sure Lady Constance agrees.'

The two young women looked towards Lady Constance, who then said, 'Could I have word with you alone for a minute, Miss Transon? Julia, do excuse us.'

Jane followed Lady Constance, who took her to a room a short way down the passageway. 'This is a rather delicate question I have to ask you,' said Lady Constance, clearly ill at ease, 'but I'm afraid it's important to me. How – how *close* are you to my son?'

Jane immediately saw through Lady Constance's fears. The elderly woman believed Jane might have designs on Courtney, and clearly did not believe Jane a suitable person for a daughter-in-law. Jane had some sympathy with those feelings. She could not see herself fitting into life at Stanton Manor on any other basis but as an employee of the household. The vast, cold splendour of the place was not to her taste. In any case, she had no intention of allowing a romance between herself and Courtney to further confuse her life. She quickly reassured Courtney's mother that her son was safe.

'Lady Constance,' she said, 'your son and I met during the war, while I was a nurse. We formed a friendship which has no romantic connotations. Neither of us has any intention of spoiling that friendship with any silly sentimentalism. We like each other, and enjoy one another's company, but that is all. Courtney is far more interested in my father, than he is in me. He – he appreciates my father's work. Your son is a kind man Lady Constance, and he wants to help a destitute woman.' Jane paused and smiled before continuing. 'I'm not really destitute, nor helpless, nor anything like that, but I must admit I shall have some difficulty in getting through the winter. It won't be fun, but I can manage if you don't wish to me stay here with Julia.'

The relief on Lady Constance's face confirmed Jane's understanding of the situation.

The elderly woman said, 'My dear, Julia is a married woman and entitled to hire whom she pleases, but I'm so glad there isn't – as you said – anything *silly* going on. I have no objection to you as a person, of course, but I believe my son has been particularly vulnerable since he came home from the war. He's not quite himself, and any liaisons he makes at the moment . . . well, they would be fragile, if you see what I mean?'

Jane smiled with relief at the news that she would be able to stay at the manor. 'Well you can rest assured that there will be no "liason" between Courtney and myself,' she said firmly.

Later, as Courtney was driving her back to the cottage to pack her bags, he asked, 'Did my mother have a go at you?'

'She was very pleasant,' said Jane, smiling. 'Pleasant, but straightforward.'

'Ah, *straightforward*. She did talk to you about me then?'

'She simply asked if there was anything going on between us:

happily I was able to assure her that there wasn't.'

Happily? Courtney wasn't sure he didn't feel a little hurt by the inclusion of that word in her reply. Still, why should she feel anything more than friendship for him? If that's as far as she wanted to take things, then he had to be satisfied with that. He needed her to be close by. He needed to see her reasonably often, so that they could talk and enjoy each other's company. If there was to be nothing more than that, then he would have to enjoy her company when he could.

'Well you must have impressed her, because she seemed to be in favour of your appointment.'

Jane said, wryly, 'I'm afraid I worked on her a little. Wasn't that wicked of me?'

'You mean you put on the charm, flattered the old bird, and insinuated yourself into her good graces?'

'Something like that.'

'Good. Did you work on Julia too?'

'No, I don't need to. I feel perfectly comfortable with Julia. I like her a lot.' She put her arm through his as he was driving, and he nearly swerved the motor car into a ditch. 'Almost as much as I like you,' she added. 'You don't mind me holding you, do you? I'm getting joggled around here by the bumps in the road.'

He could feel the warmth, the softness of her body through their clothes, and he was startled by how much it affected him.

'No,' he said, with a catch in his throat, 'help yourself, old friend.'

Chapter Fourteen

The following morning, Jane arose early and began readying the cottage for her absence, covering the furniture with dust sheets, and packing all the food and drink into boxes. Those of her clothes which she was leaving behind, she wrapped carefully in sheets of brown paper, putting mothballs into the pockets and creases. The living-room carpet was rolled up and stacked behind the sofa. By the time Courtney arrived in the car, the preparations were just about complete.

'Can we take the food with us?' she said. 'It seems a shame to waste it.'

'I'll put it in the boot of the car. I could drop it off later at one of labourer's cottages.'

'That sounds like a good idea,' she said, impressed by his thoughtfulness.

When they were in the motor car, Courtney confessed that he was beginning to enjoy driving. 'I had some more practice last night, motoring around the grounds using the car lights. Once you start getting used to doing things automatically, without thinking, it almost becomes a pleasure. It'll never replace Sheba in my affections of course,' he said, 'but I could get to like the Daimler.'

They arrived at the house at about midday. For the next few hours Jane simply familiarised herself with the large house. Unused to living in any building with more than six or seven rooms, she felt as if she were in a kind of prison. One reason for this was because the house was isolated in its own vast grounds. Also, she found that the occupants, at least now winter was approaching, rarely went for walks in the gardens, and so seemed confined to the interior. Finally,

167

the maze of passageways and the many rooms seemed to her to belong more to an institution than a private home.

When she did leave the house to go for a walk, she found the landscaped grounds extremely attractive. There were labelled trees from various parts of the world, in groups or standing alone, patterning the grassy slopes and lawns. She recognised maples, persimmons and Japanese cherry trees, her father having painted these at one time or another, but could not identify many others and had to stoop to read the nameplates. Autumn was not really a time for appreciating the beauty of the trees, and Jane looked forward to seeing them in blossom. She also found a wildflower garden behind the house, and though she could again recognise one or two by the shape of their leaves, spring would be the time to enjoy such a place to the full.

Jane found she got on well with Julia, though she found Julia's fear of her mother's criticism a little hard to take. Courtney promised to teach Jane to ride during the period he was at home, so that the two women could go out together. Julia said she was perfectly capable of teaching Jane herself, but Courtney was adamant that he should be the one to show Jane the basics of riding.

Courtney had an hour or so during the early afternoon, to put her on a horse before he left for his unit.

They brought out Lady, a gentle, veteran grey of some sixteen hands. Jane had ridden a little before, but had never been taught the skills of horsemanship properly. She was instructed to mount on the left side of the beast.

'Always on the left,' said Courtney. 'Julia, give her a leg up the first time.'

'He's so tall,' said Jane, her leg shaking as she put her foot into the stirrup.

'*She* – Lady is a mare.'

'Of course she is,' Jane said, trying to overcome her fear. 'Otherwise she'd be called Gentleman, wouldn't she?'

Once in the saddle, Jane recovered some of her courage. Julia led Lady around the stable area, while Courtney instructed Jane on the correct way to sit up in the saddle, hold the reins, guide the animal, and so on. When Julia made Lady trot, the two observers broke into laughter as Jane lost her rhythm and her buttocks repeatedly, and rather painfully, hammered the saddle out of time with Lady's movements.

When Julia let go of the bridle and allowed Lady to walk on her own, Jane's fear returned. She expected at any moment that the creature would bolt. Lady had no such intention, however, and merely strolled about the yard, ignoring Jane's attempts at steering her, and taking little notice of the jabbing of Jane's heels or the pressing of her knees (as instructed by Julia and Courtney, yelling from the sidelines), until the mare spied a fresh tuft of green on the edge of the stabling area. Lady headed directly towards it, almost unseating Jane when she dipped her head to munch at the grass.

'That's enough for one day,' Jane shouted to Courtney as he came towards her, grinning. 'I'll do it again some other time, when my bruised bottom's healed.'

He laughed. 'You'll be all right.'

'I know I'll be all right,' she said as he helped her dismount, 'but I want to be ready too. You've grown up knowing how to ride. You've no idea what it's like to start learning properly as an adult.'

'Yes, I do,' he smiled. 'It's the same with me and the Daimler you know. A horrible feeling of not being in complete control. I understand, old friend, don't worry.'

She reluctantly conceded this and went back with Julia to the house to change. An hour later, Courtney left for York, promising everyone he would be home in six weeks' time for Christmas. Julia and Jane were then driven into Saffron Walden by the new chauffeur, to do some shopping.

Late in the afternoon, when they had returned, Jane was wandering the halls looking for Julia when she came across a library in which an elderly, grey-haired gentleman sat reading.

'Good evening,' he said in very precise tones.

'Hello,' said Jane. 'How do you do. I'm Jane Transon, Julia's companion.'

The lean old gentleman began to rise with effort, using a malacca cane, but Jane motioned for him to stay where he was.

'No need to get up,' she said. 'I was just wondering where Julia was.'

He held out his hand and she crossed the room to shake it. 'My name is Buccino, er, Cesare Buccino.'

'Oh, you must be Count Buccino?' said Jane. 'Lady Constance mentioned you were a guest here.'

He nodded and smiled at her.

She could see that at one time he had been a very handsome man. He still had fine features, though he must have been in his seventies. His skin was quite pale, but the eyes were like chips of lapis lazuli, though warm and full of humour.

'Well, Count, are you enjoying your stay here?'

Again that nodding gesture. 'I cannot have a pretty girl calling me "Count". You must call me Cesare,' he said, 'if it is not too hard for you to pronounce. Do you speak Italian?'

'A little. Not as well as French, but better than German. *Cheseray*. Is that right?'

'Almost perfect,' he said. 'Now, I think I know something about you, Jane. We have something in common. Come, please sit here, on the footstool. That's it. We Italians like to be comfortable when we talk. It may go on for hours. Would you like come coffee? I would like some coffee.'

'Yes please,' said Jane. 'Shall I fetch some?'

She had not yet got used to calling servants, finding the idea a little repulsive, but the count pulled a cord near to his chair and someone appeared in the doorway with a tray within a few minutes. On it was a coffee pot, a cup and saucer, and a basin of sugar.

'You see, they know my habits,' smiled the count, 'without me having to ask them.' He said to the servant, 'Another cup and saucer for this young lady, if you please, Daphne. She would probably like some milk, too.'

Once Jane was settled with her cup of coffee which, despite the fact that she had added quite a lot of milk to it, was still as thick and strong as river mud, the count began to talk.

'Yes, I have been told things about you, by Courtney. He says you have been cultivating saffron here? Is that correct?'

'I grew some *crocus sativus* for my father to paint initially, but yes, we harvested it just a short while ago.'

The count wagged his finger. 'Ah, this is an extraordinary

coincidence. I too am a saffron grower, back in my own country. I am from Firenze . . . sorry, how do you say it? *Florence*. This is my home city, but outside Firenze I have land, fields where I grow the saffron. So,' he said, 'we are two farmers together, cultivating the beautiful flower for its riches.'

Jane laughed. 'I don't think we can be compared to one another, Count . . .'

He looked at her sternly. '*Cesare*, please, I insist. You must not call me "count", it makes me sound so . . . ?' He paused, searching for a word, and she said, 'Stuffy?'

'Yes, old and stuffy. I am not either of those. Cesare, please.'

'All right,' she smiled. 'Cesare. Anyway, what I was saying was that we're hardly in the same league. I have about eight acres of saffron, not hundreds.'

'Three thousand,' said the count.

'*Three thousand?*' gasped Jane. 'Good heavens, you must be immensely rich!'

He seemed pleased by her reaction. 'I have a little money, it's true. Tell me, did you have a good crop? Perhaps I can give you some, er, hints, yes, some hints on how to grow *crocus sativus* to produce the best chives.'

'And the processes you use to remove the chives,' said Jane, eagerly. 'I would like to learn that.'

'Of course, the removal of the chives is important, very important, but you must understand that, whereas with eight acres you probably can do it by hand, you can't with three thousand. We use the water method – beating the croci with sticks, gently, gently. Then we soak them in tubs of water.'

'I've read about that,' said Jane. 'Does it work well?'

'With quantity, yes, but the quality of course suffers a little. You are Courtney's fiancée?'

The sudden change of subject threw Jane off balance for a moment, then she recovered her wits, 'No, no, nothing like that. We're just very good friends.'

The old man pursed his lips. 'A young man and a young woman, just good friends? Is it possible?'

'Of course it is, here in England anyway. Perhaps not in Italy.'

'Definitely not in Italy. How would I marry a daughter to an eligible young man if she has already been "good friends" with another young man? It's not possible.'

'Well, it's different here,' said Jane, firmly.

They talked some more, then Julia appeared in the doorway and Jane jumped to her feet, conscious all of a sudden that she was here to keep Julia company, not chat with interesting Italian counts in the library. Julia didn't seem to mind, however, and merely suggested a walk in the garden before the light disappeared completely. Jane agreed and thanked the count for his advice on her saffron.

Later at dinner, Jane shocked Lady Constance to the core by asking, 'Cesare, could you pass the salt, please?' and receiving the reply, 'Certainly, Jane.'

'Well,' said Lady Constance, cutting her beef with some determination, 'you two seem to have found familiar ground remarkably quickly!'

The count explained. 'Jane and myself, we met in the library by accident this afternoon. We are both saffron farmers, you see, and as such we have already become good friends. Is it permissible for a middle-aged men like myself, as well as young men like Courtney, to become good friends with young women in this country?' he inquired of Jane.

'Yes, of course,' piped in Julia, before Jane could reply.

Lady Constance followed this with the remark, 'I would think it's highly questionable, if you'll forgive me for saying so, Julia.'

Sir Charles grunted. 'Lot of rubbish talked about that sort of thing,' he said. 'I agree with Cesare. No sense in standing on ceremony when we all live in the same house.' He winked at Jane, a gesture Jane was relieved to see had gone unwitnessed by Lady Constance.

'I don't agree,' said Lady Constance stiffly. 'But then I suppose I'm very old fashioned.'

'Sometimes it's good to get a balance of the two,' said Jane. 'We need to retain traditional values as well as accepting a certain amount of progress.'

Lady Constance appeared to mull over this statement for a few moments before deciding it was not unfavourable to her own point of view.

'I'm not sure the erosion of manners can be considered to be *progress*,' said Lady Constance, 'but certainly we need to be very careful about casting aside old ways. Empires have fallen through sliding into decadence.'

Julia and Stephen (whom Jane had met very briefly just before dinner) added nothing to this conversation. However, Stephen now threw in a remark which put the cat among the pigeons. Jane guessed by his eyes that he had done it on purpose to annoy his father.

'I see,' he said, 'that Nancy Astor is getting a lot of support in the by-election at Plymouth.'

Lady Constance said, '*Viscountess* Astor, dear. I don't think we know the Astors well enough to call her by her first name.'

'Oh, Mother,' Julia said, '*everybody* calls her *Nancy*.'

Sir Charles exploded, 'It doesn't matter what they call the woman, it'll be a bad day for England if a female gets elected to parliament. Never heard of such a thing. Monstrous.'

'I don't think it's *monstrous*, dear,' said Lady Constance. 'Lady Astor is quite a nice woman.'

'Quite a nice woman?' said Sir Charles, scathingly. 'She's a sharp-tongued harridan.'

'If she's going into parliament, with all the other sharp tongues,' said Stephen, 'she'll need to be able to match them, won't she? I quite like her.'

Sir Charles nodded. 'You would, Stephen. You've never had much of a head for politics. All I can say is, I'm glad my seat is not in the Commons. Turning the government of the country into a panto-mime. Get one woman in and you'll get two. Then all we'll hear from parliament is chatter about hair and clothes, and the latest facial cosmetic. Hummpphhh.' He glowered at Stephen for a moment before adding, 'And another thing' – he waved his fork at his eldest son – 'she's an *American*.'

He used the word as if he were revealing that Nancy Astor was some kind of viper in the guise of a human being.

'For myself,' said Count Buccino, 'I quite like Americans. Now, you see, this Nancy Astor might very well make a good politician, or perhaps she will simply fade into nothing – but she will not be a danger to you. In my own country this year a man formed a new party, the *Fasci di Combattimento*. I think he and his party are very *dangerous*.'

'What's his name?' said a clearly rankled Sir Charles, upset that the count had seemed to line himself up alongside the opposition.

'Benito Mussolini,' replied the count. 'A man to beware of, I think.'

Sir Charles grunted. 'Never heard of him. Anyway, he can hardly be a danger to *us* here in England, can he? While this Lady Astor creature threatens the whole fabric of British politics. A woman in parliament, indeed! I hope the voters come to their senses and send her packing.'

'It doesn't look as if that's going to happen, Father,' said Julia, a little too gleefully.

'Don't bait your father, dear,' said Lady Constance. 'You know it doesn't do his digestion any good.'

Jane found all this very entertaining. She longed to throw herself into the argument, but realised it would have been foolish of her to do so. She was still only newly arrived in the house and she felt that if she upset either Lady Constance or Sir Charles at this stage she would not be allowed to remain for very much longer. It was best to sit on the sidelines and observe, offering her own opinion only when it was requested.

Over the next few weeks, Jane gradually became more and more settled in the big house, familiarising herself with the geography of the interior, and getting to know the servants by name. Since they recognised in her a fellow employee, she was able to hold more intimate conversations with them than would otherwise have been possible.

Jane spent most of her time with Julia, of course, since that was her job, but she enjoyed doing so. She had never really had a close friend before, and Julia was rapidly filling that space in her life. Julia too was a fairly lonely woman; she said that Jane was the older sister she had never had. They went riding together, shopping, sat together in church, played with the baby a great deal and, though it was winter, went for walks in the countryside around the house.

At the end of November, Nancy Astor was elected to parliament, much to the delight of Julia and the disgust of her father. The weather turned suddenly sharp and bleak, the frost striking the landscape with sudden ferocity. Despite the roaring fires in Stanton Manor, the place was colder than a dungeon in most rooms. Jane was unused to such conditions. She developed a chill that turned to a cold, that finally put her in bed for a week with influenza.

Julia came and sat with her while she recovered.

'How's your father taking the news about Nancy Astor?' asked Jane, propped up on pillows.

'The world has come to an end,' said Julia, solemnly. 'Poor old father. Tradition crumbling, women encroaching on men's territory. The year before last, women couldn't even vote, and now there's a woman MP. He can't understand it.'

'Well, you and I *still* can't vote. You'll probably be able to when you're thirty, but I have no property, so I won't be able to. Progress is not *that* rapid.'

'He doesn't see it that way.'

'It's difficult for him. He's a product of the nineteenth century, while you and I are modern women.'

Julia smiled and said wistfully, 'Modern women? I wish I were. I feel like an old frump.'

'You're not even twenty yet, for heaven's sakes.'

'Oh, it's nothing to do with age. It's to do with things like whether you want to go to parties, or stay at home reading a book.'

Jane nodded. 'And you'd rather be reading?'

'Well, yes, I think so.'

'Don't you like to dance? With Mark?'

'Sometimes. Oh, I don't know. I suppose when I join Mark in India, I'll feel differently. It might be an exciting life there.'

'I don't doubt it is,' said Jane.

She then changed the subject. 'Could I ask what Count Buccino is doing here? He seems to have been here for ages. Is that a rude question?'

'No,' laughed Julia. 'It's not a rude question at all. Count Buccino has come to England to negotiate business transactions – I'm not sure quite what they are exactly, but he visits merchant banks in the City. I suppose it's something to do with making money out of money – commerce, things like that. I've never really understood such matters, but I know London is quite important to speculators and financiers. We're close enough to London for the count to reach it easily, and since Mother and Father are friends of his, they like him to stay with them when he's in the country.'

'Oh. I suppose once you've made a lot of money in something like saffron growing, you have to use it to make a lot more?'

'Something like that.'

As Christmas drew closer, the two women became increasingly busy, buying gifts, wrapping them, and helping the servants to decorate the house with holly and mistletoe. The old count watched them flitting about the house, commenting on the energy of the young, remarking that he would like to join them but, though his spirit was young, his body was not.

Jane bought only very small gifts for everyone except Stephanie, for whom she bought a fairly expensive doll's house. For Courtney she bought a small cedarwood box, polished to bring out the grain, in which he could keep anything from cigarettes to cuff links. She wanted him to have something substantial from her to show how grateful she was for his friendship.

Courtney arrived just before dinner on Christmas Eve. Jane was in the library, talking with Cesare, when he poked his head through the doorway.

'Hello, old friend.'

'Courtney!' cried Jane. 'How lovely to see you!'

Courtney grinned at the count and said, 'Kind of greeting I like to receive. How are you, sir?'

'I'm very well,' said the count. 'Very well. This young lady and your sister keep me awake, you know, with their comings and goings. And what about you?'

'Me? I'm chipper, as they say, now that I'm home.'

'Good, good.'

Jane said, 'How long can you stay?'

'Until after the New Year,' replied Courtney. 'Lots of time. Anyway, must go up and change, get out of these killing togs,' he gestured towards his uniform, 'and into something respectable. See you at dinner.'

Jane felt as if the sun had suddenly emerged from behind a cloud.

Seeing Courtney again made her realise how much she had missed him. That was the beauty of true friendship, she thought, when someone could go away for a couple of months and when they returned you just took up the conversation from where you left off. There was no awkwardness between them. Just a feeling of being at ease with one another. Distance was no barrier to friends, not if they were sure to meet again. It was an immensely valuable relationship to her.

She dressed with special care for dinner, putting on a maroon velveteen dress and a simple necklace. She drew her hair up on top of her head and pinned it there, allowing a bunching of the black curls at the top. It was not a way she often wore her hair, since she did not believe she had a very elegant neck and was normally loath to expose it, but the velveteen dress had a collar which helped to enhance where nature had been less generous, and she found she appeared quite acceptable.

Courtney's remark, when she entered the dining room, confirmed her judgement. 'My God, you look absolutely beautiful.'

Jane smiled, 'I wouldn't go as far as that.'

Stephen said, in his shy way, 'I agree with Courtney. You look very beautiful, doesn't she, Julia?'

Julia agreed with her brothers, while the count muttered, '*Bella, bella.*'

Lady Constance and Sir Charles were not yet in the room while this appreciation was taking place. Jane was glad of that, because Lady Constance did not approve of flattery, especially when it was not directed at her. It was the perfect beginning to a very pleasant evening for Jane. She felt she was amongst friends, and it was a warming experience. The truth was, if she allowed herself to stop and think, she found herself missing her father, so she contributed to the jolly evening by being bright and happy in her manner. She drank too much sherry, laughed a good deal too much, but no one seemed to notice or concern themselves with her over-indulgence.

Later in the evening there were carols around the piano, with Stephen playing. He was not a *good* pianist, having little musical talent, but the right notes followed each other, and that was all anyone cared about. Each of them was expected to choose a carol to begin solo. Jane was surprised that Julia seemed to suffer no embarrassment when it came to her turn: she chose 'The Holly and the Ivy.' Next was Jane. She *did* feel shy.

'Come on, Jane,' said Sir Charles, 'no one's worried about voices here.'

'But it's different for you, you're all amongst family.'

'Not me,' cried the count, 'and I am next after you!'

So she chose 'In the Deep Mid-winter', the carol with the beautiful Christina Rossetti words.

'*Earth stood hard as iron, water like a stone . . .*' she sang, while Stephen hammered out the notes, and when she had finished the first verse, the others all joined in with gusto and clapped at the end, saying she had sung very well. She knew this was flummery, but she didn't care.

The Italian count turned out to have a beautiful voice with a rich timbre, which he had been hiding until it came time for his solo. Everyone cheered him before going on to sing the next several verses with him.

By the time Jane went to bed, she was exhausted, and wondering how she was going to get through the next day.

Chapter Fifteen

In comparison to Christmas Eve, the rest of the holiday was relatively quiet. Courtney evinced much pleasure on receiving his present from Jane on Christmas morning. He gave her a silk scarf, which she protested was much too expensive for an employee of the family. She was supported in this view by Lady Constance. Secretly Jane thought the scarf the nicest present she had ever been given, and looked forward to having an opportunity to wear it, without flaunting it before Lady Constance.

Stephen was busy managing the estates, but the other three young people – Jane, Julia and Courtney – all went riding over the holiday period almost every day. They played a game with one another called 'spot the beasts' in which the first to see an uncommon wild creature scored a point. Jane saw an ermine – a stoat in its winter coat – scurrying down a ditch, the first she had ever seen. Julia was the first to see a fox, hurrying across a field. She also saw a hare, a skein of geese, and a flock of redwings, which made her the winner on that particular day. Courtney tried to argue that foxes and hares were not uncommon, but Jane supported Julia, saying that the landscape was certainly not peppered with these two particular creatures.

On 30 December, the snow came, changing the shape of the earth. Jane was always amazed at how different the landscape appeared under a thick layer of snow. It was as if the world had put on a disguise, a white sheet, to hide its face from mankind. The count was particularly fascinated by the depth of the snow for, though he said they had snow in Italy, it did not fall with such abundance on Florence.

Courtney attempted to paint a snow scene, but refused to let anyone see the result of his efforts, and the finished painting disappeared somewhere in his part of the house. Julia said he was hiding all his paintings in some chimney or secret cupboard, and no one would find them until long after his death, whereupon he would become posthumously famous.

All too soon the holiday came to an end. The New Year was seen in, and then Courtney was due to return to his unit. Jane noticed he prepared to leave with great reluctance.

Courtney was indeed very loath to return to his unit, and spoke to his mother before he left.

'I don't think I'll be doing this very much longer, Mother.'

'Do what, dear?'

They were alone in his room, where she was assisting him with his packing. She believed this to be an essential part of a mother's duty towards a son, and though her help was not required, as it once had been when he was leaving for a new school term, she still insisted on being there. It was the one time they were able to communicate in any depth.

'I don't think I'll stay in the army very much longer.'

His mother stared at him. 'Of course you will. Whatever else will you do? You have no other skills. Surely you're not going to become one of those young men who just loll around the place, waiting for something to happen to them? And what about your father?'

Courtney tried to control the flare of annoyance which had sprung up within him. 'What about my father?'

'Well, he so wanted you to have a successful career in the army.'

'That's all very well, Mother, but perhaps *I* don't want it. Father's had his life. I want mine now.'

Lady Constance sat on the edge of his bed. 'Oh dear,' she said, 'this will break his heart, you know. You're doing *so* well, too. What on earth has got into you? Was it the war, dear? Did it upset you?'

'Upset me?' he exploded. 'Of course the damn war upset me. It was a bloody massacre on both sides. You have no idea. No idea at all. Neither has father. Bloody Haig and crew! It was wholesale slaughter. Father remembers his little wars where he charged about on horseback, one or two people got killed, and they all went home satisfied. I saw battlefields *littered* with *thousands* of bodies, Mother. It was *hell*.' He calmed a little as he saw he was frightening her with the outburst. 'And I am *not* doing well, Mother. I'm a captain. Anyone can get to be a captain, especially if they've survived the Front for a couple of years. I'm sorry if this will break Father's heart, but it's my life, not his. He can't have everything he wants.'

'I do wish you wouldn't swear in front of your mother, Courtney. Whatever can you mean: he can't have everything he wants?'

Courtney laid a shirt in suitcase with infinite care before replying, 'He's had his own life, the way he wanted it. Now he wants it all over again, only through Stephen and me. He's got Stephen managing the estates, just as he wants them managed, because if Stephen tries to deviate at all from Father's methods he gets trodden on very quickly. He's even got Julia producing grandchildren for him, so that he can do it all a third time. I cheered when Stephanie was a girl, I can tell you. It must have set him back on his heels . . .'

'Courtney,' said Lady Constance sharply, 'this is not very becoming of you. If you have anything to say about your father, you should say it to him, not to me.'

'You're right, Mother, but I'm a coward.'

'Nonsense, there are no cowards among the Stantons.'

'The new Stantons are *all* cowards. Julia, Stephen and me. We do exactly as we're told, not because we want to, but because we're scared of Father. I'm not so sure Father isn't a coward either: it's his reason for doing this to us.'

Lady Constance looked shocked at this statement. She had gone white. Courtney sat on the bed next to her and laid his hand on hers. She withdrew her hand immediately.

Courtney said, 'He's afraid of death, Mother. Can't you see it? He's terrified of his own mortality. He wants to live for ever – through us.'

Lady Constance stood up, wringing her hands. 'What utter nonsense, Courtney. I won't have you speaking about your father in that way. He's been decorated many times for bravery on the battlefield. How can you say he's frightened of death?'

Courtney sighed. He did not want to point out to his mother that Sir Charles Courtney was a man of limited intelligence, and that his heroics in the cavalry stemmed from the fact that he dashed blindly into the fray first and thought about it afterwards. It was the kind of courage that won VCs – instant, unthinking valour – but not the kind that deserved lasting recognition. There was no slow, thoughtful courage in his father, of the kind that people possessed when nursing their loved ones through a ravaging illness, or the courage needed by those who were themselves facing a lingering death.

'Look,' he said, 'I don't want to upset you, Mother. Let's just forget this for now and talk about it again some other time.'

'I'm afraid you have upset me already. I can't think what's got into you, Courtney. Perhaps it's that girl? You were all right before Miss Transon came to stay.'

'I was *not* all right, Mother. Jane has nothing to do with this. Leave her out of it, if you please.'

'Jane this, Jane that. I'm sick of hearing her name.'

Courtney very unwisely let his wrath carry him through to another statement which shocked his mother even more than his attack on his father. 'Well, you'd better get used to it, because I'm going to ask Jane to marry me,' he snapped.

'Oh my God,' said Lady Constance. 'You've asked this girl to be your *wife*?'

Courtney realised what he had said. He had not even hinted any of this to Jane. He had felt this way for some time, preferring to take things slowly, allowing her to get used to his family and way of life, before he broached the question. Gradually, over the preceding months, his feelings for Jane had been growing stronger. The night he had realised Peake was on the scene was the first time he paid serious attention to his feelings. The day that he had seen Jane by the oast-houses those feelings had been confirmed and he knew then that he wanted her to be his wife. The whole purpose of getting Jane into the manor was in order to be able to see more of her and for his family to become fond of her. He now realised he had been a fool to think his mother would ever develop any affection for Jane. In his moment of anger he had let the cat out of the bag. Now he had to calm things down, to prevent his mother from saying anything to Jane.

He took his mother by the shoulders and made her look at him.

'Mother, I have not yet said anything to Jane. She doesn't suspect that I'm fond of her – not in that way – and I shan't be speaking to her until Easter. I want you to promise you'll say nothing of this conversation to her. At the moment I suspect she's marginally attracted to me, but I'm not the kind of fellow who bowls them over, d'you understand? She'll need to grow to love me gradually. I think – I *hope and pray* – this is what's happening. If you say or do anything to interfere, Mother, I promise you I'll never forgive you.'

His mother's voice was faint. 'You threaten me?'

'Mother, don't turn this into something it's not. You heard what I said, and I meant it. Now, I . . . I'm very, very fond of you. You're my mother, for heaven's sakes. But I want Jane desperately. I *need* her. If I'm going to live a sane and happy life, I need Jane with me. Just as you and Father needed each other. I have a right to such happiness, and I intend to do everything in my power to get it. I think Jane will be happy with me too, when she realises how I feel about her. I just don't want to rush it.'

Lady Constance moved away from him. His hands dropped to his sides.

She stood in the doorway for a moment. 'You seem very determined,' she said in a quiet voice. 'I don't think there's anything more for me to say.'

'You might wish me luck, Mother.'

She left the room without turning round, and Courtney stared after his parent with a growing bitterness in his breast. His mother and his father were both very selfish people, concerned only by how things would affect them. He had not even been able to say he loved his mother a few moments earlier. He felt fondness, yes. Love, no. They did not permit it, his parents. It was not something they required from their children, so it was not given. One owed duty, fondness, but not love.

His mother was right about one thing: he was determined to have Jane, whatever it cost him. If his mother never spoke to him again, and his father disinherited him, so be it. They could go their own ways, both of them, and be hanged.

Courtney finished his packing and then went to say his goodbyes to the rest of the family. He was careful not to reveal his feelings towards Jane to Jane herself. He simply told her he looked forward to Easter, when he would be home again, perhaps for good.

'You're finally leaving the army?'

'I hope so. It'll depend on one or two things.'

'What things?' she asked.

'I'd rather not say at the moment, but it will involve you,' he replied incautiously.

Her eyes opened wider. 'How will it involve me?'

Immediately he regretted the hint. 'Oh, you'll find out soon enough,' he said, laughingly, playing it down. 'Certainly nothing for you to be concerned about.'

'But you said it will involve me.'

Courtney decided this was neither the time nor the place to ask Jane to be his wife. Stanton Manor was not his idea of a romantic setting: it was a place which for him was cold and forbidding. It was the home of his parents, neither of whom had added any warmth to his life. Courtney wanted to wait until Easter, when he could get Jane to more romantic surroundings, and give his suit the best chance.

'I'm sorry,' he said at last, 'I'd rather not say any more just now.'

Jane stared at him for a moment, then asked, 'Courtney, why *did* you ask me to come to Stanton?'

'Julia . . .'

'Not Julia – there was another reason. What was it?'

He hesitated for a moment, then blurted out, 'To get you away from Peake. I don't trust the man.'

Jane appeared to stiffen. 'I'm well able to take care of myself, Courtney. My father instilled a good deal of common sense about most things in me and I don't need a protector.'

'Ah, but you do . . .' he began, unwisely, but he saw she clearly resented this intrusion into her personal affairs and since he had not yet declared himself it was difficult for him to explain exactly what were his intentions. He held up a hand and said, 'I'm sorry, I apologise if you think it was too high-handed. I was just thinking of you.'

A man had appeared at Courtney's shoulder.

'Your car is ready, sir – to take you to the railway station.'

Courtney sighed. Jane was obviously still bristling, but there was not much he could do in the few moments he had left.

'Look,' he said, 'I'll explain more at Easter, all right? Goodbye Jane,' he took her hand, but she mistook the gesture, shook his and let it go, instead of allowing her fingers to be held.

'Goodbye, Courtney – until Easter then?'

Once Courtney had gone, Jane regretted her reaction to what he had told her. The trouble was, her father had always instilled in her that she was entitled to be an independent woman in these modern times, and that she need not rely on a man to keep her safe from the world . . . 'What they will keep you safe from Jane,' Henley had said, 'is yourself and the things you might want to do or be in life. They want to keep you locked away from other men. They want to keep you in ignorance of *their* world, so that they might do as they please, while you remain innocent and ignorant, closeted from life.'

Jane had determined at a very early age that she would not become one of those creatures who were kept in the home, out of sight of all those her husband did not wish her to meet, and at her husband's beck and call. She was a free woman.

'Still,' she sighed to herself, 'I suppose I could have been less haughty with him.'

She sighed again, shrugged, and went upstairs to change for dinner.

At dinner Lady Constance was particularly cool towards her, but Jane was getting used to the mood swings of her employer's mother. One day she would be nice, the next extremely cold and distant. While Jane did not understand these changes, she accepted that there would be days of rain amongst the days of sunshine.

Immediately after dinner, Lady Constance excused herself and went to bed, which made Jane suspect that she was feeling unwell. Sir Charles also excused himself and went to his study, where he spent a great deal of his time poring over his accounts. Stephen stayed a short while to chat to the two women and the count, but his social appetite was not great, and he too left the room for parts of the house unknown.

Julia was called away to tend to the baby, and she told Jane not to stir herself. 'I'll be back in a bit,' she said.

Jane found herself talking to the count, who liked to spend some time over a few glasses of port.

'Do you have any children?' she asked him.

'I have two sons, yes. One, he is like Stephen, a little afraid of life. The other lives in Roma, with his wife. There are daughters too.'

The daughters, obviously, were not as important as the sons, but Jane did not comment on this.

'The son still at home, you sound as if you're worried about him.'

'Yes. I love him very much. He is now thirty years of age and still he is not married.' There was the sound of grief in his tone.

'Time yet,' she assured him. 'Thirty isn't old, is it?'

'No, but I see no change in my son. He is too – how do you say – too embarrassed with the girls?'

'Too shy?'

'Yes, too *shy*. He does not speak too well – like this b-b-b-b, d-d-d,' stuttered the Count.

'Oh, we call that a "stutter",' said Jane. 'It doesn't usually matter very much.'

The elderly man sighed. 'It matters to *him*, that is what matters. He thinks the girls will laugh at him. Some of them do, I know. What he needs is an understanding woman.'

'There are plenty of those around, Count. One day he'll find the right one, you'll see.'

'I hope it's true,' he sighed.

Julia then returned to the dining room. The subject was changed as they talked to the count about the beautiful Italian countryside. Like most of his countrymen, he loved his homeland deeply, and his descriptions of the Apennines were vivid and inspiring, making Jane want to return to the land she had visited as a schoolgirl with her father.

Jane went to bed that night feeling that Christmas and New Year had been a great success. She only wished her father could have been there to share it. She did not allow herself to think that any harm had come to him, but she had heard nothing since that short note posted in Gibraltar. She imagined he was trying to settle down somewhere and would write as soon as he felt able to give her some good news. In the meantime, she simply had to wait. Letters from distant lands still travelled very slowly, she reminded herself, and it might be months before she heard, even if the letter had already been written.

Chapter Sixteen

Lady Constance was sitting up in bed, a shawl around her shoulders, her nightcap down over her ears. In the background she could hear the generator chugging away into the night. By the side of the bed – on the side Charles slept – was an oil-lamp burning out a soft light. There was no electric light in the bedchambers of the house, only on the ground floor. She actually preferred lamplight in the bedrooms. It was less harsh on her complexion: not so unforgiving.

Lady Constance had a problem. Her first thought, when her son had told her of his attachment to Jane Transon, was to get the girl out of her house as quickly as possible. Initially she decided to speak to Charles about it when he came to bed that night, but after lying there waiting for him while he fiddled around in that study of his, she decided she would not involve her husband. It was not that he wouldn't sympathise with her view, but he was liable to go crashing in like a bull and upset everyone.

If Lady Constance tried to dismiss the girl herself, then Julia would most likely leave and take Jane with her anyway. And, more importantly, there was Courtney's warning, which had to be taken seriously, since she could not remember a time when he said something he did not mean. The thing had to be done cunningly, so that even the Transon girl herself would not know what had actually happened.

Julia was an obstacle though. Lady Constance had to keep reminding herself that Jane was not employed by her, but by her daughter. The house belonged to her – or rather to Charles – but she had invited Julia to stay and it would look churlish if her daughter were suddenly asked to leave. In any case, Courtney would simply go to Julia's house for his leaves instead of coming home. Lady

Constance had no doubt Julia would take Courtney's side in this affair. For some reason the children always stuck together when it came to a confrontation with Charles and herself.

Something had to be done very subtly to get the Transon girl not only out of the house, but well away from Courtney too. Lady Constance hadn't any doubt her son would soon forget this creature once she was out of his reach. She was certain he was merely infatuated with her; the girl was probably using all sorts of wiles to snare him. Lady Constance hadn't noticed anything obvious, but the pair of them often went out riding together. It was true that Julia went along too, but then Julia was just a young girl herself, with romantic notions, and would probably encourage such behaviour. No doubt it was during these rides that the girl had worked her art. Well, Miss Jane Transon had a shock coming to her if she thought she could marry into the Stantons just like that!

Over my dead body, thought Lady Constance.

Lady Constance continued to battle with the problem. By the time Sir Charles eventually decided to come to bed, she had a vague plan for ridding the house of the girl.

'Headache any better, dear?' asked Sir Charles, struggling into his nightshirt.

'Who said I had a headache?' she asked.

He shrugged, pulling the nightshirt down. 'You said you felt unwell and came straight to bed after dinner. I assumed you had a headache. Not my lucky night, eh?' he chuckled.

'Don't be coarse, dear. You've had too much brandy by the smell of you, in any case. You know you're useless when you've had too much brandy.'

'Well, I thought the headache and all that . . .'

She was still sitting bolt upright in bed, working through various machinations which might provide a solution to her problem, when he climbed in beside her. He reached over and turned off the lamp. She felt his hand rest briefly on her hip, but then it slid away, as it almost invariably did, and shortly afterward, she heard his snoring. It was at least an hour before Lady Constance removed her shawl and slid down beside her husband, pressing herself against his broad back for warmth.

* * *

Jane wondered whether it was her imagination but Lady Constance seemed a lot cooler towards her in the first days of the New Year than she had done previously. However, since Lady Constance had a cool disposition in any case, it was difficult to pinpoint exactly what the change was about, and whether indeed it had any real foundations or not. When Jane mentioned it to Julia, her companion told her that her mother often went through subtle mood changes after celebrations like Christmas and New Year.

A week after New Year's Day, Jane received a letter from Nancy, which said that Courtney had written to Jane's uncle Matthew. Courtney had requested a meeting with Matthew, saying that he wished to discuss 'certain private matters of utmost importance to my future. If all goes well and my plans are successful, it is hoped that we may enjoy a closer relationship.' Nancy wrote, 'Father says he's puzzled by the words and doesn't know what to make of them, but I think I know what Courtney's going to say to him and I'm sure you do too, dear cousin Jane. Wish me luck. I'm *so* excited, I can hardly breathe at the moment. I'm sure you understand.'

Jane was sitting in her room just after breakfast when she read the letter. She put it down on her bed with trembling hands. Was it true? Was Courtney going to ask Matthew for Nancy's hand in marriage? It didn't seem possible.

Yet Jane knew that Nancy had no reason to lie and was not the kind of girl who told untruths. Was it possible for a man to decide very suddenly that he was in love with someone? Of course it was – it happened all the time, didn't it? Jane now recalled something Courtney had said recently, which had puzzled her. 'I've made a decision which will upset my mother,' he had said, 'but one which, I hope will please you.' When she asked him what that decision was about, he had become very secretive. 'I'm not ready to tell you yet, but I shall when I come home at Easter.'

Then again, Jane thought, he had been rather effervescent. More so than she had ever known him to be before. When she had mentioned, while they had been out walking, that his limp was hardly in evidence, he had done a little jig on the turf beside the path, surprising even his sister with his childlike prancing. It had been

191

quite out of character for the serious, sad man she had met during the war.

A wave of disappointment swept over Jane. Although she could not explain it to herself, she felt in some way betrayed. It was a foolish feeling, she admitted to herself, because Courtney was free to do as he wished. It was just that they were becoming such good friends – and now? Now he was to become a cousin-by-marriage, or something. A cousin was something less than a very good friend. It would lock him inside some other world, out of Jane's reach and influence.

Why hadn't he said anything? That was the most upsetting part. If he had told her he felt passionately attracted to Nancy, she could have shared their enthusiasm. Instead, he had kept Jane on the outside, preferring to remain silent on the subject. These were not the actions of a good friend.

There was a plopping sound, and the ink began to spread on the top page of Nancy's letter. For a moment Jane could not understand what was happening, until suddenly she realised – she was crying.

Later that morning, the count sent Jane a request that she should go to him in the library. In a despondent mood, Jane obeyed the summons. She found him reading one of his favourite poems, Milton's *Paradise Lost*. He looked up and smiled as she entered.

'Jane. How are you today? I am sorry I was not at breakfast to see you. I think young people look so good in the morning and old people so very *old*.'

She smiled. 'Not you, Cesare. You just look interesting.'

'How kind you are to me. Listen, please sit down, I have a proposition for you.'

Jane was intrigued by this, and for a moment she forgot she was unhappy.

The count said, 'My proposition, Jane, is this. My son needs some assistance in managing our saffron fields. We use women pickers, you see, and they – they *tease* him. He does not manage women very well. What I would like is for you to come back with me to Italy, to Firenze, and become my manager of the pickers. You know about the saffron. I think you would be a very good manager. What do you say to this?'

192

Jane was absolutely stunned by the offer. 'You want *me* to manage your pickers? But really – I actually don't know very much at all about saffron picking. I've just muddled through with my own. No, it would be silly. There must be many more people who know much more than I do about the business.'

The count nodded. 'This is true, of course, but who can trust them? In Italy there are all sorts of people trying to wrest the business from me. Sicilian bandits who want my estates and who put spies in amongst my workers. Fascists and communists with their evil schemes. No, *you* I trust. Listen,' he leaned forward on his stick, 'you do not have to know a great deal about the saffron. My son knows it all and you would be – how do you say – a buffet . . . ?'

'A buffer?'

'Yes, a buffer between him and the workers. He would tell you what needs doing and you would tell them to do it.'

'But my Italian?'

'You said you spoke Italian.'

'Yes, but I don't know whether it's good enough to be able to . . .'

He waved away this objection before it was even fully out of her mouth.

'These are peasant people you are dealing with. They know what to do. You simply stand there, the imperious Englishwoman, and make sure they work. Oversee the fields, that's all. It's just that my son is so – shy. He needs some strong help. Another man would not do, because the women know how to get around the men. But you, I think you would make a fine manager!'

Jane was extremely flattered by the count's remarks and understood, to a certain degree, his problems. The offer was extremely tempting. What with recent revelations concerning Courtney and Nancy, Jane wanted nothing better than to leave Stanton Manor and go somewhere far away, out of reach. Although she did not want to dwell on why she was upset at the thought of Courtney and Nancy marrying, she knew she would rather be elsewhere if there was going to be a wedding. Since Henley was not in England, there was nothing to keep her there, and the idea of going to Italy filled her with the excitement of adventure.

But there was one thing which made it impossible for her to accept the count's offer. 'I'm employed here as companion to Julia. I can't just go off and leave her. That wouldn't be right.'

Jane also had her own saffron fields to consider, but her thoughts of these were mixed with those of an errant father and a bitter Petre Peake. Whenever the image of them rose to her mind, she quickly pushed it down again. Her saffron fields were, for the moment, tainted.

'Ah,' he wagged a finger and smiled, 'this I have already thought of. I have an niece, Nina, who wishes to come and stay with Julia. They know each other from past meetings. Nina will take your place here.'

'Why can't Nina oversee the fields?'

The count looked a little shocked by this remark. 'My own niece, working in the fields?'

Jane was not sure how to take this remark, but then reminded herself that this was an aristocratic family. The sons might be employed, but the women of the family were to be cosseted, protected, guarded against the world.

'Have you spoken to Julia about this?' she asked him.

'Yes, last evening I spoke to her. She says she will be sorry to see you leave, but she understands my predicament.'

Jane thanked the count for his offer and said she would think it over during the rest of the day.

She went immediately to see Julia, who was with the baby in the nursery.

'Julia, did you know that Count Buccino was going to offer me a position on his estates in Italy?'

Julia looked up from playing with Stephanie on the rug. 'Yes, aren't you excited? I would be.'

'But – is it all right with you? I mean, I'm supposed to be your companion.'

'Jane, this is a wonderful opportunity for you. Oh, of course I'll miss you enormously, but I can't stand in your way. I'll be nipping off to India soon, and then where will that leave you? You grab this with both hands – if you want it, of course. I mean, there's Courtney . . .' Julia smiled, knowingly.

Jane stiffened at the sound of his name. One of the reasons the count's offer was so attractive was because Jane would not have to face Courtney on his next leave. She wasn't sure why this was important, but every time she thought about such a meeting, her heart raced with apprehension.

'Courtney? I'm sure he won't miss me very much. I think he's got other things on his mind.'

'Jane, what are you saying? Of course he'll miss you. I think he's very fond of you. Why—'

'I'd rather not discuss Courtney, if you don't mind, Julia. This has to be my decision.'

Julia looked at her rather peculiarly and then shrugged, 'Yes, of course it's your decision. I just thought – oh, never mind. You're not going away for ever, are you?'

'Exactly,' said Jane evenly. 'Now,' she said, becoming brisk, 'Cesare says he'll replace me here with a niece called Nina. He says you know her?'

Julia smiled. 'Yes, I know Nina, bless her. She'd love to come and keep me company, I expect. They keep her locked up like a prize cow in Italy. They're so afraid their women are going to be attacked the moment they leave the house that they rarely let them out, you know. It's a terrible life for them.'

'It must be, but are you *sure* it'll be all right? I won't desert you if you want me to stay.'

'You go and make your fortune, Jane. I wish it were me. I'd go like a shot, if I weren't married with a baby.'

'You're going somewhere much more exciting. India, for heaven's sake!'

Yes,' laughed Julia, 'and the sooner the better. This house drives me insane. Oh, I shall miss you very much, Jane – very, very much, but I think this is a wonderful chance for you. You're such a strong, competent person . . .'

'I'm glad you think so,' laughed Jane. 'Personally, I feel terrified by the prospect.'

'I don't believe it.'

'Well, it's true. Anyway, I'd better go and tell the count that I accept his offer. And then I had better inform your mother: I'm not sure how she'll take my desertion.'

* * *

When Jane told Lady Constance of her plans, there was an immediate change for the better in her hostess's attitude towards her. She told Jane that she was doing the right thing, making a career for herself, and that she was sure the Count would make an excellent and generous employer. Sir Charles showed surprise when he was told, and cautioned Jane about trusting Italian males, but then seemed to lose interest.

Count Buccino and Jane sat down together in the library and talked about a salary and where she would stay. It seemed the count wanted her in his own home, and the salary he was offering her was very generous. Jane quashed any misgivings she might have felt by allowing herself to be taken along on the flood of enthusiasm she encountered from every else.

The count made the arrangements rapidly. He and Jane were to travel to Italy two days later on the Orient Express. This sounded very exciting to Jane. The Orient Express was famed for its sumptuousness. She was to have her own suite on the train. It all seemed a little unreal. The day before the train departed from London, Jane visited Wildrose Cottage to collect further luggage and to make sure everything was in order before leaving for Italy. On the mat was a letter. It was from her father who, it seemed, had settled in Hong Kong.

My dear daughter,
I hope by now you have forgiven me for my hasty departure from England, leaving you to face the music with the bank. I have convinced myself that you aren't liable, therefore the debt will be written off. I had a six week trip to Hong Kong, with several minor adventures on board – I'm sure you know what I mean – but I eventually arrived in this crown colony on the edge of China.

I'm living in Kowloon, which is cheaper than the island itself. (You'll have to look at a map, because to explain the geography of Hong Kong would take many pages: apart from a triangular peninsula, there are over two hundred islands, some bigger than Hong Kong Island itself). I love it here, though conditions are quite bad for a poor *gwailo* (Englishman) such as myself; added to that, the climate is appalling – the humidity is foul and the temperature ranges from chilly to sweltering. There are typhoons, too, though I have not yet experienced one of these.

The climate apart, Hong Kong is so stimulating! The streets are alive with people, twenty-four hours a day, and there are sights you wouldn't believe. I saw owls for sale in the market yesterday, destined for the cooking pot. They say the Cantonese will eat anything that presents its back to the sky.

You may guess that I have begun painting again with real enthusiasm for the first time in a long while, and here I am *appreciated*, for there are few western artists plying their profession in Hong Kong. The local rich *gwailos* are my patrons and I can sell everything I put on canvass. You should see what I can do with a patch of bamboo, or oleander! Did you know there are over one thousand varieties of bamboo? Such delicate leaves, like fine spearpoints: such strong stems, used for everything from beanpoles to furniture.

Finally, the Chinese are born gamblers. If you thought Hong Kong might cure me of my habit, I'm afraid you would be wrong. Happy Valley race course is one of my favourite haunts, but I am learning *mah jong*, which is the Chinese equivalent of cards. *Mah jong* is a little like rummy played with tiles – dragons, flowers, bamboo, etc, for suits – in that one collects sets. There the comparison ends, for it is a game so steeped in rituals that at first I could make not head or tail of them. I am learning fast and actually won a game last night, under the lamplight of Peking Road, where they serve shellfish and beer until the early hours and the sound of 'chattering sparrows' (*mah jong*) can be heard until the rising of the sun.

Once again, my dear Jane, try to find it in your heart to forgive this old profligate and waster, for he is still your father and loves you dearly. Please put a few flowers on your mother's grave for me?

Your father,
Henley.

There was a banker's order enclosed with the letter, amounting to just over a hundred pounds. Jane put this in her handbag along with the letter. There was no address to which she could reply, and she guessed that Henley was wary about his debt to Petre Peake. He did not want her to tell Petre where he was, probably until Henley had earned enough to cover the debt. The way he gambled, she was sure this would never happen. However, she felt certain that if she ever wanted to contact her father urgently, she could do it, because from what she knew Hong Kong was a relatively small place. As he had said, Western artists were a rarity there.

She was glad her father had found somewhere where he actually seemed to be happy. His gambling appeared to be worse, however, now that he was not under her direct gaze. Well, she thought, it is his life to do with as he wants. If it's gambling that makes him happy, then good luck to him! She knew she would not have had these sentiments were he still with her in England, but then she had changed her views on life quite radically lately. The fact that her father preferred to gamble his money away no longer seemed such a terrible thing: there were more important considerations in life. Also, the only responsibilities he had in Hong Kong were to himself, in which case it was entirely up to him.

Jane's anger and disappointment with her father had dissipated. She could accept him as he was – there was nothing else she could do in any case. It was good that he was alive and painting. And painting well, by the sound of it. His works were always better when his heart was in them.

Jane returned to Stanton Manor with her extra luggage and then took Lady out on her own for a last ride. Jane's proficiency with horses had improved immeasurably since her first encounter with them, and she was quite confident on gentle mares such as Lady. If ever Lady got in the least excited, which was extremely rare, Jane patted her neck and talked to her in low, firm tones the way Julia did with her own mare, and Lady soon settled down again.

Jane rode up across the fields to her own acres, where the saffron crocuses grew, wanting to see them before she left. She supposed they would become choked with weeds while she was away, once the spring growth took hold later in the year, but at the moment she was too heavy-hearted to worry about what this would do to the blooms. The corms themselves would be all right and she could have those raised when she returned to England. The land between was bleak and cold, the gentle switchback fields bare of all but a thin mantle of snow with brown patches showing through. Lady kicked up clouds of white, cold powder as she cantered alongside the hedgerows. Her hoofbeats thudded on the hard, drum-like earth. Once or twice a fall of snow from the branches of laden trees made her twitch a little, but as Jane showed no alarm, Lady soon resettled. Copses, still in the clear, hard light, were like tangled bristles on the backs of the rising hills, as Jane approached her own fields.

As she crossed the main ditch on to her land, Jane noticed someone standing hunched inside a heavy army overcoat, under the bough of an oak whose branches spread over the edge of a saffron field. For one moment her heart quickened as she thought it might be Courtney, but then realised it was a silly idea, because Courtney was up in Yorkshire. Then the figure stepped forward, away from the dark background of the trunk, and she saw who it was. He put his hand up to stop her progress and Lady halted.

'Petre,' Jane said. 'What are you doing here?'

His face was a grim mixture of satisfaction and pain. 'I knew you'd come here eventually. I've been here every day for a fortnight.'

Jane was appalled at the thought. She slipped down out of the saddle and let Lady stand. The mare was trained to remain where she was by a dropped rein.

'But Petre, I tried to explain. It's no good wanting to see me. Besides, I'm going away.'

'Going away?' he said, his expression becoming dour. 'Going away where?'

'I'm not telling you,' she said. 'It wouldn't do any good.'

He took his hands out of his pockets and suddenly gripped her by the shoulders. For a moment she was thoroughly frightened, until she looked into his eyes and saw only a need for herself in there. He wasn't going to hurt her.

'Jane,' he said. 'I'm desperate. I love you, don't you understand that? What we did here, in these fields, opened something inside me. You seemed to have feelings for me too, at the time, but they've

199

vanished now, haven't they? What made them go? Is it Stanton? Is that it? Are you in love with Courtney Stanton? Answer me, Jane.'

She stared at him, and eventually he let go of her arms. His own hands fell down by his sides. He looked like a helpless creature caught in a trap. His face, his eyes, reflected the unhappiness in his heart. She knew that before he had met her he had not been happy. When her father had first brought him home, she had seen the bitterness in him, his contempt for the rest of the world. But he had somehow steeled his heart against misery, preferring the guise of the cynic to the one of a man who is controlled by his own despondency. Now there was raw moroseness in his features: he no longer cared about hiding his melancholy.

With difficulty Jane said, 'There is nothing between Courtney Stanton and me.'

'You're riding one of his horses.'

'I'm companion to his sister at the moment, but I leave for the Continent tomorrow. I've been offered a job in a Mediterranean country. I'm going alone and I shan't be coming back again, not for a very long time. I'm sorry, Petre.'

He clenched his fists. 'Did you feel nothing then – out there . . . ?'

He gestured towards the place where they had lain together.

Her compassion for him in his distress outweighed her caution. 'Of course,' she said, softly. 'You were the first, you know that. That's got to mean something to any woman. I told you, I was vulnerable and confused. My father had just run away from home, for God's sake. I felt I was alone in the world.'

'I took advantage of you?'

'No, the situation did. We couldn't help it, either of us. I think we were both looking for comfort and it happened without us realising exactly why. Unfortunately, something has deepened in you, and you're suffering what you think is rejection. I'm not rejecting your love, Petre, because I never accepted it in the first place. I just don't feel the same way about you as you do about me. I *like* you. I like you a lot. But I don't love you, not at this time . . . I don't want you to think I'll ever change, because I probably won't.

'Petre, there must be dozens of women who would give their eyes to have you love them. Why me, Petre? Choose someone else.'

He shook his head and laughed harshly, then stuffed his hands into his greatcoat pockets. 'Choose someone else? As if it was that easy. By God, I don't give a snap for the whole of womankind – except you. You I would die for, *kill* for,' he said fiercely. 'The rest of them can go hang themselves for all I care. I want you, need you. No one else. There can be no substitutes. You – or no one.'

'I truly believe,' Jane said slowly 'that you are a fine man, Petre, but the fact is I don't love you – I really don't. In any case I know nothing about you, nothing beyond your name. You won't tell me, will you? You won't tell anyone.'

His eyes lost some of their fire after this and he half turned away from her. 'The truth is,' he said, 'I don't know myself.'

'You don't know what?'

He whirled on her. 'Who I am, what I am, where I come from. I don't know the answers to any of these questions. I lost my memory at the start of the war. I crashed my plane during training, so they tell me, though I remember nothing of the accident, and lost my identity amongst the wreckage.'

Instantly, she was all compassion. 'Oh, Petre, I didn't know . . .'

'No one knew. Oh, the military authorities knew of course, but no one around here knew, because I didn't tell anyone.'

'Surely there are records?'

He gave out that peculiar, harsh laugh again. 'Yes, there are records. There are records of how I walked into a recruiting office, gave my name as Petre Peake, and enlisted in the army. I was medically fit, that's all they cared about in those days. They were desperate to get more men to the Front. Then I was singled out for my potential ability as an aviator. I trained as a pilot, so they say. Then came the crash. I remember nothing about it, nor anything before the incident. I am simply Petre Peake, the cold-eyed aviator, the ace flyer who was good at shooting down enemy planes. The truth was I didn't care. That's why I was so good at it. I didn't give a damn whether I lived or died.

'I told your father that, when he asked me about the secret of gambling. "The trick is," I said, "not to care." He didn't really understand. He couldn't. How can you tell anyone that if it doesn't matter, if life itself has no meaning for you, then winning at cards is not important either? You might think that the loss of memory is just a mental thing – bothersome, but not especially crippling. In fact it's a *nightmare*. Who am I? What am I? These two questions became obsessions which never leave me alone, never let me rest, never let me sleep or dream of anything else.'

'What about your private income: father says you're reasonably well off?'

'That came from a little old lady who was the first to reach me in my crashed aircraft. She lived in a cottage on the edge of the field where I came down. She . . . well, I suppose she adopted me. She had reached that point in old age where pain and pointlessness meet: visiting me gave her a renewed interest in life. When she died, two years afterwards, she left all her money to me – not a fortune, but enough to keep me in comfort for a while. I've added to the amount with my gambling.

'But money doesn't give one an identity. It's ghastly not being anyone, not being anything. You feel as if there's no substance to you – you're a ghost. People see you there, talk to you, but you're just a ghost. Have you any idea how that feels?

'No,' she answered quietly.

'It feels like *hell*, that's how it feels. Even a dog has more identity. Petre Peake – does that sound like a real name to you? It's a name conjured up by a romantic young man to hide his real identity, that's what it is. The trouble is, I don't even know why I had to hide my real identity. Am I a murderer? A runaway from something? What?'

'Don't torture yourself,' Jane said. 'It could be something quite blameless.'

'It doesn't matter what it is, there must be something unsavoury in it. People don't hide for nothing. So I'm left with what I am. A ghost. Until you came along. You made me feel substantial again . . . if I had you, I wouldn't *care* who I really was. The obsession is already fading from me. It's you that's important to me now, not me or who I am.'

'Petre,' she said, panicking now, 'don't be unfair. You're making me responsible for your whole existence. That's not right. I just happen to be here. I'm not responsible. Don't . . . don't simply exchange one fixation for another – I don't want to be the object of your obsession.'

202

He stared at her and then nodded. 'You're right: it's me, not you. I'll be around when you eventually come home. Goodbye, Jane.'

He strode away, not looking back.

Chapter Seventeen

Jane returned to Stanton Manor in a very disturbed frame of mind. No matter what she had said to Petre, or what he had said to her, she felt guilty about turning away from him. Everything she had told him, about them both needing comfort and reassurance, had been true. Try as she might, she could foresee nothing but disaster if they were to get married, and she preferred the pain now to any future pain.

She excused herself from dinner, saying she had to pack, and had some sandwiches in her room.

The following morning, Jane said goodbye to Lady Constance, who had again become a little frosty. Sir Charles was not around but she left a message with Lady Constance to thank him for having her under his roof. Lady Constance promised it would be delivered. There was a tearful hugging with Julia and Stephanie and then she was on her way – to Italy!

Stephen drove Jane and the count to the railway station at Audley End, where they caught the train to London. At Victoria Station they boarded the Golden Arrow all-Pullman train for the Orient Express journey to Venice. Jane was very excited. Though she had travelled abroad before, she had never done so in such style, and whereas she had found the grandeur of Stanton Manor oppressing, she was prepared to enjoy a ride in a luxurious train without any feelings of shame. She knew the count would travel no other way, and she wasn't going to go separately on a pack-horse simply out of principle.

Cesare had booked a *coupé*, a small compartment, in the braking van of the British Pullman. It was more private, away from the less quiet skiing groups on their way to the Continental slopes. The count liked tranquillity.

205

'Would it be all right if I went through the train?' said Jane. 'I'd like to see the other carriages.'

'Of course,' smiled Cesare warmly. 'I'm quite able to look after myself. When we leave the station we shall have lunch, if you like.'

'I'd love it,' she replied.

She walked the whole length of the Pullman, marvelling at the magnificent décor and plush – no, she corrected herself, *opulent* – furnishings. When she felt the train beginning to move, she went back to join Cesare, to lunch on celery soup with Stilton cream, salmon with tarragon, green salad, finished off with a dessert called Tipsy cake followed by cheeses and coffee. They had only just finished this great feast when the train pulled in at the Channel port.

The luggage was checked on to the steamer for them, so all they had to do was walk on board. The Channel was rather choppy, there being a strong winter wind whipping up the water, but after Jane had got over the first few problems with her tummy, the sailing was not as bad as she had anticipated. She told Cesare she would never make a sailor, though.

'Nor me,' said the white-faced old gentleman, gripping his cane. 'I hate the ocean.'

Soon – not soon enough for Jane – Pas de Calais came into sight. The steamer docked and they left it, gladly, to join the Continental Flèche d'Or, a long, sweeping curve of graceful blue and gold carriages with Simplon-Orient-Express sleepers attached. Again, the interior was sumptuously furnished, with lavish fittings and exquisite artwork. Before long Jane was looking out of the window at French farmhouses crouched beneath low, rolling hills, not dissimilar to the landscape in her own northern Essex. When they crossed the River Somme, she felt a shiver go through her, as she remembered what had happened there such a short time ago.

It was dark when they passed through the royal forest of Chantilly, crossing the Grand Canal by viaduct, and on to Paris. By the time they left the station again, she was in bed asleep, in her own private compartment.

The morning arrived, and with it, Zürich. The express flashed through a countryside of snow-covered forests and mountains, towns and cities, scattered chateaux, and Teutonic castles, like the massive Schattenburg. The scenery was spectacular, except when they squeezed through tunnels like the Arlberg, which seemed to go on for ever.

Finally they caught sight of the Dolomites. The train swept down into Italy, eventually arriving at their destination, Venice.

Waiting at the railway station was a car to take them further south.

It was a chilly late afternoon when they arrived at an enormous red-roofed villa situated just outside the village of Molina, some thirty miles from Florence. Jane had left the bitter winters of the north for the less harsh climes of Tuscany, where winter temperatures were sometimes cold, but rarely went below freezing point.

The great villa was not fashioned for hard winters in any case, having large rooms, often with tiled floors, and high ceilings. There was a sense of light and space about the interior of the building, and Jane immediately felt at home here. There was no reason why she should, because she had lived in a cosy but cramped cottage for most of her life, but she had a sense of *déjà vu* on entering the villa, as if she had been there before in some long-forgotten dream.

It was different too, to the enormity of Stanton Manor, where the small-paned windows had kept the light at bay, and the large rooms seemed to press in and down on themselves. There was a certain oppressiveness about Stanton, which was not present in the villa, and it had something to do with the nature of stone used in the building. English stone had a damp denseness to it, which formed a grey, forbidding mass, whereas here in the villa the materials seemed lighter, more in harmony with each other and their environment. The mineral reds and yellows of tiles and bricks were warm. The rooms had an openness to them and, though they were well furnished, they were uncluttered and airy. In the upper storeys, the ceilings disappeared into thick-beamed rafters, and the deep rust-colours of roofing undertiles. There were no busy, patterned wallpapers to confound the eyes, but instead a simple wash of one colour, often white. Staircases and floors in the upper storeys were of some hard wood: walnut or oak. Windows were large, uncomplicated affairs.

207

There was a simplicity about the architecture which went straight to Jane's heart.

Jane was shown to her room which overlooked the saffron fields. These stretched outwards to the foothills of the Apennines and into the mountains themselves. There was nothing to see at this time of year hut a reddish-brown earth on the fields, but beyond these was a magnificent view of green orchards on the slopes. For a short while she felt sad that her father could not be with her to appreciate it.

When she went down to dinner, Jane was feeling extremely tired and could well have gone to bed without a meal, but she felt it would be ill-mannered of her not to take her place at the table on the first evening.

When she arrived there were seated around the table some fourteen or fifteen people, with the count at its head. The scene reminded her that Italian family life was extremely patriarchal. The count had already explained to her on the train that there would be at any one meal various cousins, uncles, aunts, nephews and nieces, and other relatives connected to him by marriage. The same people would not always be present at each meal, but would come and go according to the tides of family and business life.

'You must not think you have to learn all the names, for there is a vast ocean of relatives,' Cesare had said.

When Jane walked into the room, the noise was amazing. Just about everyone around the bare wooden table was shouting at his or her neighbour as if they were deaf. Jane took a seat which an elderly lady in black (all the elderly ladies were in black!) offered to her with a smile. She received some soup and bread and began to eat, feeling overwhelmed by the energy displayed by the other diners.

She had expected Italian aristocracy to be very much like the English upper class: genteel, quiet, distant, and stony-faced much of the time. In fact it was quite the opposite. Every time Jane looked up, someone was smiling at her, ignoring the person who was bellowing in his or her ear. They rattled away to her in Italian, some of which she understood, but a lot of which was lost in the mêlée. Cesare was too far away to talk to, but he waved to her, and with an expansive gesture seemed to say, 'Look at my family! What do you think of them?' Jane made a signal to indicate that she thought it was chaotic but wonderful, which indeed it was to her. It was like a medieval supper, with people grabbing things, yelling at each other, and swilling down tumblers of wine.

The elderly lady on her right said in Italian, 'You look tired. You must eat to get some strength. Eat. Eat.'

'Thank you,' said Jane in the old woman's language. 'I will, but this is all a little bit bewildering.'

The elderly woman laughed. 'You must not mind this lot,' she said. 'The trick is not to listen. Talk. Just talk. And if your neighbour doesn't seem to be paying attention, talk more *loudly*, until they do. And when you can't think of anything more to say, just say what you've already said, all over again. Believe me, my dear, if you stop to *listen* to anyone, you'll be lost. You'll drown.' The woman laughed again.

Jane thanked the woman for her advice, but did not have the energy to follow it. While she sipped her soup she stared around the table at the diners. One young man especially caught her attention. He was probably in his late twenties, good-looking in a gentle sort of way, but the reason Jane found herself gazing at him was because in contrast to the rest of them, he spoke very little. He seemed a bit out of sorts with the others, and when Jane caught his eye, he lowered his head quickly and stared into his soup.

Jane guessed this was Cesare's son, Giuseppe, about whose shyness she had been warned.

When the meal was over, Jane met the count's wife, Maria, who seemed to be a duplicate of the lady who had sat by Jane throughout the meal: a grey-haired woman in a black dress, with broad, smiling features. Maria stroked Jane's cheek once, and said she hoped she would be happy staying with them, then suggested Jane go to bed, because she looked so tired.

Jane thanked her, and was grateful for the opportunity to slip away from the fray.

The following morning, Jane woke to the sound of cockerels in the yard outside. A donkey brayed somewhere in the distant foothills. A weak sun brightened the room and she rose immediately, washed and dressed, and went downstairs. She found her way to the dining room again, but one of the servants redirected her towards the kitchen, telling her that breakfast was to be found there. The first meal of the day was obviously even more informal than dinner had been.

The kitchen was a large room with a stone-flagged floor. In the middle was a pine table with benches on either side. The young man who had sat across from Jane the evening before was the only occupant of these benches, and he gave her a startled look as she took a seat opposite him. He began to hurry through his bread and cheese.

'*Buongiorno*,' said Jane, reaching for the bread and jug of coffee. '*È una bellissima giornata.*'

He looked panic stricken at this, but muttered, 'G-g-good morning,' in English.

'Oh, you speak English,' said Jane, brightly. 'That's nice for me. Do you speak it well?'

'I . . . d-don't know,' he said, not looking at her.

'Well, your accent is good,' she told him. 'Much better than my Italian.'

'No, no,' he said, looking up earnestly now, 'I heard you l-l-l-last night at the table. You speak very g-good Italian.'

'It's nice of you to say so,' said Jane. 'What's your name? I'm Jane Transon.'

Two women entered the kitchen at this moment, chattering loudly, and began preparing further things for the breakfast table. He seemed reluctant to speak in front of these people, but eventually managed to say, 'Giuseppe,' in a quiet voice. One of the women stopped talking and turned round and said in loud Italian, 'Oh, it speaks!' then laughed at her companion, who also turned and looked at Giuseppe, but simply smiled without commenting further.

Giuseppe winced at this treatment, and seemed to want to hurry through his food and get away as quickly as possible. Jane wished the women had not come in, or would at least not tease him, because she wanted to make friends with Cesare's son, and she could not do so if he ran off every time she tried to engage him in conversation.

'Never mind them,' Jane said to him in a quiet tone, so as not to be overheard. 'I wanted to ask you something.'

He nodded, reluctantly it seemed.

Jane quickly searched her mind for a suitable topic, because she simply wanted to engage him in conversation, to find out more about him. Finally, she said, 'This is a large house. Has it been in the family for generations?'

'No,' he replied. 'M-my father bought it when he became rich.'

'Oh, I see. I thought it might be the Buccino castle,' she smiled. 'A home built by an early Italian knight.'

'Yes, yes, it was,' he said with that same earnestness he had displayed earlier, losing his stutter as he became more interested in the conversation. 'A very great noble.'

'But not a Buccino?'

He smiled shyly at her. 'The Buccinos are really just farmers – my grandfather was almost a peasant.'

Jane said, 'I don't understand. You mean Cesare is not a count?'

Her gentle probing seemed to have the desired effect, because Giuseppe began to open up, even looking at her while he spoke. 'My father was lucky. He had a patron who paid for his education, a wealthy man whose land my father worked. Sometimes it happens, here in Italy. When my father was eight years old, he surprised the man with his intelligence. The man paid for my father's schooling.'

'I see,' said Jane. 'So Cesare was the first Buccino to go to school?'

Giuseppe nodded enthusiastically. 'This is the truth. So, we are not a noble family, you see. Not from the past. Ten years ago father bought the title from another man, when he became rich from being a lawyer. The land and the house too, he bought. My mother thinks it is all, what is it, *silly*? Yes, she thinks my father is silly to call himself "Count". But then she doesn't mind, and she loves the house.'

This was a revelation indeed. Jane wondered how the snobbish Lady Constance Stanton would take the news that Count Cesare Buccino was actually a jumped-up peasant! That would be one in the eye for dear old Connie! However, Jane was not going to be the one to tell her. She wasn't that vindictive.

'I didn't know all that,' said Jane to her informant.

Giuseppe said, 'D-d-does it make a difference?'

'Certainly not,' laughed Jane. 'Why should it? In fact, I feel much more comfortable now that I know I'm not in the house of an Italian aristocrat.'

'But you are,' insisted Giuseppe, 'because my father is now a count.'

Jane accepted this quietly, but in fact Giuseppe's information had answered a lot of questions for her. She had been puzzled about the arrangements for dinner and the behaviour at the table the previous evening, because it had been more in the nature of an ordinary Italian family meal. There were other indications of Cesare's origins, too, such as the way the villa was furnished. There were few elegant, stylish pieces. Instead most of the rooms were filled with reliable, solid, rustic furniture. There were oil paintings on the wall, but they were not portraits of aristocrats. They were landscapes, mostly, of different parts of Italy. There were hanging tapestries, but the weave was coarse. Only in the Turkish carpets was an excellence of quality which Jane might have associated with an aristocratic household.

'I'm sorry, I didn't mean to insult your father,' said Jane, 'because he's been very kind to me. I understand you and I will be working together. Your father says I'm to manage the women pickers when the time comes.'

'What will y-you do until then?'

'I don't know what your father has in mind. Perhaps he expects me to help around the house or something?'

One of the women at the sink said loudly to her companion, 'Look at little Giuseppe, talking away in a foreign tongue! You'd think he was born to it, wouldn't you? I expect it's because he wants to make love to the English girl.'

This was too much for Giuseppe, who made a bolt for it from the kitchen.

Annoyed, Jane snapped at the woman in Italian, 'Why can't you leave him alone?'

The woman stared at Jane, mouth agape for a moment, obviously not expecting her to speak Italian. Then the woman recovered her composure and shrugged. 'He's a silly man. He gets embarrassed too easily.'

Jane said, 'Well, you're not helping to cure him of that by teasing him, are you?'

'Why should I want to? He's thirty years of age – a man, not a child. So far as I'm concerned, men are fair game. What does it matter to you, anyway? Are you soft on him?'

'Look, I'm a newcomer here. It's really not my place to tell you this, but I just don't think it helps him to keep making fun of him. If you ignored his shyness, it might go away of its own accord. Instead, you seem to make it worse.'

The woman shrugged again and went back to cutting vegetables. Over her shoulder, she said, 'So what's it to you? I'm his sister. I'm entitled to treat him any way I wish. You? You're just a guest here.'

Jane realised this was true and kept quiet after that, wondering how many children the count had and whether she was going to have any more embarrassing encounters with them.

An hour later the count, accompanied by Giuseppe, showed her over the estates. They drove around in a huge Benz motor car, which kept getting its wheels stuck in the ruts on the edges of the dirt tracks between the fields. Jane had the window down on her side of the car, and the sunlight slanted into the vehicle adding to the warmth from the engine. The count had insisted that they all have blankets over their legs, but it was really quite pleasant compared to an English winter.

'Where did you go to school?' Jane asked of Giuseppe as they trundled along a track between fields.

'I went to Roma, to a Jesuit boy's school.'

Jane thought, that's one of the reasons why he's so shy. He probably didn't have anything to do with girls until he was in his late teens, and by that time the shyness had set in. I'm a bit different, though, she decided, being a foreign girl. That's probably why he can speak to me more easily than he can to his own countrywomen.

'Did you enjoy it at the school?' she asked, when nothing more was forthcoming.

'No, not very much. I was beaten by the monks. Everyone was. They said it was good for us.'

Cesare nodded. 'I think this is correct. One must have discipline.'

Jane protested. 'Oh, but not punishment for its own sake. That's just sadistic. I went to a town school – in Thaxted – you must know it, Cesare? We were given the cane if we did something quite bad. I got it once for throwing an apple at another girl. I suppose I deserved it. But I don't agree that boys should be beaten just to make them into men or something. That's wrong, Cesare.'

Giuseppe looked at his father quickly, and Jane guessed the

count's son was thinking: *this English girl has overstepped the boundaries of propriety, telling my father he is wrong.* Jane knew that Italian women were supposed to defer to the men in all arguments except those concerning the kitchen. More especially, hired help did not offer radical opinions to their employers, unless those opinions were specifically requested. However, she wasn't going to have her principles stamped on without some sort of protest.

Cesare merely smiled, perhaps a little thinly and nodded in a way which suggested that these foreign ideas were all very well for England but not for Italy.

'But did you hit her?' asked the count after a short silence.

'Hit her?' asked Jane.

'With the apple? She must have done something to anger you, because I know you well enough now to realise you do not do things like that without good cause.'

Jane laughed. 'Oh, yes! The apple made a bruise on her forehead, poor girl. She was the class bully. I'd been teased by her for weeks. One day I just snapped and threw my lunch at her with all the strength I could muster. It just happened to be an apple.'

'G-good,' Giuseppe said fervently. 'She deserved it.'

The rest of the morning was spent touring the vast saffron fields. Jane asked Cesare what she was supposed to do until the time came for the picking, several months away. He told her she could improve her Italian with one or two hours study a day, and also help his grandchildren, and the children of the servants, with lessons in the English language.

'That doesn't sound very much, for what you're paying me.'

'You do not know my grandchildren,' he smiled. 'I have three daughters, all married, who live with me here. There are already thirteen grandchildren, all ruffians, who give their parents a great deal of trouble.'

'Well, I'll be happy to help with their English, but you must tell me where I'm allowed to go on the estate, what my hours are to be, and the arrangements I need to follow for things like meals.'

The count gave Jane a peculiar look. 'Why, you are free to go anywhere you please, Jane. Your hours are what you wish them to be. As for your meals, you must eat with the family, of course. You must think of yourself not so much as an employee but as our guest here. I thought this was clear in our agreement.'

'Well, it's very generous of you,' she replied, humbly.

'No, no,' he said, looking at her with young eyes set in an elderly face. 'I remember you came and sat with me in the library at Stanton Manor, for many hours, talking, listening. You were very kind to an old man. Many young English people would possibly have been polite, yes, but not so patient, not so understanding towards a foreigner, especially an old one. The Stantons are very civil people, but they have no . . .' He paused for a while and Jane said, 'Warmth?'

He nodded. 'Yes, the baronet and his lady are not warm people. Julia was too busy with her new baby, and Stephen – Stephen spoke to me only once . . .'

'And Courtney was not often there?' suggested Jane.

'Exactly,' nodded the count. 'So, I was lonely and I often went to read in the library. Then you came to stay and you talked to me. You listened.

'When I was invited to stay with the Stantons, after we had done some business together, I thought, now is the chance to see how an English family live! Now is the chance to live like an Englishman!' He shook his head sadly. 'It is not like Italian family life. So very different. In an English house, everyone goes to different rooms and stays there until dinner. And dinner! So quiet sometimes you could hear a mouse eating. I did not like it very much.'

Jane smiled at the old man. 'You chose the wrong family, really. Many English families are as noisy as Italians.'

'Is your family like that?' asked Giuseppe.

'Well, not exactly. There's only my father and me, and he's an artist. Artists are temperamental people. During the day he would go to his studio, or outdoors, to do his painting.'

'And in the evening?' asked Giuseppe.

Jane was silent for a moment, remembering her struggles with Henley over his gambling. 'Well,' she said finally, 'we would have dinner together and be quite lively, I can tell you. I would make a statement about something, and he would usually disagree with my point of view, just for the sake of debate. Or the other way around. We're both a bit controversial, my father and I.'

'Ah,' cried Cesare, '*this* sounds more like an Italian family!'

Giuseppe said, 'Your father is now living all alone?'

Jane decided not to tell the whole truth about her private business, because it would open up for discussion many things about which she did not want to talk.

'No, he's gone away – to paint. He wanted to do some work in the Far East, painting. That's where he is now.'

'He left you all alone in England?' said Giuseppe with disbelief in his tone.

'No,' she replied carefully, 'I went to stay with the Stantons, where I met your father.'

At that point the car arrived back at the villa, and Jane was able to make an excuse and escape to her room.

Chapter Eighteen

After the initial excitement of being in a new place, life gradually settled into a routine for Jane. She rose at around seven-thirty and had breakfast: sometimes with others, but generally alone. The rest of the household seemed to get up with the first crow of the rooster. Jane couldn't think why it was necessary for them to rise so early, because the work did not seem that demanding, and talk seemed to take precedence over everything else. However, there was always a great deal of bustle and chatter going on in various parts of the house before Jane had even stirred. She felt like a sluggard, but could not think what she would do for two hours if she got up any earlier.

Breakfast over, she then went to her room and tidied it. Choosing what she was going to wear was not a great problem, since the amount of luggage she could carry had limited her wardrobe to what she could manage on the journey to Italy. She had separates – skirts and blouses and jumpers for when it became chillier, but only a couple of dresses. She also had two suits, but they were far too formal to wear around an Italian villa.

After leaving her room, Jane would read and practise her Italian until it was time to teach the children English for two hours. She split the lesson into two sessions, with a break between, because she found the children got tired by the end of the first hour and their attention lapsed. Jane surprised herself by finding teaching more fun than she thought it would be, though she realised she had an easier time of it than would an Italian. Because she was English, the children were a bit in awe of her, and by the time she had become familiar to them, they were already making progress and interested in learning more. It especially pleased some of them, the children of the servants, that they could do something their parents could not.

When she entered the room designated as a classroom, they would all rise from their chairs and chant, '*Buongiorno, Miss Transon. Comé sta?*' To which she would reply in English, 'Good morning children. I'm very well thank you. How are you?' The children would then switch to English with, 'Very well, thank you,' though once they got more confident, her question prompted them to list their minor ills to her.

'I have a bad cold, Miss Transon.'

'Miss Transon, I slept not well this night.'

'My brother has the spots on his face.'

She encouraged this for she saw their confidence as a reward for her endeavour.

The afternoon was hers. Mostly she tended to seek out work around the house, or out in the fields if there was any to be done. She also took any opportunities that presented themselves to go into Florence. She was fascinated by the architecture. She wandered the streets with her head at a permanent upward tilt, and at first suffered a crick in the neck as a result. The thirteenth-century cathedral of Santa Maria del Fiore was an instant success with her, and she loved the campanile of Giotto. She also discovered the art galleries, chief amongst them the famous Affizi gallery, and immersed herself in Michelangelo, Donatello, Masaccio, Fra Angelico, Raphael, Titian, Botticelli, and many others.

Once or twice, when he discovered Jane preparing for one of these trips, the count suggested that Giuseppe went with her, to show her the most interesting sights. The thirty-year-old Italian was obviously excruciatingly embarrassed the first time he had to sit with her in the chauffeur-driven car into Florence, but by the end of that afternoon he was much easier in her company. He obviously loved his native city, because he spoke with such enthusiasm and energy, rushing her round the streets so that they should not miss anything before darkness came. She had to say to him, 'Giuseppe, there will be other afternoons. I don't have to see it all today.' He had laughed at this, replying, 'Y-you are right. I'm s-sorry. We shall go a little more s-s-slowly.' But in fact, he forgot this within two minutes, and Jane had to suffer being dashed from one building to the next at high speed.

Like her father, Jane was no great letter writer. In fact, it almost took a disaster to get her to put pen to paper. She did write to her father in Hong Kong, addressing the letter to the Foreign Correspondents' Club, hoping that at some time he would be invited to this famous meeting place. It was likely that he would get to know some of the correspondents, in the course of showing his paintings, and that one of them might pass the letter on to him. There was nothing really important on the pages, simply an account of her life in Molina.

She had asked Julia Stanton to ensure that the post office had her forwarding address, so that any mail from her father would be sent to her in Italy, but none arrived. This did not concern or surprise Jane; if anything terrible happened to him, she would get news of it soon enough.

She received a slight jolt one day when a letter arrived from Courtney, the content of which puzzled Jane.

Dear Jane,

I hope you are well and happy in your new job.

Italy! It's a wonderful country, isn't it? I can well imagine why you were easily persuaded to leave Stanton for Florence, especially during the winter. Shortly after you left, Julia took a passage to India to join Mark. [Jane was aware of this; the count had received a cable telling him that Nina was no longer required.] The house was not finished but, according to Mother, Julia said she missed Mark too much and would 'sleep in a native hut if that was all there was to be had'. Naturally Mother did not approve of this last remark, though I consider it admirable. I was not at the house at the time and so, as well as missing your departure, I was also not present at my sister's leaving. I grieve, and beg forgiveness, for both omissions.

I'm sorry if my mother upset you by pre-empting what was in my mind. It was a foolish thought, I grant you, but I did have hopes. I would still like us to remain friends, if that kind of situation is not distressing to you. If it is, and we *must* say goodbye at a distance, I shall wish you all the luck in the world and hope you have a happy life. You must know that I shall be here, to help in any way I can, if you should ever need my

219

assistance. Enjoy Italy! I envy you. The regiment is on standby for Ireland, where the troubles are increasing. So while you are enjoying the Tuscany sunshine, I have the prospect of Irish mizzle!

Your friend,
Courtney.

The first two paragraphs were comprehensible enough, but the third was very perplexing. What had been in Courtney's mind? To marry Nancy, so Jane thought, but Lady Constance hadn't mentioned it. And it sounded as if Courtney's hopes had been dashed. Was it possible that something had gone wrong with his plans? Perhaps Matthew had forbidden the match, since Nancy was under the age of consent? This seemed unlikely. Matthew would surely not have objected to so eligible a suitor.

Nancy had sounded excited by the prospect of marrying Courtney – and well she might have done, thought Jane, because Courtney was an extremely nice man and would no doubt make a wonderful husband for any woman.

Then there was that bit at the end of the letter about remaining friends, even though the situation might distress her. What was Courtney thinking about? Of course she wanted to be friends with him. The fact that something had gone wrong between him and Nancy was no barrier to their friendship, surely, but quite the reverse?

Jane thought grimly that it was entirely likely that Lady Constance had scotched the whole business in some way.

It sounded as if Courtney had been badly upset by his failure, whatever quarter it came from, because he seemed to be rambling a little. Jane was a little disturbed to hear that violent incidents in Ireland were on the increase, and hoped Courtney would not be sent there. He had seen enough of the horror of violence in France.

She sat down at once and wrote a reply, knowing if she left it, it might never be sent. She told Courtney that of course she wished to remain friends with him, and regarded their friendship as one of the more treasured aspects of her life. She did not mention her cousin for two reasons. One, she was not sure what had passed between them.

Two, she did not want to remind him of anything unpleasant in what would probably be the only letter he would receive from her. She added a brief description of her life at the count's villa, some lines about her walks around Florence, and then ended with, 'Oh Courtney, you mustn't ever think I would want to lose you as a friend, because I value that friendship above everything. With fondest regards, Jane.'

Apart from Courtney, no one else wrote to Jane. Jane was quite surprised that Nancy had not written to tell her about what had happened between her and Courtney, but then no doubt Nancy had her reasons for remaining silent on the subject.

In the early summer, when the Italian heat was at its height, the corms were lifted from several fields, split, and then replanted. Jane assisted in this operation, overseeing the women whose job it was to separate the corms. She had expected them to resent an Englishwoman directing work which they were far more qualified to understand, but in fact it was as Cesare had told her they accepted a foreigner more readily than one of their own, which would have raised personal jealousies. Besides, though many of the women had been doing the job for years, Jane's work was more on the organisational side. She made sure the women were in the right place, at the right time, in the right numbers, rather than actually telling them what they should be doing with the corms. They knew what to do once the *sativus* bulbs were in their hands.

It was also Jane's job to pay them at the end of the day, according to individual work effort, in the way that she had her gypsies in England. When she suggested to Giuseppe that the women should be paid weekly to save time and money, he grinned at her.

'They have always been paid at the end of the day. Some of them live day by day and need the money to buy the evening meal. They would be eating the corms by the end of the week. These are *poor* people, Jane.'

Suitably chastened by Giueseppe's words, Jane never again tried to change a system which had been in operation long before she had been born, and would no doubt continue long after she was gone.

Since they had become friends, Giuseppe no longer stuttered when he was talking to Jane. He still did so with some of the other women, but his confidence had grown since Jane had arrived, and he did so with less and less frequency. She had told him she was no different from any other woman, and if he could talk to her without his impediment, he could surely talk to any female on the place in the same manner.

She found that the women liked her, once she showed them she could exchange Italian oaths with the best of them. When she had visited Naples with her parents as a child, she had played in the backstreets with the urchins, and had learned enough swearwords to swamp the goodness of a Pope. These expletives and richly descriptive southern-Italian street phrases were sometimes unusual enough to the northern women to make them laugh and want to copy them.

In the presence of the men, the women chattered about everyday things like cooking and housework, but once the men were out of earshot, they swore and discussed each other's sex lives, and attacked the reputations of local burghers, schoolteachers and shopkeepers with vigour and inventiveness.

'Hey, Jane,' one of them called one day after an official visit from an ambitious politician, 'what do you think of our new mayor?'

'He has the eyes of a pig's orphan,' Jane shouted back. 'I wouldn't trust him with your new heifer, let alone your daughter. He's probably a bastard child from the union of an unfrocked priest and a Sicilian whore.'

They shrieked in delighted laughter at this, and Jane had one or two pangs of conscience as she wondered what the gentle and polite Courtney would make of his 'old friend' if he heard her exchanging obscenities with these Italian field-workers. She suspected that Cesare would be shocked, too, even though he probably had a good idea what the language was like out in the fields.

Giuseppe seemed terrified of the women workers, and stayed out of range of their remarks as often as possible. They were merciless when it came to verbally castrating timid menfolk who wandered within their sphere of attention. Giuseppe would have a blush on his face even before he approached the field, and by the time he left it would be almost burning.

Though Jane got on well with the peasant women, it was a little different with Giuseppe's sisters. They were members of the household, and therefore higher in status than Jane, whom they regarded as an employee. She understood this, though she did not intend to be walked all over. They tried at first to trample her, but Jane would have none of that, and one or two quarrels arose, after which Jane left them in no doubt that they could not get away with being impolite. So long as they were civil to her, Jane did not mind, but if she had been looking for friendship from them, she would have waited for a very long time. But they appreciated what Jane was doing for their children with her English classes, and so finally settled for a position in which they expected to be accorded some respect as the daughters of Jane's employer, but were always careful to speak politely to her.

Maria was different again. As the wife of the count she could have been expected to be the most resentful of Jane's presence in the house. Jane had been brought to the villa without Maria's knowledge or consent: there had been no time for the Count to consult his wife on the issue. He had simply turned up with this English girl in tow and dumped her on his household. In truth, Jane felt she could not have blamed Maria if she had been as frosty as Lady Constance.

On the contrary, Maria was a naturally warm and welcoming person, quite unlike her daughters, and treated Jane as if she were one of those daughters. Jane certainly did not think of her as a countess – Maria was too motherly and homely for such a title – but her respect for the elderly lady exceeded any Jane felt for Lady Constance Stanton.

One sweltering day in August, Maria and Jane were sitting on the balcony. Maria was drinking wine that was so diluted it was almost coloured water. Jane stuck to iced lemon tea in the afternoons, though she drank wine at dinner. She found that wine in the day made her head spin; especially in the deep summer heat. Out in the fields and foothills the heatwaves were rising in tendrils from the ground, and wriggling away into invisibility somewhere in the hard blue sky. There was a sharp edge to the distant horizon, especially around the mountain peaks, which made it appear to Jane that the day only needed a crack with a rock to shatter it.

Maria said in a weary voice, '*Whaaa – che caldo, eh? So hot.*'

'Very hot,' agreed Jane, finding even the effort of speaking a bit too much for her.

Maria wanted to talk, though. 'My eldest son and his wife are coming to stay soon. My son Antonio, he is thirty-seven years of age, and still a child.'

'What do you mean?' asked Jane.

'Oh, still a little boy, you know? He wants the fast motor car, the best fashion clothes, the scented cigarettes – still a boy. That wife of his, a *gelato*, you know? Fancy, fancy, but no work in her.'

Jane knew that *gelato*, literally the word for ice-cream, meant the equivalent of the English word 'tart' when used to describe a woman.

'Still,' said Jane, drinking her lemon tea, 'you'll be happy to see your son?'

Maria shrugged and made the typical Italian gesture of sticking out her bottom lip to indicate, maybe yes, maybe no.

'He causes trouble,' she said to Jane. 'In Roma he is the big man with selling motor cars. Sometimes I think I don't know my own children. When he was a little boy, still in *pannolini*, he was nice to his mamma. He bring me the wild flowers from the roadside. A lovely boy. Dark eyes like black stones, you know? What happens to them? They become men with bad ways. When? How? Who knows?'

'Perhaps you see his faults because you expect him to be like he was then? Maybe to other people, he's not that bad?'

'Huh!' said Maria. 'Just you wait and see. Your bottom will not be safe from his hands, I can tell you. He is a woman-chaser, this boy of mine. You must lock your bedroom door.'

Jane thought that Maria must be exaggerating a little, but when, a couple of days later, she saw the long, square-bonneted sports car come to a skidding halt on the new gravel driveway, and a tall, smooth man leap from one of the bucket seats, she knew instantly that this was Antonio and that Maria had been speaking the truth.

Jane just happened to be on her way into the house from the stables when the car drew up.

'Hey, baby,' he called to her in Italian. 'Come and carry my wife's things into the house.'

His wife, a languid creature with too much lipstick and a ludicrous hat, allowed herself to be assisted from the car by her thoughtful, smiling husband.

'Carry it yourself,' snapped Jane. 'I'm not a servant.'

He looked up at her and frowned. 'You work here, don't you?'

'Not for you I don't,' snorted Jane. She could tell by his expression that he was preparing a little speech, and so she added quickly, 'And before you tell me you're Antonio, the eldest son of Cesare and Maria, let me tell you I am Jane Transon, the children's English teacher and the women's field supervisor. I don't carry cases, especially for people who call me *bambino*.'

He gave her a mock bow. '*Scusa, scusa*. I did not know I was talking to an English princess. Please forgive me,' he said.

'Sarcasm won't get your luggage moved either,' said Jane in a contemptuous tone. 'I suggest you either call for a servant or carry them in yourself.'

She left him then, while his wife rattled away in a rapid southern-Italian accent, asking him if he was going to take such back-chat from an English nanny, or was he going to do something to put Jane in her place? Jane did not wait for the outcome but hurried to her room. She was partly amused by Antonio and partly concerned by his presence in the house. He *was* a trouble-maker, she could see that at a glance, and so was his pert little wife. Jane hoped they were not going to spoil her time at the villa.

At dinner that night he sat opposite her. His wife, whose name Jane had learned was Anita, inquired loudly why the servants were eating with the family.

Cesare looked up, his face thunderous as he realised what was being implied. 'What?' he said menacingly. 'You dare to call my guest names? Who the hell are you, you little trollop, to call anyone "servant"? You were a shopgirl when my son met you, but you don't even have a shopgirl's manners. You have the manners of a breeding sow. If you speak like that at my table again, I'll have you thrown into the pigsty where you belong.'

Anita burst into tears under this tirade, and looked at her husband as if she expected him to do something. Jane could see he was terrified of his father, though, because he kept his eyes straight ahead, and sipped his soup carefully. When she realised she was being ignored by everyone, Anita sniffed herself dry and then began talking loudly with one of her husband's sisters about clothes and city life.

Half-way through the meal, Jane felt a sock-covered foot between her bare legs. She jerked backwards, instinctively, and when she looked up Antonio was smiling vacantly. Then his eyes rested on hers. Jane tapped her fork meaningfully against the side of her plate and he understood the gesture immediately. If he tried it again, he would be stabbed in the foot with Jane's fork. He stared at her darkly and then turned his attention to one of his cousins.

Before coffee, Cesare retired to another room, having apologised to Jane for his outburst. Maria was in and out of the room supervising the clearing of the table, when Antonio said softly, 'How does my little brother find the English girl, eh? Have you bedded her yet, or are you still not a man?'

Giuseppe went bright red at this remark, which fortunately Maria had not heard.

He replied in a choked voice, 'That is not appropriate talk. You have a foul mouth, Antonio.'

'Oh, really?' sneered his elder brother. 'Well most men would consider it highly appropriate, but then it is only *men* who appreciate these things.'

Jane felt the need to intervene here. 'You consider yourself a man, do you Antonio? Does a real man need to insult his younger brother in front of other people to prove how powerful he is? I think not. Does a real man need to make eyes at every woman except his wife? Of course he doesn't. Does a real man need the outward show of fine clothes and fast cars to prove he is virile? Not at all. The trouble with you, Antonio, is that you don't know what a man really is, because you're not one yourself.'

Antonio hissed, 'You be careful, English lady. Don't overstep the mark too often, or you'll find out how much of a man I really am.'

Jane was taken aback by the ferocity of his tone and she found herself afraid for a moment.

It was Giuseppe's turn to step in. 'Listen, my brother,' he said evenly. 'If you so much as *touch* Signorina Transon, I shall kill you.'

This was all becoming much too serious, and Jane was beginning to get worried.

226

She said lightly, 'Well, he's not going to touch me, are you Antonio, because his wife wouldn't let him, would you, Anita? Let's all leave the table as friends, or it will be very uncomfortable. Antonio, Anita, I'll apologise if you will.'

The brothers continue to glare at each other for some time, until Maria returned to the room. Then Giuseppe got up without another word and left. Antonio shrugged at Jane and then smiled, as if to say, what can you do with such a brother? Anita was again busily talking to one of the other women. Jane got up and went to her room. For the first time since she had been in the house, she locked the door.

Chapter Nineteen

The following morning, Antonio was waiting outside Jane's room. The day was already very hot and his brightly coloured silk shirt was damp with sweat around the armpits. He was wearing a vast array of thick gold rings and bracelets on his hands and wrists; Jane felt his arms must ache with the weight. She could see his black chest-hair, glistening with oil, sprouting above the neckline of the shirt.

Jane said, 'Good morning. I wouldn't fall in any lakes today, if I were you.'

He grinned at her, clearly not comprehending.

'You'll sink and drown,' she stated, pointing to his jewellery.

He laughed. 'Oh, you're joking with me?'

When she walked past him, he fell into step beside her and said, 'I shall accompany you to breakfast. I have to apologise to you for my behaviour yesterday.'

'If you wish,' Jane said.

They entered the kitchen together, Antonio steering her by her elbow at the last minute. Giuseppe was just finishing his coffee. Antonio smiled and shrugged at his brother in a way that made Jane want to smack his face. His motives for entering the kitchen with her were now obvious. He wanted his brother to think they had come from the same room.

'We met on the landing,' Jane said wearily to Giuseppe.

Giuseppe nodded in understanding. Ignoring the presence of his brother he said in English, 'Perhaps, Jane, you would like to tour the fields today? The crop is just showing through the earth.'

'Anything to get me away from the villa while Romeo here is wandering around loose. Can you pick me up after I've given the children their lessons?'

'Of course,' Giuseppe said as he left the room.

Antonio made an Italian gesture after his brother, then smiled at Jane. 'I'm a bad man,' he said. 'My wife doesn't care, you know, if that's what worries you.'

'I'm just not interested,' said Jane. 'If that hurts your ego then I'm very sorry, but it happens to be the truth. I prefer men like your brother.'

'How can you like my brother?' he said, genuinely mystified. 'He is a woman.'

'Giuseppe is a sensitive and intelligent man and I enjoy his company.'

'Oh, *intelligent*. Most of the women I know don't want intelligence. They want a good lover.'

'Oh,' said Jane airily. 'He's that too. Now, if you'll excuse me?'

She left without eating any breakfast, satisfied to see that Antonio's mouth had dropped open. Later, when she met Giuseppe, she told him. 'I'm afraid I've given your brother the wrong impression of our relationship,' she said as they rode to the fields. 'I left him with the idea that we are lovers.'

Giuseppe blushed, but then he actually laughed. 'That will stick in his throat,' he said. Then he turned to Jane and said, 'It could not be true though, could it?'

Jane realised she had entered dangerous ground. 'I don't think so. I like you very much, Giuseppe, but I'm not in love with you.'

'Nor me with you,' he said, in a satisfied tone which might have been hurtful if Jane had been feeling vulnerable. 'But this will disappoint my father very much, I think.'

Jane patted the neck of her mount while she absorbed this piece of information. 'Your father wants us to fall in love?'

'It was one of the reasons why he asked you to come here. Lady Constance Stanton spoke to him when he told her he was worried about the fact that I am not married. He thinks I should be, at my age. Perhaps he's right.'

'Lady Constance suggested that your father should take me to Italy, so that we could fall in love?'

'Yes, Lady Constance Stanton said you would make a good wife for an Italian saffron farmer.'

'Did she now?' mused Jane, wondering why on earth Lady Constance should bother to do such a thing. There was something not quite right about all this, but Jane couldn't put her finger on it. Unless Lady Constance had been thinking that Jane was a bad influence on her daughter? So to get Jane out of the house and Julia out of Jane's sphere of influence, she had persuaded the count to take Jane back to Italy with him? That made a little bit of sense, but not a lot. There was something else, Jane was sure of it, but for the moment it would have to remain a secret between Lady Constance and her conscience.

Jane turned her attention to Giuseppe as they rode along, side by side, in the heat of the day.

'Giuseppe,' she said, 'do you think you will ever fall in love?'

He turned and smiled at her. 'Of course,' he said. 'Once I meet the right woman. Unlike the rest of my family, I'm a patient man. What does it matter if I'm forty or fifty when it happens, so long as she is the right woman for me? To me that's the most important thing of all.'

'Most people would agree with you. I certainly do.'

'You mean most *women* would agree with me?'

'No, men too. I have a man friend back in England who would agree with that philosophy – if it can be called a philosophy.'

'Would that be Courtney Stanton?' said Giuseppe with a smile. 'Is he the boyfriend to whom you refer?'

She had in fact been thinking that Petre would subscribe to Giuseppe's view. At the mention of Courtney's name, however, she experienced an unexpected jolt of sadness, for while they were discussing Giuseppe's love life, Jane had been subconsciously examining her own feelings. It was not the first time she realised she was missing Courtney, but usually she pushed any such feelings back down inside her, out of reach. Now she let them well up, and found them very uncomfortable. Why should she miss Courtney in this way? They were just friends, after all.

'You mustn't say *boyfriend*, Giuseppe,' she told him, 'it can have more serious connotations in English. It implies that the two people are lovers, or will probably become so.'

'And you and Courtney are not lovers?'

She jerked her head up. 'No, why do say that?'

Giuseppe shrugged. 'I don't know. Something in your eyes a

231

moment ago. I'm sorry, I don't mean to be rude and inquisitive. Your private thoughts are your own.'

While Jane allowed herself to examine her feelings to a certain degree, she felt wary of stirring up some of her deeper emotions; she was afraid she might hurt herself and make herself miserable. Italy was a country where one could wile away a lifetime and never find the need to revive old dreams.

It was hot and dusty at this time of year, but the shadow of the mountains was not far away, where the conifer groves grew tall. Jane promised herself a ride out that way later in the month, where she could give herself a lecture in the quiet of countryside. She was resilient, if nothing else. A gentle trot through the vineyards, along the bank of the river, and up into the apple orchards would give her time to reflect on how lucky she was to be in such a wonderful country.

'You weren't really intruding,' said Jane, to put Giuseppe at his ease. 'You just touched on a tender place, that's all.'

'I could tell that by your face,' he replied, but they left the conversation there and turned to more practical matters.

Over the next ten days, Jane had to repel Antonio on numerous occasions. He seemed to follow her everywhere she went, even out riding, and she learned the trick of not putting on her riding clothes, pretending to go out into the fields, then cutting back to the stables when she was out of sight of anyone in the villa.

There were one or two occasions when she found him in her room. Once he was even going through her things and had found the letter from Courtney.

'Get out of here,' she snapped at him in frustration. 'This is my room.'

He laughed. 'I don't mind whose room it is. Who is this man "Courtney" anyway? What kind of a name is that?'

'He's a friend,' said Jane. 'Have you no shame? How can you just read someone's letters?'

'It doesn't matter to me,' he said. 'Why should it?'

When she ordered him out of the room he tried to fumble with her blouse, and she threatened to call his father. This was the only thing that had any effect whatsoever on the persistent Antonio. Jane was thankful that Cesare was around, or she feared she would be in real trouble. However, she did not want to upset Cesare or Maria by informing them of their son's behaviour, so she kept it to herself, hoping she could cope with any moves Antonio made without bothering anyone else with her problem.

One day Jane was passing their room when she accidentally overheard his wife complain about him chasing after 'that English bitch'. Antonio had quickly subdued her with a tongue-lashing and told her to mind her own business: he seemed to have complete control over his wife, and if she ever tried to argue with him he would simply shout louder.

The whole thing was wearisome, and one day Jane decided to ride out into the countryside, as she had promised herself she would do ten days earlier, to get some peace from the stupid man. She used her old trick of wearing her field-clothes to walk away from the villa, then she doubled back and collected her mare from the rear of the stables.

She headed towards the blue line of the mountains, passing field-workers out toiling in the late afternoon following their siesta. There were midges and other insects about, which bothered her a little, but she was not one to fret about things over which she had no control. Italy in the summer was like that, and there was nothing for it but to put up with it.

She rode for a long time, mostly following the main tracks, but then left the winding trail behind altogether and set off over the scrublands, into a line of trees. Breaking out of the woods there were orange groves on the other side which seemed to have been abandoned, the bushes covered in vineweeds, and a thick twitch grass growing between the neglected trees. She found a narrow gorge with a stream, and followed this through foliaged cliffs and over rocky outcrops. At one point a bee-eater bird with bright plumage zipped down the gorge like an arrow startling her mare, but she had ridden quite a lot recently and was able to get her mount under control with reasonable ease.

Finally she came across a cool-looking lake like a mirror in a glade of pine trees. A soft pastel evening light was easing in, and she realised she could not stay much longer. She dismounted and splashed some water on to her face, and then sat down to admire the view for a few moments.

Beyond the lake, on the far shore, the foothills rose sharply, their folds producing steep-sided valleys in the creases. A buzzard wheeled above a show of rocks, where the heat caused thermals to spiral upwards and carry the large bird, with minimal effort on the creature's part. All it had to do was spread its ragged wings and be lifted to the heavens. It finally soared away over a spread of pines and into the purpling sunset.

The mosquitoes were coming out now: a very different proposition to the midges. Jane buttoned the collar of her blouse and pulled her field skirt well over her legs. Still they attacked her neck and face. She slapped at them in a half-hearted way, knowing they would go when the darkness fell.

She was just thinking about mounting her mare again, when she suddenly caught a whiff of cigarette smoke. She looked around her, but could see nothing. However, there were some tall bushes not far from where she was sitting, and she guessed someone was behind them. Then a lighted end flew past her towards the lake, landing in the dry grasses there and smouldering.

Her eyes had instinctively followed the arc of the burning cigarette end and, before she could turn around, she felt strong hands gripping her shoulders. She was flung forward on to the bank of the lake. She cried out in fright as she landed awkwardly on her front. A man climbed heavily on to her prone body, pinning her to the ground, crushing her breasts, and she let out a scream of fear.

'There's no one to hear you.'

She recognised Antonio's voice immediately, and could feel the gold chain-bracelet digging into her shoulder-blade. His whole body-weight was on top of her, with his legs bearing down on the backs of her own lower limbs. She tried to wriggle out from under him, but he laughed and pressed down harder. She could feel his hard erection through her skirt, pressing into her buttocks.

'Let me go. Please let me go,' she cried.

'Ah, *please* now, is it? I don't think so.'

She struggled against him, but he was quite strong and his weight kept her pinned to the dust. He squirmed his hand between the ground and her chest and began squeezing her flattened breast. His mouth was next to her ear, and she could smell the garlic on his breath.

He growled, 'You like it, don't you? You like a real man?'

'You're disgusting,' she hissed, her face pressed painfully against the gritty soil. 'Get off me.'

Antonio shifted his weight and, holding her bunched hair, tried to pull her blouse from her skirt. Jane kicked out and caught his ankle. He swore violently and yanked harder on her hair until she thought it would come out. Her eyes watered in agony and she screamed. Antonio then reached down again and whipped her skirt up before trying to force his knee between her thighs. With all her strength, Jane resisted him, refusing to allow her legs to be parted. He became savage, punching her in the back, still gripping her hair with his other hand and bearing down on her buttocks with his knees.

Jane started crying with the pain of the blows. After a few minutes he reached down again, wrenching frantically at her underclothes, trying to tear them off. But they were made of strong material, and finally, in exasperation, he pulled them to one side. Realising he was fumbling with his own clothes, Jane managed to hunch her back and kicked, hard, succeeding in throwing him to one side at last.

He rolled away from her, still holding her hair. The effort in throwing him off had exhausted her for the moment, and she expected him to be back in an instant. Instead he tried to pull her towards him through the dust. Jane was then dimly aware that there was a lot of smoke in the air. She dug her fingernails into the hand that held her hair, hard between the knuckles. Suddenly he let go and shrieked at the top of his voice.

When she sat up, Antonio was beating at his trousers with his hands to put out a smouldering flame. His cigarette had caused a fire. A line of flame had crept towards the pair of them through the short, dry grass, and Antonio had rolled into this advancing wildfire.

Jane's horse, tethered to a bush not far away, was whinnying and jerking at its rein, obviously terrified by the smoke and flames.

Jane got to her feet and staggered towards the frightened mare. She soothed it with one or two words before climbing into the saddle. As she rode away, Antonio was getting to his feet. He ran from the fire towards a group of trees, where Jane guessed he had left his own horse. Jane allowed the mare to gallop away over the uneven ground, at a very great risk to them both; but luckily the horse kept its feet, and soon they were a mile from the scene where the black smoke rose into the rapidly darkening sky.

After some hard riding, Jane's boots felt slippery against the mare's flanks. She looked down to see that the horse was lathering, the white froth squeezing from beneath the saddle. There was also some foam flying in flecks from the mare's mouth. Looking fearfully behind, her she made sure that Antonio was not following close behind, and then allowed the poor, exhausted creature to walk the rest of the way back to the villa.

When she got back to the stables it was dark. There were lamps lit for her to see by, and she removed the mare's tack herself, hanging it behind the stable door. Then she put the mare in its stall. One of the grooms appeared at the other end of the stables, and she called to him, asking him to look after her horse. Then she ran towards the house, anxious not to be seen in her present state.

Her heart was beating wildly, and there was a leaden feeling in her stomach as she made her way to her room. Just before she entered, however, Giuseppe emerged from the shower-room. His hair was wet and plastered down on his head, but he was fully dressed in a long-sleeved shirt and slacks. He stared at Jane in the dim electric light of the landing, obviously puzzled by her dirty and dishevelled appearance.

'What happened to you?' he asked.

'Nothing,' said Jane, quickly. 'I got thrown.'

'Then why is your blouse ripped?' he said in a disbelieving tone.

At that moment there were hoofbeats outside. Giuseppe went to the landing window and looked down. Presumably he saw his brother, because he looked back at Jane significantly. Then he strode towards the staircase.

'No,' said Jane. 'Don't! He . . . he didn't manage to do anything. I'm all right. It'll just cause more trouble.'

But Giuseppe took no notice.

Jane did not want to be seen in an unkempt condition by any other member of the household. She ran into her room, washed her face

236

and hands in the basin, and brushed her hair. Then she quickly changed her clothes. Then, as swiftly as she could, she made her way downstairs. Happily, most of the occupants of the house were either busy somewhere or had retired for the night.

She stood at the top of the steps to the house. At first she could not see or hear anything untoward. The crickets and cicadas were making their usual racket, but there were no sounds of men arguing. Then she thought she heard a muffled sound like a *crack*, coming from the direction of the stables.

Jane ran towards the stables. When she got there she heard the cracking sound again. Someone screamed. The walls of the stables were of thick stone, however, and the sound did not penetrate much beyond the stable area.

Oh God, she thought, I hope that's not a pistol shot!

She tried one of the doors to the stables, but it appeared to be locked from the inside. Frantically she tried other doors to stalls, all the way along, but they were closed tight. When she got to the end of the building, she could see a light shining through a window no bigger than a castle arrow-loop, about twelve feet off the ground.

Jane looked around for something to stand on, and finally saw an empty barrel which had been used to store oats for the horses. She ran to it and rolled it to the side of the building, turned it upside-down, and stood on it. In this way she was able to peer through the window-slit.

At first she could see very little, because the lamps inside the building were few and not very bright. Then, as she stared into the gloom, she discerned two figures standing off from one another, in the alley between the stalls. The horses were kicking and shuffling on either side of these two motionless people, as if alarmed by their presence. Then, as Jane watched, one of the figures stepped forward. She heard the *crack* again, and the second figure hunched and shrieked, lashing out wildly with something in his hand. It whistled through the air, failing to find a target.

The horses went wild for a few moments, crashing around in their stalls in fear.

As her eyes got used to the light, Jane recognised the man furthest away from her viewpoint. It was Antonio, bare to the waist, rubbing his chest and cursing softly. With his back to her, facing this opponent, was Giuseppe, also bare to the waist. She could see the shadows thrown by the lamp in the hollows of his muscular back. Then she saw what each man had in his hand. They were holding buggy whips. These long, slim, flexible whips, as tall as the men that held them, were normally used with the pony and trap. On the end of each whip was a six-inch leather thong that was used to flick the pony's rump. It was this short piece of hide that made the cracking sound when one of the two men used his weapon on the other.

Jane had a lump in her throat as she stared at the two combatants. Giuseppe was obviously trying to punish his brother for attacking her. But Jane was afraid for the younger man: Giuseppe was not as tall and thick-set as Antonio, who had inherited his father's build. In the lamplight below, Giuseppe looked much smaller of stature, and to Jane it seemed that Antonio must be the stronger.

However, as she continued to gaze on this scene, Antonio stepped forward, clumsily lashing with his whip. The blow caught Giuseppe on the upper arm, but Giuseppe sidestepped neatly and flicked out with his own whip, catching Antonio across the right shoulder. The older man gave out a sound like a sob, and Jane saw a slim weal appear on the smooth flesh of Antonio's clavicle. Antonio rubbed his wound and tried to inspect it, but Giuseppe took advantage of this lack of concentration. He stepped forward deliberately, and Jane heard the hiss of the whip being wielded three times in rapid succession – *crack crack, crack*. All three strokes caught Antonio in the tender area under his left arm, at the top of the ribcage. The flesh split and opened to reveal white bone beneath.

Antonio screamed in agony and in a temper started lashing this way and that, trying to land a blow on his brother's unprotected body. Giuseppe was amazingly fast; what he lacked in muscle power he made up for in lithe athleticism. He skipped neatly from side to side, avoiding every stroke of his opponent's whip, frustrating the user even more. Antonio went into a blind rage, thrashing away at the air, sometimes striking the walls of the stalls, or one of the centreposts. His fury was evident in his face, which was twisted with anger, as he failed repeatedly to land a single blow on his younger brother.

Then Giuseppe tripped backwards over a bucket and fell to the ground. With a yell of triumph, Antonio was on him, the whip lashing down several times. But Giuseppe had his right arm raised, warding off the blows, and he managed to parry most, so that only one or two were in any way effective.

Finally, Antonio threw down the whip and reached for a pitchfork resting against one of the stalls. It seemed to be what Giuseppe had been waiting for. He leapt to his feet and the buggy whip lashed out, slashing Antonio's fingers. The older brother withdrew his hand from the haft of the pitchfork with a terrible yell. Giuseppe stepped closer to him, and began to lash his body with a series of quick, hard strokes that had Antonio trying to protect his chest, stomach and back with his arms. He was openly sobbing now, with the occasional scream as the thong of the whip bit deeper than usual into his body.

Antonio fell to the floor amongst the dung and straw. Still Giuseppe did not stop hitting him, causing criss-crossed striations to appear over his brother's shoulder-blades and lower back, but carefully avoiding his face, neck and head. Antonio squirmed and let out renewed shrieks under the attack as Giuseppe moved around him, carefully placing each new stroke so that it landed somewhere new on the wriggling body.

Jane could see Giuseppe's face now. It was devoid of any emotion. His features were hard and uncompromising. He continued to deliver the strokes deliberately and efficiently, as if he were thrashing a sheaf of corn. The whip was making a *swack* sound now as it bit into the writhing figure on the floor of the stable.

Jane shouted through the slit, 'No more, Giuseppe. Please, please, don't hit him any more.'

Giuseppe looked up to where she was calling from. Another person stepped out of the shadows and into her view now. Two more people. They were stable hands, presumably guarding the doors in case anyone heard Antonio's cries and came to the stables to investigate. One of them reached for the whip in Giuseppe's hand and made a motion towards the door. Giuseppe looked down on the sobbing Antonio and nodded to the groom, relinquishing his grip on the buggy whip. Then he strode through the stalls and out of Jane's view. A few moments later she heard his voice below her.

'You'd better come down from there,' he said.

Jane allowed him to help her from the barrel.

'What are you doing, watching men fight? This was for me and my brother to settle.'

Jane said, 'I wanted to make sure you didn't come to too much harm. It was over me – over what Antonio had tried to do to me.'

'Not entirely,' said Giuseppe. 'This has been building up for a long time – ever since we were children. Antonio was always threatening to whip me, so I gave him his chance. Well, he found out that the soft life in the city renders you a poor opponent when it comes to such fights. He's a weak man anyway. He might have a bully's body, but he has a weak man's mind.'

'What about the stable hands? Won't they tell Cesare, or Maria?'

'No, they won't say anything. This was between Antonio and myself. No one else is involved.'

Jane said, 'You keep saying that, but there are other people involved. *I'm* involved, however much you say I'm not. I *am*.'

'Does it bother you? Would you rather I hadn't whipped him?'

Jane thought for only a moment before surprising even herself with the reply. 'No,' she said fiercely. 'I wanted him to suffer. He frightened me badly tonight. He needed someone to warn him off, because I'm sure he would have tried it again, if not with me then with some other woman; perhaps a young girl not as able to protect herself as I was. Perhaps he'll think twice now before trying to rape someone.'

Giuseppe put his hands on her shoulders and looked into her eyes. 'Are you hurt in any way? Did he . . .'

'No, really, he didn't manage it. I got away from him before he could. But I'm shaken up inside.'

'I can feel you trembling. You must go to bed. You've had a shock. I'll send one of my sisters to you.'

'No,' Jane said, 'don't do that. I'll be all right. Thank you . . . thank you for helping me, Giuseppe.'

'Go to your room now. I'll see you in the morning. He'll be gone by then.'

'Are you sure?'

Giuseppe laughed. 'Do you think he's going to be able to face you over the breakfast table after a beating like that? He knows you saw it. He'll be so humiliated he won't want to see anyone for a while.'

'What about his wife? Won't she cause trouble? She's bound to see his wounds.'

'I doubt it. She does whatever Antonio tells her to, and he won't want this to go any further.'

Jane nodded and made her way towards the villa. The sound of chirruping crickets still rose from the gardens and the crevices of the house. A horse whinnied noisily, but the stables had gone remarkably quiet now. Just before she climbed the steps to the villa, she called to Giuseppe, 'He'll hate you now, won't he?'

Giuseppe smiled and shrugged. 'He hated me anyway.'

Chapter Twenty

In mid-September of 1920, Courtney returned home by train to Stanton Manor. He was not expected, since his regiment had gone to Ireland. His father demanded an explanation. Courtney faced his father across the breakfast table. Stephen was in reluctant attendance.

'I'm not interested in a career in the army any longer,' said Courtney. 'I've handed in my resignation.'

Sir Charles looked as if he had been physically struck. 'You've what?' he said, utter disbelief in his tone.

Stephen, on the same side of the table as Courtney, moved a little away from his brother, as if anticipating a storm which might engulf him as well if he did not take steps to protect himself.

Courtney sighed. He knew he was going to experience stiff opposition to his resignation from the army, especially from his father, but he was determined to go through with it. He had had his fill of the military, and he wanted to get down to full-time painting. This aspect too was going to cause some controversy between members of the family.

'I can't put it any more plainly,' he said. 'I've resigned from the army.'

'I don't understand,' said Sir Charles. 'Why have you resigned? Have you done something wrong?'

'No, I haven't embezzled the officer's mess funds, or anything like that. I've just had enough of the army. I don't want to make it a career. I've done my bit.'

Stephen said, 'I think he means what he says, Father.'

'But,' protested Sir Charles, 'it *is* your career. You have no other, do you? What do you intend to do? Go into the Church? Join the diplomatic corps? Politics, perhaps? You're not suited to any of them you know. You're a born soldier . . .'

'No, father,' said Courtney, *'you're* the born soldier, not me. It was *your* career. I want to paint.'

'Paint?' there was a bewildered expression on the old man's face.

'I want to paint pictures, become an artist.'

'But you haven't had any training for that sort of thing. You can't just pick up a brush and be another Rubens, you know. One needs talent, inspiration, that sort of thing. Good Lord boy . . .'

'Father,' snapped Courtney, 'I'm not a *boy*, I'm a man. Of course I don't expect to become a major artist overnight, but I have sought advice, and the kind of advice I get is that talent is not the most important aspect of it all – though I think I have a little of that too – but hard work is the necessary ingredient. Hard work and persistence. Dedication. I intend to dedicate myself to my painting.'

'Do you now?' thundered Sir Charles. 'And how do you propose to live during this dedicated period?'

Courtney glanced at Stephen and was surprised to find a lack of support in that direction. His older brother frowned and shook his head a little, as if to say, 'Don't pursue this, Courtney', but Courtney was too far in now. He could not drop the matter, nor could he retreat. He had to see the thing through to its conclusion.

'Why, I have a little money coming, Father, when I reach the age of thirty.

'There is no money,' growled Sir Charles.

There was silence between them for a few moments, then Stephen said quietly, 'What Father means, Courtney, is that the estates are in trouble. We were stung for some pretty stiff taxes last year – and the year before – which are the result of accumulated problems incurred by our grandfather. We've gone into debt with the bank, and we're relying on rents and crop-yields this year just to make ends meet.'

Courtney was stunned by this announcement. 'We're broke?' he questioned.

Sir Charles had lost his florid pallor and was now a little calmer. It was a calmness that revealed a lot of misery beneath his normally bluff exterior. For the first time in his life, Courtney felt sorry for his father. Sir Charles looked like a beaten old man, hammered down by unseen forces.

Sir Charles said, 'What your brother has said is true. I don't like to use slang words like "broke" but I suppose it's as good a phrase as any. The estate is mortgaged up to the hilt, and beyond, and Stephen is struggling to make the farmlands pay for their existence. We're being whittled down to nothing. Each year the taxes get worse, and our income just isn't keeping up. We've sold off some of the northern pasture-land, but we can't keep selling. We're almost tenant farmers ourselves now.'

'Not quite as bad as that yet, Father,' said Stephen, 'but we're heading that way.'

'But surely,' Courtney said, 'we can start to make a profit soon? I mean, food is essential. Everyone wants it.'

Stephen replied, 'You never were much good at the practical side of management, Courtney. Food might be essential, but you have to sell it in a very competitive market. The colonies, Australia and New Zealand, are producing more meat than the country needs. They're strong on dairy produce, too, now that refrigerated ships are running between continents. Cheap beef is coming in from South America. Agricultural products will still sell, but they don't make a vast amount of money. The only thing that seems to be constant is the rise in taxes.'

'So we really are in trouble,' Courtney said.

'Yes, we are,' said Sir Charles, 'so you see why it's essential that you remain in the army?'

Courtney felt his hackles rise. 'No, I damn well don't. I'm not going to make enough money as a captain in the army to save the family fortune. I said I'd resigned and I meant it. I'm going to paint, Father, and that's that, whether I starve doing it or not.'

'Very melodramatic, but not at all reasonable.'

'It's reasonable to me. You did want you wanted to do: you went into the army and had a glorious time. Now I want to follow my dreams, not yours. Stephen here seems stuck on the land . . .'

'I *like* what I do,' said Stephen.

'Well, good,' continued Courtney. 'Good for you, but if you

wanted to take up ballet, I would still say good for you, go and do it. I want to like what I do, too. I don't think that's unreasonable at all.'

Courtney stood up, just as his mother was entering the breakfast room.

'And how *are* you going to keep yourself?' said Sir Charles. 'It's a serious question.'

'I don't know yet,' replied Courtney, 'I'll give it a great deal of thought.'

Courtney went upstairs to his room and dressed in his riding clothes. He felt he needed to get out into the fresh air, to be able to think. He went to the stables, saddled his mare, and then rode out into the undulating farmlands that surrounded Stanton Manor. He allowed the horse to canter at first, but then slowed it to a walk so that he could contemplate the beauty of the countryside and consider carefully what he should do in the near future.

The horse followed the line of ditches up hill and down into the shallow valleys between, skirting oaks and hawthorns. At noon, Courtney was no nearer to a solution to his problem than when he had started out, but the ride was pleasant enough, and it had taken him far beyond lands that belonged to his family. Suddenly, as he reached the brow of a rise, he heard voices on the wind, saw colourful figures in the fields ahead of him. He stood ln his stirrups to get a better view, and realised he was staring in the direction of Henley Transon's land.

Curious, he spurred his mount on to investigate.

When he arrived at the saffron fields, they were full of gypsies, picking the crocus flowers. So far as Courtney was aware, Henley was in the Far East and Jane in Italy. What were all these people doing in Jane's fields?

'Hey there,' he called to a woman. 'What's going on here? Who's in charge?'

'The master's up there,' returned the woman. 'Go on to the end if you want to see him.'

Courtney put his mount into a trot. Soon he reached the top of the fields where the carts were waiting to take away the bundles of flower heads. Standing by the carts with a clipboard, was a man Courtney vaguely recognised. At first glance he looked like a gypsy with his swarthy skin, but then his clothes were smarter and tailored to a modern style and not gypsy men. When he looked up, Courtney saw that he had startlingly blue eyes.

Courtney dismounted and led his mount up to him. 'Don't I know you?' he said.

The man looked up again and frowned; it was then that Courtney recognised him. Petre Peake, the intruder at Wildrose Cottage that time. The man who had warned Courtney to stay away from Jane.

'Yes,' nodded Courtney, answering the question himself, 'we had a bit of a do last year, at the Transon place.'

'That we did,' confirmed Peake with a tight mouth. 'Can I help you now?'

'Yes, you can. You can start by telling me what you're doing with the Transon land?'

'What's it to you? What business is it of yours?'

Courtney said, 'The business of a neighbour who has been asked to watch over things. Now, do you give me an explanation, or do I fetch the police? Miss Transon isn't here, and neither is her father, so I can only assume you're trespassing.'

For a moment Courtney thought that Peake was going to hit him, because the man's eyes darkened and there was a look of action about him. However, he must have thought better of it, because he rocked back on his heels before answering.

'It's true I'm here without permission.' He waved at the activity around him. 'I thought it was a shame that the land should be left to go to waste when it was producing good saffron. I've consulted Saltash, of Coleman's Seed Company, and he's agreed we should continue to farm the land in the absence of the owners.'

'And the money you receive for the saffron?'

Peake's face hardened again. 'It goes into an account of course, at the bank, ready for Jane's return from Italy.'

Courtney felt a bolt of jealousy go through him. 'You know she's in Italy?'

Peake smiled now. 'Yes, of course. We're not in constant communication. She's not the world's greatest letter writer. But I know where she is, and I know that she would prefer the land to be put to use while she's away. I'm not keeping anything for myself, you know, even though Henley Transon is in my debt to the tune of – well, a few thousand pounds. It's all going into an account for Jane.'

Courtney saw by the other man's eyes that this was true.

'Why? What do you get out of it?' he asked, almost afraid of what the answer would be.

Peake's face hardened. 'I don't want anything out of it at all. I'm doing it for her. Only for her. You can understand that, can't you?'

'I can understand that,' said Courtney, quietly. 'I wish I'd thought of it. It's a very laudable thing to do, even though you do have a motive.'

'What motive?'

'You know very well,' replied Courtney. 'It would be my motive, if I were you.'

He mounted his horse now and nodded his farewell. Then he was off, galloping beside the hedgerow, allowing the horse to get some wind around its ears and himself some distance between himself and his rival. When he stopped his mount, he knew he was still upset. There was a hotness behind his eyes which was very irritating to him. He tried not to think too hard about how he stood with Jane, because he knew the answer inside-out His mother had told him that, when she had accidentally disclosed his plans for marriage to Jane, Jane had immediately asked to leave Stanton Manor.

'She was most put out,' Lady Constance had told him. 'She seemed quite anxious to get away.'

He might not have believed his mother, except that the proof was in the pudding: Jane *had* left for Italy.

'Well, damn Peake and good luck to him,' said Courtney, patting the neck of his horse. 'If she loves him, then there's an end to it all, but I'm damned if I'm going to give up my friendship with Jane until I hear wedding bells, whoever they're for, and that's a fact.'

Sheba whinnied in agreement.

When he arrived back at the manor, Courtney was still no clearer about how he was going to manage financially.

Chapter Twenty-one

The gathering of the saffron croci was in full swing, and Jane had no time for thoughts of home. She was busy from the moment the cockerel first cleared its throat, to when the last lights were put out in the evening. Every night she fell into bed exhausted, not concerned any longer about whether she was earning her keep. She knew she was, if not through expertise, then through sheer hard physical toil. Being an overseer did not exempt her from manual labour.

The lilac-hued flower heads were bundled into bales and were taken to the washing sheds, where they were lightly beaten with sticks and then immersed in tanks of water. This caused the chives to drop to the bottom of the tank. They were then gathered and placed on drying racks in kilns and turned into bricks of saffron. The saffron was not as pure as that which Jane had produced with her hand-picked chives, but it was commercially valuable none the less; and what the Buccino saffron lacked in quality, it made up for in quantity, for the vast numbers of acres yielded huge amounts of saffron and the harvest was enormous.

At dinner each evening, everyone talked saffron.

'In early times,' Giuseppe told Jane, 'saffron was mostly cultivated in Persia in Asia Minor. Then the Arabs brought it to Spain. By the thirteenth century, it was worth more than its weight in gold.'

'Before that it was grown in Kashmir, and the Mongols discovered it and introduced it into China. It's mentioned in the *Pun Tsaou*, the ancient Chinese book of medicine. It's still the world's most valuable spice, of course,' added Cesare as he tucked into his pasta.

Jane felt she was part of some secret society, some special group, and it was intensely exciting. She was a saffron grower – a 'croker', as they had once been called in Essex – and hers was the magical knowledge of the wonderful spice. Even the word 'spice' sounded exotic, lying alongside such words as pearls, ivory, diamonds, silk. It was a word which was weighed carefully and in small amounts, like gold-dust, to be treasured by the purchaser. Giuseppe had shown her the biblical verses of the *Song of Solomon*, which read: 'Spikenard and saffron; calamus and cinnamon, with all trees of frankincense; myrrh and aloes, with all the chief spices.' A chief spice! And she was a chief spice-grower. She felt special.

The villa was a pleasant place once more, now that Antonio and his wife had returned to Rome. If Cesare knew why his eldest son had left so suddenly, he did not mention it. Neither did Maria. Jane felt it was a sad thing that a baby could grow into such a man, to disappoint his parents, to make the world an uglier place. Still, she could forget him. It was doubtful that Antonio would return while she was still at the villa. Giuseppe had thrashed his brother so soundly that Antonio had had difficulty in walking to his car the next day.

Giuseppe and Jane did not talk of the incident again, at Jane's request.

One evening, when the frenetic days of the crocus harvest were almost over and they could begin to relax a little, Jane and Giuseppe were sitting on the balcony of the villa, looking down on the fields.

'How long are you going to stay?' asked Giuseppe. 'I suppose you must think of going home sometime?'

Jane thought about this for a while. 'I don't know,' she said at last. 'Though my father is in Hong Kong, there are people I would like to see, people I miss. You've all been very good to me here, but as the old saying goes, there's no place like home. I shan't go yet, though. I want to prove myself here with at least one more harvest.'

'You've already proved yourself.'

'It's nice of you to say so, but I still feel like an amateur – I *am* an amateur. There's still a lot to learn. Oh, I know I can go back home and make a good job of growing saffron, but I want to be an *expert*.'

Giuseppe laughed. 'Well, you can stay here as long as you like as far as I'm concerned, so long as you are not missing your relations too much. You English are not like the Italians in that respect. We miss our people.'

'Oh, I do miss them,' said Jane. She thought of something. 'Wait here. I'll show you a photograph of my father.'

She left him on the balcony and went to her room. Still in her suitcase, away from prying eyes, was a framed photograph of her father and herself, Uncle Matthew, Aunt Sybil, Nancy and Jonathan, taken on her eighteenth birthday.

When she returned to the balcony, Giuseppe had turned up the lamp and the light was brighter. She sat down beside him and began pointing to the figures in the photograph.

'This is my father. Do you think I look like him?'

'No, you look more like this man,' said Giuseppe, pointing to Uncle Matthew.

'Oh, well, he's my father's brother. It often happens like that, doesn't it? One turns out looking like a cousin or an aunt, rather than one's immediate family.'

Suddenly, Giuseppe snatched the picture from her and stared hard at it, under the light.

'Who is this?' he said, quietly but with excitement in his voice.

She tried to see which of the figures he was pointing to. It looked like Jonathan.

'That's my young cousin, Jonathan.'

'A girl named *Jonathan*?' cried Giuseppe.

Jane laughed out loud. 'No, no. The girl in the picture, that's my other cousin, Nancy. She's sixteen there.' Jane realised Nancy's birthday had just passed. 'Nineteen now,' she added.

'She's beautiful,' breathed Giuseppe.

Jane made a face. 'Oh, really? I suppose she's quite nice. A bit of a wallflower, though, because she's so shy.'

'I like shy women,' said Giuseppe firmly, still staring at the photograph and seeming unwilling to let it go. 'I think shy women are like – like princesses.'

Jane managed to get the photograph out of Giuseppe's fingers with difficulty. She stared at her cousin's features, trying to see them through Giuseppe's eyes. Yes, Nancy was quite pretty in those days. Perhaps she was *beautiful* now? Obviously she had made a big hit with Giuseppe, who was now plying Jane with dozens of questions.

'Where does she live?'

'On the edge of London.'

'Is she betrothed? Spoken for?'

'Neither, as far as I know.' Jane didn't care to go into the details of what had happened between Nancy and Courtney, because she didn't really know herself, but also because it seemed that any romance was now over in any case.

'I should like to be betrothed to such a girl,' said Giuseppe.

Jane felt things were going a bit too fast.

'Hold on, hold on, Giuseppe. You mean to say you haven't seen or met one woman in the flesh you could love, yet here you are proclaiming undying love to a *picture*? It doesn't make sense. You don't even know Nancy. She might be a monster.'

'How could someone who looks like an angel be a monster?' remonstrated Giuseppe. 'Don't even speak of such a thing. She is all I ever wanted. That hair, those eyes . . .'

Jane stared at the photograph again. 'Surely,' she argued, 'you have to like her as a *person* too?'

'It cannot fail,' said Giuseppe firmly. 'I can feel it in my heart. I *know* we could be happy together. She is the woman of my dreams. I have seen her, spoken with her, a thousand times in my fantasies . . .'

He continued to rhapsodise in this fashion for a long time, revealing to Jane the difference between Italian lovers and their English counterparts. She could not imagine Petre or Courtney using the phrases that Giuseppe was employing at the moment. They would rather die. It would be nice, she thought, if someone were to drool over her in this way. It sounded so romantic in Italian, too. Like something out of an opera.

'So what are we going to do about this great love you've found?' said Jane practically. 'Shall I write and tell Nancy to come out for a holiday or something? You might find you loathe her on sight.'

'In that case, I don't want to see her,' said Giuseppe. 'I shall have this photograph to keep by me for all my life.'

'No you won't' said Jane, clutching her property. 'This is mine.'

Giuseppe stared at her for a moment, as if she were trying to come between him and his newly discovered love, then he nodded emphatically. 'When you return to England,' he said. 'I shall go with you and meet this angel.'

'What happens if someone else thinks she's an angel in the meantime and beats you to her?'

'In that case, I shall mourn for what I have lost. Have you no soul, Jane? This has to be done slowly and carefully, so that the dream remains intact. Dreams are flimsy. One has to be delicate. I must spend time with the idea that the woman of my dreams is actually alive, somewhere, waiting for me.'

'Waiting for you?'

'I think so. I think so,' he said, seriously.

Jane was both amused and astounded by Giuseppe's conviction that fate had presented him with his future wife. It seemed so ludicrous to her that he should fall in love with a picture in which the figure and features of her cousin Nancy were not even terribly clear. It was as if he had been taken by storm, by the *idea* of Nancy, rather than by the person. However, who was she to criticise? She knew less about romance than she did about growing saffron croci.

Over the next few months, through Christmas and New Year, Jane remained at the villa, working with the children's English and any other task which presented itself. Soon enough the season was on them again, and she was thrown into the work once more. During this time she began to become increasingly more lonely, which she decided was strange because she had Giuseppe and others to keep her company. One day she rode out into the hills, took a dusty path through the evergreens, and dismounted on a high place.

Below her, she could see the red roofs of individual villas scattered over the plain, sometimes guarded by cypresses. Here and there a village sprouted from a clutch of shrubs and low trees, terracotta and whitewash, brilliant in the sun. To the west there were rows of vines strapped to wooden crosses: a scene which echoed faintly an Ancient Roman punishment. A blue patch of water, a lake or reservoir, nestled in a pocket on a stretch of undulating ground.

The warm air from the plain blew dusty and perfumed with oleander, up the slopes, to stir Jane's hair and clothes. Moments like this were rewards for her hard work in the fields and she wished someone like Courtney were there to share it with her: he would have enjoyed painting such a scene, while she sat idly by, sipping a cool drink and watching him.

She shook herself, deciding this was a foolish dream.

She sat on a rock, holding the reins of her horse, allowing the heat of the early afternoon to make her drowsy. A field hand on his way from work in another valley, crossing by the high road, walked by with an adze on his shoulder. He stared at Jane curiously and when she smiled his face broke into a grin. He touched his straw hat, murmured, 'Good day,' and walked on.

What a nice people, she thought. *What a wonderful country. What a shame I was not born Italian.* As an Englishwoman she could appreciate the country, be friends with its people, but she could never be part of it, one of them. She would always *feel* outsider, even if she stayed long enough for them to forget where she was born and bred. It was evident to her that one could assimilate aspects of another culture, with time, but to be thoroughly native one had to be immersed in a place from birth.

After a long rest she mounted her mare and took the dirt road down to the hot plain below.

It was not until the spring of 1922 that she decided to go home again. Giuseppe was still intent on going with her, and the preparations were made. Cesare and Maria were disappointed that Jane and Giuseppe were not in love, but were delighted that Giuseppe had his eye on another woman. They had hopes he would bring a wife back to Italy. Jane wasn't so sure. Giuseppe was a fine-looking young man, but there was no guarantee that Nancy would fall for him. Even now she might be courting someone else, someone from her own area. And then there was Courtney; Nancy might still be carrying a torch for him. It was all in the melting pot so far as Jane was concerned.

On the day they were to depart, Maria was in tears.

'Goodbye, Maria,' said Jane, hugging her. '*Arrivederci*. I'll miss you. You've been like a second mother to me.'

Maria stemmed her tears and gave Jane a reproachful look. 'I *want* to be a second mother to you.' She looked significantly in Giuseppe's direction and then back at Jane. 'You know what I mean.'

Jane shook her head sadly. 'I do know what you mean, but

Giuseppe and I don't love each other. Sad, but true. We'll always be good friends, though: you can count on seeing me again.'

Cesare, standing nearby, said, 'There's no doubt about that, Jane. This is your second home. You come to us whenever you're feeling bad. We want you here, remember that.'

'I'll remember,' said Jane, getting a little sniffy herself now. 'You're very kind.'

'Not kind, we like you. We do it for selfish reasons. We like having you near us.'

So Jane and Giuseppe were driven to the railway station where they were to take the train to Venice. Jane watched the saffron fields flash past the car in silence. Giuseppe, for whom this was the beginning of an adventure, not the end of one, understood her feelings and left her to muse.

Chapter Twenty-two

Jane found going home almost as exciting as leaving for Italy, but not quite. They did not travel by the Orient Express, though they had first-class tickets on the ordinary trains. It took longer. The sea crossing was calm, however, and Jane was thankful for that. On arrival in London, Jane telephoned Matthew and Sybil, explaining that she was in the company of Giuseppe and they needed somewhere to stay. Could they come to Green Lanes?

'I can't take Giuseppe back to Wildrose Cottage, Uncle, it wouldn't look right. The villagers would gossip. And in any case, the place must be damp. It's been unlived-in for nearly two years now.'

'No, of course you can't take him to the cottage,' said her uncle Matthew in a shocked voice, 'that wouldn't do at all. I'm just surprised you're travelling together, but then you always were an unconventional girl, and since you're not my daughter, I can't tell you what to do. This Giuseppe, can't he stay in an hotel?'

Jane obviously did not want to tell Matthew the real reason for taking Giuseppe to his house: in order that the Italian could make romantic love to his daughter. That might shock him to the very core of his correctness.

Jane said, 'Well, of course he *could* go into an hotel, but that wouldn't be very hospitable. Don't forget the Buccino family has put up with me for a long time.'

'His father's a count you say?'

Jane smiled to herself, picturing her uncle on the other end. Matthew was a very cautious man, who would do anything for 'family', but was wary of strangers. Most men, especially salesmen looking for business opportunities, would have jumped at the

257

thought of entertaining the son of an Italian nobleman in their own home. The story alone would be worth something when they were on the road.

'Yes, Uncle, his father is Count Buccino, a wealthy Florentine, with a huge house and millions of acres of land. He won't steal anything.'

Matthew's voice was stiff. 'I never suggested he would, Jane.'

'I was teasing you, Uncle. Can we come?'

'Of course you can come.' The voice changed now and was charged with a tone of pride. 'I shall pick you up from the station in my new car.'

'You have a car?'

'Yes, as Senior Sales Manager I'm given a motor car. It's an Austin Tourer.'

'Uncle, how wonderful. You must be very pleased. We'll see you in about an hour.'

Uncle Matthew was at the station when they arrived. Jane introduced them.

'Uncle, this is Signor Giuseppe Buccino. Giuseppe, this my uncle, Mr Matthew Transon.'

Giuseppe gave Matthew a short bow before shaking hands. 'I am very pleased to meet you, Mr Transon. You are very kind to come to the station.'

Matthew huffed a little. 'Oh, no trouble, no trouble. You must call me Matthew.'

'So,' smiled Giuseppe, 'and I am Giuseppe.'

'Right,' said Matthew, 'now we've got all that sorted out, let's get you back to the house. You must both be very tired.' He turned to Jane. 'Your aunt Sybil has made up a bed for you in Nancy's room. Giuseppe will have the guest room, of course.'

Outside the station, Matthew paused, presumably to let Jane guess which of the cars parked outside were his. There were only three. One was a sports car, quite unsuitable for a travelling salesman. Another was too big. Jane went up the most obvious of the three and saw by the words on the front that it was indeed an Austin Tourer.

'Uncle, it's beautiful.'

Matthew beamed. 'Yes, isn't it? I've worked hard for that beast. Twenty-three years with the same firm. Still, I've made it.'

'Yes, Senior Sales Manager. You must be very pleased – and Aunt Sybil quite proud of you.'

'I think she is. I think she is.'

The drive to the house was slow and careful, with Matthew continually swivelling his head to see what else was on the roads and where the dangers to his wonderful motor car might lie. He was particularly wary of horse-drawn vehicles, because, as he explained to his passengers, animals were unpredictable, and not like machines at all.

Jane noticed that there were far more cars on the road than when she had left for Italy. She said to Matthew, 'But surely, the motor cars have an animal driving them?'

'What?' asked Matthew. 'How do you mean?'

'Well, men are animals, aren't they?'

Matthew said he would have to think about that statement, which was difficult while driving and concentrating on the road. It wasn't easy, he told them, to go at twenty miles an hour *and* talk to his passengers. That was how accidents happened.

Finally he said, 'Biologically speaking, man is an animal, yes, Jane. But we're not as stupid as horses, are we?'

'I think sometimes we are even more stupid,' said Giuseppe, but Matthew let this radical statement slide away without further argument, because they were entering Green Lanes.

Aunt Sybil must have been waiting at the curtains, because the door flew open to reveal her presence, and then her arms flew open in a visual echo of the movement.

'Jane, my dear.' She came down the steps, still with open arms.

Jane got out of the car and allowed her aunt to hug her fiercely.

'Hello, Auntie. How are you? How are Nancy and Jonathan?'

The very last part of the question was answered immediately, when a tall young man appeared in the doorway at the top of the steps. Jonathan had climbed upwards a good twelve inches since Jane had last seen him, and was now a willowy sixteen-year-old with a smile almost as wide as his mother's. He came down the steps and shook hands very formally with Jane, saying, 'Nice to see you again, cuz.'

'Cuz? Is that me? No hugs for your *cuz*, then? We shake hands, do we?' asked Jane, laughing.

'Don't embarrass him, Jane,' said Matthew. 'He's at that age when all young females are threatening. He's still an awkward young stripling.'

'I am not,' said Jonathan hotly. 'I'm virtually a man now.'

To let Jonathan get over his self-consciousness, Jane then introduced Giuseppe to Sybil, and then to Jonathan himself. The Italian was charming, giving Sybil an effusive smile and telling her that she looked 'quite lovely', causing Matthew to swing round and stare at his wife.

'Yes, Uncle,' said Jane, amused, 'it's Aunt Sybil he's talking about. You just take her for granted.'

Matthew looked slightly affronted. 'No, no. I think she's, er, quite lovely, too. It's just that I don't get the opportunity to tell her so, these days, what with the pressure of work and all that.'

'Of course you don't, dear,' said Sybil, bestowing a kiss on her husband's cheek. 'I know you think I'm lovely.'

In the meantime, Giuseppe shook hands with Jonathan and said very seriously, 'I am most pleased to meet you, Mr Transon. I have heard a great deal about you from your cousin, Jane. She tells me you are good at hunting and fishing?'

That was not what Jane had said – she had told Giuseppe that Jonathan was mad about killing things – but she could see that the Italian was trying to win friends quickly.

Jonathan looked suitably pleased. 'Well, I used to do it a lot, but not so much lately.'

'Indeed. But if you ever come to Italy, and I urge you to do so, you may stay with my family. I shall show you some hunting you will not forget for a long time.'

Jonathan's face lit up. 'Really? Well, that's awfully good of you, isn't it, Mother? Gosh. When?'

Matthew laughed. 'Not so eager, son. Giuseppe's just being polite.'

'No, I really mean it,' said Giuseppe, 'but we can discuss it later, when we have more time.'

'Where's Nancy?' asked Jane.

Sybil said, 'Oh, she's at work of course. Didn't you know? Nancy works in Harrods, in the perfume department. Quite a coup, getting work in Harrods, you know.'

Jane thought it was a waste of a good education to settle for being a shop assistant, but didn't say so because she knew it would upset her aunt and uncle.

As they went up the steps into the house, Jane whispered to Giuseppe, 'What happened to that *shy* Italian that I met in Molina eighteen months ago?'

'Me?' he whispered back. 'This is my *life* I am fighting for now. I have no time to be shy.'

'Faint heart never won fair lady, eh?'

'Exactly, Jane. You are a very clever woman. I would not have thought to put it like that.'

She had no time to tell him that she had simply used an English cliché, because they were taken upstairs and shown their rooms. Giuseppe said he would like to freshen up before he did anything else. Matthew showed him where the bathroom was and then took Jane back downstairs to talk.

While Giuseppe was in the bathroom, Jane chattered about her time in Italy, telling them just who Giuseppe was and all about his family. She did mention Antonio, and that she did not get on with him, but did not go into details. All three of her relatives were suitably impressed by her descriptions of the villa and its occupants. By the time Giuseppe appeared again, they had a good picture of where and how he lived.

Jane then went to the bathroom, bathed, changed into some fresh clothes, and then rejoined the others in the living room.

At six-thirty there was the sound of a key in the lock and then of someone in the hall. 'Hello everyone, I'm home,' called a voice.

A few moments later, Nancy entered the room. Jane was astonished at the change in her cousin. Nancy looked bright-eyed and confident, not at all like the shy young woman she had been at eighteen. Her hair was cut short and stylishly, the suit she wore was smart and fashionable, and her make-up had been applied with care. She looked chic and sophisticated. Jane wondered what Giuseppe was going to think of this cosmopolitan young woman who had appeared in place of the shy sixteen-year-old he had fallen for in the old photograph. She quickly stole a glance at the Italian.

Giuseppe was, however, looking entranced. He rose to his feet as Matthew made the introductions, and shook Nancy's hand, his eyes never leaving her face. For her part Nancy looked happy to meet Giuseppe, but then announced that she had to leave them all because she had a date to go to the pictures.

Giuseppe looked crestfallen. 'Ah, you have a young man,' he said. 'Congratulations.'

Nancy laughed. 'No, I'm going with a friend from work, to see a Buster Keaton film. Do you know Buster? He's wonderful. Buster's a comedian, like Charlie Chaplin.'

'I have never been to the cinema,' admitted Giuseppe.

Nancy's eyes widened. 'Never been to the pictures? Then you must come with Jill and me tonight – and you, Jane.'

'Can I come too?' said Jonathan.

'No, you can't. This is adults only,' replied Nancy a little unkindly. 'How about it, Jane?'

Jane did not particularly want to go to the cinema, because she was feeling the effects of the journey, but she knew that Giuseppe wanted her to go with him. He needed her support to woo this cosmopolitan Nancy who worked in Harrods and talked of film stars as if she knew them personally.

'Fine, yes, I'd love to. How long have we got?'

'About five minutes,' laughed Nancy, dashing out of the room and up the stairs. 'It starts at seven. Come on, shake a leg.'

'What about your dinner, dear?' called Sybil, going to the bottom of the stairs.

'No time for that,' yelled Nancy. 'Sorry, Mum. I'll have something when I come in.'

Jane and Giuseppe fetched their coats. When the others were out of earshot, Jane said to him, 'Changed your mind about your angel? They do grow up, you know.'

'Changed my mind?' he breathed. He turned to look at her, his eyes shining passionately. 'Are you mad? She's like a princess.'

'Angel to princess? Isn't that a sort of drop in status? Sublime Being to Mortal?'

'I don't know what you mean,' replied Giuseppe, who was too love-struck to be teased. 'She's so . . . so—'

'Sophisticated?' said Jane.

'Yes, that's what she is. Sophisticated.'

Jane refused to rise to his mood of seriousness. 'But not at all the little violet you expected, surely? I mean, will she make a good Italian wife? Don't they have to be timid and submissive?'

Giuseppe snorted. 'Good Italian wife – bah! Submissive? Timid? They're all little flowers *before* they wed, but afterwards they soon change. At least I can see what I'm getting before I marry.' He sighed in satisfaction. 'A woman of the world!'

'Yes, she's so urbane she even goes to the cinema,' Jane said with a straight face.

'Yes, exactly,' he answered, as if she had hit the nail on the head.

Her attempts at poking fun at him were all wasted. He was having none of it. The woman of his dreams was not only as beautiful as a princess, she was as worldly as a star of the silver screen. What man could hope for more? Jane only hoped he would not put Nancy on a pedestal, because the Nancy she knew would be quick to take advantage of such a position.

Jane left Giuseppe at the bottom of the stairs, and went up to see Nancy in her room. When she entered, Nancy was changing her stockings. Her cousin looked up and smiled.

'Hello, Jane, who's the boyfriend?'

Jane said, 'Giuseppe isn't my boyfriend – he's just a friend, as you well know.' Despite her earlier ideas on the subject, she decided to come clean straight away. 'In fact, Nancy, I ought to warn you. It's you Giuseppe is interested in.'

Nancy looked up quickly, and Jane could see by her reaction how much her cousin had matured. She didn't go red, or go into a flap. She simply looked a bit taken aback.

'Crikey, that was quick. I don't usually have that sort of effect on men.'

'Yes, well, he saw your photo a few months ago, so it's not all that . . . He's been dying to meet you and since – er – since he had to do business in London, he asked me if I would help him.'

Nancy smoothed down her petticoat thoughtfully. 'No harm in

263

meeting, I suppose,' she said, shrugging her shoulders. Then she stood up and gave Jane a hug. 'But what about you, Jane? Italy! It must have been *really* exciting. Tell me all about it, please, while I get ready?'

Jane did as she was asked, describing her life in Italy while Nancy whizzed around. When Nancy was almost ready, Jane went downstairs to rejoin Giuseppe. Nancy came down immediately afterwards.

'Try not to worship her,' whispered Jane, as Nancy skipped down the stairs, wearing a blue dress and looking even prettier than she had before.

'It will be difficult with such a divine creature,' mumbled Giuseppe, obviously awestruck by this vision descending the stairs as if from heaven, 'but of course you are right. One mustn't prostrate oneself on the altar of beauty, for that would be opening the door to ridicule.'

... stupid, after all. Jane need not have worried. Then again, thought Jane, Nancy may have changed completely. Perhaps the old Nancy was simply a selfish, adolescent version of what appeared before them now? It was possible. There was also the possibility that Nancy might find Giuseppe completely unattractive, so all that adoration would go to waste in any case. This was an aspect which Giuseppe could not afford to entertain if he was to win her, but one which to Jane seemed just as likely as Nancy falling in love with this son of (newly purchased) Italian aristocracy.

The last thing she muttered to him, in Italian, before they left the house was, 'Don't tell her your father bought the title. Not yet, anyway. Save the truth until later.'

'Are you mad?' he muttered back. 'Of course I shan't tell her that it was purchased. She might spit in my eye.'

'What are you two whispering about?' asked Nancy, as they went down the steps. 'Was that Italian?'

'I was saying to your cousin,' replied Giuseppe smiling, 'what an attractive hairstyle you have. It suits you very much.'

Giuseppe is not daft, thought Jane. He's not wading in with purple poetry, but testing the water gently.

Nancy beamed at him. 'D'you really think so? I had it shaped only last week.'

'Charming – on you, of course. It wouldn't suit Jane, because her looks are darker than yours. You seem to have that touch of – of the individual, which most English, and Italian women lack: a personal style that I have witnessed only in the ladies of Paris.'

Thank you, thought Jane, too dark to be stylish, eh? Loyalty had gone out of the door with the entrance of true love, had it? Dark looks were to be betrayed in order to praise the fair? And the ladies of Paris! So far as she knew, the only French women Giuseppe had ever laid eyes on were those he had seen when he leaned out of the window while the train stood in Aix-en-Provence railway station. But of course he knew Nancy would like being compared to the Parisians, who exemplified style.

They met with Nancy's friend, and the four of them went in to the cinema. Giuseppe confessed afterwards that he was not fond of slapstick comedy, but only to Jane, not to Nancy. Jane had to admit that Giuseppe had handled everything very well. He had made an impression on the parents, and had progressed at just the right speed with Nancy.

Jane felt a little guilty, having brought Giuseppe into the household in the full knowledge that he was probably going to woo Nancy. The truth was, Jane had been curious to see how it progressed, and now that it seemed apparent that Giuseppe might possibly achieve his aim, she wondered if she had done the right thing. After all, Giuseppe would take Nancy away from her family, away from her city, away from her country. If Nancy did fall for Giuseppe, get married and go to Italy, would she be happy living there? It was impossible to say. Jane was going to have to bear some of the blame if it did all happen as Giuseppe wished and it resulted in an unhappy Nancy.

Some time later that night, when the women were in bed, Jane asked Nancy what had happened with Courtney.

There was a silence from the other side of the room, and then Nancy said, 'I don't honestly know, Jane. I mean, I told you what he said in his letter to Father. The next time I heard from him, he asked me to forget what he had written previously, because circumstances had changed for him. I mean, he was so *cryptic* over the whole thing. I must have read his letters a hundred times and I still couldn't make up my mind what he actually meant to tell me.'

'Oh dear, I am sorry, Nancy.'

'Oh, don't be sorry. It all worked out for the best anyway. It was only a crush. I was not much more than a schoolgirl and he paid some attention to me. That was all.'

'Well, I'm glad you didn't get too hurt,' said Jane.

'No. I was wounded and puzzled for a while, but I soon got over it. Giuseppe's nice, isn't he. Are you sure you two . . . ?'

Jane said, 'Good heavens, no, I told you. Nothing like that, though his parents wanted us to get together. We're just – well, just good friends, that's all. As I said, it's you he's interested in.'

'But he doesn't even know me.'

'That doesn't seem to matter to him.'

There was silence from the other bed once more and Jane bit her lip, thinking she had knocked things sideways for Giuseppe by revealing his intentions too early, just when he was proceeding at a leisurely pace and doing so well.

'Well?' demanded Nancy at last. 'And now he's met me?'

'I think – I think he still likes what he sees,' said Jane, desperately trying to play it down now.

'You think?'

'I *know*. He told me he thought you were even more beautiful than your picture. It was that one I have of the whole family – when you were sixteen.'

'Did he really say that?'

'Yes. Do you mind?'

Again that infuriating silence, then, 'No, I don't think so. He's not slobbery, is he? I mean, he didn't exactly fling himself all over me. He's – a gentleman.'

'I'm sure he'll go as slowly as you think he ought to. He seems good at judging those sort of things. You won't have to fight him off or anything. You could get rid of him tomorrow, if you wanted to.'

Nancy did not answer this, and after a while Jane guessed she was not going to. The conversation was at an end. Jane felt she had done what she felt was right, which was to warn Nancy that she was the object of this Italian's desire. Now it was up to her cousin to play it whichever way she wanted to.

* * *

The following morning, Nancy went to work before any of the others were even awake. She left a message to say that it would be nice if the three of them could go for a walk along the Thames' embankment. Jane wondered if she was supposed to cry off, but then decided that if Nancy had wanted it that way, she would have left her a separate note in the bedroom. No, Nancy was curious, that was all, about this young suitor that had come all the way from Italy to woo a sixteen-year-old in a photograph. Jane was needed as a chaperon.

When the evening came, the three of them took a bus to the Strand and walked down to Waterloo Bridge and then along the riverside from there. They proceeded westward along the north bank, past Cleopatra's Needle, towards Big Ben and the Houses of Parliament. As they approached Big Ben, Giuseppe stopped at the statue of Queen Boadicea in her chariot and asked who she was, creating a bit of a crisis.

'She was a queen of an ancient British tribe of Celts, called the Iceni,' Jane told him. 'When her husband the king died, the Romans confiscated her lands and raped her and her daughters, so she took up arms against them and slaughtered a whole . . .'

Jane stopped because Giuseppe was looking at her rather strangely. It was then she realised what was the matter. Giuseppe was an Italian and therefore would feel an affinity with the Ancient Romans.

'Italians would not do this,' he said, starchily. 'They do not steal and rape. You are thinking of Norse people. The Viking men.'

'Oh, but they did,' said Nancy. 'Queen Boadicea rallied the British tribes in the region – it was out in Essex, near Colchester – and attacked and destroyed Roman camps.'

'Supposing I believe you. What happened to her?' asked Giuseppe, still in that affronted manner.

'She was eventually killed, north of London, and the rebellion was squashed,' said Jane.

Giuseppe appeared to read the words on the plaque, though Jane was not sure he could read English as well as he spoke it. Finally he stepped back, looked up at the fiery bronze queen in her chariot and shook his head wonderingly. 'I still cannot believe this.'

Jane laughed and said, 'But it was so long ago, Giuseppe. And there weren't even any Italians then, not as such. If you'd been alive then you'd have probably been an Etruscan. They weren't the same people as the Romans. They were much nicer. The Etruscans were very artistic.'

This seemed to salve his wounded pride a little. 'Yes, you are right. I would have been an Etruscan. I never liked the people of Roma very much. They are like my brother, shallow and full of . . . what do you say when people believe owning *glioggetti* is the most important thing, of more value than the spirit of man?'

'Materialism?' suggested Jane.

'Yes, they are like that, like my brother. He prays to his car and his new wireless set.'

This having been settled, they walked on to see Big Ben, the Houses of Parliament and Westminster Abbey. Giuseppe was suitably impressed by all he saw, and the Victorian idea of Boadicea was soon forgotten.

Perhaps it was Jane's imagination, but Nancy seemed to be very attentive to Giuseppe, studying his gestures and listening to his every word. It was to Nancy he turned for information about Westminster Abbey and the people who were buried there. Though her knowledge was somewhat limited, Nancy did her best to satisfy his curiosity, and seemed to enjoy doing so.

On the way back to the bus stop, via Trafalgar Square, the girls walked one on either side of Giuseppe, with an arm through each of his. They steered him along Whitehall and marched him up to the fountains. There he insisted on throwing a coin into the water, saying it was an Etruscan custom. Then they went home.

In bed that night, Nancy said to Jane, 'He's very nice. I don't know. I don't know what to do.'

'Just take things as they come. He's not expecting you to fall in love with him immediately,' said Jane. 'If you think it's not going to work out at any time, then break it to him gently and send him home.'

'But I don't want to hurt him. I mean, I've been thinking about it. What if I *did* like him – enough to marry him if he asked me – what then? I'd have to go and live in Italy, wouldn't I? He wouldn't come to live here.'

'I suppose so, yes.'

'But would I like it in Italy, Jane?'

'Well, I did, but I was only there for a relatively short time. I mean, you'd be there for life, so you've got to be sure about it. You wouldn't see a great deal of your mum and dad, or your brother. It would be a great adventure in the beginning, but that would wear off in time. You'd have to love him an awful lot, I suppose – unless the idea of living in a foreign country really attracts you. It does some people. There are women who would give their eye-teeth to be in your position – a wealthy, aristocratic Italian ready to sweep you off your feet and carry you back to his estate on the slopes of the Apennines!'

'I'm not the sort to go into ecstasies about a foreign country. We had a girl at our school who was absolutely desperate to get to Japan: I never understood why.'

Jane said, 'I think I can understand it. If you're captivated by the culture of another race, then perhaps going to live in their country is perhaps your idea of heaven? I don't feel like that about anywhere else, myself. I think I could live abroad permanently, but it wouldn't matter where, so long as there was lots of sunshine. Otherwise, I might as well live in England, which I like too.'

Nancy sighed and shuffled in her sheets. 'I don't know. I'll have to think about it some more. I suppose there's no chance he'll change his mind, now we've had another evening together?'

'I don't think so. Did you see how animated he was when we linked arms with him? That wasn't because of me.'

'I know. I quite liked it too. He's very *warm*, isn't he?'

Not really sure whether Nancy was talking about Giuseppe's personality or the physical side of being touched by him, Jane did not answer. Instead, she said, 'I think I'll go to Wildrose Cottage soon. Leave you to sort it all out. Is that all right?'

'Oh fine,' replied Nancy, with what sounded like light sarcasm. 'You bring him here and then dump him on me.'

'What would you have done if someone had said they wanted desperately to meet *me*?'

There was a silence in the room.

Finally, Nancy said, 'The same, I suppose.'

'I'll take him with me if you want me to,' said Jane. 'I told you, you can call a halt at any time.'

'No,' said Nancy quickly. 'Don't do that. It'll upset him.'

'You might have to do that anyway.'

'Perhaps, but not now.'

'Better now than later, if you're sure.'

'I'm not sure, that's why I want him to stay for a while. I don't know, I really don't know. I can't get things straight in my mind at the moment.'

Leaving it at that, Jane eventually fell asleep.

Chapter Twenty-three

The next day, Jane spoke to Matthew and Sybil alone.

'I think I've got to go to the cottage now, and see what needs to be done there to get it in a liveable state. Obviously I can't take Giuseppe with me. Could he stay here with you for a while? I'm sure he'll pay for his keep.'

Matthew and Sybil gave each other significant looks and then Matthew turned to Jane and said, 'I don't think that's quite the point, is it, Jane?'

Jane sensed the storms gathering around her. 'What do you mean?'

'I mean, this Giuseppe chap. He's paying an awful lot of attention to Nancy, isn't he? They've gone out somewhere now – down to the park I think.'

Sybil said, 'We've a feeling you know more about what he's doing here than you let on, Jane.'

Jane, who was dressed up ready to go out to the shops, took off her gloves and sat down. Her aunt and uncle remained standing for a while, but eventually Sybil sat down, and then Matthew. Jane felt it was time to come clean and tell them why Giuseppe was here.

She said, 'I thought Giuseppe was being very discreet, but you obviously saw through that.'

Matthew went red. He was obviously quite angry underneath, and was trying to hide that fact. 'Are you telling me we're right to worry about him and Nancy?' he asked. 'If anything happens to Nancy, I shall hold you responsible, Jane.'

'Uncle, he's not here to seduce her,' said Jane. 'He wants to ask her to marry him.'

'Marry him?' said Sybil faintly. 'But we don't know him.'

'And how could you, when he's been living in Tuscany for all his life? How are you going to get to know him unless he stays here with you for a while? How is Nancy going to find out whether she can ever fall in love with him, unless he is here to be seen and heard? Don't you see, he *had* to come. It was the only way. Oh, he could have stayed at an hotel, but then the whole process would have taken that much longer, wouldn't it? This way you'll find out pretty quickly whether Nancy wants him or not, and you've got him under your roof to observe for yourselves that everything's above board.'

Matthew shook his head. 'It all seems very unconventional.'

'And how does a conventional romance go? Boy walks into Harrods, sees girl? Boy asks girl to go out? Boy and girl fall in love? Is that how you want it to go, Uncle? You'll still have to find out who the boy is, where he comes from, who his parents are. You wouldn't be satisfied with less, I know you, Uncle Matthew. And you, Aunt Sybil. So what's different here? Except that you already know who he is, where he comes from, and who his parents are – and they're mighty respectable, aren't they? On top of that you have my word that he has the most honourable of intentions.

'Giuseppe is without a doubt one of the most moral men I've ever met. If I'm sure of one thing, it's that Giuseppe would do nothing to harm any girl, let alone Nancy, who he's head over heels in love with. He'll be loyal, courteous and kind, and she'll want for nothing – if she wants *him*. And if she doesn't, why, Giuseppe will just say "thank you for having me", and get back on the train and return to Italy.'

Uncle Matthew paced the floor. 'I can't just take the word of a . . . of my niece. You might be smitten by him too, and so besotted you can't see his real character. It happens all the time with young women.'

'It happens to young men too, Uncle. Except that, if I had wanted Giuseppe, and he had wanted me, we could have married long ago. His father wanted it – but Giuseppe and I are *not* in love – and neither of us would be so irresponsible as to marry someone we do not care for in that way. His passion is for Nancy, and has been ever since he saw her photograph.'

Aunt Sybil said, 'So you *are* responsible for him being here, Jane?'

'If you want to put it that way, yes, but I didn't *engineer* it, Auntie. I was showing him a picture of my father, and your family was in the photo too. It wasn't a deliberate ploy to get Nancy to Italy. Why on earth would I do that?'

'But it's your fault, really,' Sybil persisted.

'And if it ends happily, I shall be glad of it.'

'What if it ends unhappily?' snapped Uncle Matthew. 'Nancy isn't a woman of the world, like you.'

'I wouldn't describe myself in those terms either,' said Jane, 'but Giuseppe himself is no cosmopolitan gentleman. If it ends unhappily, I shall not only be very sorry, but also extremely surprised. You don't give your daughter credit for her good common sense, which I have to say she's inherited from both of you.'

'Yes, but *Italy*,' said Sybil, making it sound like Milton's version of Hell.

'Italy isn't the ends of the earth, or a den of iniquity, or anything like that, Auntie. I've already spoken to Nancy about it, and warned her she might be lonely if she goes, and that there will be a lot of different things to get used to – the food, the way of life – but in the end it'll be up to her.'

Sybil said, 'Are they Catholics?'

'Yes, but it can't matter to them that we're Anglicans.'

Uncle Matthew said, 'It might make a difference to *us*. Have you thought of that?'

'Yes,' said Jane, 'but I dismissed it, because you haven't been to church in donkey's years, Uncle.'

'That's not the point,' he grumbled.

'I think it is. Anyway, we're all jumping the gun a bit here, aren't we? Nancy may never fall for him.'

Sybil, who was fussing around with some garment or other in the corner of the room, said, 'Let's be sensible about this, Matthew. We have to trust our daughter's judgement. If Giuseppe asks her to marry him, and she wants to, I don't think we should stand in their way. Let's leave them alone to sort it out between the pair of them, shall we?'

'I'm not so sure about that,' said Matthew.

'If you go barging in now,' Sybil said, 'you'll only make matters worse. You know Nancy's stubborn streak. You'll drive her in the opposite direction, even if she doesn't want to go there.'

Matthew appeared to think about this for a while, then he nodded. 'You're right, Sybil. If I told her to do something, she'd always do the opposite, just to assert herself, whether she wanted to or not. That's exactly right. So you think the best thing is to leave them alone? That's what we'll do then.'

He turned to Jane, 'But I think you've taken advantage of us here, Jane. You should never have brought him.'

'He would have come anyway, sooner or later. I'm sorry, Uncle. I don't get anything out of this, you know. I'm not doing it for my own gain. I know him to be a good man and I didn't see any reason why he shouldn't be introduced to Nancy.'

'Well,' said Matthew, 'you get on to your cottage now and we'll take care of him while you're gone. I've made my point and we'll leave it at that.'

So it was with mixed feelings that Jane took the train to Audley End that day. She was conscious of being in the middle of one of those affairs which there is no *right* method of conducting. It was true she probably should have warned Matthew and Sybil of Giuseppe's intentions before she brought him to England, but then Matthew would have given her a flat 'no' without even considering the matter further. He was not without his prejudices, and he was still not out of that stage of fatherhood where he saw it as his duty to protect his daughter from 'doing the wrong thing'. Nancy was well able to make her own sensible judgements on such matters, but the distance between fifteen and twenty years is very short for a man of Matthew's age, and it probably seemed like only yesterday to him that Nancy was a silly young girl. It took longer than the span of five years for a father to make the jump from *telling* his daughter what was good for her, to accepting that she had a right to determine her own future. It was an age-old battle, and one Jane remembered fighting with Henley, though at an earlier age than her cousin's.

Jane took a bus from the station to Howlett End and found her cottage just as she had left it. She was startled, as she approached, to see that the garden was in beautiful condition, full of spring flowers and not a weed in sight. That it had been recently dug and turned over, and new plants put in, was obvious. She wondered who could be responsible for such kindness and decided it must be the Blatchers. Sally or Alex must have sent a farm-hand to do it for her. But how did they know she was coming home? Very mysterious, she decided. She would speak to them later.

Inside, the cottage was as damp and dreary as she had expected it to be. She began by lighting fires in all those rooms which had fireplaces – the living room, the bedrooms and the kitchen – and leaving the doors open for a free flow of warm air between them. Then she removed all the dust covers from the furniture and began a spring clean.

By eight in the evening she was exhausted, and decided to put off her visit to the Blatchers until the following day. She went to bed in partly aired sheets, hoping she wouldn't develop any rheumatic pains or a cold. Despite the damp atmosphere she fell soundly asleep, and did not wake until eight o'clock the next morning.

Once again, she relit the fires, and the airing process continued. By lunch-time she decided the place was liveable in once again. There was some recent mail on the doormat, but none of it very exciting. Just a few notices.

At ten o'clock she visited Sally Blatcher, who welcomed her with open arms. 'Lovely to see you back, love,' she laughed. 'The place hasn't been the same without you. Is your father with you?'

'No, so far as I know he's still in Hong Kong, Sally. I don't suppose we'll see him for a while.'

Sally began making a pot of tea from a kettle that was permanently on the boil. The steam wafted round her solid form. Sally's kitchen range was always red-hot; Sally was always cooking something, no matter what time of day it was.

Once the tea was made and they were sitting at the large oak kitchen table, marked with a thousand knife cuts and stained by the juices of the berries of a thousand summers, Jane said to Sally, 'Thanks for looking after the garden, Sally.'

Jane received a peculiar look for this remark, and decided that the praise had been given in the wrong quarter. 'You didn't send a man round to do the garden?'

'No love, I didn't need to anyways. That young man's been doin' everything.'

'What young man?' asked Jane, startled.

'Tall one.'

A flush of pleasure went through Jane. 'Courtney? Courtney Stanton?'

Sally laughed, almost spilling her tea. 'Bless you, no Jane. I can't see none of the Stantons doing people's *gardens*, can you? They're gentry, aren't they? They get other people to do theirs.'

'Well, who then?' cried Jane, mystified.

'Tall, blond one, friend of your father's. Used to gamble with him at the pub.'

Petre! Petre had been to the cottage.

Jane described Petre to Sally and discovered that yes, it was him who had been looking after the garden.

'He did it last year too – all through spring and summer, like he was your regular gardener, dear. Doing it as though he expected you at any time, or perhaps he wanted it to be up to snuff if you *did* decide to walk in. I thought maybe you'd left him with instructions, though you didn't say nothing to me about it, it's true, which was why I asked him what he was doing the first time I saw him there.'

'And what did he say?'

'Well, first off he says, "None of your damn business, woman."' Sally's face darkened at the memory of the insult.

'Yes,' said Jane, hollowly, 'that sounds like Petre. What happened next? Did you leave him to it?'

'I certainly did not,' said Sally. 'I folded me arms and set me feet. Then I told him that if he didn't get out I'd have him run off for trespassing, as I was given strict instructions by you to look after the property. Then he went polite – as polite as that young man *can* get, I suspect – and says that he's sorry, he didn't know who I was. He says that it was his job to look after the garden, keep the hedges trimmed, and such like. "Perhaps Jane mentioned the fact to you?" he says.'

'"No," I comes back, "she didn't." But I thought, well, if he's just doing the gardening, there can't be much harm in that, can there? So I left him to it. I knew who he was, so I didn't think he'd go stealing nothing...'

'Oh no,' said Jane, quickly, 'he wouldn't do that.'

Sally took another sip of her tea and looked up at Jane over the rim of the cup. 'Somethin' else,' she said. 'Alex says he's been doing things with your fields too.'

Jane's heart began racing now. 'Doing what things?'

'Same as the garden. Looking after them, raisin' the corms, replanting, harvesting them. All that. Alex had a go at him, but the young man told Alex he was doing what you'd asked him to. Did you?'

'Did I what?' asked Jane, faintly, trying to sort out in her mind how she felt about this unexpected development.

'Did you ask him to do it?'

Jane shook her head. 'No. Frankly I don't know anything about it. He's taken it all on himself. No doubt he's been making a bit of money out of the saffron. That's only right, I suppose. Dad owes him quite a bit.'

'Well, I think it's a bit of a cheek,' Sally grunted. 'Though I'm bound to say that doing your garden was nice of him.'

'Yes, yes it was, wasn't it?'

Jane left Sally with her mind in a turmoil. What did Petre think he was doing, working the saffron fields? Was he really trying to recoup his debt from the crocuses? It seemed a very strange thing for a gambler to do. After all, in order to make the fields pay he would have had to work extremely hard, and manual labour was not normally the favourite occupation of gamblers. Jane's impression of them was that they were usually happier indoors, behind closed curtains.

Jane went back to her cottage and put on her boots, before setting off for the saffron fields. As ever, once out on the soil of her county, Jane felt part of the natural world again. A plover flew up from a ditch and a hare bolted before her, cutting zig-zags over the field, its bullet head boring through the wind. She had missed the gentle slopes of Essex, the mild earth, while in Italy. The scents were all different here: the smell of the chalk, the odour of freshly turned arable land, the water channels and the mossy copses. Once or twice the tangy scent of early-summer fungi – morel, shaggy ink-caps or tinder – found her sensitive nostrils. She had forgotten how much she loved the broad skies, now streaked with mares' tails, and the rolling reaches of soft landscape.

When she got to the fields she discovered that indeed they were clear of weeds and neatly furrowed. Someone had put in a lot of work, and that someone needed to be asked a few questions. She was extremely touched that he should do the garden, and keep doing it in expectation that she might walk down the path at any moment, but the fields were different. They were hers, her idea, and very special to her, like a favourite child. She hadn't been able to avoid leaving them, but she simply didn't want anyone else interfering. However much he might have had a certain right to the proceeds from those fields, Jane felt they had been violated and she wanted an explanation as to the exact reasons for that violation. She set out immediately to walk to Saffron Walden. Her father had told her Petre had lodgings in Castle Street.

His rooms were accessible from the street, through an open front door and up some back stairs. She climbed the stairs and stood outside his door. Someone was playing a piano in the room and she recognised the tune. It was the recent popular song 'Limehouse Blues' which everyone was humming or singing. The player was injecting such a quality of sadness into the tune, though, that it was almost unrecognisable from the versions she had heard from whistling tradesmen and young London girls singing to themselves on their way to work down Green Lanes.

Jane knocked tentatively on the door and the piano playing stopped abruptly.

The door flew open and Petre stood there, saying, 'If you've come to complain...' The words died in his throat and he stood there staring for a moment before saying, 'God, Jane – it's you.'

She smiled at him and stepped into the room. 'Hello Petre. Did you think I was one of the neighbours?'

He closed the door behind her. Wearing a paisley dressing gown, he crossed the room and took a cigarette from a silver case lying on the piano top. He lit it with trembling fingers and then said, 'Yes, they're bloody bores. I can't play anything without someone knocking the door down.'

'It sounded lovely to me. They should be grateful. I didn't know you played the piano.'

'Sit down,' he said, motioning her to an armchair and sitting down

in another himself. 'There's a lot you don't know about me...'
He paused before saying. 'There's a lot I don't know about myself.'

She sat in the chair. 'Still no memory?'

He shook his head bitterly. 'Nope. It's a funny thing, isn't it? I
know how to fly a plane and play the piano, but I can't remember my
own name. I find that very peculiar.'

'You also know how to garden and grow saffron,' said Jane.

He looked at her sideways, 'Ah, you've been to the fields?'

'I've been to the fields. You're quite welcome to whatever you
make from them. I should have said that before I left for Italy.
Whatever it takes to cover father's debt to you and any interest that
you feel necessary. I just wish you had asked. And I'm very grateful
for the garden. That was kind.'

'Is that why you thought I'd done the fields?' he said. 'To recover
my debt?'

'I must admit I was surprised that you should put in so much
manual work, but yes, what other reason could you have?'

Petre gave her that bitter look with which she was now familiar. He
stared at his feet, encased in leather slippers, for a moment. Then he
took a long draw on his cigarette before replying, 'The money from
the harvest is in the bank, Jane, in an account which bears your name.
There's quite a lot there. We had a good harvest and there's another
expected this year. The corms had to be raised and split of course,
then replanted, but they're good for another two years now. Saltash
has been working with me on this, so he must take some of the
blame.'

'Blame?' said Jane, faintly. 'But why, why have you been doing
this, Petre?'

He turned fierce dark eyes on her. 'For you, of course. Why
else?'

'But Petre...'

'Oh, don't worry,' he said, giving a short, caustic laugh, 'there's no
obligation on your part. I did it for you because I wanted to, simply
that, so you don't need to worry.'

She was silent for a moment, studying her hands, wondering what
to say. She was overwhelmed by his feelings for her, and found it
difficult not to experience a flood of affection for him. He was a kind

man, to her if not to others, and it was impossible to deny that she felt quite a strong emotional tie to him because of it.

To do her garden for her! To maintain it so that she would see it at its best, no matter when she came home. That almost meant more than cultivating the saffron fields, even though the work involved in the latter was obviously much greater. It was that little extra gift, beside the main one, that showed how deep his feelings actually ran: to be able to search his mind for some small extra effort that would add to the pleasure of her homecoming.

A rush of warm feelings went through her as she realised how enormously difficult it was to resist the love of someone. You could fight against hate and bitterness, reject those easily, but it was much harder to fight against devotion and passion.

Almost involuntarily, she rose from the chair and kissed him. 'Thank you, Petre,' she said. 'You are a real friend.'

'I would like to be more,' he said, quickly.

'I know, but you said I had no obligation,' she reminded him.

'You don't. But will you think about it? Promise me you'll think about it? Did you meet anyone in Italy? I don't care if you did, just tell me.'

Of course he cared, but she had the answer he wanted to hear. 'No, no one in Italy. No one here.'

He took her hands in his own, his black eyes boring into hers with a ferocity that made her legs go weak. 'Then think about it. Marry me, Jane.'

'Yes . . .' she said.

'Yes, you *will*?' he cried, the light in his eyes brightening to brilliance.

'Yes, I'll *think* about it.'

They dimmed a little again, but he seemed happier than she had ever seen him before. That, too, was difficult to resist, and she began to wonder if she was going to say yes after all. Petre was so insistent, so loving, so completely hers: it was difficult to see how she was going to turn him away. He had the battalions of love on his side, and she had very few defences against them except the thought that perhaps she could not fall in love with him in the same way. Did that matter? Perhaps affection was enough?

'I really will think about it,' she repeated, stepping towards the door.

'When? When may I know?' he asked.

'Come to the cottage in . . . in two days' time,' she told him. 'I'll give you my answer then.'

'I'll be there,' he said. 'I'll be there.'

When he had waved her down the stairs, she stopped and stood on the landing below, wondering what was happening to her. Perhaps, she thought, this was how it happened between people? How was she to know? She knew she was not in love, because she had an idea she knew what love felt like, but she certainly *liked* Petre a great deal. He made her feel special and valuable. It was a good feeling. One which could be enjoyed.

The problem was, she admitted to herself, Petre wasn't Courtney. She had looked at love through a crack in the wall, and the person on the other side had been Courtney. Since she could not have Courtney, since he was unobtainable, she had sealed the crack over again, determined not to allow herself to peek at something which was impossible to grasp. Thus, she knew what real love looked like, but knew she was going to have to settle for something less.

As she reached street level the piano-playing began again, but this time the tune had a lilt in it, a happy air, and again it was one of the most recent melodies to hit the music world. It took her a minute to recall the title, but then it came to her: 'I wish I could shimmy like my sister Kate.' Petre was not only quite talented, but also very up to date. She thought that was right for a man with no memory. He lives for the present, she told herself, because he has no past. Now he was reaching for a future and he wanted it to be her.

Chapter Twenty-four

Before Jane left Saffron Walden, she telephoned Stanton Manor to try to contact Courtney. The call was answered by Lady Constance, whose voice immediately went frosty when she heard it was Jane on the line. Jane tried to be congenial, but it was difficult when talking to someone who was determined to be quite the opposite.

'I wondered if I could speak to Courtney?' Jane said, once she had inquired after Lady Constance's and Sir Charles's health, and found them both to be well.

'I'm afraid you can't,' replied the voice at the other end with some satisfaction, 'he's not here.'

Jane wasn't going to be put off like that. 'Might I inquire where he is?' said Jane, sweetly.

'I'm afraid we don't broadcast the whereabouts of family members, unless they wish it.'

'Lady Constance,' said Jane, losing her temper a little, 'I would like to contact Courtney and I know he would wish to speak to me. I don't know why you're being so obstructive, because I shall find him in the end, and I shan't hesitate to tell him that you seemed determined to prevent me from reaching him.'

There was not only frost on the voice that came back, but a thick layer of ice. 'Don't you dare take that tone of voice with me, young woman, or I'll hang up immediately. I think I'm entitled to some politeness—'

'And so am I,' said Jane with just a trace of ice in her own reply. 'You seem to think that because your husband has a title you can treat people like dirt. I would like to contact my friend Courtney . . .'

The line went dead.

'Damn, hell, bugger,' snapped Jane. 'Bloody woman.'

She waited for about ten minutes before ringing again, hoping someone else would answer.

'Stanton Manor. This is Stephen Stanton speaking.'

Thank God, thought Jane. 'Hello, Stephen. This is Jane Transon.'

There was a slight pause on the other end before she heard, 'Oh hello, Jane. How are you? You'll want to speak to Courtney, but he's not here at the moment.'

'Can you tell me where he is?'

'Yes, he's in Egypt.'

'Egypt?'

'Yes, there's a man, an archaeologist called Howard Carter out there, about to open up a tomb at Luxor – supposed to be the grave of some ancient Egyptian king or other. Somebody called Tutankhamen. Anyway, Carter's sponsored by the Earl of Carnarvon, who's asked Courtney to do a series of paintings and sketches to illustrate the progress of the dig. They have an official photographer, of course, but Carnarvon's niece Elizabeth persuaded her uncle to hire Courtney as well. He's out there now.'

Disappointed as she was that Courtney was not in England, Jane was pleased for him. He seemed to have got what he wanted at last. He was an official artist. Something in Stephen's tone was puzzling her, however.

'You say Lord Carnarvon's niece persuaded her uncle to hire Courtney? Is she a friend of the family? Perhaps I shouldn't ask that? It's really none of my business, I suppose. Does Courtney know her well?'

There was some hesitation on the other end of the line, then Stephen said, 'Jane ... I, well, they travelled out to Egypt together... Elizabeth wanted to join her uncle and Courtney escorted her ... They ... they became friends when Elizabeth stayed with us. Mother invited her to the house, you see.'

A pang of emotion went through Jane. Had Lady Constance told her this news, she would have put it down to vindictiveness, but this was Stephen, trying to explain the circumstances of Courtney's absence to her. Jane bit her lip and forced the feeling down, deep inside her, where it could no longer affect her.

'That's all right, Stephen. Courtney has already told me about ...

about Elizabeth. Thank you for explaining, anyway. I do appreciate it.'

'Jane . . . ?'

'Goodbye, Stephen. Thanks again.'

She replaced the receiver and stood there for a moment, gathering herself. Of course Courtney had never mentioned this Elizabeth, but Jane did not want Stephen to speak about her further. It was not that Jane was upset by the news, but that she had other, more important things, to think about.

Jane left the post office, feeling she had done what she could to get hold of Courtney. She wished he were here now, so that she could ask his advice about Petre, but he was not. He was in Egypt, accompanied by Lord Carnarvon's niece, Elizabeth, who was no doubt hanging on his arm this very instant, twirling her parasol, asking Courtney his opinion on this and that. Just as Jane wanted his opinion. That was what friends were for, after all. It was a cruel world sometimes, when two . . . two good friends could not get together for a talk after they had been parted for nearly two years. She tried to imagine what Courtney would say if she were to ask him whether or not she should marry Petre.

As she walked back across the fields, the clouds moved to a greyness and a drizzle began to descend. The world around her was quiet for a while as beasts took shelter, travelling along the animal highways worn into the grasses, and birds went to roost. Jane herself sheltered for a while under a broad oak, but when it looked as if the sky were set for a few hours, she decided she would have to get wet and put up with it.

As she passed through a gap in a blackthorn hedge, scratching the back of her hand in the process, it suddenly came to her that she knew *exactly* what Courtney would say if she asked his advice about marrying Petre. He would say, 'If you have to ask me, then the answer is, don't do it.'

That was the answer, but she still couldn't accept it. She did have feelings for Petre. They were not as deep as to be able to say, yes, this is the man with whom I want to spend the rest of my life, but they were there. She felt immensely grateful to him for what he had done for her, and she was extremely flattered to be so loved. It would take more than an unspoken censure from an imaginary conversation with Courtney to convince her that such a marriage was not right.

Over the next day or so, Jane considered the proposal, first settling on one answer, then on the other. She visited her mother's grave in Thaxted churchyard, but she could gain no guidance here. She talked to Sally about it. Sally was a practical woman.

'Well, he's a gambler, so I hear, which isn't good, is it? But he's changed – you've changed him – because he's done all them things for you while you've been gone, hasn't he? I mean, how many men would even *think* to do what he's done? I'm lucky if me birthday gets remembered, let alone someone doing all that for me. 'Course, he's new in love, which makes a difference, but just the same, it wasn't just a bunch of flowers, was it? It was fields of 'em, and gardens of 'em, and all on the off-chance that you'd come back and see 'em . . .'

Finally, when Jane was half-way through attacking the lonely job of blacking her kitchen range, she made up her mind. She *would* marry Petre. He was an intelligent, thoughtful man and would make her a good companion. She dropped the blacking and went out to telephone him, to ask him to meet her at the saffron fields in two hours' time. She knew if she left it until he came to her the following day, she might change her mind again.

It was a clear blue sky when she started out, but again the greyness came drifting over from the north in different shades. The rain held off, but by the time she approached the saffron fields, the spinneys had turned dark and gloomy and the landscape was hunched like a great sulking beast with a ridged back. The ditches had grown shadows in their depths and the hedgerows were still.

Jane passed a gamekeeper and his lad as they entered a thicket. The keeper had a twelve-bore shotgun in the crook of his arm, while the youth carried what looked to Jane like a .22 rifle. They were obviously going to shoot rooks: it was common practice for keepers to cull the birds by shooting them through their nests high in the elms using a .22 rifle, which made only a *snapping* sound, not loud enough to disturb the whole colony and scare it into flight.

The keeper tipped his cap to her and Jane nodded back.

When she reached the saffron fields, she looked towards Saffron Walden, and saw not one, but two tiny figures moving over the rounded hills, occasionally disappearing into the shallow valleys. The first of these was obviously Petre. The second looked like a woman, about half a mile behind him. It seemed from Jane's perspective that they were moving terribly slowly, like small creatures over a vast wasteland, and they took an age just to travel the length of a brown or green field. The nearer they got, the more apprehensive Jane felt.

Behind them and around them was an immense Essex sky, bland and featureless, which emphasised their pale, slow progress over the undulating terrain.

Instinctively Jane felt that the presence of a second figure was ominous, perhaps even threatening. It appeared that Petre, probably deep in thought and intent on reaching the saffron fields as quickly as possible, did not know he was being pursued. He could not know, unless he turned to look, and the woman was too far behind for him to hear her.

Of course, thought Jane, this third person might have some completely innocuous reason for following Petre. Perhaps she had mistaken him for someone else? Jane's thoughts ran wildly around various reasons for the woman's presence, none of which seemed in any way satisfactory. It was as if the woman were a predator, tracking its quarry, and Petre the prey, unaware of the danger he was in.

When Petre was two hundred yards away, she could see his fixed smile. She had merely told him on the telephone that she wanted to see him. He had asked her if it was good or bad news, and she had replied that she did not want to say anything on the phone or there would be no point in the meeting. So his smile was frozen: he did not yet know his fate.

He waved and Jane waved back, then she gestured, indicating that he was being followed.

He did not understand the signal at first and stopped, looking puzzled. Then finally he turned and saw the woman, now about three hundred yards behind him. He stared at her for a while, then continued his journey towards Jane.

When he reached her, he said, 'Well Jane, have you got some news for me? An early answer? Tell me quickly.'

'Hadn't we better find out who that is?' asked Jane.

Petre frowned and looked over his shoulder at the figure struggling up the length of the field. She looked weary, as if she had travelled a greater distance than from Saffron Walden to Jane's fields, or else she was ill in some way.

Petre said, 'Do you know who she is?'

'No,' Jane replied. 'I've never seen her before.'

'Neither have I,' Petre said. 'Perhaps she wants work when the season comes – in the fields?'

Jane immediately felt a sense of relief wash through her as a plausible explanation for the woman's presence was presented to her by the man she was going to marry.

As the woman approached them, Jane saw that her blonde hair hung in limp thongs from her head, as if it had been wet and had dried under the sun. She seemed to be in her mid-twenties, dressed for town in a fawn topcoat. Her eyes were light blue, though the effect of them was masked by the heavy make-up around them. She appeared of a slighter build than Jane, with a daintiness about her which Jane envied, and a waist that looked impossibly trim. She was wearing smart black shoes with heels, now clogged with mud, and was having immense difficulty in walking in this unsuitable footwear.

When she reached them, the woman stopped, needing time to catch her breath.

Then she spoke, not to Jane, nor even to both of them, but to Petre alone.

'I've been looking for you for so long I can't believe I've actually found you,' she gasped.

'Do we know one another?' asked Petre, in a voice so cold it sent a chill through Jane.

The woman's mouth dropped open in what appeared to be disappointment. 'Jim – you don't even recognise *me*?'

Petre looked startled. 'Jim?' he said.

'Yes – that's your name. Has that gone from you too? The army said it had. Oh, Jim, I'm sorry it's taken me so long to find you. You should have left an address with the army. Mother has been so worried – all these years. It's taken me I don't know how long to trace you to Saffron Walden. Then, when I came to the place where you live, I saw you racing off to the back of the church and over the fields . . .'

288

The woman looked close to tears, and Jane felt moved by her obviously emotional state.

Petre said, 'Who are you? Tell me your name.'

'Lisa . . .'

'Lisa who?' he interrupted sharply, as if he were interrogating an enemy prisoner.

'Walthing – you're Jim Walthing. You don't remember – oh, I'm so tired, so tired.' The tears began flowing down the woman's cheeks now, and Jane went to her and put her arm around her. Lisa almost collapsed in Jane's arms, and Jane had to support her. She seemed completely exhausted.

Petre's puzzled face gradually revealed comprehension, and he suddenly cried out with a kind of frenzied pleasure, 'You're my sister! You must be my sister! In God's name, why didn't you say so first off? Jane, it's my sister.'

The girl stumbled from Jane's arms and fell into Petre's, resting her head on his chest. He held her awkwardly, like a man holding a baby for the first time. He seemed embarrassed. She mumbled something into his shirt front.

'What?' he cried, wildly. 'What was that?'

There was a moment's silence, then Jane heard the words distinctly.

'I'm your *wife*,' Lisa moaned.

The words seemed not only to stun the listeners, but the whole landscape. It appeared to Jane that even the birds, the seagulls and rooks, had been numbed by that short admission. Jane felt out of touch with reality for a moment, on the edge of some kind of madness.

'My wife,' repeated Petre tonelessly. 'I have no wife.' He tried to peel her away from him, but she clung to him. She needed comfort in her distress, Jane could see that, and Petre wanted her away from him. They seemed to struggle there silently for a while, before the woman named Lisa Walthing lifted her head and spoke again. This time her voice was calm and even.

'I'm your wife, Jim. You married me and then went off to the war. You ran away when I became pregnant. We have a son: his name is Francis.'

Petre groaned. 'Impossible,' he said. 'I was too young – surely I was too young?'

'We were *both* too young, Jim, but it's true. I've waited all these years. This is the seventh year. They told me to divorce you – that you were dead – but I knew you weren't, Jim. I knew in my heart you weren't. It must be a shock for you,' she admitted, 'to find you have a wife.'

'It's – it's a – a *terrible* shock,' he said hollowly. 'Jane and me – we . . .'

Lisa flashed a look at Jane which appeared to be a mixture of sudden hate and deep hurt.

Jane said quickly, 'We have been good friends, Petre – that is, Jim and myself.'

'More than friends!' shouted Petre, pushing Lisa from him at last. 'We made love in this very field. We – we were . . . we had *passion*. Oh my God, what are we going to do? Jane, answer me. What were you going to say to me? Tell me.'

'I can't,' said Jane. 'It doesn't matter now.'

'It matters to *me*,' he shouted. 'It matters to me.'

Jane took a quick look at Lisa and then took a deep breath before saying, 'I'm sorry, but the answer is no. I'm very fond of you Petre, but I don't love you. I thought you knew that.'

Petre ran forward and gripped her by the shoulders.

'It can still be yes, can't it? If you're fond of me – love would come later. I don't know this other woman. I don't know her, I tell you. She could be lying . . .'

'She's telling the truth, Petre, you know that.'

'But I don't love her, Jane. I don't know her and I don't love her. I love you. I've always loved you.'

'Not always,' said Lisa, interrupting him sullenly. 'You loved *me* once, not her. You told me so. You used to tell me all the time that you loved me.'

He turned to her, his anguish evident in his twisted features. 'Always, always, always. I *never* loved you. I don't *know* you, don't you understand that? I don't even know you. That was someone else – someone else loved you. Not me. I'm *not* the man who left you. This may be his body, but the mind belongs to me, not to him. You've got to understand that this fellow Jim, whoever he is, he died in a crashed plane. Petre Peake, *me*, I crawled from the wreckage of that aircraft. I was born in its twisted, mangled womb, in amongst the bent wires and broken struts. That machine was my mother. I'm Petre Peake, not Jim Walthing. I'm *me*. Me, me, me.'

Jane stared at Petre as he raved at his wife, and knew he was speaking the truth. He had been given birth, a new life, by that biplane. That was his belief. It accounted for his cold attitude towards his fellow men. Petre Peake was a machine, born of a machine; he had no human ancestors, only antecedents formed of metal, wood and canvas.

Lisa began crying again. 'I don't know what you're talking about.' She appealed to Jane. 'What's he talking about? Please tell me.'

Jane went and put her arm around the other woman.

'Petre,' she said, firmly. 'You've got to get a hold of yourself, please. I'm going to take Lisa with me, back to the cottage. She's distressed enough as it is, without you ranting nonsense at her . . .'

'It's not nonsense,' he cried.

'It is to her,' snapped Jane, 'and you're going to make her ill, do you understand me? I know what you're saying, but she's tired and overwrought, and I'm not sure she could take it in anyway. Leave her alone. Come to the cottage later.'

'I have no obligations – none. I don't know her. Jane, we must get married.'

'You're already married.'

'No, I'm not. Or perhaps I am, legally, but not morally. You can see that, Jane. Can't you?'

She could see something in the words, but turned away from him.

'A divorce then. I'll get a divorce,' he said with panic in his tone. 'Jane?'

Jane said, 'I don't love you enough for all this. Petre, please get a hold of yourself. You'll send her insane.'

He suddenly seemed to go limp and lifeless, his arms dangling by his sides. Then he walked to the middle of the field and just stood there, his head hanging down, staring at the ground. He appeared to be looking for something.

Jane led the sobbing woman away. Lisa was reluctant to leave at first, but allowed herself to be persuaded. She was almost dead on her feet.

'You need some rest,' soothed Jane. 'Then we'll sort this mess out.'

When the two women had been stumbling along together for about five minutes, having crossed one field and a ditch, there was the sound of a shot. Lisa screamed. Rooks flew up, cawing, from nearby trees. Jane's heart jumped; then she remembered the two men.

'It's only a local keeper,' she reassured Lisa. 'He's out shooting rooks.'

Both women looked back though, towards the saffron fields, and could see no tall figure standing there.

Petre's gone down the slope, Jane thought. He's simply walked off towards Saffron Walden. That was a shotgun blast I heard. I know a shotgun when I hear one.

Lisa began running back, though, despite a plea from Jane, and then Jane followed. The two women reached the edge of the saffron field together, and saw the body lying slumped sideways, almost in the middle of the row of furrows. It was twisted into a funny shape, as if Petre had been sitting, leaning forward, when death came. Even from where they stood they could see the raw wound where part of his head was missing. His service revolver was still in his hand.

Jane knew then what Petre had been searching for, as he had roamed about in his grief while the two women had set out for Howlett End.

He had shot himself on the very spot where he and Jane had made love.

Chapter Twenty-five

Shortly after Lisa began screaming the keeper and his lad arrived. Once he had found that there was nothing they could do for the dead man, the gamekeeper said he would stay with the body while the other three went for the police. The youth who owned the .22 rifle, white and trembling himself, helped Jane get Lisa Walthing to the main road. There they flagged down a car driver who took them all into Saffron Walden. Jane took Lisa to the police station and the police called in a doctor for the distressed young women, at the same time as sending two men out to investigate the suicide.

When the doctor arrived, he treated both women for shock, giving them a sedative. He contacted Jane's local doctor and asked him to look in on Jane later. Jane was more worried about Lisa than herself. The police assured Jane that they would send someone back to London with Lisa Walthing. She lived there with her mother-in-law. Jane was then taken by police car, back to her own cottage, and told she would be contacted in the morning.

Once her own doctor had been, Jane sat in her living room, staring out over the fields, until the sun went down behind the hills. She went over and over things in her mind, searching for a way in which she could have prevented the man she knew as Petre Peake from killing himself. But Lisa Walthing was the wild card in all Jane's reshuffling and redealing of the pack. There was no way Jane could have known about Lisa Walthing. There was no way Lisa could have been kept out of the situation, having tracked down her missing husband. Fate was a funnel down which all the ingredients for a tragedy had been thrown; eventually they had come together at the narrow neck of that funnel.

Jane knew, had always known, that Petre had been a complex character. Perhaps if Jane had said no to marriage, even without Lisa Walthing in the picture, Petre would still have shot himself? It was entirely possible, for Petre had been an unstable, unpredictable character. Jane suddenly felt guilty, then angry *because* she felt guilty. She was angry at Petre for making her responsible for his death. He had set her up to be the one who ordained whether he lived or died, and Jane knew this was not fair. It was not fair at all. She had tried to avoid him after that encounter in the saffron field, but he had worked himself back into her life, and then killed himself, leaving her to shoulder the blame. It was the despicable act of a thoughtless, selfish man.

'Oh, why, why, did I let him make love to me that day?' she cried, weeping into her hands. 'Why was I so stupid? If that hadn't happened, he would have been alive now.'

Was that the truth? She had no way of knowing. Now there was a widow and a fatherless son, mourning the loss of a loved one. Someone they thought they had found after seven years of searching. Seven years! Yet Petre had run away from them in the first instance. If he had owned his memory at the end of the war, would he have gone back? It was probably better for them, in the long run, that he had been found, even if he was now dead, thought Jane. To have to live with a missing husband and father was probably worse than knowing for certain that he was dead.

Jane went to bed later, but did not sleep. The thoughts just whirled around her brain. In the morning the police came and took her statement. She told them everything that had happened, except that Petre and she had made love in the saffron fields three years previously. There was, she decided, no sensible reason for them to know that. Lisa Walthing might tell them, if she remembered Petre's outburst at the saffron fields, but that was up to her, and Jane did not think that 'Jim's' widow would want to rake muck, especially since there was nothing to be gained from it.

The police said they would be in touch once they had other statements.

Jane telephoned Matthew that day, but did not tell him of events in Essex. She did not want the family descending on her at this time, and she could not leave until after the hearing. Matthew grumbled a little about Giuseppe and Nancy, saying they were getting on too well, which gave Jane hope for her cousin and her suitor. It's time for some pure romance in the family, Jane thought, unbesmirched by ugly stains. Let the pair of them fall deeply in love, get married, and have some nice children. Never mind uncle Matthew's disapproval. His turn had come and gone. It was now his daughter's hour.

'Mind you,' said Matthew, already softening a little, 'he's a nice enough chap, for all that. He's very polite to your aunt and me. I just wonder when he's going home.'

'Have you asked him yet?' said Jane.

'Well, I *did*, but your aunt told me to hush up. She said he could stay as long as he wanted, and since she did the cooking and made the beds, what was it to me? She said I wasn't around enough to be bothered by him . . .'

Jane smiled to herself. Giuseppe had already won over the daughter and the mother. With Matthew beginning to melt, there was no stopping the Italian lover. She put down the receiver in the knowledge that at least Giuseppe's story might have a happy ending.

Three weeks later, Jane had to repeat her statement about events at the saffron fields to the court, under the eyes of Jim Walthing's family. Lisa Walthing, dressed in black, was also called to the stand and corroborated much of what Jane had said, with some additions of her own. She looked small, weak and defenceless in the witness box. Jane had sensibly decided to wear a grey suit, so as not to identify with the family in mourning, nor to arouse their antagonism as the 'other woman' and the person responsible for their Jim's death.

Lisa Walthing was resentful of her, going by the tone of her testimony, but did not blame her for her husband's suicide. Lisa remembered the things Jane had said at the saffron fields, about not wanting to marry Jim, and seemed to accept that Jane was completely ignorant of Jim Walthing's real name or previous history.

There were also witnesses to testify to the victim's loss of memory, his subsequent career in the Royal Flying Corps, and an army psychiatrist stated that Lieutenant Petre Peake had been discharged from the army as medically unfit at the end of the war, due to the officer's unstable mental condition.

'He was my patient for the last six months of his service career,' said the doctor, 'and I diagnosed a personality disorder. It was on my recommendation, and with Lieutenant Peake's agreement, that he be discharged as medically unfit.'

The coroner delivered a verdict of 'Suicide while the balance of the mind was disturbed'.

Jane was not encouraged to speak to Jim Walthing's family after the hearing, and had no desire to do so. She went home alone on the bus. She was still very shaken at the end of the journey, and wondered if she would ever completely recover from the shock of such an experience. It still haunted her dreams, turning them into nightmares occasionally, and there were times when she was completely overcome by remorse and guilt. Since she had no one to turn to except Sally Blatcher, who was well-meaning but not a very effective counsellor, Jane was gradually slipping into a morose and depressed state.

As she walked up the lane to Wildrose Cottage, she heard the whinny of a horse. She lifted her head, feeling a tremor of hope go through her. Could it be Courtney? Then she remembered Courtney was probably still in Egypt, and disappointment swamped the hope inside her. The horse she could hear was probably one of the Blatchers' shires.

But when she turned the bend, there he was.

Courtney was standing by the gate, dressed in his riding breeches, a grey shirt with rolled-up sleeves, and tall riding boots. His normally pale complexion was tanned a light brown, presumably from hours in the sun in Egypt. His hair was longer and less groomed than usual, but he looked well, if slightly anxious, and as she walked towards him he took a seemingly involuntary step forward. He smiled, warmly, and then held open his arms in a tentative gesture of greeting.

Suddenly, Jane felt an overwhelming need to be comforted. Without thinking further she choked back a sob and rushed forward, flinging herself into his arms. The action was a pure emotional response, which she would never have carried out in her normal state. She clung to him, crying into his shoulder for several minutes, while he hugged her gently, and made soft soothing noises in her ear.

'Oh, Courtney,' she said, 'it's been *horrible*.'

'I know,' he replied softly. 'I read about it in the local paper. I came over as soon as I arrived home. It must have been terrible for you.'

'I'm sorry, I really shouldn't be wetting your shirt front like this. It's nothing to do with you.'

'I want it to be,' he said in a firm voice. 'I want it to be to do with me. Everything about you. I want you to let me help you through this.'

'My old friend,' she said, sniffing back the tears. 'You're so good to me.'

'Not *just* your old friend. More than that. I'm in love with you, Jane, always have been. I don't know why it's taken me so long to tell you – probably because I thought you wouldn't want me. And when my mother told me you had left for Italy to avoid my offer of marriage . . .'

Now she felt the shock of a thrill go through her. Love? He said he was in love with her. That was something she had never dared hope for, had so often pushed away into the corners of her mind because it seemed impossible. How could a man from a family like Courtney's love the daughter of an impoverished artist? It still seemed an impossible dream.

'What?' Jane cried, as she absorbed the last piece of his statement. 'Avoid your offer of marriage?'

He looked at her grimly. 'She lied, didn't she?' he said. 'I realise that now.'

Jane nodded. 'I'm afraid so. And I thought you wanted Nancy. You wrote something in a letter to Uncle Matthew which made it sound as if you wanted to marry *her* – at least, she thought so. After that I put all romantic thoughts of you out of my mind. I refused to allow myself to think of you in that way. A friend, a close friend, that's all I could let you be.'

Courtney groaned. 'My stupid coy way of communicating with people. You can blame my parents for some of that. I always have to test the water first, make sure I'm not going to be laughed at or rejected out of hand. I'm a victim of my own stupid, tentative ways. Since your father wasn't here, I was going to speak to your uncle about us, once I'd asked you to marry me, and was in the possession of the right answer . . .'

297

'You silly traditionalist.'

He smiled down at her. 'Yes, I know, but that's my upbringing, I'm afraid. I suppose I wanted to talk to someone who would actually be happy at the thought that we were going to be married, instead of horrified, as I knew my parents were. Then when I returned home, you'd gone. My mother told me you'd jumped at the chance to go to Italy, because you found me threatening, so I thought you didn't want me.'

Jane nestled more deeply into his arms again. 'Courtney,' she said in a small voice, 'there's something else. I didn't know I was in love with you. I didn't really know until now.'

'And now?' he said, a catch in his voice.

'Now I know what a fool I was. I've been in love with you for ages, but couldn't see it, or wouldn't let myself see it. I knew I wasn't in love with Petre, but I took *you* for granted. I thought, whatever happens, my old friend will be there.'

'Darling Jane,' he said. 'Oh God, you don't know how wonderful that sounds to me. If only . . . if only I had spoken sooner, I might have saved you from all this grief.'

'Or got yourself shot by Petre,' she said. 'Who knows what he might have done, poor man? It's so very sad. Such a waste. I hate what the war has done to young men.'

'Those that were lucky enough to come through it alive,' said Courtney.

'Or unlucky enough . . .'

He nodded, then said, 'Jane, will you marry me?'

'Yes,' she replied, 'whenever you like.'

He held her for a long time.

Then they went into the cottage where they told each other everything that had happened to them since they had last parted from one another.

'What about Peake?' said Courtney. 'You were going to marry him?'

'He was very kind to me. I wanted to repay him for that kindness. I wanted to give him something back. He was a very unhappy man, Courtney, and I thought I could help him.'

Courtney leaned forward and put a finger on her lips. 'Always a mistake, Jane. You can't help people by forming that kind of relationship with them. People are not simple machines with logical behaviour. They're complex beings, often guided by feelings they don't understand themselves. Sometimes they get into the most unlikely fixes, out of no real fault of their own, and for reasons they don't comprehend. So far as you and I are concerned, if you want to talk about him, you can. But if you want to keep some things secret, Jane, if it hurts you to talk about them, or if you simply don't know how to put them, then that's fine too. You understand?'

'Thank you, Courtney. I ... I'd rather let things lie for the moment.'

'That's fine. Take your time. Let it come out naturally, when you feel you're able to talk about it – or not, as you please. You're entitled to tell me as much or as little as you want. As long as we're together, now, the past can take care of itself all in good time. It doesn't matter to me what has gone before, only what's to come.'

She stroked his cheek. 'You're so nice to me, you know. I don't deserve it after the mess I've made of things. However,' she put on a brave face and smiled, 'what's your mother going to say about all this? And Elizabeth. How is she going to take it?'

Courtney frowned. 'Elizabeth?'

'Lord Carnarvon's niece,' Jane reminded him.

'What's she got to do ... good lord, you didn't think she and I were ... ?'

'Stephen said she'd got you the job with Carter and Lord Carnarvon, and that you'd travelled out to Egypt together. I didn't know how far the attachment between you went.'

'Attachment?' cried Courtney, looking genuinely upset. 'Elizabeth and me? No such thing. Anyway, she didn't get me the job. She mentioned they wanted an artist and I applied along with a dozen others. Then, when I was appointed, she asked if I would escort her to Egypt. Look, Jane, I'm sure she had no other motive than joining her...'

'Really, Courtney? I think I'd better marry you very quickly – you're quite gullible, you know.'

Courtney laughed. 'I am *not*! It was all very proper. I admit she's very attractive...'

'Is she?' said Jane, quickly.

'. . . but she can't hold a candle to you, darling, and that's a fact. As for my mother, we've already had it all out. I told her I was coming to ask you to marry me, and she went into the sulks. She's refused to have anything to do with the wedding. Good job, I think. By the way, I've told her that if she mentions this Peake business, I'll never speak to her again. She knows I mean it, so I don't believe she'll embarrass you with that.'

'Oh, Courtney, poor woman. She had such high hopes for you. Now here you are, marrying a notorious woman with no money and no breeding, involved in an ugly local scandal. I can well understand why she's so upset.'

'Listen, don't have any sympathy for my mother, Jane. Don't forget she was responsible for keeping us apart before. We would probably have been married now, and this Petre Peake affair would never have happened if it wasn't for her. I hold her entirely responsible for that.'

'But her plans for you?'

'Yes,' he said grimly, 'I was supposed to marry a general's daughter and follow in my father-in-law's footsteps. Anyway, Father likes you, he told me so, and you're a favourite with Stephen and Julia, so we haven't got a great deal to worry about with the rest of the family. What would you like, a whacking great wedding or a quiet one?'

'A quiet one, please.'

'My sentiments exactly. Which is your church? Saffron Walden?'

'Thaxted.'

'Well, mine's Walden, so we'll have to have the banns called at both. I'll bring the car around tomorrow morning and we'll go and see both vicars. Exciting, isn't it?'

'Wonderful,' she sighed, moving over to the sofa and sitting close to him.

After a moment he put his arm around her and pulled her gently towards him. She lay her head on his chest and took her feet off the floor to stretch out fully on the sofa. Soon Courtney was also lying lengthways over the cushions and they were kissing. Jane's face felt hot and her legs were trembling as she and Courtney began moving together, stroking each other through their clothes. Then they began to shed some clothing, awkwardly, while still on the sofa.

Finally, still half-undressed, they pressed together with some urgency. She could feel his warm flesh against her abdomen. She touched that part of him which was now hard and smooth, while he kissed her bared throat and breasts, at the same time running his fingers down her spine, stroking her buttocks through the thin satin slip, and then her naked thighs. His breath began to quicken, hot and damp, as his lips met hers again.

'Oh Courtney,' she said in the back of her throat, then closed her eyes as their separate rhythms quickly merged into one. All the while he was murmuring into her ear, words which hardly had any meaning, but which burned through her, firing her passion for this man she knew she loved.

This time it felt entirely right to Jane. She was moved spiritually as well as physically – every aspect of her was involved in the lovemaking. She loved the feel of Courtney inside her, and was able to respond with enthusiasm and energy. They looked into each other's eyes without embarrassment or awkwardness, as they each reached a climax, finding a strength in each other.

'Oh my darling,' he moaned into her ear. 'I love you so, so much.'

'I love you, too,' she whispered. 'I want you to stay in me for ever . . .'

The rhythms of their bodies were like compatible currents and tides, flowing into and through each other. Two warm oceans that mingled in an inseparable embrace. Jane knew that they were now part of one another, for the rest of their lives and, no matter what happened, would remain so.

When they got their breath back, they lay in each other's arms, and talked.

Once they had thoroughly investigated the seemingly inexhaustible subject of how they felt about each other, and the enjoyment they derived from each other, she asked him about his painting in Egypt.

'Well, I'm still much better at sketching than painting,' he said, 'though I did do one or two oils. Carnarvon asked me to go along mainly to create an artistic record of the discovery, alongside the official photographer, rather than to produce great works. However, I didn't stay for the summer because, when I telephoned last, Stephen told me you had come home again, unattached.'

'Courtney, you must go back now!' she cried, holding his naked body to her own.

'With you clinging to me like this?' he laughed. 'That would start a few tongues wagging. I can see the headlines now: '*Naked artist hurries back to Egypt.*' What a wonderful effect that would have on my mother.'

'Don't be frivolous. This is important. No, no. I'll be unselfish. I'll let you go. I'll detach myself from you and allow you to get dressed and go.'

'It's not that important to me,' he said, still laughing. 'What is important is that we get married. Then I'll consider going back, but only with you. They won't open the tomb for some time yet – perhaps not even until November – there's plenty of time.'

'Are you sure that's what you want? Now that we know we want to be together, I don't mind what happens.'

Courtney said, 'Well I do. If you think I'm going to trot back to Egypt now, you've got another think coming. Not until you're safely in the net . . .'

He stayed until very late that night, then went back to Stanton Manor, only to reappear at the crack of dawn the next day in the car. They drove to the two churches and made arrangements with the vicars to call the banns. The wedding would take place in one month's time, at Thaxted church. Jane rang the Transon household at Green Lanes to give them the news. After speaking with her aunt and uncle, both of whom were delighted, she talked to Nancy.

'I have some news too,' said Nancy. 'Giuseppe and I are engaged.'

'Oh, that's *wonderful*,' cried Jane into the mouthpiece. 'I really didn't mean to eclipse your good tidings.'

'It doesn't matter,' said Nancy, the happiness bubbling up in her voice, 'we're not rushing things like you – what I mean is, the wedding won't be for at least six months. There're lots of arrangements to make. Well, you know all that. I just wanted you to know about us.'

'Of course, and congratulations, both of you. I know you'll be very happy. You do *love* him Nancy, don't you?'

'Of course I do,' said Nancy, 'I wouldn't be marrying him otherwise.'

'Good,' Jane said, feeling relieved, 'don't just go into it because he loves *you* and you feel it's a good idea.'

'Jane, I'm not stupid.'

Not as stupid as me, thought Jane.

Next, Jane spoke with Giuseppe. 'Well done,' she said. 'I'm so pleased for you.'

'And I'm pleased for you, too. I shall make her very happy, Jane, you must know that. In three days' time I go home to Italy. I will call on you before I leave. I am very grateful to you, for what you have done for my Nancy and me.'

'Like what?' laughed Jane. 'Introduced you? I'm sure fate would have done that somehow, without my help.'

'I think not. I think you are God's angel, bringing us together . . .'

Lady Constance and Jane were alone at Stanton Manor after dinner the week following the first calling of the banns. The first thing Lady Constance said to her was, 'There won't be any money, you know. His father's about to go bankrupt.' The words were spoken with a certain amount of relish, as if they were meant to upset Jane and send her away in a temper.

'It makes me very sad to hear that,' said Jane. 'Not for me, but for you. You're used to having money – I'm not. Courtney and I will manage all right. We're both able-bodied and intelligent people. It must be awful for you and Sir Charles, though. Will you lose the house?'

It was only at these words that Lady Constance appeared to crumple a little. They were sitting in the morning room, while Sir Charles, Courtney and Stephen were discussing business in the library. In an effort at covering her obvious distress over the Stanton financial position, Lady Constance sipped at her sherry very quickly. She seemed to be fighting back the tears.

'I'm sure you won't be able to manage without money either, Miss Transon. Nobody can.'

'Jane, you have to start calling me Jane. "Miss Transon" will sound ridiculous, coming from my mother-in-law. Whether you like it or not, you will have to treat me with more familiarity.'

Lady Constance winced at these words, but nodded slightly, as if to acknowledge the sense in Jane's request.

Jane continued, 'Some people can manage on a lot less money than others. We'll be fine at the cottage. The rent is fairly low and there are things we can do.'

'You think Courtney can live at a *cottage* when he's been used to this?' Lady Constance gestured at the grandeur around them.

'He might have had trouble adjusting if he hadn't been away to the war,' said Jane. 'But he's lived in trenches half filled with stinking water, in the middle of winter, so I don't think a cottage will appear a great trial to him. If you believe it will, you don't know your own son, Lady Constance.'

Lady Constance merely sniffed in reply to this statement.

However, later that day, Jane thought about what her future mother-in-law had said about the ruinous state of the Stanton affairs. She spoke to Courtney about it as they walked around the grounds of the estate.

'You needn't worry,' he said. 'Things *are* in a bad way, but Father and Stephen will just have to sort it all out by selling something. I know they don't want to do it, but that's nothing to do with us.'

'Have they thought about saffron?' asked Jane.

Courtney stopped in his tracks and looked at her. 'What do you mean?'

'I mean, as a main crop. I made a very handsome profit when I grew it, and I only planted eight acres. The Buccino family have made a fortune from it. I'm not saying it will be the answer to all your family's prayers, but you could mention it to them as a possibility.'

'Come with me,' said Courtney, taking her hand. 'I want you to talk to my father.'

He took her to the library, where Stephen and Sir Charles were still battling with their accounts.

An hour later, Jane looked up from the figures she was scribbling on a piece of paper, while Stephen and Sir Charles leaned over her shoulder, studying her projected accounts.

'Good Lord,' said Sir Charles, straightening his back. 'We might do something with this.'

'It may not work, of course,' said the practical Stephen, 'but we can give it a try. Thank you, Jane. Now, the only other thing is this: are you and Courtney planning to go away? You're the only one around here who knows anything about growing saffron, Jane, and I would appreciate it if you would act as our advisor until we get the hang of it.'

Courtney looked at his future wife and raised his eyebrows.

'What do *you* say, darling?' she asked him.

'I think we can stay around for a while,' he smiled. 'Get this lot on the road. Then I thought we might go out to India, by way of Egypt, to see what we can do with some saffron-growing there. I understand its a good climate for that sort of thing, and Julia and Mark seem to be having a fine old time out there on the tea plantation. What do you say?'

'A saffron farm in India?' she said, excited.

'Why not?' Courtney replied. 'If you agree to the scheme, of course . . .'

'Oh, yes, that would be an adventure, Courtney.'

'I hope our marriage is one *long* adventure,' he said.

Sir Charles was looking from one to the other of them with a little pique in his expression.

'Here, I say,' he said. 'You're not thinking of setting up a rival company before we even get started, are you?'

Courtney put an arm around his father. 'Not immediately, Father and, in any case, I'm sure the world market can stand more than one saffron farm.'

'Hmmmm,' grunted Sir Charles, not looking entirely convinced.

Jane left them discussing the finer points of future business, in order to answer a summons from Lady Constance. When Jane reached the morning room, she found Lady Constance in the company of Giuseppe Buccino.

'Giuseppe!' she cried, running to him and giving him a hug, a demonstration which earned her a look of disapproval from Lady Constance. It was likely that, in Lady Constance's mind, Jane was a seducer of all men who came within her reach, and this sort of behaviour was proof of that opinion.

'How are you?' Jane asked, once they had let each other go.

'I'm very well,' said a plumper-looking Giuseppe, smiling all over his face. 'You know my news, so you must realise how happy I am at the moment.'

'Nancy hasn't changed her mind?'

'No, not yet,' he smiled. 'It is to be hoped her mind remains constant until I return to Hornsey to take her to Italy, tomorrow morning.' Then he turned to include Lady Constance in the conversation. 'I thought also that, as I was in this part of the world, good manners required me to pay my respects to this lady and her husband, as friends of my father.'

Lady Constance acknowledged this with a slight bow of her head.

At that moment, Courtney entered the room. Jane went to him and took his hand, leading him over to Giuseppe, who stood waiting with his hands behind his back, smiling.

'Courtney, this is Giuseppe Buccino. You know his father, the count of course.'

'He is count no more,' smiled Giuseppe, bringing forth a hand and shaking Courtney's. 'My father has renounced his title. We're peasants again. We thought it advisable – Mussolini, you know?'

Lady Constance gave a little gasp, but Courtney said, 'Ah yes, the Fascists. Very wise of him.'

Jane said, 'Peasants? Surely not?'

Giuseppe smiled wrily. 'Common people then. We are keeping our money, house and lands, of course. It's just the title that's gone. My father sold it to a man he hates the Italian way. The man once robbed us of some land and he hasn't the foresight to see what is happening in Italian politics. He still thinks the nobleman is at the top. Well, if you're going to make a profit on something, make sure you do it at the expense of your enemies.'

Jane said, 'Sounds a bit bloodthirsty to me.'

'I know,' said Giuseppe. 'You're English.'

Courtney said, 'I have to thank you, Signor Buccino, for being so kind to my future wife while she stayed with your family in Italy. I have heard nothing but praise of you and your parents.'

'Pooh,' said Giuseppe, waving this away. 'We are to be relatives. You may have heard I am to marry Jane's cousin? One does not need to be thanked for being kind to one's family.'

306

'I believe one should be especially grateful, in those circumstances,' replied Courtney, his significant look rather lost on his mother.

'Not in Italy,' Giuseppe insisted. 'In Italy one's family comes first and last, in all matters.'

Sir Charles and Stephen joined the four people in the morning room, and they went in to dinner together, spending a very agreeable evening in one another's company. Even Lady Constance melted under Giuseppe's charm, and though she occasionally stole a slightly cool glance at Jane, she was for the most part as close to amiable as she would ever become. Courtney told Jane later that it was one of the best evenings he had ever had with his parents.

Chapter Twenty-six

Giuseppe returned to Italy, and preparations for Jane and Courtney's wedding continued apace, despite opposition from a certain quarter of Courtney's family.

Lady Constance said she was not at all displeased that it was to be a quiet affair involving only close family. This disclosure did not surprise Jane. Jane told Courtney later that she quite understood why Lady Constance preferred not to involve her friends and distant relations in such a sordid affair as a marriage between her youngest son and the daughter of an artist and gambler. Courtney had had the bad taste to laugh.

When the day arrived, Jane and Courtney flouted convention and went along to the church together, in the same car, driven by Stephen. Sir Charles and Lady Constance followed behind in a chauffeur-driven car. Also in the second car was Nancy, the only bridesmaid. Jane said she hoped her cousin wouldn't be devoured by Courtney's parents before she reached the church. Sybil and Matthew were already at the church, accompanied by Jonathan. There were no other guests.

It was a gloriously warm day in the first week of July, and the bride's bouquet consisted mostly of carnations from the manor gardens. The wedding couple had insisted on saving money where it was possible, to keep down the cost. Though both Jane and Courtney had some money saved, there were other priorities to consider, such as travel expenses.

Before they entered the great church, Courtney said to Jane, 'Are you sure you want it like this? We could make it a big occasion, you know. There's still time. It's supposed to be the bride's day.'

Jane, wearing a simple white dress with a white pillbox hat and no veil, shook her head and smiled in contentment. 'This is the way I want it, darling. No crowds. Just us. It's a pity that the saffron isn't yet in bloom – it would have made a perfect bouquet; but, as for people, well I'd prefer we did without them.'

Courtney grinned. 'I hoped you would say that.'

Courtney went into the church with Stephen, who was the best man. Uncle Matthew was to stand in for Jane's father and, when they got the signal, the pair of them stepped through the doors and walked down the long aisle.

Jane was feeling very happy. The sun was shining outside, and shafts of brilliant light came through the stained-glass windows, filling the church with colour. Since there were so few wedding guests, the church had an empty feel to it, the interior being so vast. However, Courtney was there by the altar, waiting, and his presence was enough for Jane.

When she and Matthew reached the waiting groom and best man, her uncle relinquished her.

'We are gathered here . . .' began the vicar.

Suddenly there was a commotion at the back of the church and a voice cried out, 'Stop this wedding!' The words echoed around the relatively empty church.

Heads swung round, Jane's amongst them.

Hurrying down the aisle was her father, Henley, with a small, tidy Chinese lady in tow. They both looked hot and bothered. Both too, appeared to be dressed for travel, and it seemed they were the worse for their journey.

'I found the cottage empty,' said Henley, gasping for breath, while the lady with him wafted a hand in front of her face and blinked, 'so I went round to the Blatchers'. They told me about the wedding. Has it actually started yet?'

Jane, the calmest person in the church, said, 'We've got as far as, "We are gathered here . . ."'

'Good. Good,' cried Henley. 'Then if someone will relieve me of my wife, Mai Ling? How about you, Matthew? Could you just see that she feels comfortable?'

'Your wife? You've married again? Um, does she speak English?'

whispered his brother, not moving an inch.

'Of course I speak English,' laughed the lady, adjusting her fashionable lilac suit. 'Don't worry about me, Henley. I'll be all right. You just get on with the wedding.'

Mai Ling winked at Jane, who could not help smiling back at her father's new wife. Then Mrs Transon squeezed herself in next to Lady Constance, forcing that lady and her husband further along the pew.

Mai Ling turned and smiled into Lady Constance's face. 'Lovely day for a wedding, isn't it?' she said, picking up a copy of the Order of Service and fanning herself with it.

Lady Constance looked at her with wide eyes and made a little more room for her.

'I have to sit on the end, to see what's going on,' confided Mai Ling, peering at the altar. 'Bit short-sighted, you see. Are you all right there?'

'I'm fine,' said Lady Constance, faintly.

'That's lovely,' said Mai Ling. Then looking round added, 'I like these big English churches. Bigger than Christ Church, Kowloon, isn't it, Henley? Are all the churches here this big?'

'Father, would you mind telling me what you intend doing next?' called Jane patiently from the altar.

Courtney said, 'Yes, we would like to get married, sir, if you don't object.'

Henley laughed. 'Bit late for objections, isn't it? Anyway, she's over the age of consent.'

'I was being ironical,' said Courtney. 'I meant, can we get on with the wedding now?'

'No, not yet. We've got to do the whole bit again.'

The vicar, who had been standing by looking bewildered, said, 'Do what again?'

'The whole bit,' gestured Henley, waving his arms at the entrance doors. 'Down the aisle, and all that. I'm grateful to my brother Matthew for standing in when he believed me to be absent, but I'm here now. I want to lead my daughter down the aisle myself, if you don't mind.'

'It is getting late,' said the vicar, looking at his watch, 'and I have another wedding . . .'

'Two jiffies,' said Henley, taking Jane's hand and pulling her back towards the doors. 'Less than two jiffies. Start the music and we'll be on our way back.'

And so it was that Jane and Courtney were eventually married. When they all left the church, there was a group of Morris dancers, jingling their belled legs and clashing their staves up and down the street outside the church. Flowered hats, coloured baldricks and rosettes filled the street with bright colours. The Fool danced over the wedding group, and began whacking everyone in sight with his inflated pig's bladder on a stick. Sir Charles protected his wife as best as he could, but even Lady Constance came in for a couple of humiliating blows on the buttocks. She gave the Fool a look that would kill an elephant.

Mai Ling Transon thought it was all hilarious, and kept asking, 'What is it? What is it? A festival? Like August Moon Festival in Hong Kong, eh, Henley?' Henley yelled something at her about pagans, and then, to avoid the Fool's bladder, Jane's father ducked underneath the flailing sticks and jigged along with the dancers for a few moments, much to the delight of his clapping wife. Henley then narrowly missed being decapitated when he ran through an arch of swinging staves. At the end of the arch was the Betty, a man dressed in a woman's clothes, who grasped Henley and swung him backwards and forwards to the rhythm of the fiddler's tune.

It was very colourful, and for Jane it added to the joy of the occasion. She said jokingly to Courtney, 'You didn't need to put on this wonderful show just for *me*.' And he replied with a grin, 'No expense spared, old friend.'

Afterwards, at the reception, they learned that Jane's father had stepped off the boat from Hong Kong only the day before. He and his wife, a middle-aged lady from the Mong Kok district of Kowloon, had arrived at Audley End by train, taken a taxi to the cottage, and the rest had already been explained.

'Close thing,' said Henley, chuckling. 'Very close thing. Still, we made it.'

Courtney lifted his glass to his new wife. 'And so did we,' he said. 'At last.'

'At *last*,' Jane repeated in contentment.

Later, Nancy asked Jane, 'What do you think of your new stepmother?'

'Is she that? I suppose she must be,' said Jane, looking across the room at the neat little lady who was at that moment possessively straightening her husband's tie. 'I must get to know her better before we go away. I hope dad treats her well, but she looks as if she's not the sort to stand a great deal of nonsense. I like what I've seen of her so far. She seems to have a very warm personality, doesn't she?'

'Unlike your new ma-in-law.'

Jane said, 'Oh, she'll defrost a little in time. What about you, and Italy? Are you happy?'

'Oh yes,' said Nancy earnestly. 'You told me that his family are delightful . . .'

'Well, Mum and Dad are. His sisters are all right, once they get to know you. But beware of the older brother. He's a rake.'

'So Giuseppe warned me. I can take care of myself.'

Jane looked at her smart cousin and nodded. 'I do believe you can. From wallflower to rose in three short years. I still can't believe it.'

Nancy laughed. 'Was I that bad?'

'Worse,' said Jane, wrinkling her nose.

Courtney came and separated them at that moment, saying, 'Excuse me, Nancy, I have to take my wife outside to kiss her.'

'Why not in here?' asked Nancy, arching a brow.

'Wouldn't be approved of by one's guests, not the way I'm going to do it.'

'People have got to get used to it, Courtney,' Nancy said. 'Unless you only intend doing it once.'

He looked at her and narrowed his eyes, then took his new bride around the waist.

'You're quite right, Nancy,' he said, looking into Jane's eyes. 'Time to show the world.'

With those words he pulled Jane close and kissed her the way a lover kisses his sweetheart after having been parted from her for three years. A silence fell over the whole room as the wedding guests stared at this spectacle. There was a shifting of feet, several of them belonging to embarrassed owners. Jonathan laughed self-consciously. Matthew coughed. Then, when the couple had finished and parted a little, their eyes shining, someone let out a great 'Hooray!' Jane recognised the voice of her father, the artist and gambler.